Praise for the historical suspense

Ava Dianne Day

BEACON STREET MOURNING
"With her independent spirit and youthful determination,
Miss Jones is invincible."
—*The New York Times Book Review*

"Plunging into the rich atmosphere of the upper-crust Boston in
the winter of Day's tale mesmerizes with long-festering secrets."
—*Booklist*

"What is immensely appealing is the care Day takes to re-create
the period and differentiate two very different cities on bays
3,000 miles apart. The expert crime-solving, it turns out, is
something of a bonus."
—*Chicago Tribune*

THE STRANGE FILES OF FREMONT JONES
"One of the most refreshing heroines to appear in years . . . Day
rates top marks for her crisp, witty dialogue . . . cleverly
conceived plot, and darkly menacing touches." —*Booklist*

FIRE AND FOG
"This delightful mystery begins with a bang . . . and things get
more and more complicated from there."
—*San Francisco Chronicle*

THE BOHEMIAN MURDERS
"A special treat. Highly recommended."
—*Chicago Tribune*

EMPEROR NORTON'S GHOST
"A lively and atmospheric mixture of sharply observed detail and high drama." —Amazon.com

DEATH TRAIN TO BOSTON
"An extremely appealing book . . . great fun to read."
—*The Book Report*

Cut to the Heart

Clara Barton and the
Darkness of Love and War

Ava Dianne Day

BANTAM BOOKS

CUT TO THE HEART

A Bantam Book

PUBLISHING HISTORY
Doubleday hardcover edition published June 2002
Bantam paperback edition / March 2003

Published by
Bantam Dell
A Division of Random House, Inc.
New York, New York

Map by Laura Hartman Maestro

ISBN 0-553-58559-2

Manufactured in the United States of America
Published simultaneously in Canada

OPM   10 9 8 7 6 5 4 3 2 1

*This book is dedicated
to all people who,
in the true spirit of
Clarissa Harlowe Barton,
do their work
for the love of the work itself,
regardless of how much
or how little
they may be paid.*

This book is a work of fiction set within a framework of historical fact. Some of the main characters, for example Clara Barton and John Elwell, are people who really lived. I have to the best of my ability brought them fictionally to life in a way I believe is consistent with their true natures, as reflected in their own writings. I have researched in primary sources as much as possible, including unpublished letters and diaries.

At the back of the book, in addition to Acknowledgments and References, there is a list of which characters are real and which are fictional.

— AVA DIANNE DAY

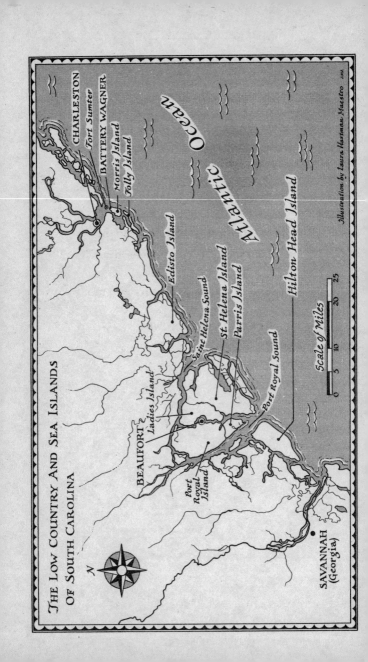

THE LOW COUNTRY AND SEA ISLANDS OF SOUTH CAROLINA

CHARLESTON
Fort Sumter
BATTERY WAGNER
Morris Island
Folly Island
Edisto Island
Saint Helena Sound
St. Helena Island
Parris Island
Port Royal Sound
Hilton Head Island
BEAUFORT
Ladies Island
Port Royal Island
SAVANNAH (Georgia)

Atlantic Ocean

N

Scale of Miles
0 5 10 20 25

Illustration by Laura Hartman Maestro 2002

Sunt lacrimae rerum et mentem mortalia tangunt.

"These are the tears of things, and the
stuff of our mortality cuts us to the heart."

— VIRGIL, *THE AENEID,* ON THE NATURE
OF WAR
(TRANSLATOR UNKNOWN)

Cut to the Heart

1863

Prologue

". . . monster . . ."

In a mean alleyway, narrow and dark, that served the grand houses looming tall above the water, a man whispered to a woman, and from his whispers one word carried clear upon the air: "monster."

That word was overheard . . . by the Monster himself.

The woman died not long after that, with a thin-bladed knife in her heart. Her man watched it all, even to the cutting-up. He cringed and cried and hid in the shadows, hating himself for his own will to live, which surged so strong in him while the life flowed out of his woman along with her blood onto the alley's dirty, rutted ground.

He felt her soul brush by him, screaming as she had not, for she'd died in silence; felt her soul rise out of her body and go up from the foulness of the alley, up through the great oaks trembling with Spanish moss, up and up.

Then the Monster summoned him, and he obeyed.

This dead thing that was left wasn't the woman anymore, although it looked like her . . . so it was hard for the man to take her severed hands, hands that had touched him and in their touching had brought so much pleasure, and put them in the black bag. Her feet too, whose high arches he had caressed, whose toes like black pearls he had kissed.

His tears fell on the white, protruding bones.

April 1863

I confess I am confounded, literally speechless with amazement! When I left Washington everyone said it boded no peace, it was a bad omen for me to start. I had never missed of finding the trouble I went to find, and was never late— I thought little of it.

—FROM THE UNPUBLISHED DIARY OF CLARA BARTON, DATED "APRIL 7TH, 1863, TUESDAY"

Chapter 1

HILTON HEAD ISLAND

"Here," I said, just loudly enough to be heard over the cries of seagulls and their bass counterpoint, a continuous throbbing hum that comes from all the unseen life hidden in these marshes. I raised my hand until I felt the boat slow, then pointed a finger to indicate that I wished us to move deeper into the cover of the sea grass, which even now at high tide loomed above my head.

I gave my directions serenely, without turning to look my man Jack in the eye; he was at the moment out of favor with me. I had no need to look—I could feel his sullen acquiescence behind me just as easily as I felt the small boat creep into the grasses at the merest pointing of my finger.

I know Jackson obeys me only because he fears me. I've given this man a home and work to do for which I've paid him wages, even back before Emancipation, when he was nothing but contraband. He didn't understand the value of money, so I taught him how to spend it wisely. Yet if he were not afraid of me he'd run away in a minute.

I can't allow the man to run. I need him because he's

strong, healthier than most, and he knows these Low Country marshes so well that he can navigate the creeks even on a dark night—a skill they say must be learned from an early age or it cannot be acquired. Then too, I need to keep him close because he's seen too much. If I let him leave he'll carry tales—and his tales would be of only one side, the more gruesome side, of my work. Of course that gruesome aspect is why he fears me, and so I must let it be; but sometimes it pains me to be so misunderstood, even by a poor black man.

Jackson can't be expected to comprehend the grand purpose, the noble aim of my life's work. How could he, with his lack of education, understand when my own professional colleagues did not? No one else has my clarity of vision, not to mention the sheer level of my skill. They could not keep up with me, therefore they excluded me.

I am accustomed to feeling alone.

Yet after all I've done for Jackson, one would think the man could give me devotion, if not love. Not so. Instead, he has so little sense that he mourns after his former owners, who abandoned him. I deserve better.

I have always deserved better than I get; such is all too frequently the curse of having a brilliant mind.

Jackson called me a monster not two hours earlier this day. He was talking to a woman outside the Freemen's Clinic in Beaufort, and I overheard him say that word, "monster," an appellation I truly abhor. Of course I had to put a stop to that kind of talk right away, and I did. As a result, his fear of me has been reinforced, and that is a good thing.

Even as I raised the spyglass to my eye and trained it on the military settlement at the northwest end of Hilton Head, I wondered fleetingly if my man Jack had loved that woman. She was pretty, if one measured her looks only in comparison with her own kind. A pity I could not have saved her head, as it was the most attractive part of her, but I had no use for it.

The parts I can use are in my black bag, here in the bottom of the boat not far from Jackson's bare feet. He knows all too well what is in the bag. I do not think he will call me a monster ever again. I have taught him a lesson.

"Jackson," I said politely, as I generally do him the honor of calling him by the longer version of his name, "can you move us any closer without our being seen? I'd like to know what's going on over there."

Some kind of ruckus had arisen over at the military base. I couldn't quite make out what. Though I doubted if it could have any relation to the matter that had brought me here spying this day, any disruption of normal routine on the post was interesting and bore watching.

"Yassuh," Jackson said and pushed off, using his long oar like a pole.

The boats these Gullahs fashion are sharp-prowed and flat-bottomed. They part the tall sea grasses with a swish that can be eerie or silky, depending on one's mood. My mood was silky this afternoon, despite that brief disruption to take care of Jackson's woman friend. Dismemberment, the way *I* do it, is hard, exacting work—but in its wake it leaves a sense of the greatest satisfaction.

I returned my attention to the activity captured in the glass.

For some months now Hilton Head Island has been headquarters for the Union Army's Department of the South. All the Sea Islands to the south of Charleston were abandoned by the plantation owners about a year ago, when Union ships found their way into Port Royal Sound—the

white gentry just took off. They left almost all their posses-
sions behind them: mansions, furniture, field slaves and all.
On the mainland near the coast it was the same—every
house in the rich old town of Beaufort had been left empty
of people but fully furnished. And everything—*everything*—including the abandoned field slaves, became contraband. Beaufort and all the Sea Islands, as far south as
Savannah, all were seized and occupied by the Union without so much as a single shot having been fired.

As for me, I came here to the Low Country by luck, at
one of those times in life that reinforce the truth in apho-
risms such as: It is always darkest before the dawn. I've
always been a lucky man, though I do not mean with
gambling and cards; rather I am supremely confident that
luck will in time make things break my way. I do not believe in a loving God who watches over us, because I am a
scientist; Lady Luck is the goddess who takes special care
of me.

Therefore I was not at all surprised to soon find, through
my spyglass, the small figure of the very woman whom I
sought over there on Hilton Head. In town I had heard that
she'd arrived, and I'd said to myself: *Ah, she has come to me.*

She stood on the long veranda that runs across the whole
second story of the former plantation now known as Headquarters House, looking down on that ruckus of unknown
origin. I could not see her features, but by her dark hair,
slight stature and neat appearance in a wide-skirted black
dress I knew her. Her identity was further confirmed by the
simple fact of her standing there, as if she had every right to
be the only woman in a company of soldiers—she alone
among the hardest of men.

I sharpened my focus, yet still could not make out her
face.

Never mind—from secret observation at Fredericksburg four months past I remembered her well: Her face was piquantly pretty, with an indentation at the point of her chin; her eyes were large, dark and lustrous; her cheekbones wide and prominent. Before Fredericksburg, at Antietam (the first time she got in my way), I'd lingered long enough to learn her name: Clara.

My Clara.

I had always known I would see Clara again someday. Now luck had brought her to me, without the slightest effort on my part. Idly I wondered how much time I'd have with her, how long I'd dare to keep her before she had to die.

"Whatever is going on over there, it seems to involve a number of your people, Jackson," I said.

They couldn't have found that woman's body already, I thought. *They aren't likely to find it until it starts to stink.*

Colonel John Elwell bit his lip. His mind was not on pain, and he was able to stay his hand only with difficulty.

He wanted to stroke her dark brown hair *now,* this very minute, while her attention was focused on his leg wound; wanted to touch her before she could see it coming or sense his intent, and with a frown or the merest narrowing of her eyes, shame him into stone.

For a moment John fantasized: *If I were to touch her just once, even the merest, lightest touch, then like magic the attraction between us would take hold—must take hold, for it's truly irresistible—and so we should be forgiven, also like magic, whatever might come next!*

But then Clara did something that caused such a sharp twinge in his thigh that he gasped, and groaned as the twinge dissolved into an only slightly lesser wave of pain that traveled all the way down his leg into his very toes. And up the other way as well.

She tilted her head and looked over her shoulder with a little worried frown, at the same time applying a gentle pressure on his wound that brought relief.

"I'm sorry, Colonel," she said, "but I have to change the dressing, and it was stuck. I should have warned you this might hurt."

"You just changed dressings yesterday," John grumbled.

"I know," she agreed, gathering up some strips of cloth that he had to admit did look rather nasty, "but I've observed that wounds heal faster the cleaner they're kept."

Clara whisked the old bandage out of sight and produced a clean length of cloth that she began to fold expertly, without looking. She smiled, her brown eyes lit with a mischievous glint. "It's like kitchens."

"Kitchens?" John felt his own lips twitch in amused response, though he had not the slightest idea what she was talking about. Who could resist this woman, who was not much taller than a child, had the hands of an angel—and, to boot, a wicked wit?

"The best-tasting food comes from a clean kitchen," she said, "and the neatest, fastest healing comes from a clean wound."

John thought about this as he watched her bind the white bandage around the deep hole where the broken bone had opened up the skin of his inner thigh—how surely her hands moved over those angry, red, raggedly sewn together edges. She had not done the sewing, of course, because she hadn't yet arrived when the wound was inflicted; he was certain she'd have made a much neater stitch. It was true that soldiers and their male nurses tended to ignore dirt. There was something manly, in fact, about the ability to ignore the muck and the mud along with all the other hardships.

Clara's insistence on cleanliness seemed a purely feminine thing—and she'd saved his leg, against a lot of odds. If there'd been a surgeon available when his horse fell on him, most likely he wouldn't have that leg anymore. Amputation, then cauterization, was the preferred method of treatment when a broken bone pierced the skin. But to the Colonel's everlasting shame, his was not a battle wound—for there was no battle in the area yet, and so no medical personnel on Hilton Head Island. He'd only been out pleasure riding and his horse had stumbled; he'd lost his seat and landed wrong, and so had the horse. A sickening snap of bone was the last thing he'd remembered before blacking out.

John suspected he might have lost not only his leg, but his life as well, if Clara Barton had not arrived a week ago and seen how things were with him. She'd immediately taken over his nursing. He'd been too weak and wracked with fever to protest that no lady should have to tend a man whose wound was in such an intimate place.

She touched *him* all the time. Her touch itself was healing. He fancied—or was it mere fancy?—her touch was not always impersonal.

Yet John, being a gentleman, had never allowed himself to touch her at all.

It's not fair, he thought grumpily.

"There!" Clara said with a note of satisfaction. She pulled the afghan back over his lap and straightened up. For a few moments she bustled about, washing her hands, tidying things, putting a small bag of refuse outside the door.

Then from one of the pockets inside her voluminous skirt, which seemed to contain any number of wondrous things, she produced a small bottle of some sweet-smelling cream. This she proceeded to rub thoroughly into her hands, taking time to go between each finger.

Aha, John thought, enchanted, *that is how she manages to work so hard yet keep those little hands so white.*

At last Clara looked around and asked, "Now, where is that book of poems we've been reading?"

It was the moment he'd been waiting for all day.

"Did you hear that?" Perhaps half an hour after she'd begun to read to the Colonel from his favorite volume of Keats, Clara paused in midpoem. She lowered the book to her lap and cocked her head, listening hard.

John Elwell frowned. "It sounds like some sort of disturbance outside."

"I'll go see what's happening, shall I?" she offered, unable to keep eagerness from her voice, yet so immediately ashamed of it that she forced herself to remain in her chair. It was not Colonel Elwell's fault that the war seemed to have come to a halt on the Sea Islands, making Clara feel as if the army must have sent her—and more important, all the supplies she'd gathered for the fighting men—to the wrong place.

"If you like," John said, "but it's not necessary to trouble yourself."

"Oh, it wouldn't be any trouble," Clara said, biting her lip and keeping her seat. Her whole body suddenly seemed to itch and she wanted to fly out the door to see what was happening.

"Go and find out, then come back and report to me,"

John said at last, in a tone somewhere between command and his usual soft-spokenness.

Even as Clara rose—slowly, so as not to hurt his feelings—and handed him the book, the noise grew louder: Many voices cried out, haphazardly different in tone and pitch, sounding all together, as if they must be working up to something, perhaps some sort of riot.

But not a battle.

"It's some domestic thing, I'm sure," she said, as much to herself as to him. Nevertheless he'd given a command of sorts and, grateful, she was on the way to the door. She flung it open, stepped out and left the door standing wide, momentarily not thinking about drafts and their possible effect on the Colonel's fragile state of health.

As headquarters, the former plantation house had been divided so that the working offices of the Quartermaster Corps were below on the first floor, and the officers' living quarters were on the second floor, which was accessible only from the veranda that ran across the whole facade. As commandant, Colonel Elwell occupied the two best center rooms, so Clara emerged midway on the veranda.

She stepped quickly to the railing and looked down. The enclosure on the grounds below, usually patrolled by silent guards, was now a mass of motion, swirling with noise and color and people the likes of which she had heard about, but never seen before.

Their thin arms waved above their dark heads like a writhing thicket of naked, blue-black branches. Their bodies too were thin, clothed in splashes of color that made an exciting contrast to the somber uniforms of the soldiers who stood aside, warily looking on.

Gullah, Clara thought, *they are the former slaves, now freemen and women, called the Gullah.*

Her first few contacts with the Gullah, she'd been warned, would not be easy—their language was difficult to understand and almost impossible to speak, though the words were a dialect of English. Sure enough, though she tried hard, she couldn't make out a single intelligible word rising from the crowd below. But the syntax and cadence of the Gullah speech were exotic, melodious—in fact, bewitchingly beautiful—in spite of the sense of urgency she felt coming from them.

They chanted and keened incomprehensibly, and all the while a sense of grief, of mourning, ebbed and flowed in a palpable rhythm, as if through a heavy vocal sea. Most of the voices were high-pitched, the cries of women . . . and one woman stood out from all the rest.

Swaying near the center of the crowd, she was taller, her uplifted arms rose higher, and she was dressed all in white, even to a turban headdress. The tall woman threw her head back and howled—momentarily a hush fell—and then she broke away. The others parted to let her pass, as she rushed toward the staircase.

Soldiers followed, brandishing their bayonet-tipped rifles and yelling, "Halt! Halt!" But the woman was already halfway up the stairs, propelled by her own great momentum.

"Let her come!" Clara yelled down. "I take full responsibility!"

The soldiers, though their heads jerked up as if in surprise, responded either to the tone of her voice or to the words "full responsibility." They backed off and arranged themselves in a barrier at the foot of the stairs before anyone else in the crowd could follow.

The woman who emerged onto the veranda must be nearly six feet tall, Clara judged by making a swift comparison with her own height, which was just under five feet. And the woman was so thin that she seemed even taller. Her eyes were enormous, their whites having a clear bluish cast against her dark skin, and she carried her head in the white turban with perfect grace, like the queen of a far-off land.

Yet this queen became an immediate supplicant, bending double, babbling and imploring in words Clara could scarcely make out.

George, she thought she heard, and *cunnel,* no doubt for "Colonel."

"Shush for a moment," Clara said kindly, holding out her hands with the palms up in a pleading gesture. "Please, I want to help but you must speak more slowly."

Twice more she repeated both her plea and the gesture, before the woman's words tumbled to a halt and she raised her head. Clara was finally able to ask, "Can you tell me your name?"

The woman, calmer now, unfolded to her full height. "Annabelle," she said.

"And who is George?"

One large tear spilled from Annabelle's right eye and rolled down her cheek, leaving a silvery track on ebony skin that glowed with a purple sheen. " 'E mah boy," she said.

"Something has happened to your son, George," Clara interpreted. She understood the tone, the facial expression, the outpouring of sorrow all too well—these were a common language that needed no words.

Annabelle drew in a sharp breath and nodded. " 'E don' binnah los'," she said.

"And you've come to see the Colonel, is that right?"

Annabelle nodded again.

"Colonel Elwell has been injured, he is hurt, do you

understand? His horse fell on him and broke the colonel's leg bone, high up above the knee." Clara tapped her own thigh, though her full skirt and petticoats made the gesture fairly meaningless. "It hasn't been healing right and he's confined to his room."

Confined to his bed, and in a weak and precarious state of health if the full truth be known—but generally it was not. The Colonel could not leave his bed to receive this woman, nor would it be at all seemly to show her into his bedroom, and so Clara did not know what to do.

Annabelle hung her head, clasped her hands tightly together and brought them to her lips. Whether she was thinking, praying or crying was impossible to tell. All three, perhaps. Within the enclosed grounds below, the other Gullah still moaned, their voices rising and falling as if in an agreed cadence, with occasionally a single wail that soared high and chill on the winds of the afternoon.

Clara reached into the deep pocket of her skirt and took out a palm-sized notebook and a lead pencil. Making notes was second nature to her, though most often she did it in a field hospital, or walking the battlefield to find soldiers still alive among those who'd been left for dead.

She flipped past pages of names of sons, fathers, husbands, lovers, all of whose messages she had promised to deliver and someday she would—until finally she found a blank space and in it she wrote: *Annabelle*. Then she drew a two-headed arrow, and at its other end she wrote: *George, son*. Along the shaft of this arrow she wrote: *missing*.

Then Clara moved closer, tipped her head to one side and looked up into Annabelle's face. Above the Gullah woman's clasped hands her cheeks were shiny-wet with tears, and the skin around her eyes was creased with sorrow.

"Is George the only one who's lost?" Clara asked quietly, urgently compelled by some sort of sixth sense she had about people who'd gone missing. "Are there others?"

Annabelle did not reply. Instead she closed her eyes and began to sway ever so slightly forward and back, forward and back.

"Do you understand what I'm asking?" Clara pressed.

The tall woman stilled herself, opened her eyes and wiped her cheeks with the back of her hand. Slowly she shook her head back and forth—a negative reply.

"George don' binnah los'," she insisted. "Uh tole oonuh. Dem tek um. 'E don' binnah onlies' dem tek."

Clara bit her bottom lip in frustration—now she was the one who did not understand.

The Colonel shoved his elbows back hard against the pillows and struggled to raise his shoulders and neck off the bed so as to see through the doorway. He hated not knowing everything that was going on.

Damnation! He still couldn't see.

Beads of sweat popped out on John's forehead as he tried harder, leaning all the weight of his upper body first on one elbow, then the other, until at last he'd dragged himself more or less upright. Then he bent forward from the waist—a position that produced instant nausea in the pit of his stomach—reached back and quickly balled the feather pillows up behind him for support.

Aaah! Better.

Sitting up he felt less like an invalid. Though he still couldn't see her—she'd moved out of range. By craning his neck to the left, he got a glimpse of her black skirt. And he could hear some anguished-sounding outpouring of the Gullah language, in a woman's voice.

It would be good experience for Clara to handle it as much as she could, whatever it was—even though he was jealous of his time with her.

Within two days of her arrival, John had freed up a room beside his own in the big house and assigned it to Clara. He'd raided some of the officers' rooms to provide her a rocking chair and some other, smaller luxuries; he'd ordered that a handsome chest of drawers with parquet inlay from his own room be moved into hers, as well.

All without her knowledge. If he'd asked, she might have declined, and he wasn't taking that chance. He was the commanding officer, he could give what orders he liked, and if the men made rude remarks behind his back about all this fuss over a woman (he was pretty sure they did), well then, let them.

John's next step had been to assign David Barton, Clara's brother and travel companion, to share Sam Lamb's quarters. Both men already shared the rank of captain—they might as well share a suite of rooms. Better two officers together than force a brother and sister to live in a two-room cabin that had been assigned before their arrival, in the mistaken belief that David Barton and Clara Barton were man and wife.

Anyway that was the rationale of the new arrangement, and there was no one entitled to complain about it—no one except John Elwell's occasionally aching conscience.

Rumor had it that the two captains were not entirely happy, but they had no choice other than to obey orders. Major Lamb was Colonel Elwell's second in command, and what with the Colonel out of commission, he had too much to do. So John had made Captain Barton Samuel Lamb's assistant. It had seemed a good idea, but was not working out, and their living together only exacerbated the situation.

The Colonel grimaced when he thought of Clara's brother. He didn't like the man, who was much older and yet had so little experience as a soldier that John wondered how he'd earned his rank. Of course John also didn't like that David was always watching Clara. . . .

Which was why John had put him in a room on the other side, where it was much harder for him to know his sister's every move. Smiling at his own cleverness, the Colonel again craned his head to see as much as he could of the pair on the porch. Clara had bent toward the Gullah woman, a motion that set the hoop under her skirt swaying and provided a rare flash of ruffled petticoat.

That's the trouble with war, far too few petticoats. John was appalled by the frivolousness of his thought . . . but it was nice to smile for a change.

Clara's reputation had preceded her, along with her clearance papers—but she'd turned out to be far different from what any of them had expected. She had her own permits issued by the U.S. Congress, including a battlefield pass that allowed her to go anywhere, even to the front lines, to distribute her supplies and to assist the medical corps. No ordinary citizen got a battlefield pass that circumvented the whole military chain of command, especially not a woman. Such a thing was unheard of. So they'd anticipated some sort of Amazonian bluestocking, and got an energetic little angel instead.

Clara Barton's battlefield pass was legitimate—John had seen it with his own eyes.

Amazing woman! Smiling again, he shook his head.

Amazing or not, it was time he offered to help in the present situation. He'd been listening, thought he'd recognized the voice of the Gullah woman, who was a kind of leader in their community. And now, he'd just heard Clara say his name.

John cleared his throat and called out: "Clara! Miss Barton!"

After a beat or two there she was, a small woman in a skirt so wide she took up the whole doorway.

"Yes, Colonel? I'm sorry I forgot to close the door. I hope you're not feeling a chill."

"Nonsense." John felt himself smiling. It must be years since he had smiled so much. "I'm enjoying the fresh air. I've been cooped up in here for far too long."

"I'm sure that's so."

"Bring the woman on in. I think I know her, and I'd like to help."

Chapter 2

Through my field glasses I watched Clara on the veranda of Headquarters House—she had been joined by a Gullah woman whose height made Clara look like a dwarf. The Gullah flung herself into an obeisance resembling a puppet out of control. Fascinating. I wondered what she wanted—they're always wanting something. Too bad I couldn't hear as well as I could see.

My field glasses are of German manufacture and excellent quality; they came to me some months back through an artillery officer whose mangled arm I did my best to save. This same officer got me in a pack of trouble by dying before I'd finished repairing him—to this very day I cannot bear to think of all that trouble—but having inherited his fine optical instrument gives some consolation.

I felt the most curiously urgent need to know what the two women, Clara and the Gullah, were talking about now that Clara'd gotten the woman to her feet again. My ears burned as if they might be discussing *me,* but of course not—the very idea only comes from the sort of superstition one picks up all too easily from these Gullah people. Nevertheless, by the time Clara gestured for the tall woman to precede her through a door into the house, I'd grown anxious and disturbed.

"Jackson," I said, lowering the field glasses, "get us out of here."

He obeyed without a word. I felt the boat begin to move stealthily backward. My man Jack was no more eager to be seen than was I; I didn't have to tell him to keep the boat hidden in the grass.

"Take us home the long way," I instructed; "cut through Trenchard's Inlet, around behind Fripp Island, and go up St. Helena Sound."

He mumbled something I couldn't understand.

"I beg your pardon?" I won't tolerate sloppiness, verbal or otherwise.

"Yes, *suh!*"

Jackson snapped his words out smartly this time, and the boat moved sharply back. The tall sea grass closed all around, only inches in front of my eyes; I'd been standing but took my seat in the prow quickly, so as not to get my face slapped—they aren't called "blades" of grass for nothing.

Eventually we reached a wide patch of water among the concealing grasses where Jack could turn the boat around and take us properly forward, and then I started to relax. Moving backward makes me uneasy—I prefer to see whatever's coming at me.

My ears were not much use for helping me orientate myself, and did nothing to relieve my unaccountable anxiety—there were far too many sounds, all of them alien and offensive to my delicate sense of hearing. The ubiquitous insects were the worst offenders: They whirred and chittered and jittered, and occasionally they shrieked.

Surely that *was* some strange insect shrieking?

At length I found myself swatting at a swarm of bugs so infinitesimal I could not see what they were, but they bit. Then I realized the boat was no longer moving—Jack had hesitated at some juncture of these incomprehensible creeks.

"Well, go on, go on!" I said impatiently.

Jackson shook his head. "Thinkin' best we go t'other way."

"We will *go* the way I told you to go!"

"Tonight be the dark of the moon," he said, sticking his long oar straight down into the muddy bottom like an anchor.

My heart gave a treacherous lurch in the direction of my throat, for I had not the slightest idea where we were—but of course I did not betray one iota of concern.

"Is this information supposed to be of some significance to me?" I inquired, busily swatting, as if bugs were my only care in the world.

"Massuh, if we go roun' up St. Helena Sound, we won't get to the landing till after dark."

I know Jackson does not like to walk through the woods surrounding my plantation after dark; indeed, this irrational fear of his has often been useful to me. But open defiance of my order? That would never do!

"We have a lantern here in the boat with us," I reminded him, "and I have a packet of sulfur matches in my vest pocket. The phase of the moon makes no difference whatever, except to your superstitious mind. Now stop complaining and carry on."

"Dark of the moon's when debbils walk."

I swear the man's hand trembled on the oar.

I laughed. "If that's all you're worried about, then don't. *I'll* protect you."

He darted me a strange look, but a second later his big chest expanded in a deep breath, and with a mighty shove he pushed off. His oar came up out of the water with a rushing, sucking sound.

Again he mumbled.

"Speak up, man! When did you pick up that irritating habit? What exactly did you say?"

"Suh, I said I 'spects you can do whatsomever you wants."

An interesting remark, even if I wasn't quite sure what he meant.

HEADQUARTERS HOUSE, HILTON HEAD

"Good news, Annabelle," Clara said, smiling and slipping the notebook back into her pocket. "Colonel Elwell wants to talk to you. He's invited us into his room, so come along."

The Colonel—Clara found it hard not to think of him as John, although even thinking his first name on such short acquaintance was not entirely proper—had gotten himself up into a sitting position. Not much short of a miracle, since only a few days ago he'd been weak as a kitten.

Oh, good for you, John! Clara thought, as she guided the Gullah woman into the room.

"Colonel Elwell," she said with a smile, "this is Annabelle."

Turning to Annabelle, she apologized: "I'm sorry, I forgot to ask your last name."

When Annabelle didn't provide the information, Clara prompted, "Your surname, or family name?"

Annabelle ignored the question in favor of going down on her knees beside the Colonel's bed.

Clara thought: *Oh dear, more self-abasement—if she prostrates herself in front of the Colonel I swear I shall be sick.*

Fortunately the woman did no such thing—she sat back on her haunches and her white skirt billowed around her, as if she'd come down on her own personal cloud.

He held out his hand in greeting, but she apparently didn't understand his intent, and merely settled herself. So the Colonel turned his movement into a gesture toward Clara, along with an explanation:

"The Negroes in the South very often do not have surnames, or if they do, then they're called after their masters. Of course, that practice no longer seems appropriate now that they are free. The problem is to get them to understand that they can do what *they* want now. They're still reluctant on that score, perhaps especially when it comes to choosing their own names."

He shifted his gaze. "Do you have another name, Annabelle?"

"Jus' Annabelle," she said, "f'um Mas' Cawfud plantesshun obuh Parris Ile."

"I know the place, the Crawford plantation on Parris Island," John nodded. "I think you and I have met before when I was over there on Parris. I expect I'd gone to see the Gages."

"Yassuh," the woman nodded. "Oonuh sed ennyting trubble we, fuh come yuh."

John chuckled, cocked his head just enough to throw a glance Clara's way and remarked, to neither of them in particular, "Whatever I said, let's hope I don't end by regretting it!"

The woman rocked slightly back and forth, her eyes fixed on the Colonel.

He continued in a more serious tone, "Before we talk anymore, Annabelle, I want to be sure you understand: That plantation where you live on Parris Island doesn't belong to Mr. Crawford now, nor do you, nor does anyone who lives there. You know that, don't you?"

"Yassuh, Cunnel, we knows 'Mansippashun. Miz Frances Gage an' Miz Mary Gage teach we."

Clara bit her lip to keep from blurting out, *Please! Just say* yes, *or* yes, Colonel! But at the same time she knew it would never happen. Even white Southerners said yes, sir or yes, ma'am. All that fancy speech seemed unnecessary, even offensive, to her spirit of Yankee plainspokenness.

"I'm sure Frances and Mary are very good teachers," John said.

So who were Frances Gage and Mary Gage? Clara wondered. Surely not Southern women, if they were teaching the Gullahs. She opened her mouth to ask the Colonel, but immediately closed it again.

Too late: John was already asking his next question, in a manner so slow and patient she found it almost . . . what? Well, maddening. Perhaps even patronizing. Or was she just being terribly critical?

"Now Annabelle," he coaxed, "I want you to talk to me in English—not Gullah—and tell me what you've already told Miss Barton out on the veranda. Start from the beginning and tell me everything you can."

Quietly resuming her place in the chair, Clara slipped the notebook back out of her pocket and held her pencil at the ready. Whether it was the Colonel's manner or the authority of his rank, the woman's eyes and facial expression reflected rapid thought.

Annabelle began to speak, and went on haltingly but ever more clearly, with much use of her hands:

"Mah George, he be almos' a man. He daddy binnah dead—ah—his daddy been dead a long time gone. George git—he gets us food to eat, looks after his mama. He a good boy. Soon he be a good man. George be strong an' fine, all dey gals gwine—all the girls will be wanting him."

For a moment she forgot her sorrow and her fear as pride in her son shone from her face, along with her love. With such an exotically beautiful mother, George was certain to be a handsome young man.

"You must be proud of him," John said.

"Yassuh, Colonel suh."

Oh drat, there she goes again.

"Excellent. Tell me more," he encouraged.

The longer Annabelle spoke, the better her English became, or so it seemed. Gradually Clara found her own ears attuned to the Gullah cadence and phraseology, until the mixture of English and Gullah seemed increasingly easy to understand.

"So last week," Annabelle was saying, "George went over t' Lady Ile t' hunt coons and possums, and he never did come back. Me and lots other peoples, we went on search party—one day, overnight and 'nother day, but we never did find nary a sign what happen to him."

"What about his boat?" John asked.

He glanced at Clara, explaining, "He must have had one. George couldn't get to Lady's Island from Parris Island without a boat. In fact, no one can get much of anywhere around here except by water."

Clara nodded; a point well taken but continually hard to

grasp, because one's eyes suggested otherwise. The Sea Islands were deceptive.

On either side of Port Royal Sound there appeared to be no islands. Instead there were rippling plains of lush green grass flanking the Sound's deep-water channel, by which boats of moderate draft could sail up to Port Royal Landing, and then on up the Beaufort River to the town itself. Here and there clumps of woods sprung up among the surrounding grass, sheltering a hut or two; and in the distance among the treetops one might occasionally glimpse the tall chimneys of a big house.

Yet the grassy plain was ephemeral, teasing, without substance. Beneath all that grass there was only water, laced with twisting waterways Clara had learned were called "creeks," which rose and fell with the tides. There *were* islands out there—just enough solid land to serve as anchors for the patches of trees and the occasional house—but she had an uneasy feeling about these Sea Islands, as if even here on Hilton Head they were living in a mirage, where everything could at any moment sink beneath the all-consuming grass as if it had never been.

Sound and motion from Annabelle brought Clara out of her uncomfortable musings. The woman had clapped one hand over her mouth, as if to stanch too great an emotion. But she couldn't hold back her tears, and now she dropped her hand to draw a shuddering, gasping breath.

On its exhalation words poured from her hard and fast, but raggedly: "Yestiddy buncha dem fum ober Mas' Yenkins—"

Elwell interrupted: "In English, please, slowly. Take your time."

Annabelle stopped abruptly, gulping, almost choking.

Tears cascaded down her cheeks. "S-s-sorry. He boat, yestiddy he boat—"

John Elwell bent from the waist and reached out until he could place his hand over Annabelle's—a movement Clara knew must be painful for him. Indeed there were lines of pain alongside the sympathy etched deep in his face.

"Take your time," he said again. "Whenever you're ready, tell us about the boat."

The woman gathered strength: wiped her cheeks, smoothed out her white skirt, took herself in control. When once more she raised her head on its long neck, Clara thought of a black swan.

"Thank you kindly, Colonel," Annabelle said. "These people from Jenkins plantation, they come yesterday over to Parris Ile with our boat. Jenkins place been over to Lady's Island. They found the boat way up by Beaufort town. Knew it be mine by my mark on the side. But nobody never seen my boy."

Clara held out her notebook. "Please, Annabelle, will you make your mark in my book for me?"

Suspicion immediately gleamed out of the black woman's eyes, and she lapsed back from English to Gullah. "Whuffuh?"

Elwell too shot Clara a sidelong look and said, with uncharacteristic sharpness, "Never mind that now."

Clara felt rebuffed as she returned the notebook to her lap, and puzzled. What had she done that was so wrong?

"Annabelle," the Colonel said in an insistent tone that forced the woman's eyes away from Clara and back to him, "did George take a gun?"

"Gun, suh?"

"On the day he disappeared, did your son take a gun to hunt with, a shotgun or a rifle?"

"Nossuh. We got no guns. George, he hunt with net and pole. Catch mos' ennyting—most anything—that way."

The Colonel proceeded, in his excruciatingly slow way, to quiz Annabelle on people and places and possibilities that meant nothing to Clara.

She'd been taken aback by his rebuff, which had seemed all the more harsh because he was usually so gentle and soft-spoken. Her mind began to wander. That was something she did not allow very often—normally Clara kept a strict discipline even over her own inner thoughts.

But now a voice—the voice of doubt—said inside her head: *What on earth am I doing here?*

In a sudden, heart-stopping instant, Clara felt lost.

It was as if a circle of darkness opened up right in front of her face and continued to grow. There was no way to escape it, no way out. The room, the man, the woman in white—they all faded, overwhelmed by the darkness that was now *inside* her. It had swallowed her, pervaded her, just as it would soon swallow everything.

Her ears seemed stuffed with cotton, and her skin crawled as if thousands of tiny worms had worked their way beneath it to run along her bones. The voices of that man and woman receded as if down a tunnel, drowned out by the noise of her own blood rushing through her head.

Once again into her mind came the dreadful question: *What am I doing here?*

Clara stopped breathing. The self-doubt she usually kept behind the lock and key of a strong will had escaped, and was threatening to run out of control.

They've sent me here, where there is no battle happening; I am of no use here yet I've given over everything to my mission for this war; if I cannot help the soldiers between the battlefield and the hospital, then I have no purpose left to my life. . . .

A small, blessed remaining bit of rationality reminded Clara that she had felt this way once before. Long ago, it was—almost twenty years ago. She'd been lost in the blackness then too, of no use to anyone, with no purpose to her life, and therefore no reason to live. She'd wanted to kill herself back then, and ever after, could not be sure she hadn't tried.

"Clara?"

What? Her mind registered that someone had called her name, but she did not speak.

"Miss Barton?"

She blinked, and came back to an awareness of the breath in her nostrils, the sunlight in the room, and the two people—a pale, brown-haired man with large, kind eyes, and a woman with the most extraordinary skin, the shade of aubergines—both of whom were looking expectantly at her.

"Yes, Colonel?" To her own surprise the voice that came from her throat sounded quite normal.

"I noticed you were making notes and wondered if you had questions, something I may have omitted to ask?"

Glancing down at her notebook, Clara saw she had indeed automatically made some scribbles, and had marked with a star one point on which she wanted clarification. Quickly she tried to decipher the "battlefield scrawl" that was so different from her normal handwriting.

"Yes, yes—just a minute."

Meanwhile Annabelle, apparently feeling finished, unfolded herself from her place on the floor by the Colonel and now towered over them both.

Clara glanced up, felt herself at a decided disadvantage, so she too rose before asking her question.

"I was wondering about Mrs. Tubman, Harriet Tubman—I heard she came through Beaufort a few months ago. Annabelle, do you suppose your son might have decided to follow her up north? By any chance did Mrs. Tubman visit you on Parris Island, or did you and George go into Beaufort to hear her speak?"

"Miz Tubman a fine woman," Annabelle said. "She been here before, we hear her talk, know she help peoples and do good. But George have his own place with we. He not be wanting to leave."

Frowning a bit, Clara crossed off her question. After a brief hesitation she added, "Thank you. I have nothing else."

Colonel Elwell said, "I'll look into your son's disappearance, and I'll send Miss Barton, or one of my men, over to Parris with a report as soon as possible."

Annabelle gave Clara a look piercingly keen. "Miz Barton, she work for you, Cunnel?"

He smiled at that. "No, Miss Barton works only for herself, but occasionally she gives the Union Army a hand with this and that, and she has been most kind to me lately. So I expect, since I cannot do it myself, she might be willing to carry a message to you."

"Yes, of course I will," Clara said, "and m-maybe more. I—I have a kind of a gift," she went on reluctantly, almost unwillingly, as if the words were pushing themselves out of her on their own. "I'm rather good at finding people who have been separated from one another by this awful war. That's why I keep these notes"—she dangled the notebook, its pages riffling in the breeze that came through the still-open door—"and I have made some for you now, and for your George. Certainly I'll do what I can, even if it's only to carry a message."

Gravely Annabelle inclined her head. "God blessum,"

she said, and then with two strides of her long legs was gone before Clara had time to even begin to think of showing her to the door.

After a hesitation Clara followed, shut the door after the woman and leaned back against it.

"Give a penny," said John Elwell.

"Pardon?" she looked up, distracted.

"I'd give a penny, or more, to know what furrows that lovely brow—and where you'd gone away to in your head there a few moments back."

"Oh. Well, for one thing, I was wondering why you snapped at me about asking Annabelle to make her mark in my book. I always do that when someone asks me to find a loved one. It has become a habit of mine to ask for a signature from those who can write or make their marks."

"Why? If I may ask."

"It forms a bond. And in the few cases so far when I actually have been able to deliver messages, bring people together, having that signature helps as proof that the person I've spoken with—it's always an injured soldier, except now for Annabelle—is still alive. Or was, when we spoke. I don't understand why she would act like that."

John Elwell rubbed thoughtfully at the bridge of his nose. "I could easily be wrong, doing the woman a disservice, but—I trust you to be discreet and not to jump to any unwarranted conclusions. All right?"

Clara nodded. "Of course."

"Annabelle is a kind of native priestess among her people."

"Priestess?"

"Oh, if you asked her or anyone in her congregation about their religion, they'll tell you they're Christians. But their religion is at least half something else. Something probably more akin to their African roots."

"You mean, as one hears of the Negroes in New Orleans . . . *voodoo?*"

"Something like that, yes, only here they don't call it voodoo. I don't even know what collective term these Gullahs have for their beliefs. But I can tell you this: To them, a name has power. And writing, the written word, is still mysterious to them. You must ask the Gages. They know much more about these things than I do, because their life's work is teaching the freed slaves to read and write."

"All right, when I get to know these Gage women I will certainly ask them. But I still don't understand why Annabelle wouldn't make her mark, especially if it might help her find her son."

Again John rubbed at his nose before replying.

"Suppose that mark stood for more than just her name."

"I'm not following you."

"When you were young—remember, the Gullah have a very direct way of thinking, somewhat akin to the simplicity we had when we were young and incapable of guile— did you ever write, perhaps in a book, 'This belongs to Clara Barton, keep out!'?"

"Well, yes." Clara smiled. "Or something similar."

John nodded. "The Gullah believe Annabelle has a certain sort of spiritual power at her command. I would expect she projected some of that into the mark she put on her boat. And she wouldn't want to be reproducing that mark in your notebook on the spur of the moment—nor would you want her to."

"Oh. You mean something like 'Cursed be he who steals my property.' "

"Something like that, yes."

As Clara's understanding deepened, a chill began at the back of her neck and proceeded down her spine all the way into her toes.

ST. HELENA ISLAND

In my experimentation I have found that, for greatest success, specimens must be dealt with while they are fresh. Even when I have taken them myself with the greatest of care, if they are allowed to stand for much time at all, a certain amount of deterioration will set in. The ends of the small veins will collapse, and nerve endings seem to—how shall one say—frizzle up and simply disappear.

They are very shy, nerves. Hard to locate in the first place, hard to grasp with even the finest of instruments and impossible with one's bare fingers. I swear nerves go into hiding once they are severed.

Yet who is to say but what the nerves, being connected in some way with the seat of *feeling*—for it is the nerves that are the vehicles for delivery of both pleasure and pain; my experiments have proved it—I repeat, who is to say but what the nerves may not be the key to stimulating regrowth?

My man Jack had outdone himself at the rowing, and so we'd arrived at Coffin Landing—my estate (I refuse to call it a plantation, though of course that is what it was before I took it over) formerly belonged to a family named Coffin and I've kept the nomenclature because its singular appropriateness amuses me—as I was saying, we'd arrived at my landing in the twilight hours. Thus it was not yet full dark when we took the walk through the woods that Jackson so dreaded. Out of a certain degree of perversity, which I admit I enjoyed, I left the lanterns in the boat. But I am not without pity: I told Jackson he could run on ahead as fast as he pleased.

I myself was preoccupied, on that walk, with thoughts of wanting to write a letter to Clara Barton. Indeed my desire to write had been whetted to an almost unbearable degree by knowing that she was now so near.

Just think: no more waiting, no more of never knowing if my missives had found their mark or not. (Mail delivery is so annoyingly uncertain in these times of war.) Why, I could have a messenger deliver my next letter right into her hands! Or, if I were very daring, I could deliver it myself.

I played with this tantalizing idea for some time, reckoning it should be relatively easy and safe—for of course Clara has not the slightest idea who I really am. Nor will she, until I decide the time is right.

However, by the time I'd reached the house I had accepted the inevitable: I could not write yet. First I must discharge my duty to my specimens. Therefore, after I'd locked Jackson into his part of the house, I went on to my laboratory, bagged specimens in hand.

The laboratory occupies an outbuilding behind the house. Due to the overhead canopy of live oaks, with their thick, weirdly gnarled branches dripping curtains of Spanish moss, night had already overtaken the path from house to lab. And as I said, I'd left the lanterns in the boat.

Never mind, I knew the way well enough; yet I was sufficiently haunted by remnants of that earlier anxiety that I set the bag of specimens aside and spent the first few minutes lighting all the lamps in the laboratory. It was a process that gave me the most eerie feeling, a sense of what the French call *déjà vu,* a sense of being both in the present and the past at the same time.

What was this? Lamps . . . light driving out darkness . . .
what was the cause of this feeling? I felt the oddest mixture
of both pleasure and a kind of torment, with the sizzle and
sharp odor of each sulfur-headed match I struck.

The answer, the cause, came to me as I touched flame to
wick of the final lamp and I stood transfixed, remembering.
It was Clara, of course. Clara and her candle lamps, after
the Battle of Antietam:

*I am standing back in the woods near a farmhouse that be-
longs to a man with the ridiculous name of Poffenberger. I'm
waiting for the dark to come. I am low in spirit; I know I need
the cloak of darkness to survive, to do what I must do and be
gone.*

*I'm also low on rations and supplies, reduced to pursuing my
all-important work in a piecemeal manner. The uncertainty
and the interruptions leave me feeling ragged. I know I can get
what I need here, in the tents surrounding the house or, if need
be, in the house itself. But not until dark.*

*This farmhouse is now a battlefield hospital—and the battle
to end all battles so far has been fought here today. When they
count the dead in that cornfield between the house and Antietam Creek, they won't stop till they reach twenty-three thousand. This whole countryside stinks of the blood and excrement
of dying men.*

*Another smell hangs like a miasma over the farmhouse: the
unmistakable meaty odor of burnt flesh. It is not a stench, but
the smell of cautery. A smell that excites me even though I know
what butchers these surgeons are. Butchers, brutes, men of little
knowledge and less vision. Cut it off, throw it away, seal up
what remains and bring on the maggots to eat the decomposing
flesh off the stumps—that's all they know how to do.*

I feel not the slightest qualm about the so-called criminal acts that are necessary to support my work. It cannot be a crime to steal from such unenlightened men.

And so I stand back in the trees, observing that the screams of the soldiers' amputations have ceased, and knowing that this is because it has grown too dark inside the farmhouse for the butchers to operate. It is always darker inside than out. This is what I have been waiting for: that brief period just as darkness falls when they are mopping up the blood from the floors and gathering up all the severed flesh in baskets. That is the precise time when I can slip into the supply tents unnoticed. A perfect time when it is still light enough out here for me to see, yet inside the house they are too much occupied by the last tasks of their exhausting day to pay me any mind. That time is fast approaching.

I'm ready, energy surges through my body and I forget the emptiness in my stomach and how every muscle aches. I begin to move. But just as I approach the edge of the clearing, I hear the creak of a screen door, and I must hide behind the thick trunk of the one tree that stands between me and discovery.

A door opens—I see its opening as a blacker rectangle in the black bulk that is the farmhouse. And in that yawning rectangle looms something white, which floats out into the yard, toward the tree where I am hiding.

What is this, an apparition?

It is a face, apparently bodiless; is it then a ghost?

Perhaps it is the disembodied spirit that wakes me in the night with its crying, that torments me until I go looking, looking, looking . . . but never can I find the one who cries.

Closer and closer the face floats toward me. I want to turn and run but I am chilled to my bones in spite of the heat of the late September night and my feet are leaden blocks that trap me on the ground. In that moment I am as afraid as I have ever been.

Lady Luck steps in and saves me: The ghostly face turns away at the last moment—any closer, I should have either dissolved of fright or been discovered—and as the face presents its profile I see this is no apparition, but a woman. A real woman of short stature, with dark hair. She wears a black dress, and her hands are covered with dried blood; I can smell it on her. She might as well be wearing black gloves. Only her white face reflects the last available light—from a distance she had appeared to be bodiless.

I hold back a huge sigh that comes with the relief flooding through me, and I watch with interest as the woman folds back the canvas flap on the nearest tent. She enters, then closes the flap behind her.

As I am debating whether I might take a chance and follow her—it's a long time since I've had a woman—from inside the tent a light blooms and turns the canvas walls to gold. The woman's shadow moves against the light, more gracefully than she can know. She unbuttons her jacket and slips it from her shoulders, pours water into a bowl, washes her hands and arms. I watch all this like a pantomime show, her silhouette in black against a golden ground.

She stirs me to erection; this is pleasurable. She stirs something in my soul too; but this I neither like nor wish to understand.

I take a step toward her tent, and then another—and once more my Lady Luck saves me, for I am still in the shadows when again I hear that creak of the door opening. This time I hear as well a heavy tread descend the porch steps, by which I know it is a man following the woman.

He wears the uniform of a Union officer. His clothes are too clean for him to be a doctor, yet an officer cannot be a nurse, so I wonder what he is doing here at this field hospital. For the first time I wonder too, what is the woman doing here? There are no females allowed at the front, all battlefield nurses are men. She should not be here.

I shift my weight from foot to foot, the minutes are passing by, my special time will soon be gone. I try to be patient, reminding myself that I can still achieve my purpose as long as I have the cover of night. But I am tired, hungry and thirsty; the woman, and now the man, is an impediment.

The man approaching the tent is tall and fair, but he has the look of a weakling. I could take him. He is stupid too: He raises his hand as if to knock on her door—but of course a tent has no door—and now he looks at his hand for a moment as if he does not know what to do with it—

Idiot! *I silently curse him. Above all else I despise stupidity.*

Then he drops his hand to his side, leans his cheek against the canvas flap and calls out: Clara?

Clara. *It is the first time I have heard her name.*

I swayed on my feet with the power of the memory.

That, a memory touched off by the act of lighting my own lamp, was the source of my strange feelings. In truth I was still both angry and a bit in awe of what Clara did to me that night at Antietam—the night she stole my darkness— the dark I needed to do my work.

This was how she did it: From a seemingly bottomless coffer inside her tent, she brought forth lamps. Small candle lamps in glass chimneys, lamps by the dozens, which she lit one by one and passed to her stupid helper, who carried them into the house. Back and forth and back and forth he went, as lamps and still more lamps poured from Clara's hands, until the whole farmhouse even unto its very porch stood ablaze with light.

The doctors worked on through the whole night. And

without my cloak of darkness, I was forced to leave with empty hands and an empty stomach.

I have hated that woman ever since; it gives me the greatest pleasure to hate her, almost as much pleasure as I feel in my work.

Oh, I have plans for Clara Barton.

Chapter 3

The next day Clara sat in her room by the back window, sewing; the bright sunlight was helpful, flashing upon her silver needle as she made tiny stitches in black thread upon the black linsey-woolsey that had not been her first choice in fabric, but the best she'd been able to obtain. Sun or no, it was tedious work, and she stopped from time to time to rub at the place on her forehead where an age line threatened to form.

She was making a new skirt to go with the jacket of her riding habit, because she'd promised Colonel Elwell that she would ride with him when he was well enough to sit a horse again. Sewing her own clothes was not only necessary, since for her war work she drew no salary, but here on Hilton Head it occupied the time—kept her fingers nimble and her hands busy—though to be truthful, she would have preferred an activity that also occupied her mind. A good book, for instance—but alas, she had not seen a bookshop or the inside of a library for a very long time.

Clara unconsciously sighed, held her seam up to the light to be sure it was straight, and sighed again.

Through the open window on the back side of the house she could hear the surf breaking on the ocean side of the island. She could smell and taste the salt-tang of the sea. The Atlantic's gray-blue waters were visible, but not the beach itself. Nor from this particular vantage could any of the several hastily constructed buildings that comprised the army's ordnance and supply depots be seen. In the near distance, obscuring a view of the sands oceanside, rose a tangle of low-growing vegetation. All the plants and trees out there were of wild or peculiar appearance, at least to her eyes, and most had no fragrance. For the first time in her life Clara was living in a place where she could not identify the local flora. The only plant native to Hilton Head that she could easily recognize was the palmetto—a short, spiky little palm that seemed more bush than tree.

Clara let her hands rest in her lap for a moment and stared out toward the horizon, searching keen-eyed for a boat. Any kind of boat, sail or steam, large or small. But today there was nothing out there, no sign of activity of any sort upon the ocean. A warm breeze curled through the window frame and caressed her face so gently that she could not help but smile.

On such a spring day it was hard to believe that somewhere else—*many* somewheres else, and some of them not too far away—at this very moment brave men were shooting and slashing each other to pieces. Fighting, falling, screaming, dying, each for his own chosen cause. The noise and the stench would be horrific, and the sights unspeakable.

Here one heard only the calls of seagulls out over the water, and the twittering of house sparrows under the eaves.

The everyday human sounds—footsteps, conversations that through her four walls became distant murmurings, with the occasional punctuation of a sharply barked order—these were so constant Clara scarcely heard them at all anymore.

She picked up her sewing again. She'd taken only a few stitches when there came a perfunctory knock at her open door.

"Sister?"

"Come in, David," Clara said to her brother, recognizing his voice before she'd turned her head. Many of the men called her "Sister"; it was a common term for a female nurse.

The sight of her brother tugged at her heart today, as it so often did: David was an exceptionally handsome man, even at past fifty with his black hair going gray and lines of exhaustion beneath the high cheekbones all the Bartons had in common. In him the family's inherited physical characteristics had come together most harmoniously: He had their father's light eyes, whereas she had their mother's dark ones; and where Clara had only an indentation like a thumbprint upon her chin, David bore a deep cleft so striking that he had never worn a beard. He grew thick sideburns instead, and Clara easily forgave him that small vanity.

"Sister . . ." he said again, hesitating on the edge of she knew not what.

"You seem uncommonly reticent today, brother." She'd set aside her sewing and came forward now with open arms, going up on tiptoe to kiss his cheek.

He did not kiss her back. For all his good looks David was shy and undemonstrative, always had been. His eyes darted around the room, avoiding hers.

So, are you looking to see what new gift the Colonel has lav-ished on me? Clara wanted to ask, but of course she didn't. Instead she said, with a reserve equal to his: "Shall we sit?"

"I suppose."

Clara gestured David to the rocking chair, and brought over the ladder-back chair from the window for herself.

David leapt up. "Let me get that."

"Don't be silly, I already have it. This chair is light as a feather." She sat and regarded him expectantly.

"I have, er-hum," he nervously cleared his throat, "two things. The first is Army business. The second is, I suppose you could say, family business."

"And in which order would you like to take them?" Clara asked, with amused affection.

She and David had a strong brother-sister bond with a unique twist that stemmed from her nursing him through a long, serious illness when she'd been only eleven years old to his twenty-four. Since then he'd often said—oblivious to the less-flattering aspects of the remark—that his sister Clara had been born old. Whereas she often thought, without say-ing so, that in many ways David had never grown up.

At her question he chuckled; Clara ignored the fact that it sounded forced.

"If I don't tell you the Army business first, I doubt you'd pay much attention to the other. You're too eager to see some action."

"Quite right." She folded her hands. "But only so that we can get this war over with as quickly as possible. Pray, pro-ceed."

"I've just come from a meeting of the officers with Elwell. He formally requests that you provide him with a list of donated materials you can make ready for the arrival of casualties."

Nothing could have surprised her more. "What?"

Too agitated by this sudden news to sit still, she jumped up from her chair and paced a few steps while her mind rushed ahead.

"When?" She turned back to David. "And how? There is nothing, David, absolutely nothing going on around here! There cannot be a battle without some sort of visible preparation—ordnance, men, *something*—flowing through the Quartermaster Corps!"

"A hospital ship, a steamer, is to arrive in our harbor sometime in the next three days—depending on when the battle takes place, exactly. This ship is to receive the wounded as they are transported. They don't want to send the hospital ship ahead or the Rebs may spot it, and the plan will be given away."

Clara paced again. This was what she had been waiting for, but somehow it didn't seem right.

"But still . . ." She started her objection, then couldn't find the precise words to finish it. "All right. Where are we talking about?"

David leaned forward, elbows on his knees. "They're going to take Charleston Harbor at last, Clara. It's to be entirely a naval battle. The ships are coming down from the North. I don't know the details because Elwell doesn't either."

"Who is in charge?" She sat, somber now. "What number of ships?"

"I don't know. If the Colonel does, he didn't say. That's none of our concern anyway. The point is, you're to get your supplies ready. The casualties, if there are any, will be brought in by boat."

If there are *any!*

Clara seriously worried about her brother when he made

such remarks, which showed his lack of experience. He was new to his commission and to military service; at over fifty, who would have thought he'd volunteer? But he had, and she'd lost her previous assistant to typhoid, so she'd done the logical thing—campaigned to get David appointed as the male military escort her battlefield permit required. She only hoped he'd never find out she was behind his commission in the Quartermaster Corps, the army branch that handled her assignments.

David couldn't provide her with answers or even with grounds for discussion—it had been pointless to ask. She'd been in the thick of Washington politics herself since the beginning, and on a few battlefields since. Clara had a far greater base of experience than her brother—even though, to her everlasting frustration, as a female she was not allowed to take up a gun and fight. She was a dead-straight shot, taught by both her father and her brothers; oh, how she longed to be a soldier.

Yet Clara calmed herself and said quietly: "I understand. I'll begin as soon as we've finished our conversation. Now: The other thing you wished to tell me was . . . ?"

He shifted in his chair, glanced away, then back without quite meeting her eyes.

Uh-oh, Clara thought. Oh, how she missed dear Cornelius Welles, who as her assistant had been irreproachable because he was an ordained minister. Even more important, Cornelius had respected her as a woman who'd lived alone in her own apartment in Washington City for more than a decade, and had worked as the only female clerk in the Government Patent Office. He did not, for instance, make a fuss when Clara chose to sleep alone in her own tent. But David was another matter. All too often he interpreted his role as one of guardian and chaperon.

"As I said," David began, "it is in a way a family matter."

Case in point, Clara thought, hard-put not to roll her eyes. With great restraint, she merely nodded.

Her brother set his jaw and raised that cleft chin slightly—in determination, she supposed, to see to his family duty. He said, "It's about Colonel Elwell."

"Yes?" She raised her chin higher than he had—an old habit when challenged by either of her brothers, sign of a possible fight to come.

"Did you know he's a married man?"

"No, I did not, but it doesn't surprise me. Most officers are married men, including yourself."

"Captain Lamb is a bachelor," David said too eagerly, "and he is near to you in age. He finds you quite attractive."

"So you're matchmaking again, is that it?" Clara's voice held an icy edge that David would have heeded, had he been anyone else. But secure in their unique relationship, he didn't even hear it.

"I suppose I am, yes." David smiled. He was utterly charming when he smiled, but she was left untouched.

"Leaving aside the fact that I know exactly what I'm doing with Colonel Elwell," Clara said carefully, "and I daresay he feels the same with regard to me, you must—*absolutely must*—stop this kind of thing. If you don't, you and I will never be able to get along for the rest of this tour of duty, never mind for however long the country may remain at war."

She might as well have been talking into the wind; David plunged on with his argument.

"Elwell is entirely too taken with you. Everyone has noticed. They talk about the two of you."

"I'm a little taken with him too, but that's not the point. The point is your unwelcome matchmaking. I am *never* going to marry, and there is nothing you can say or do to change that. As a matter of fact, I prefer to *avoid* eligible men for that very reason!"

"But Clara, you *must* marry! Father didn't leave enough money to provide for you for the rest of your life. You know that! Your attitude is stubborn, and, and, worse than unconventional—it's irresponsible. Just as Mother used to say."

He'd pushed her too hard. Their father, a much-loved man everyone in their town had called the Old Soldier, had not been dead long and Clara still actively mourned him. Yet their mother, who'd died first, she had not mourned— for good reason. Clara had been an accidental baby, born during her mother's menopause, and her mother had completely rejected her. All Clara's lessons, and all her nurturing, had come from her father and brothers.

Her deepest, darkest secret, which she generally kept even from herself, was how much she had longed for her mother's approval, if not for the love that now remained forever out of reach.

So Clara whirled on David: "I can provide for myself! I do not need a legacy. When the war is over I'll go back to work and draw a salary again. I don't need anyone to look after me, nor do I need to be reminded that you were Mother's favorite. I swear, David, if I'd known you were going to pry into my private life I wouldn't have wanted you to come south with me in the first place!"

Oh dear, now she'd done it: lost her temper, hurt his feelings, and come much too close to spilling the truth about his appointment. Now Clara did roll her eyes, but in self-reproach. At the same time she quickly reached out to touch his arm, and altered her tone of voice as she tried to make amends.

"Please don't misunderstand," she said. "I know how

lucky I am to have you since Cornelius fell ill with the typhoid and hasn't yet recovered. But I'm a grown woman, David. I don't *need* you to look after me."

"Clarissa," he said gravely—it was her full given name, but she hated it; only their mother had consistently called her Clarissa, which right now made it a very bad choice on David's part—"that's the very nature of the problem. You're a grown woman, and if you get much older before you marry, it's likely you'll be unable to have children. That is why you must marry soon. Can't you see that? Since you can't possibly marry John Elwell, your time would be far better spent elsewhere."

"I am not going to marry," she said with her hands clenched and her jaw tight. "I will never have children. Since I never had any mothering to speak of, I do not know how to do it. I would make a terrible mother if I were to try it myself, and I do not intend to inflict such an experience upon an innocent child."

"But—"

"I know you, David Barton—what really bothers you is the gossip. And there would be less gossip if I were spending my time *elsewhere,* isn't that right? For the sake of some small-minded propriety, I am supposed to disregard the fact that I enjoy Colonel Elwell's company for the quality of his mind and for the liveliness of our discussions. Captain Lamb is a sweet man but nowhere near the Colonel's intellectual equal.

"You might also consider, brother, that I have far more time available right now to spend with the Colonel than anyone else on Hilton Head. He is the commanding officer, and he needs the stimulation I can provide to hasten his recovery."

David's cheeks colored slightly, but he was not quite

ready to give up yet. "You're doing damage to your reputation," he insisted. "There is already talk that the two of you are having—"

"An affair?" she suggested, taking right out of his mouth the words she knew he would find distasteful. She felt a hundred years older than he. "You may take my word for it: The Colonel's wound is in such a location that he could not bear the type of physical contact that is necessary to perform the act you, and the other gossips, have in mind."

This time David blushed outright, though Clara's own cheeks remained as cool as always. She was not a person who blushed, nor did she show any emotion she chose to suppress—an ability she'd fought hard with herself to achieve.

"I do not wish to discuss this further," she said. "You'll have to trust that I know what I'm doing, and if my behavior causes you distress, you may request reassignment. I won't hold it against you, David. I'll understand if you leave."

"But—"

"As Shakespeare or someone once said," she smiled, and more playfully than she felt she grasped both her brother's hands and tugged him to his feet, " 'but me no buts.' This discussion is over. I have work to do now. If this hospital ship arrives tomorrow, I doubt I can be ready."

David allowed himself to be tugged along toward the door, where he stopped, bent and most uncharacteristically kissed Clara on the cheek. "Do you need my help?"

"No, thank you," she said, because she wanted to be alone; and even if she were to need help, the last person she wanted it from at the moment was David—unusual kisses notwithstanding.

Then she had an inspiration: "But there is one thing you could do."

"What's that?"

"Ask Captain Lamb if we might hire one of those young black boys who are always hanging around to help me shift boxes, load the wagon, and things of that sort. There are far better ways for you to spend your time.

"As I'm sure," she added with a twinkle, "Captain Lamb himself will be glad to tell you."

ST. HELENA ISLAND

Come the dawn, as they say, and there I was standing in one of my experimental subjects' rooms, whose barred door I had apparently left open last night. The experiment itself was nowhere to be seen. The bed was empty, but there were drag marks, and a nasty bandage on the floor.

Tch, tch, I said to myself. I wondered where it had got to. Not likely to have gone anyplace on its own. It wouldn't have survived—surely I had gotten to the point in my examination where I'd seen that much, before I'd been interrupted?

Hard to remember . . .

It had been Clara who'd interrupted me, of course. The necessity of writing that next letter had grown too huge to ignore.

Now, puzzled by what had become of my experiment, I tried to remember step by step what I had done last night.

First I'd lit the lamps, and then I'd seen to those specimens I'd brought home, the hands and feet of Jackson's female friend. But they were no good, they'd gone high on me—it's a pity how fast things spoil outdoors in this humid climate.

So I'd put the useless specimens aside, in the usual place, for Jackson to bury later. And then I'd proceeded to examine my experiments one at a time. As well as I recalled, there had been no surprises until I got to the last one. . . .

"Hmm," I said aloud, in the tone of the proverbial head-scratcher, although I myself did nothing so uncouth as scratch.

I'd seen this experiment wouldn't last much longer, but it was moaning, so I'd decided to change its binding.

Yes. I looked down now and saw the old binding on the dirt floor. But last night, hadn't I applied a new one?

By golly! I snapped my fingers. I had not!

I'd *intended* to do the job right, hopeless though I expected it to be—I'd taken care to go all the way back to the laboratory for clean cloth and some of my special powders—but then once in the laboratory I'd been distracted by the lamps. . . .

It was her fault, all those memories that had beset me earlier when I was lighting the lamps. Then suddenly writing to her that very minute last night had become far more urgent than anything else; I'm afraid the truth was the experiment had gone clean out of my head. I'd sat down to write the next letter, instead. I'd seen so clearly that it was the perfect time to ratchet up the tension to the next level.

Not, you understand, that I would ever intentionally set about to *terrify* anyone—that is not my way. But Clara Barton got in the way of my higher purpose, and so for her I have been making an exception.

I'm sure she expects no less—Clara is accustomed to having exceptions made for her, she insists upon them—so one has heard. Only woman on the battlefield and all that.

Well, in fairness (I do try to be fair), I've seen her there for myself and so I know it's true. But being *true* doesn't make it *right,* especially when she insists on getting in my way.

The method of my plan for Clara is to apply pressure slowly, and with steadily increasing tension, as well as increasing consequences. Consequences for *her,* of course.

Due to geographical necessity I began this process from afar several months ago, which at first was frustrating. But I had not remained frustrated long, for soon I'd realized how appropriate it was, in fact how delightful, to be able to create a sense of dread in another person without my actually having to *be* there, or to overtly *do* anything.

It was all only words. Words, words, words. Yet words in themselves have power, especially over a woman whose very reason for existence hangs upon her ability to write a good letter.

She has a reputation as a fine letter writer, Miss Clara Barton. A champion letter-writer. That was one of the first things I'd found out about her after learning her last name, the "Barton" to go with the "Clara" that her fair friend, the weakling, had called out. One of her damn letters had undoubtedly procured the supply of lamps she'd used to prevent my work that night at Antietam.

How utterly clever of me to turn her very own tactic back on her!

My source in Washington (for I do still have acquaintances there, some who have stood by me while the rest turned traitors) had told me that both Clara and her friend the weakling had caught the typhoid fever in the fall of last year, sometime after Antietam. Served them right; perhaps my Lady Luck had a hand in their ill fortune—or perhaps not, for almost everyone in the front lines gets typhoid sooner or later. No one knows why this happens, though there are plenty of theories.

I'd been right about the weakling: He *was* weak—he didn't recover from the typhoid but Clara Barton was back on her feet at the Battle of Fredericksburg sans the weakling in December. With my own eyes I'd seen her come out into the yard of the Lacy House, another field hospital where I'd been lurking for the usual purpose, in search of supplies. She'd stood there wringing blood out of the hems of her skirts just as calmly as a woman doing the wash. There'd been a veritable hill of amputated arms, legs, hands and feet not a yard from where she stood, but she hadn't glanced that way—not even once.

Admirable woman . . .

But, of course, quite damned.

I came out of my rememberings with the conclusion that I must have left the door to the experiment's room open when I'd rushed out to get more bandage material, but had ended up writing to Clara instead.

Hmmm. I looked about, tapping my foot. This was not good, not good at all.

My laboratory is some distance from the house, and the little rooms where I sequester my experiments are back still farther into the trees that encroach upon the Coffin Place, *my* place, from every side. I assume the little rooms are abandoned slave quarters, built all in a long row, side by side. I had them cleaned out and put on brand-new doors— I spared no expense—with bars to let in the light and to allow me to observe any time I want.

It is no great task, even for a city fellow like myself, to track through woods where every step disturbs the clutter on the forest floor, breaks little branches and so forth; to track an animal (man *or* beast) that is leaking body fluids, even an idiot could do. I am far from an idiot; therefore in very little time I had found what remained of my experiment.

Tch, tch, I thought, shaking my head, *predators.*

It was not a pretty sight, but I'm used to that; what bothered me the most was the predators had dragged the grafted part clean away. I spent some time looking for it, broke off a long stick and poked about in the undergrowth, but to no avail.

Pity. Now I'd learn nothing from this one. Its death was to no purpose. What a waste.

Nor would I ever know—from the signs on the ground it was impossible to tell—whether it had dragged itself out here on its own, or the predators had gotten in and done the dragging.

Either way it was more work for Jackson, who does not particularly like to dig, and I went back to the house calling his name.

HILTON HEAD

"Well, I declare!" Clara exclaimed with her fists on her hips. It was about as close as she ever came to swearing aloud. There was no one but herself in the storage shed to hear—she could with impunity have recited every swear word she knew, and certainly the war had increased her vocabulary considerably in that regard.

"The Colonel will get an earful from me about this!" she mumbled, furious at seeing her territory invaded. She glared disgustedly at the key in her hand before thrusting it back into her pocket. Obviously someone else also had a key to this shed, and that someone had shoved her things back where she wasn't even sure she could get to them.

Clara was small but she was strong. Hard physical work did not put her off. In fact, she believed her physical strength to be the main reason she'd recovered relatively quickly from the typhoid.

She rolled up her sleeves, tucked her skirt up an inch or two at the waist—for real work she never wore a hoop and kept the petticoats to a minimum of one or two—and then she got vigorously to the task of clearing herself a path.

That illness, the typhoid, had been an awful experience. Especially for dear Cornelius, who the last she'd heard was at least alive but still confined to the hospital. He was in the same hospital where Clara had refused to go, insisting she could recover at home just as well. Hospital space was precious, and she was only a woman; the soldiers transporting her in back of a flatbed wagon had been only too happy to comply with her wish to go back to her apartment in Washington. Most likely it had never occurred to them that she lived alone.

There had been days when she lay in bed in her apartment, shaking with fever, thinking she'd made a mistake in assessing her illness and she might die after all; sometimes she'd drifted in and out of consciousness, wondering if she did die, how long it would be before someone came and found her body; finally in the end she'd decided it didn't matter if she died and decomposed right there in her bed, because she'd caught the typhoid doing the one thing she had most wanted to do: She'd been to the battlefield. Been to more than one. She had walked those battlefields and found men still alive who otherwise would have been left for dead. She'd fulfilled a promise she'd made to her father on his deathbed—she had gone to war in her own way, even if her sex would not allow her to be a real soldier, a hero like he had been.

"And I did it even if that drat-blasted woman Dorothea Dix wouldn't let me in her blame nursing corps!" she muttered, uncharacteristically letting loose with some more of the milder swear words in her increased vocabulary.

Oh how it still rankled that Dix had turned her down! It was well known that Miss Dix accepted only married women, or else spinsters she considered "plain"; in Miss Dix's opinion the unmarried Miss Barton had not been plain enough to qualify. But Clara took no consolation from such a backhanded compliment. Who did Dorothea Dix think she was anyway? What human being in her right mind could give a fig for such false standards of propriety in dire times like these?

On her own Clara had gone to the Washington headquarters of the U.S. Sanitary Commission, which ran the medical corps. She'd been appalled by what she saw, how few doctors they had, and far less supplies than they needed to keep up with the casualties. So she'd volunteered to bring in supplies on her own, to solicit donations, to organize and distribute whatever she obtained—and soon her whole project just grew like Topsy. The Sanitary Commission gave her an official designation of "relief worker."

Still the need was so great that Clara became a nurse de facto.

Everyone, from Senator Henry Wilson, who was her staunchest advocate, right on down to the lowliest army private on Hilton Head, thought of Clara as a nurse and called her "nurse" or "sister." Her lack of nurse's training she placed square on Miss Dix's head. Clara did what was needed as best she could, as she was told. Every way she assisted the doctors came from common sense, or from something she'd learned by watching them. Some things she'd learned long ago, in the course of nursing her brother David and becoming the Barton family nurse thereafter. Her mother had abdicated that role, though in most families the mother was also the resident nurse.

At least her mother hadn't lived long enough to see Dorothea Dix turn her down—Clara would never have heard the end of it.

While thinking about all this she had made some progress at stacking piles of linked wooden slats up against the front wall of the storage shed. What she really wanted to do was throw them every which way out into the dirt road.

Someone, some extremely inconsiderate and no doubt boorish person, had filled up every obtainable inch with the blasted things, totally blocking a neat space she'd intentionally left as a narrow aisle. She'd known from experience she might, at any time, need to be able to walk back among her labeled boxes of donated materials in order to get quickly at whatever was most needed, whenever it was needed.

She understood the purpose of these cumbersome, heavy slats—they'd be laid down over muddy ground to form a kind of temporary road, over which the troops could march much faster than through sucking mud. But this presumed that someone would be ordered ahead to lay the road, which further presumed someone in charge knew where they were going, and that in turn presumed an even-higher-up-the-chain-of-command person actually knew where the next battle would be fought.

Hah! Not too very likely, not anymore . . .

So the damn slats were just so much excess baggage, in her way—

But her anger was not really about the slats. Was it? Was

it really so important that someone had filled up her shed, blocked her way?

Clara paused, panting. The humidity was making for sweaty work. She wiped the back of her hand across her forehead, probably leaving a smear of dirt because the slats were as encrusted with old, dried mud as one might expect from something that had been used that way. For once, though, she didn't care about her appearance.

What she cared about was losing control of her feelings. Letting her temper run away with her like this, for instance. She stood in the stifling, smutty-smelling shed and instead of taking inventory of her stores, she took an inventory of herself.

Clara came quickly to the obvious conclusion: She was on edge, no doubt about it. The evidence was there.

Yesterday the Colonel had delivered her a slight rebuff, to which she'd completely overreacted. She'd come dangerously close to some old feelings of hopelessness that were completely unnecessary in the present situation.

Earlier today she'd almost lost her temper with David, which in itself wasn't that unusual—but the fact that she'd come so close to throwing the truth about his appointment in his face, that was a great concern. David must never, ever know how hard she'd lobbied to get him made captain and appointed to escort her down to Hilton Head. He wouldn't believe she'd done it with his best interests at heart. As his sister she knew better than anyone how, all his life, David would never fight about anything except as a last resort, how much he deplored violence on principle. Attached to the Quartermaster Corps, with any luck he could remain behind the lines in times of battle.

Spare us from our brothers and sisters! she thought, as an irony struck her. She slowed a bit, pondering.

The irony: David must have told himself the very same thing, that he had her best interests at heart—when instead he was severely trying her patience by harping all the time on marriage. Not to mention children.

Well, there was nothing she could do about it now, any more than what she had already done. She made a mental note of the irony and went back to work.

Soon Clara was working harder and faster than before. She cleared a path halfway down the aisle she'd left between her boxes. Then instead of neatly stacking she began to sling the slats behind her, where they clattered loudly on the wood floor; she could go back and stack them later.

At least, she reflected, this shed *had* a proper floor—it had been raised up on blocks so that a tidal overflow wouldn't ruin the things stored inside.

Clara worked faster still—she intentionally made a lot of noise, the more crashing the better—and she *loved* the noise, it felt highly satisfactory, a kind of antidote to the quiet that had reigned on Hilton Head for long enough.

Who are you, a voice whispered inside her head, *to decide when it has been quiet for long enough here, or anywhere?*

That voice stopped her cold. She stood trembling, feeling the rage that drove her—and again the strength of her emotions was frightening.

She sneezed, her eyes watered, she wiped her hands and then her face with the hem of a petticoat. But she knew it was not the dust that made her eyes water—it was the beginning of tears.

Clara blinked them back, and as she did, at last she named the reason for her loss of emotional control: *those damned letters!*

Chapter 4

"Ma'am? Ma'am?"

"Oh!" Clara turned too quickly, betraying how much the unexpected voice had startled her. "I'm sorry, I didn't hear you at first."

It was only a boy, all gangly limbs and white teeth.

"Cap Lamb says go hep Miss Clara," he said, grinning wider, his smile bright as a lantern in the storage shed's dim and dusty atmosphere. "You Miss Clara?"

"Yes, I am," she answered, wiping her hands on her skirt and smoothing it down, "and I certainly could use some help."

"I be Razzmus." He ducked his head, tipped it to one side and seemed at once both innocent and sly. He was about Clara's height, just under five feet. "My momma say I be *Ee*-rasmus, but mos'ly I likes jus' Razz."

"Then I shall certainly call you Razz—at least, mostly." Clara grinned too, for his good humor was infectious.

She extended her hand to the boy, who looked at it for a moment, puzzled, as if he didn't know what to do. Then one side of his wide mouth curved up, tentatively, and he lightly placed his long, skinny fingers against her palm. She grabbed his hand and gave it a hearty shake.

"Thank you for coming, Razz. Shall we get to work?"

"Yes'm! Cap says I works for pay!"

"Of course you do."

"He say now I be on payroll!"

Clara felt glad along with the boy because he was so obviously pleased, but a part of her also felt slightly sick over the meaning behind his delight. She reminded herself: *This is what we're fighting for, so that when Razz grows up to have sons and daughters of his own, it will never occur to them that anyone might expect them to work without being paid.*

Like Clara, Razz was stronger than he looked. He was also quick, smart and practical. Once he'd identified the long links of wooden slats as unwanted material, she didn't have to tell him what to do. He quickly and correctly calculated there was not enough room in the shed for all the slats, no matter how neatly they might be stacked, and began to stack them outdoors to one side of the shed instead.

"Them needs a tarp'lin," he eventually observed.

Assuming what he meant was a tarpaulin, she agreed with him. She took her small notebook out of her pocket, scribbled a note of authorization, and sent Erasmus off in search of one.

Notebook still in hand, Clara got started on her inventory and immediately forgot everything else. She didn't hear Razz return, but when it was time to shift boxes so that she could read her marks on the sides of the wooden crates in the next row back, Razz was right there, quietly waiting for her to call on him.

A willing helper and an easy companion, she couldn't have asked for better even if Razz was only, she estimated, about fourteen. They worked well together. When she was quiet, so was the boy; when she spoke, he replied, and as the afternoon wore on he began to anticipate her wishes.

Eventually, and inevitably, visibility in the windowless storage shed dwindled down to near dark. Clara looked out the doorway and saw long shadows amid the burnished light cast by the setting sun.

Razz came and stood by her. He said, "I could maybe get a lamp, or a candle."

"No, that's all right. These are the last crates and I know what's in them. They're all blankets."

She scribbled the word "blankets" at the bottom of her list, folded the notebook, and slipped it into her pocket. With her other hand she searched in the other pocket for the key to the shed. They'd worked hard and she was tired—but far more important, she had a feeling of accomplishment for the first time in at least two weeks.

"I wisht I could do that," Razz said wistfully as they went out and Clara locked the door.

Somehow she didn't think he meant locking a door, so she asked, "Do what?"

"Make them marks like you do in that little book you put in your pocket. You reads 'em later, right? What for?"

"So that I can tell the Colonel exactly what I have in the boxes."

Razz thought about this, then nodded solemnly. "That be a good way."

So, Clara thought, *Erasmus does not have Annabelle's aversion to writing. Interesting.*

The shed, due to its being up on blocks, had one step. Clara glanced at him and said, "Sit down here with me. I want to rest for a while, and we can talk. I'd like to know more about you."

He looked shocked. "You wants me sit on that stoop with you?"

"Yes, please." Clara smiled, arranging her bulky skirts to make room and patting the empty spot beside her. "I want to ask you some questions."

The boy pulled at one long earlobe. He cocked his head to one side, in that engaging way he had. Apparently concluding there was no harm in her rather unorthodox idea, he suddenly plopped down beside her.

"What you wants to know?"

Wiser now for her experience with Annabelle, she began with: "Do you have another name, or is it just Erasmus?"

"Razz be good enough for me, but my momma, she called Miz Ettamae Sullivan. That 'cause my pappy—he be gone in Gen'ral Gillmore Negro regiment—he Race Sullivan. So I guess if I needs 'nother name, it be Sullivan."

"Erasmus Sullivan. My whole name is Clarissa Harlowe Barton, but like you, I have a name I prefer to go by, which is Clara. You said your father's name is Race?"

"He name Race Sullivan on account he take care Massa Sullivan racehorses. He maybe have 'nother name but . . ." Razz frowned mightily, "I forgets. Everybody, Momma too, call him Race. Massa Sullivan place be way far from here, past Drayton Plantation, 'bout twenny mile to inland. Massa Sullivan, he lost lotta money on them horses when I'se a baby, an' he sell my momma an' me over here to Miz Penny. So I never see my pappy much anyhow."

"You and your mama live here on Hilton Head, then?"

"Just me. My mama gone now. She a house slave. Miz Penny done took her off inlan' but not me. I stays in our ole cabin down Penny Place. Lots us field hands stay there. Some works here fo' the army, some jes sets around." He shrugged, as if he didn't quite approve of the last.

Clara decided not to remind Razz that he and his mother weren't slaves anymore. She didn't want to interrupt the flow of their talk, nor to make him feel as if he'd been reprimanded. So she went on:

"Penny Place is here on Hilton Head?"

"Yes'm." Razz turned and pointed toward the southwest, and the sunset flowed over his dark skin in a coat of bronze. "Down thatta way. Where they build up all them walls, and put the big guns, and all."

The far end of Hilton Head faced a Rebel-held section of the mainland, and had heavy fortifications. Clara had been down there only once and had seen the walls with their gun emplacements, but not the plantation where he said he lived.

"You have a long walk to get here," she observed.

"Yes'm, but here be where the work is."

"Quite right." She resisted a strong impulse to reach out and tousle his hair—not that the wiry black bush on his head would react much to tousling. "And you're a good worker. We did well together today."

The boy hung his head for a moment, then looked up at her with an expression that would have been coy if he'd been a long-lashed girl, but instead merely registered a little embarrassment.

Clara decided to risk a question she'd been wanting very much to ask: "You're not Gullah, are you?"

She was learning a lot, very quickly, on her first trip into the Deep South. In her Yankee ignorance she'd thought of the Negroes as belonging to one black race, all much the same. Now she'd begun to see differences, even in the small sample on this one island. Razz, for example, spoke a dialect different from the Gullah language. And his skin, while very dark, lacked the purplish sheen of the Gullah.

Razz frowned at her question and suddenly became very interested in his bare, dusty toes.

Eventually he replied, still studying his toes, "Nome."

This she took for no. She wanted to ask more, but as it was obviously a touchy subject for him, she refrained.

The boy continued on his own: "Over to Sullivan plantation, where I be born, peoples come from 'nother, different part of Africa. Long time ago. But the Gullah, they been here longer than we. They *ancient.*"

"I see." Interesting, his use of the word *"ancient,"* and his emphasis upon it. Could there be a hierarchy among the Negroes, in which by virtue of having survived in slavery longer, the Gullah were at the top—and were they somehow enforcing their hold on their top position?

Erasmus interrupted her speculations.

"Miss Clara, you know where Africa be?"

She answered his eager question with one of her own: "Have you ever seen a map of the world, Razz?"

"Nome." He looked at his toes again. "Couldn't read it nohow."

"A map is like a big picture. You don't have to be able to read the words on it to understand a map. It shows you what parts of the Earth are covered with water, and what parts are land. Some maps show where the mountains are on the land, and rivers too. And lakes, and cities and so on."

"Miz Penny must don't have no maps," he mumbled, digging his long toes into the sand. "Else she keep 'em hid."

Now why would he say that? Clara had an idea, and someday she'd find out, but for now she merely said, "Africa is far, far away. On the other side of the ocean out there. One of these days I'll show you."

"You really do that? When?"

"Yes, I will, as soon as I can lay my hands on a map of the world. Right now I only have maps of the United States.

"And I'll tell you what else I'll do," she went on, "that's even better. The very best of all."

Clara got to her feet. The sun had gone down, the sky was deepening and the breeze picked up, as it always did at twilight.

"Now you gone make Razz a promise?" There it was again, that bright grin.

"Ohhhh, I might," Clara teased, "let me think a minute."

She shook dust from her skirt and pushed back a few strands of hair that had come loose from the tightly rolled figure eight she wore at the back of her head. With a clean handkerchief from one of her well-supplied pockets, she wiped her face.

Erasmus stared, his grin fading as he waited, watching her.

Clara believed she could sense his thoughts: Erasmus Sullivan, or just Razz, was a boy who'd been let down by white people and their promises all his life—a life that might be short so far in years, but must seem long to him after all he'd been through. Sold away from his father, put to work in the fields at God knew how young an age, and now his mother had been taken from him too.

Clara wanted to be careful she didn't lead the boy to expect more than she could deliver. She asked, to be sure: "You want to learn to read and write, don't you?"

"Yes, *Mam!*" The boy jumped up. "Most of all; that's what I wants most of all! I wants to read books! Miz Penny, she got a whole room in the big house all full of books an' they all jus' there. No peoples, jus' books an' sticks of furniture. Oney I can't read a word on them books."

"Erasmus, why do you want to read so much?"

His desire to read and write was unusual. She'd heard for months, from many different sources, how hard it was to motivate the freed slaves, how their spirits had been broken by their former masters. Erasmus was different from everything she'd been told to expect.

And so, she thought, *is Annabelle.*

He pulled at his ear and gave her question careful consideration.

Night was coming on fast; the watch commander barked an order for the change of the guard; sounds of marching feet soon followed his bark. The gates of the palisades, the outermost fortifications that lay beyond the fenced enclosure immediately surrounding Headquarters House, clanged shut. The sound of their closing reverberated like a deep bell through the purple air. When Erasmus looked at Clara again the whites of his eyes seemed to glow.

"I wants to know things," he said. "Like where Africa be, and what do it look like. And where Nu Yok City. Where the Miss'ippi River. How them stars get up there?" He pointed to the sky. "How come they stay up there an' not fall on we heads? Things like that be in books, so my momma tell me."

Tears came to Clara's eyes. She didn't know how to respond. She wanted to take the boy's hand, but that would be far too familiar. So blinking back the tears, she began to walk in the direction of the main gate, knowing he would follow along.

"Yes, it's true," she said when she could be sure her voice was steady. "Books are full of all kinds of wonderful things. I have an idea, Razz, and if you like my idea, we can try to make it happen. But you mustn't think of this as a promise, exactly, because in wartime promises can be very hard to keep. Do you understand what I'm saying?"

" 'Course I knows we in a war! That why my pappy be in Genr'l Gillmore regiment. That why my momma be gone an' Miz Penny an' all them be gone too. That why sodjers be all over this here islan', buildin' walls and makin' messes. Razz ain't no baby, 'course I understands!"

In his indignation he had somewhat missed Clara's point, but never mind, she went ahead:

"I was thinking there are two women—ladies"—changing the word grated, but she'd learned it was best to call females "ladies" in the South—"on Parris Island, who are teachers. Their name is Gage. Perhaps you've heard of them?"

"Nome." Erasmus shook his head.

"Well, I've been wanting to meet them"—she had only been wanting it for the past few minutes, but that was enough—"and I was thinking, if I can get a boat, perhaps you could row me over there. Do you know the way through the marshes?"

"I know them creeks good as any Gullah!"

"In that case, if you'll help me get over to Parris Island on a regular basis, I expect one of the Gage ladies could give you lessons in reading and writing while we're there."

"When you wants to go?" Razz wouldn't need a lamp to light his way home if he kept on smiling like that. "T-marra?"

"Not tomorrow." They'd reached the main gate now and she lowered her voice, wary of the patrolling guards, who might or might not know as much as she did. "Remember about the war? I can't leave Hilton Head tomorrow, and maybe for a couple of days after that, because we're waiting for a certain ship to come. But I promise you—"

Oh dear, that word had slipped out anyway. She let it be, hoping this was one promise she would never have to break. "—we'll go to Parris Island just as soon as I possibly can.

Meanwhile, you come see me first thing every morning. I, or Captain Lamb, can always find work for you. Will you do that?"

"Yes'm."

"I know you have a long walk, so just get here as early as you can."

"Yes, *Mam!*"

"Tell the guard on the gate you're to work with me, and he'll tell you how to find me. Now let's get you a lamp and send you on home."

"I don't needs no lamp. Razz see in the dark." He grinned at his own exaggeration, and Clara waved him out the gate, thinking: *I wouldn't be surprised if he can.*

Someone had tacked a note to her door advising that supper would be a cold collation served by buffet in Colonel Elwell's room. Expecting that both David and Samuel Lamb would be present, and not feeling in the mood for polite conversation with her brother, Clara went immediately next door in spite of her accumulated dust and dirt. Swiftly, and with a smile, she explained that she'd been working all afternoon and asked to be excused from the meal.

John Elwell said—a warmth in his voice that no doubt caused David to inwardly cringe—"Miss Barton, I think I'll call you my Bird because you eat like one! You must promise to take a full plate of food with you, and then you may be excused."

Clara thanked him most kindly, touched Captain Lamb briefly with her smile, and avoided David's eyes altogether as she loaded her plate willy-nilly. It was true she didn't care much for food. True too, she flew back to her own room as quickly as any bird.

With her door closed safely behind her, she put the plate aside and began to unbutton her bodice, smiling quietly to herself. *My bird,* he'd said. *My Bird.* She liked the Colonel's comparison, found it apt, especially as she was about to take what she called a "bird bath."

There were tricks, she'd learned, to keeping as clean as she liked while traveling and living in close quarters with soldiers, who were generally less meticulous about these things. She made it a point to obtain her own large pitcher or bucket of water every day, wherever she happened to be. If necessary she'd hoard it, so that come evening she always had enough to wash herself. She hadn't seen a hip bath since she'd left Washington.

Of course at Headquarters House on Hilton Head they did not stoop to buckets. In her room Clara had a real washstand, with a china bowl and matching pitcher. The pitcher was still full of the water she'd fetched herself this morning, according to her habit. She closed all the curtains and disrobed to perform her ablutions. Then she dressed again from the skin out.

That was another thing she had learned early in her army experience: She never knew when they might call for her, so she remained completely dressed even at night in her own room—or in her tent if they were on the march. Her concessions to the comfort of an evening alone were few: no corset, just a chemise and only one petticoat under one of her daytime skirts, and on top a loosely fitted wrapper rather than her usual tailored blouse and jacket.

Dressed again, with a grateful sigh Clara pulled out the pins and let down her hair—her last and best concession to the evening hours. Her hair was thick and heavy; such a relief to no longer feel its coiled weight upon the back of her neck. She brushed and brushed, and with every stroke of the brush relaxed a little more.

Eventually she remembered she hadn't eaten, and took her plate to the back window, where she opened the curtains and pulled up the sash a few inches to let in the fresh, sea-scented air. A three-quarter moon cast a pale, wavering path over inky ocean waters. She sat with her plate in her lap and picked at her food until she noticed how good it tasted—ham that was salty but relatively fresh, a salad of potatoes with chopped egg and pickle, some kind of yeast rolls—and then she began to eat as if famished.

Even a bird, she thought, amused by a sudden dread of incipient gluttony, *must enjoy its worms occasionally.*

Far out to sea, a tiny light bobbed in the darkness. A boat? A ship? Her heart leapt, but only briefly; for even if that were the hospital ship they expected, it was far away and would not attempt to make harbor until morning. Then the little light winked out.

Clara left the window, resisting a desire to stand waiting to see if it might reappear, as it would if it were truly a ship that had only dipped into the trough of an ocean wave. But she had finished her meal, and to stand staring out of windows was not her way. She didn't intend to allow the relaxed customs of Hilton Head to creep into her routine any more than had already happened.

Evenings, Clara routinely wrote letters—the letters that, one way or another, procured the contents of more boxes like the ones in the storage shed.

Of course, it was possible Colonel Elwell might send for her to read to him. . . .

Clara put that enticing thought out of her mind, but not without effort.

The afternoon's work had left her feeling pleasantly

tired all over, which she considered an affirmation of her belief that physical activity made one strong, and was therefore good for women as well as men. Not a popular view, by any means—especially not in a region where one could not even say the word "women." Southern ladies, needless to say, did not do hard work.

Well, she thought, *without their slaves they may have to learn.*

With the thought came a certain amount of satisfaction, which she hoped was not too vindictive. She couldn't forget those hoopskirted Virginia belles who'd stood on the bluffs of the Potomac to watch the batteries of guns fire in the early days of the war. As if the killing of men were a spectacle staged for their entertainment, with a picnic to follow.

No one was picnicking now.

Well, that was not quite true, was it? There was picnicking on Hilton Head. Only the day before yesterday, Captain Lamb had proposed that she join him for one down at the south end of the island, on the ocean side.

"Oh dear God," Clara murmured, and for a moment she leaned against the wall resting her head in her hands. She was thinking how much she would have wanted to go if only it had been John Elwell doing the asking; thinking that just being in the South was turning her into some kind of idle hypocrite.

She lifted her head, pushed away from the wall and resolutely retrieved her portable writing desk from under the bed, where she kept it out of sight, at least, if not exactly hidden. She opened its sloping lid and took out paper and pens, then fitted the ink bottle into its place.

As she touched the paper she shivered a little, and she could have sworn that for a moment the lamps flickered and dimmed. But the shadow was only in her mind.

Those damned letters . . .

She wouldn't think about them.

She took the stopper off the ink bottle, held her pen up against the lamp to inspect its tip—of course the light was as strong as ever. Imagination can do strange as well as wonderful things.

Besides, he—for the person who wrote the awful, unsigned letters to her was surely a man—might not find her here. He'd written to her through the Army of the Potomac, to which she'd been previously assigned, and during her bout with typhoid his unwanted letters had arrived at her Washington City apartment right along with the many that were welcome. But how could he know that she'd gone to the Department of the South? Clara had told only her regular correspondents—all people she was close to, or who for reasons of helping in her work had a need to know. Surely none of them had such an evil, twisted mind.

The anonymous letter writer had to be a fanatic, a stranger who had read of her work in the newspapers and disapproved. . . .

I won't think about it anymore.

"No sense borrowing trouble," she added aloud, for emphasis; and then she dipped pen in ink and began to write to her childhood friend Mary Norton, who still lived in North Oxford, Massachusetts.

> *Dear Mary,*
>
> *I am on Hilton Head Island, where our Army keeps its Department of the South. Everything here is quite peaceful and splendidly gay. I live in an abandoned mansion, now called Headquarters House, in the most excellent situation—indeed it is all so excellent that I very much fear*

I should quite forget there is a war going on, if it were not for the constant presence of men in uniforms, carrying rifles and shouting orders, even though there is no need to shout.

David is somewhat discontent, I fear. He has begun to talk of getting a pass to go to North Carolina, where he wishes to inquire after our older brother. You will remember our brother Stephen, I'm sure. We've been told, but not with certainty, that Stephen's manufacturing business near New Bern has been seized by the Confederacy and turned to the Rebel cause. As Stephen himself would never swear allegiance to the Confederates, we are concerned for his fate. Nevertheless I have counseled David against going, for he does not seem to understand the dangers of travel in these times. My gentle brother is, I am sure, a good husband and father, but he is most impractical about the ways of war.

Our days of idle leisure on Hilton Head are numbered—you know from my last letter, which I recollect was written while I was waiting for passage on the Arago, I have something of a nose for battle. But since I may not write of these things until after the fact, for fear my letter may fall into the wrong hands, I will move on to another topic.

When I arrived here a few days ago, I found the commandant of the Quartermaster Corps, Colonel John Elwell, bedridden and in a very sorry state of health. He had fallen from his horse—not in battle, it was an accident—a bridge collapsed and he fell into a gully with the horse on top of him. The thighbone in his leg was broken. It pierced the skin and left a nasty wound after the bone ends had been forced back into proper place. By the time of

my arrival the poor Colonel was wracked with fever, dripping with sweat and occasionally delirious. I took over his
care immediately, and can say with good nursing he has
grown stronger every day.

Mary, Colonel Elwell is the most agreeable man I have
known in many a year. Though at the moment he is rather
pale and wan and has of course lost a great deal of weight,
he has an essentially strong constitution and a broad masculine build. When standing—though mind you I have never
yet seen him stand—I should think he must be well above
average height. Yet it is not only his physical attributes that
are so harmonious, but also his kindness and the quality of
his conversation. I do believe, if there were not a war going
on, I could talk to him forever. There is a restlessness, a spirit
of inquiry in his mind that quite matches my own.

The Colonel comes from Ohio, and he has had more
than one profession; how he landed in the Quartermaster
Corps I cannot fathom. Most recently he was teaching in
the field of medical jurisprudence at the Western Reserve
College in Cleveland. This extraordinary man is by training both a doctor and a lawyer! And he has served a term in
the legislature of his state.

But I must not run on so—for when my time on Hilton
Head is up, I am sure I will never see John Elwell again.
Now to business: I did an inventory of my stores today. . . .

From time to time, as she wrote, Clara felt a chill in the hol-
lows of her bones that had no cause in nature. When the
chill came she'd catch herself looking up from her writing,
and more than once she thought she saw a shadow slink

across the ceiling and hang there in the corner, like an evil spirit watching her.

BEAUFORT TOWN

In the afternoon, wearing my best clothes and a benevolent gentleman's persona, I went by horse and ferry from my place up to Beaufort—a trip that on a good day takes about an hour and a half. Each way, of course.

In an inner pocket of my jacket I carried my latest letter to Clara Barton, where it made an interesting warmth all the way through waistcoat and shirt, on into my skin. I mused over this peculiar phenomenon, supposing that warmth must come from the thrill of having a secret correspondence, one-sided though it may be. My scientific mind told me two pages of paper could not spontaneously generate heat—yet the heat is definitely there, and moreover has a sexual edge.

I daresay I shall be reluctant to part with the letter for that reason, when I have found a messenger I can trust to take it to Hilton Head—that being the primary purpose of this outing.

I sighed like the bored gentleman I pretended to be, took off my hat and ran my fingers through my hair. In truth I was not bored, I was enjoying the pleasant breeze that swept over the flat-bottomed ramshackle ferry—a conveyance that hardly deserves the name of "boat," but it's the only way across the river to Beaufort from Lady's Island.

I twirled my hat in my hand, enjoying the lovely spring weather in spite of a few minor annoyances. Such as: one of the ever-present insects, this one a long-legged affair that kept circling my head and landing upon the side of my face, but never long enough for me to slap it dead. Such as: the fact that I had no choice but to stand downwind of the ferryman, a pitch-black fellow of such powerful personal stench he made me vomitous.

Those things aside, it was quite a nice day.

Old Beaufort looked especially handsome from this distance, with the sun glinting off the tall houses facing the water along the far end of Bay Street. The sunlight struck at such an angle you couldn't see how the Yankee occupation had already—in just over a year—turned all shabby the grand facades with their parapets and pillared porches.

I don't take sides in this war, but there's no question the Confederates are more cultured and refined, have better houses and take better care of their things. Except their slaves. Some of the things I've seen done to those former slaves, who are now among the contraband, are as bad as any battle injury.

I recall one old fella who was brought to the Freemen's Clinic with his feet nothing but festering stumps below the ankles. Said his "massa" made him stand with his feet in the fire for some reason, I forget what, he'd made Massa mad somehow. Little wonder his heels fell off and his toes too— by the time I saw him he had only one toe left and that one, not for long. He wouldn't die, though; if he were going to die he'd have done it already by then. They're hardy, these people. Their blood can get so thin from the poor food that their skin turns dusky; they're starved right down to the bone and their eyes have gone dead—but still they live on. Their women live the longest of all.

For these reasons they make good experimental subjects, when I can get one. My scientific studies have shown that the Negroes are not much different physically from the rest of us, except of course for the color of their skin. They react to stimuli the way we do—to borrow and paraphrase from the immortal Shakespeare, "If you prick them they do bleed"—with blood just as red as anyone's. Their meat and mucosa, the inner parts not normally exposed to sunlight or air, are also decidedly pink to reddish; it is truly the most curious thing. A black woman's vagina is pink as can be.

While I had been engaged in these scientific ruminations, the ferry had completed its crossing of the placid Beaufort River and was now bumping at the dock. I led my horse off and left him tethered down by the waterfront, where I was interested to observe that Nature knows her seasons and nothing of war, for there was a fine crop of grass. It had a fresh odor that cleansed my nostrils of the ferryman's stink. The horse was delighted and set in to graze while I strolled on into town.

I started up Charles Street, reminding myself that at some point I should stop by the clinic—but I couldn't remember if today was, or was not, an open day. Petty details are such a bother. . . .

Never mind. The first order of business was to find a messenger to take my letter to Hilton Head, and I was far more likely to do that downtown, so I backtracked and turned up Bay. I strolled on into John Cross Tavern, which was as good a place to start as any; at the very least I could have a drink and hear the latest gossip, or maybe if I was lucky, a bit of real news.

The tavern's a mean, dark place—"mean" in the sense of small and stingy of space, but that's because it's so old. I like the darkness, find it cozy, and besides, everybody gathers there. Upstairs are a couple of rooms for rent by the night, handy if a man's too drunk to find his way home. Rumor has it those rooms have sheltered many a fellow in need of it, drunk or not. The John Cross may carry gossip, but tells no tales.

I don't much indulge in wines and spirits—I like to be in control and the drink interferes with that—but I went on up to the old mahogany bar, ordered a shot of the best bourbon and took it to one of the little tables far to the back of the room. Gradually my eyes adjusted to the gloom, and my ears to the whispers and grunts that came from another table.

My hearing's acute but still it took a while to piece together what they were talking about: the navy, this time. Monitors, those ridiculous-looking ironclad ships that don't do much of anything so far as I can tell but fire from too far out in the water to hit anything on land, and sink like stones when they're hit themselves. Seems the Union had done it again, tried to take Charleston in a naval battle, with the usual result.

I didn't listen to the rest of what they were saying, though the man at the center of those clustered at that table, the one with all the news, was a stranger. Probably fresh from Charleston—he'd been riding hard from what little I could see of him, so no doubt his news was good. But I didn't care, because I had my own goals and my own thoughts.

Hospital ships . . . tons of supplies . . . open stores . . . soldiers brought upriver to recover in the big houses turned to convalescent hospitals. It was all quite wonderful, and certainly about time!

In fact I was so elated I decided I would deliver my letter to Clara myself. Tomorrow. In the thick of it, nobody would ever notice me; and even if they did, well, I had the perfect cover.

Chapter 5

Hell could not be much worse than this, Clara thought—right down to the flickering orange flames, which in this case came from torches that provided the only light.

The severely cramped confinement of the hospital ship belowdecks magnified everything, especially sounds and smells. The air was thick with the cloying, metallic odor of blood—and to breathe it was to taste it. Screams of the men's pain down here reverberated round and round the ship's hull like mad bells, and their groans became a constant drone that dragged at one's soul.

She found herself wanting to run away for the first time since she had come to war.

It wasn't lack of experience that made her want to run. Clara had walked battlefields with her skirts tucked up yet still her hems got bloody; she'd thrown away more pairs of shoes than she dared count because blood and gore had soaked through their leather soles and never would come out; she'd seen men, some of them still alive, who didn't even look human anymore. But all that had been under open skies, though she'd never even thought about the sky being overhead at the time.

Down here it was worse, a thousand times worse.

David hadn't lasted long; she'd sent him on an errand after the third time he'd choked on his own bile. How long she'd been at her task of simply doing what she could, she had no idea. It seemed like forever.

The boy beneath her hand—he did not look old enough to be a man, and yet his eyes were haunted, ancient—babbled the same thing over and over again: "We never had a chance, we never had a chance, we never had a chance—"

"Hush," Clara said, bending over him more closely, "look into my eyes and tell me your name."

"We never had—"

"Look at me!"

Finally, he did.

"My name is Clara. What's yours?"

He didn't reply, but he continued to look at her, not through her, which she considered a good sign.

"This will pinch," she said. "It will hurt, but not for long, if you can just be still. I'm going to sew up your arm." She threaded a needle with thick black cotton thread—not an easy task in the constantly flickering torchlight.

The boy shrieked: "It ain't my arm, it's my leg, my leg, my leg! We never had a chance!"

His leg was smashed below the knee. He'd been lucky—either the heat of the ball that hit him had seared the veins closed, or (more likely) someone had gotten to him and tied them off. The doctors would amputate his lower leg eventually, when they could get around to him; but meanwhile if Clara didn't sew up the gash in his arm and stop its slow bleeding, his recovery would be all the harder.

She explained this to him, after a lot of shushing to get

him to listen. "You can't afford to lose any more blood," she concluded, "so be still now and let me sew you up."

Finally he understood. "All right," he said, "I guess."

Clara smiled at him. "I'm so glad you didn't say 'yes, ma'am.'"

He tried to smile, but didn't quite make it.

"You're from somewhere in the North then?"

"Yes." He screwed up his face as she pierced the closest intact piece of skin she could find at the border of the long wound and drew the thread through.

She prodded with words, to take his mind off the prodding of the needle: "My home state is Massachusetts. What about you?"

"Maine. Home's in Bath."

"And your name is . . . ?"

"Tim. Oww!"

"Sorry." Clara smiled at him again. She wasn't worried because she knew the pain he felt from her stitching was relatively minor, and would take the boy's mind off other, far worse things.

Her own head was reeling with the noise and the lack of fresh air, which made it hard to continue even the most elementary conversation. For a moment she couldn't even recall the name of the hospital ship, but then it came to her and she asked: "So Tim, how long have you been aboard the *Comstock*?"

"Just since it happened. I dunno, I was out cold."

Of course. She wasn't thinking straight—he'd have been transferred to the hospital ship from his own ship, which might or might not have gone down. She wished she'd been told more about the battle. All anyone on Hilton Head seemed to know was that the Union had lost, in the most humiliating way: They'd quickly seen they could not win and had pulled out their ships almost as soon as the battle had been joined.

But not before all these poor boys had sacrificed either life or limbs for the Cause.

Tim's blood ran down Clara's bare arm; she'd rolled her sleeves up to her elbows, which was as far as they would go. She ignored the bloody trickle.

He was calmer now, but still obsessed. "We never had a chance," he insisted again. Shock was like that: Some men babbled, some became mute. The babblers seemed overall to have a better chance at recovery than the silent ones, so she encouraged him.

"Tell me about it, then, while I finish up."

"They had these long guns on shore, big cannons with more range than anybody thought."

"The Confederates, you mean?"

"Yes. The balls from them guns went clear through our armorplate. Wasn't just us, either—before I got hit myself, I saw other ships with holes torn through their armor abovedecks. We got our turret shot off, that's how I got hit. But our guns in the turret was useless anyhow. We couldn't get in close enough to hit the enemy."

"You're a gunner?"

"That's right. When Cap'n give the order to retreat, reverse engines, wasn't nothing else he could do. They'd of sunk us all. Might have sunk some anyway, I dunno, because I passed out right after that. I thought I was dead. My leg . . ."

He started to glance down but Clara caught his eye and held it, saying firmly: "You were a very lucky man, Tim. You're going to be fine."

"If you say so," he responded glumly, dubious.

"I know it." Clara tied off the thread in a knot and

placed the needle in a packet with others she'd used. She would wash the needles with soap when she returned to her room. Used needles went into her left pocket, clean ones came from the right pocket. It was only common sense, no matter what the doctors said.

Now came a moment when she could have used David's help, but he hadn't returned, so she'd just have to manage alone. In the close quarters and with the roll of the ship to the waves, handling liquids was a problem. Ideally she would have had one or more bottles of water, a basin and an assistant to do the juggling. But on her own, Clara had her pockets, and in her pockets were flasks—one of laudanum and one of fresh water.

"Here," she handed Tim a flask, "take a big swallow. It will ease your pain." The laudanum.

She wet a clean rag with water from the other flask and gently wiped the arm she'd just stitched. For his leg she could do nothing more than hope the drug dulled his pain.

"Now sleep for as long as you can," Clara said, knowing that if he slept, when he awoke it would be to the knife and the saw and the stench of his own burned bone.

She went on to the next man, who, from the size of the dark, viscous pool beneath him, had silently bled to death— perhaps he'd even taken his last breath while she was talking to Tim. She hoped not. But she'd learned not to blame herself, for it was simply not possible to be in more than one place at one time, or to do all she wished she could do.

Clara closed his eyelids with a soft sweep of her palm, murmuring, "Rest in peace."

With nimble swiftness her small fingers searched the man's pockets until she found a wallet. It was blood-soaked but she could read the name, and that was what she wanted:

Jeremiah Hartshorn, she wrote in her notebook, *died abd.*
Comstock, *14 April 1863.*

David Barton had not quite made the escape his sister intended when she'd sent him off. The horrific novelty of it
all astounded, almost paralyzed him. Clara's world, this life
she'd chosen—he couldn't get over it—his little sister, and
all this, *this* . . .

He could not find the right words, not even in the privacy of his own head.

Up on the deck of the hospital steamship *Comstock,* canvas that on a sloop or a barque or a cutter would have gone
for sails had been tacked to common poles in lieu of masts,
forming a tentlike shelter. Under the canvas the doctors and
surgeons did their grisly work, aided by men David could
only assume were male nurses. Men who seemed the very
antithesis of his sister Clara.

Their main attribute appeared to be physical strength, so
far as David could tell. Certainly they had nothing of
Clara's gentle touch. He watched in a kind of grim fascina-
tion as a pair of the burly nurses handled the wounded,
who'd been lined up along the deck like sacks of cotton
waiting to go under the cotton gin. The nurses didn't
bother with stretchers or litters; they took the patients—
David frowned, for somehow the word "patient" seemed all
wrong for this situation—under the arms and under the
knees and slung them, one at a time, onto the next available
operating table. The "tables" were slabs of bare board, set
on sawhorses.

It was horrible. But it was not as bad—he realized as he
stood riveted to the spot, reluctant to watch, yet unable to

look away—as belowdecks. Here a breeze took away most of the smell.

And . . . and . . . something else was very different from David's expectations. He couldn't quite put his finger upon it, but then suddenly he did: It was quiet. *Too* quiet. The only sounds of amputation were the cutting and sawing and sizzling, but no screaming. None.

Eerie . . .

The wind shifted, his nostrils caught a strange, cloying, chemical smell, and suddenly he realized why it was so quiet: ether. This hospital ship had somehow obtained ether, the new miracle anesthetic. These doctors, and the wounded men especially, were unusually blessed.

"You there!" someone said harshly, and at the same time clapped a hand on his shoulder. "If you've got time to stand around gawking, then you've got time to do something for me!"

David turned, drawing his dark eyebrows together in a scowl even as he jerked away from the offending grip. He wasn't accustomed to being addressed, much less physically accosted, in such a fashion.

"I beg your pardon." David's response was automatically polite.

"I suppose I should beg yours." The other man's eyes scanned him quickly once up, once down. "I didn't realize you were an officer. But never mind, I need help and you'll do. On the double, can't waste time!"

"I . . ."

David started to say he already had a job to do for Clara Barton, but something about the man stopped him, made him think fast.

Clara had emphasized that they were here—she as a relief worker and he as her assistant—to serve in whatever capacity was required, to the best of their ability. The way Clara interpreted her role, her primary service was to the wounded men during that most critical period—"between the battlefield and the field hospital" was how she herself described it. In order to do that, she had to work closely with the doctors, who were seriously understaffed and undersupplied. That gap was where Clara and her donated stores came into action.

This man could be a doctor; if so, Clara wouldn't want to put him off, no matter how rude he acted. His Union blue trousers were faded, and he'd traded his uniform jacket for a butcher's bib apron over a shirt of linen worn thin but of good cut and quality; jacketless he was without insignia, so David was unable to tell his rank. The bloodstained apron, however, suggested the man was a surgeon.

Therefore the ever-cautious David swallowed what he had been about to say and said instead, "I have my own duties, but if you'll tell me what you need, I'll see what I can do. Allow me to introduce myself." He pulled himself up to his full height. "I'm Captain David Barton. Whom have I the honor of assisting, sir?"

"Dr. Matheson, first name Revel, rank of major. Let's get out of the thick of things, shall we? After you."

Dr. Matheson gestured toward the gangway that had been lashed up between the *Comstock* and the smaller supply ship, the *Rector,* a sailing vessel. The *Comstock* drew too deep a draft to come all the way to Hilton Head's dock. Rowboats plied continually from the dock to the *Rector,* which served as a way station and transfer point to and from the larger *Comstock.*

David said, from caution or politeness or both, "Doctor, I insist: after *you.*"

The doctor gave him a look, but David made a grand,

sweeping gesture that seemed to please Revel Matheson, for he nodded, grunted and went on ahead.

Revel. Interesting name, David thought as he followed across the sagging insecurity of the gangway. Rather than think about falling into the sea below, he thought about the name and the man.

David dabbled in genealogy, and tried to place where or even if he'd ever heard the name Revel before. He didn't think he had. But then again, he wasn't sure. Somehow it had a familiar ring.

The man who bore this curious name was tall, perhaps over six feet. He was lean but muscular. The most remarkable thing about him was his hair, which was a rich, dark auburn, worn long and wavy to his shoulders. His beard was equally luxuriant and wavy.

When Matheson stepped down on the *Rector*'s deck and turned back to watch David do the same, David saw he had the pale skin that typically went with auburn hair. Still thinking along genealogical lines, David surmised he'd be either a Scot or an Irishman. Yet neither Revel nor Matheson sounded Celt in origin.

David was intrigued. It seemed an inopportune time to ask a personal question; but on the other hand he might not have another opportunity, since the doctor had obviously arrived with the hospital ship and would also depart with it.

"I hope I'm not being too familiar, Dr. Matheson," David ventured, "but the study of names and families is something of a hobby of mine. May I be so bold as to ask you, what is the origin of your name, and where are you and your family from?"

The doctor's eyes were such a pale gray they were almost clear, like the still waters of a lake on a day of high, thin cloud cover. He said:

"Revel is a family name, Captain Barton. As for where I'm from originally, I prefer not to think about that until this war is over. Meanwhile I live as the war disposes me. I'm sure you can understand."

"I think so, sir," David replied, still studiously polite.

Many families, especially from the border states, were fighting brother against brother, friend against friend. He offered, as if by way of apology:

"My own brother, Stephen, lives in North Carolina, in a manufacturing town that has been named after him. Yet his son, my nephew Samuel, lives and works for the government in Washington City. Stephen's town is called Bartonsville, near New Bern, in the eastern part of the state. Perhaps you know it?"

Of course Stephen could not possibly be made to fight for the Confederacy; he'd go to prison, or choose to die first. That was something to worry about, and they all did—especially poor Sammy.

"No," Matheson replied, "I can't say I've ever heard of Bartonsville. Nor have I more time for chitchat. I've got to get back." He jerked his head, with hair glowing richly in the sunlight, toward the *Comstock*. "We've run through our ship's store of several things, and one piece of equipment broke, my bone saw, absolutely essential. Is your memory good, man? Or have you paper and lead pencil on you?"

"I assure you, Doctor, my memory is excellent," David replied truthfully.

The list Dr. Matheson recited was not long. David made a mnemonic of it, greatly aided by the fact that the list contained ether, represented by an *e,* the most frequently occurring letter of the alphabet. Then he gave his best imitation of a salute and was on his way to do the doctor's errand first, as he thought Clara would have wanted.

Clara continued to work her way through the mass of men crowded belowdecks. They all fell into one category or another: Either they were so severely wounded their survival was seriously in doubt, or they were like the boy Tim—who not only would survive, though with only one leg, but in future would probably look back and mark this as the day he truly became a man. She firmly believed the endurance of pain could turn a weak person strong; yet at the same time she also believed people should not needlessly suffer. If a means existed to relieve suffering, then it was the duty of those who could do so to provide it.

On through the cluttered rows of bodies she went, with little touches and murmurs of encouragement, cleaning where she could (though she fast ran out of water—where *was* David?), sewing up cuts and gashes where that was possible, holding a few hands until last breaths, already near, were taken. Writing names in her book.

Many had died. More than she liked to see. And if the male nurses came down from time to time to take some of these men up onto the deck where they could be treated, as they should, she had not seen it happen.

Clara's ears had begun to hurt from the relentless nature of the noise in such confinement. Someone cried out sharply and she winced, as the cry hit both her eardrums like an arrow that plunged straight through her head. In reaction she gasped, drawing in a deep breath that inflated her rib cage—and popped a stay in her corset.

"Oh drat!" she swore aloud, then bit her lip for shame.

The broken sliver of whalebone pierced the corset cover

and dug into the underside of her left breast, where in no time at all it was sure to rub that tender skin raw. But there was nothing she could do about it now, and she'd be very foolish indeed to let it bother her.

Still, it did hurt, and as is often the way of just one thing too many, brought tears to her eyes.

She blinked them away and shook her head at her own trivial foolishness, stretched her neck from side to side to relieve some of the tension—and just as she was about to move on to the next man, Clara realized she was not the only person moving through the ranks of the injured and the dying and the dead.

She frowned, trying to see better in the flickering light. It was a man, of course, not David returning with bandages and salves she didn't really need—at least, not yet—and not a nurse, because they came in pairs, as necessary to shift their human burdens.

Now he had seen her too and was working his way toward her, much too rapidly for the comfort of the men he walked over and among—and for Clara's comfort as she had to watch him.

She couldn't stand it and called out: "You, sir, have a care where you put your feet! These men are hurting and your stepping on them will not make them feel any better!"

One of the wounded in the row behind her gave a weak cheer.

"I'm a doctor," the man, still at some distance, snapped back in a baritone both loud and clear, "I don't need *you* to tell *me* what's going on here. If my eyes do not deceive me, you're a female."

Clara bit her lip again. She knew trouble when she heard it, and saw it coming toward her. With an effort she held her tongue.

He came on and she stood her ground, wishing that she didn't have a piece of whalebone digging into her breast, and that her hair felt less like a dead rat on the back of her neck, and that it could be possible to look after smashed, slashed, bleeding and dying men while wearing one of the hoops that made her waist look even smaller than it was. She had these ludicrous thoughts because of a lesson she'd learned years ago:

When a man makes as if to cause you trouble, *be your most charming.* Always smile. Keep your voice low. Be feminine as feminine can be. Flirt, cajole, appear to give way to him . . . yet never, ever yield even a fraction of an inch—because if you are charming enough, and feminine enough, he will naturally assume it was entirely his own idea, when you get your way after all.

So Clara smiled and lifted her chin when this new man, who rather oddly wore an out-of-date army officer's uniform on a navy ship, came and stood too close, too tall above her. She still smiled as the angles of his thin, almost ascetic face turned satanic in the constantly shifting torchlight.

"Doctor," she said, taking an initiative before she lost her nerve, "I'm so glad you've come. I was feeling quite abandoned, all by myself with so much to do down here!"

"Well, you needn't feel that way anymore." His voice was beautifully modulated, yet had no depth to it.

Clara made a little dip of a curtsey, the best she could manage given the surroundings, and steeled her mind against everything inside herself that cried out against this charade. She played her part and gave him his cue: "I fear we haven't been properly introduced, but I expect we'll be forgiven in the circumstances."

He took it up, placing a gloved left hand to his chest and inclining his head.

Gloves? Clara thought numbly. *He's wearing gloves?*

He cleared his throat and spoke:

"Allow me to introduce myself. I am Colonel Claude Fontaine, doctor of medicine"—at this point his voice changed harshly—"and I *know* who *you* are!"

Clara blinked and her throat closed up, most helpful in the necessity of holding her tongue.

"I will thank you to leave this ship and get out of my sight, Miss Clara Barton. Now that I have arrived, your assistance is no longer either welcome or necessary."

If she hadn't had a piece of whalebone torturing her; and *if* she had not already been at work more hours than she had bothered to count—in early days she'd worn a man's watch on a chain at her waist, but had given it up after she'd found that knowing the passage of time somehow made things all the harder—and *if*, furthermore, she were not somehow slightly off-kilter lately, Clara might have stayed.

She might have tried harder to charm Colonel Fontaine out of the irrational dislike he had taken to her, sight unseen. Because it was all very unfair, really. She'd turned men around before in similar situations; some were now her champions. It was a bother to deal with such men, especially when they were doctors, and it was time-consuming—but it seemed there was always one like him at every post.

Another case of my reputation preceding me, she thought.

But on this particular day there'd been more "if's" than she could handle, and so she decided the best way to handle him was with quiet acceptance and seeming obedience.

Clara merely murmured, "As you say, Doctor," and backed away, as if leaving a royal presence. Slowly she backed, until she had room to turn and walk as straight a line as was possible, given those of the men who were conscious, and in pain, were not too good about keeping to orderly rows upon the flooring.

Nor did it help her dignity that the ship swayed, so she had to lean this way or that to compensate, or else lose her balance. It was most heartening, though, that some of the men to whom she'd already given her attention reached out to touch her skirt or her hand with their fingertips as she passed.

She tried not to hurry, to keep her confidence high, even when her heavy-laden pockets dragged her skirt down at the waist as she tried to climb the ship's ladder to the upper deck. In fact, the weight of the pockets threatened to partially disrobe her, as her skirt sagged further with every step up, and finally she felt the buttonhole begin to tear and give way.

What to do? The contents of her pockets were too precious to unload and leave behind. She refused to go back into Fontaine's dominion to look for a basket, which in any case would have been just another encumbrance. So it was either take off the skirt, roll it into a bundle and carry it, or be permanently consigned to this hellhole for nothing more than modesty's sake.

The choice was obvious: She unbuttoned the button, not a moment too soon either, and took off her skirt. It was an old one that she had made herself of good, sturdy, dark blue gabardine of cotton. She folded it up carefully, so as to protect the pockets' contents from falling out. Then Clara ascended the ladder one-handed, with her bodice points coming down over only one full petticoat, and she didn't give a rat's behind if anyone was looking. Including that damn Dr. Fontaine, who was probably back there gawping up the skirts of that one petticoat that was all she had left to cover her nether limbs.

The one person whose opinion she did give a rat's behind about—besides Colonel Elwell, who had to be still safely tucked up in his room—was her brother David. And there he was on the deck of the *Comstock,* large as life; his cheeks turned pink from three feet away when he saw Clara, folded skirt clutched to her chest, come up through the hatch.

"Don't just stand there, David," she said crossly, "come and give me a hand."

She teetered on the top step of the ladder, not wanting to put her skirt down on the filthy deck, but needing more than one hand to boost herself up that last step over and out of the hatchway.

"And none of your criticism, whether you think I've earned it or not," she cautioned under her breath when he drew close enough.

"But what in the God's earth are you *doing,* Clara?"

"Just pull me up!" she insisted, in a hissing whisper.

David complied, though he nearly parted her arm from its socket.

"Are you going to enlighten me?" he asked.

"Let's just say that very heavy pockets, a small-boned woman and a ship's ladder do not make a harmonious trio."

He looked puzzled; she didn't care, he'd soon enough figure it out. She said, "Now turn your back, if you please."

"Whatever you say!" David put his hands in his pockets and turned himself around.

It was a ridiculous request, given that she was standing on the deck of a ship in broad daylight, but Clara had made it more for her brother's sake than for her own.

With every movement of her arms, as she worked the

heavy skirt over her head and down past her shoulders until, with some clanking of pocket contents, it settled around her waist, the broken piece of whalebone jabbed at her. She refused to permit herself so much as a single frown line, but that small spot beneath her breast hurt as much as it was annoying, and maybe even more.

"You can turn back around now." She had done up the button and was now as presentable as she was going to be until she'd washed.

"But—I'm sorry, Clara, but I still don't understand. I mean, I find my sister coming up out of the bowels of a ship half undressed—well, how do you expect me to feel?"

"I *expect* you to trust me, the same as Cornelius did, David. For heaven's sake, it was only that my pockets were too heavy for me to climb the ladder without tearing my skirt off."

David considered this while Clara smoothed the dark blue folds of that skirt and rearranged the contents of her pockets to her liking.

"That doesn't make sense," he insisted. "Your pockets should not be any heavier when you're climbing a ladder than they are when you're walking around."

"Well," her chin came up, "they were. At least, that's how they felt. And the buttonhole was right on the verge of ripping."

"I can understand how heavy pockets might throw you off-balance, but—"

"Oh David, enough!"

They had always argued like this, ever since she was a child with a ton of common sense in her precocity, and David was the older brother with almost none, but much book-learning instead.

"All right," David conceded amiably. "But tell me this:

Why are you leaving just now, when I've brought the things you asked for?"

She could have charged him with taking too long on a simple errand, or asked what had delayed him, but she didn't. She merely consigned her brother to the hell below.

"Go on down, David, and meet Dr. Claude Fontaine. He will have use for the bandages and salves, I'm sure. He has most graciously given me the rest of the day off, but since you are a *man,* I'm sure he will welcome your assistance."

In spite of her weariness, and her anger, Clara felt guilty to be leaving the hospital ship when there was so much work left to do. The doctors and surgeons would be working as far into the night as they could, as long as they had light to see by. But she had no choice—she had to go, and not only because she'd been ordered away by a doctor whose right she lacked the strength to challenge. At least, for today.

She hurried across the precarious gangplank to the *Rector,* wove her way through the people who milled about its deck with only one minor collision, and found someone to help her down the rope ladder and into a rowboat that would take her back to the dock at Hilton Head. The sun was going down, casting long shadows across the marshes, but she didn't notice; nor did she hear the frogs that began to sing in a myriad of pitches this time of evening. Her fingers clutched the side of the rowboat so tightly her knuckles turned white, which she did not notice either.

Inside herself, Clara had become a mass of seething emotions. She felt as if some essential inner order-keeping mechanism had recently broken, and now she could no longer remain disciplined, in check.

More than anything else, Clara feared a loss of self-control. She was frightened by the force of her anger with the Colonel Dr. Claude Fontaine, or whatever his name was; also frightened by an increasing sense of dread about David, that something bad would happen to him here in the Department of the South. So there was guilt too—all the worse, guilt over a brother she loved so dearly.

As soon as the rowboat touched the side of the dock she scrambled out and yelled back her thanks to the rower, for the first time noticing that he was black, a Gullah. She gave him a quick smile over her shoulder and then rushed on, supporting the contents of her pockets in the palms of her hands on either side of her skirt—because no matter what she had said to David, the buttonhole at her waist would not hold much longer.

Clara did not notice the cream-colored sheet of paper folded so that it became its own envelope, which had been slipped beneath the door of her room. She passed right over it and continued on straight to her washstand, along the way giving the door a shove with her shoulder, so that it closed on its own behind her. She dropped her skirt—but not without inspecting its buttonhole first, which was indeed torn at one side and would have to be mended—then her petticoats, and soon every other article of clothing joined the pile upon the floor at her bare feet. She had taken to going without stockings whenever she thought no one would notice; the war had made the cost of silk too dear, and cotton stockings in this warm, humid climate felt awful.

Scented soap, tepid water, a large, silky sponge—Clara focused on these and on their purpose, nothing else. When she had done washing her body, she washed her hair—even though she knew the half pitcher of water she had left was not enough for a thorough rinse.

Give complete attention to whatever you are doing at the moment; that is the secret to keeping a clear head, she thought. Her friend General Sturgis had taught her that lesson, in the midst of the worst of Fredericksburg.

The worst of Fredericksburg had been very bad indeed.

Finally she was done, clean, her mind calm, her fingers no longer trembling, knees no longer shaking. She dressed again, choosing a skirt that was slightly gay, in that it was made of chintz with an ivory stripe, alternating with a narrower black stripe that had little blue flowers woven into it in a ribbonlike pattern. Following her usual evening fashion, she topped the skirt with a loose ivory blouse. Her body would thank her for going without a corset for a few days—that sore, raw spot on the underside of her breast was in a difficult place for healing, where the air could never get at it.

But would her vanity survive, corsetless? Clara smiled in gladness, as she felt her sense of humor return.

She brushed her wet hair until it began to dry. By this time it had grown quite dark out, and she'd heard Colonel Elwell knock upon their adjoining wall more than once. To his second knock she'd replied with three rapid little taps, which meant she was coming as soon as she could.

She left her hair down, but she did stop to gather up her dirty clothes from the floor. That was when she noticed the letter.

The letter—only one person wrote to her on that exact kind of expensive, heavy paper, folded in that very exact way. When Clara looked down at it, lying in a creamy evil glow upon the dark hardwood floor, she felt a tremor deep in her recently reconstructed inner self.

"I won't deal with it!" she said aloud, resolutely, and with the toe of her shoe she swept the folded paper across the bare floor. She didn't even look back to see where it came to rest.

Instead she went to the Colonel and found him alone, sitting propped on his couch with a bright patchwork-quilted coverlet over his legs and a book in his hand. His room was warm with candlelight, and more, with the warmth of his own presence.

"Well," he said, "my little Bird has at last flown home."

Clara felt her chin tremble, and she thought, *Oh, no! I can't—I'm not—I won't cry, I'm all over that!*

She closed the door behind her carefully, not quite meeting his eyes. She couldn't yet trust herself to speak.

He'd noticed, of course.

"Clara," he said softly, "my dear Miss Barton, what's wrong? Was it so bad today? Surely not, after all you've already been through."

She shook her head, still mute, chin still trembling, fighting for the control she'd thought she had regained.

He waited, wisely letting her fight her own silent battle with herself.

At last, Clara raised her eyes and gazed at John Elwell's kind face. In a curiously small voice she heard herself say:

"Colonel, your little Bird finds herself in need of a nest."

He opened his arms to her, and she flew to him.

Chapter 6

Annabelle had an old bandanna with good juju on it—she got it from her pa, who never said where he'd got it from. It was a big purple cloth a yard to each side, with white dots and lines in a pattern around the edges, a pattern that looked like it might hold the juju but if it did, Pa had gone to his grave without telling her the secret. Still Annabelle used the bandanna for the same things Pa had: Carry dem ting fuh wukkum.

"Carry the things for . . ." Annabelle mumbled. She tried to keep her promise to Miss Frances and Miss Mary Gage that she'd use the buckruh words, the white man's words, not the Gullah's. But she could hear her dead pa's voice in her head . . . and even with her best effort, there was no other word meant the same as "wukkum."

Nobody on Parris Island, or Hilton Head, could do a wukkum but Annabelle, who'd been taught all the old ways by her pa, who'd been the Conjuh Man. She didn't know was there anybody could do it up Beaufort way, since she didn't much get up that far. On St. Helena was a fella claimed he was a hoodoo man, but 'e dint mekum nem-mine, he didn't make a nevermind. She wasn't concerned about him.

Tek 'ee brack fedduh—Pa's voice went on in her mind as she took a black raven's feather—not that from the common crow but from a real raven, a much bigger bird, much harder to find, harder still to track, until the raven shed the feather that was the key to unlock something Annabelle didn't entirely understand, but only knew it worked—and stroked the feather against the back of her hand. The raven's plumage was the same color and had the same depth of sheen as her own skin. Same as the skin of most all Gullahs.

Tek 'ee seb'n stones tumblety smood en roun'—Take seven stones that have been tumbled in the ocean till they're smooth and round—

With her pa's voice directing every motion, she assembled everything she'd need. She tied it all up in the juju bandanna and slung the bundle over her left shoulder. In her right hand she carried a thick wooden pole, longer than she was tall, carved all over with faces of people and shapes of animals and birds and fish, and suns and moons and stars. Pa'd carved it mostly, and maybe somebody else before him; she didn't know and there was nobody more to ask because they were all dead.

Wuk ebry day tell det shet out dey light. They'd worked every day till death shut out their light. Until they died. A slave's life. Things would be different now there was Emancipation.

Annabelle firmly believed that things would be not just different but better, when Gullah peoples learned all the things Miss Frances and Miss Mary had to teach. Maybe not for herself, maybe she wouldn't live long enough to see the changes come. But George would have that better life. Oh yes, he would!

George would have it better, but not unless she found him and brought him home.

She couldn't wait anymore now, not for the help of the good Cunnel, or the Cunnel's little Yankee lady, or even for the help of her own Gullah friends. Things were happening and there was no more time.

Annabelle guessed she'd known it in her bones, that it would take the old ways to get George back. Not just any of the old ways neither, but the hardest and most dangerous. She hadn't done a wukkum for a long time. Maybe she'd been hoping she wouldn't never have to do one again. Truth was, Annabelle was only halfway a conjure woman—her heart was in leading the shouts at the Praise House. Still she carried on with doing for the peoples most of the things her pa had done. And for George, Annabelle would do anything.

She'd been waiting, but now she couldn't hold off. Today she'd seen a big steamship and a littler sailing ship set down in the harbor at Hilton Head, and lots of little boats going back and forth to the bigger ships. As if that weren't enough, later on one more sail ship had anchored outside the breakwater; when the others cleared the way, that one would come on in. Pretty soon there'd be sodjuhs everywhere.

War coming closer now to the Low Country and the Sea Islands. Boats going up Port Royal Sound into Beaufort River, carrying sick men to the hospitals in Beaufort town, up and back, again and again. But something else was coming too, besides the war, some very bad thing stirring itself up, going on the move. She didn't know what it was, but right now, this very day it had been close by. She'd felt it.

All afternoon when the wind blew onshore and carried the sounds, she'd heard the moaning and crying coming from that steamship in the harbor—but she hadn't really needed to hear it to know what was happening out there. She could feel the massive suffering in the air, feel the dying and the pain. Especially the pain. Other people's pain went through Annabelle like a knife and stuck in her backbone, around behind her stomach.

This other thing was not that kind of pain, it was worse. When pain stops, it's plumb over. This other thing felt more like one of them dark clouds you first see out on the edge of the ocean, that just keeps coming closer and getting bigger, until the next thing you know it's all over you.

Annabelle felt other people's pain because she had the power. Having to feel their pain was its price—that's what Pa had said when he taught her the old ways while she was still a little girl. Taught her, not her brother, because she had the power but he didn't. Bredduh wanted to be the next Conjuh Man. He got 'e mout' all box-up, he made a sour face an' ran away after that, and none of them had ever seen him again, from that day to this.

Wukkum was the last of all the old ways Pa'd taught Annabelle; she'd been a grown woman by then and had thought she already knew all the old ways, thought there was nothing more for Pa to teach her. She was happy being the shout leader in the Praise House, where they had a big picture of God's son Jesus as a baby with his ma, Mary.

W'en 'E binnah leetle lap-chile on 'E ma knee, Annabelle thought, smiling as she went out the door of her cabin; she always did like that picture. Would of give a pretty penny to have one at home, if she had any pennies at all. She left her door on the latch so if anybody came calling they'd know she'd be back in a whiles.

She set off walking through the twilight, using the pole like a staff. Most likely she'd have a long way to go. She didn't know how long it would take to find the right spot for this wukkum, but it had to be deep in the woods, which meant she had to cross over the crick onto Port Royal Island. There was sodjers all over Parris Island now, and Yankees, all these buckruhs chopping down trees, not having enough sense to stay in they houses after dark, invading her secret places where she practiced the old ways. It was worrisome.

Pa had died right after teaching wukkum to Annabelle. Sometimes she'd wished it was the other way around, that if he had to die anyway he would've died first, because then she wouldn't know and wouldn't have to do it. The old Gullahs, they knew she'd got the power and after Pa died, they came to her. She didn't like wukkum—she'd be left with a bad feeling for days after. So she'd raised her price and raised her price again, until finally the peoples only asked if they need was truly great.

Her own need was truly great: For George, Annabelle was going to make the biggest, most powerful, most dangerous wukkum she had in her. She just hoped when it was over nobody, Gullah nor buckruh, ever found out exactly what she'd done.

Something cold went running through Annabelle, and the juju bundle on her shoulder got heavier. She hefted it and straightened up all the taller, and went on through long and longer shadows as evening turned to night. She'd never asked to have the power, but she had it, and all her life she'd accepted it. Now she was gonna use it for her boy. The Ma Mary with the Jesus lap-chile would surely understand.

Annabelle felt a kinship to the Ma Mary, and most of all she liked to be in that Praise House leadin' the shouts. She liked to be with all the peoples, liked to get them voices coming all together on the *same* word at the *same* time in the *same* way. Liked to get that rhythm going, with the clap-hands and the shuffle and the sway up, sway back, every-body moving *all* together.

Oney trubble was (with apologies to the Ma Mary), the Lord God and the Growed-Up Jesus Christ didn't seem any too inclined to do much in return for all that praise. They just soaked it up and didn't give nuthin' back, so far as Annabelle could tell. Not to the Gullahs. You could pray and praise till your face turned bluer than black and it wouldn't make no difference, not unless you was buckruh, and maybe not even then.

The old ways gave back. But on their own terms.

For Annabelle the hardest of those terms wasn't the pain, whether the pain was physical or the other kind that seemed to start in her head and then run everywhere, even into her dreams. What was hardest of the old ways was do-ing it *alone*. No singing no shouting no clap hands all to-gether. Alone. 'Specially for wukkum.

Most spells and magic and such, if anybody came up on you, only harm done was you had to start over. But on wukkum if ennyting mess wit' the power, anything break you out from you trance, you could be dead.

It was that dangerous.

That danger drove Annabelle deeper and deeper into the woods on Port Royal Island. St. Helena would have been easier, she knew her way better over there; but lately she had a bad feeling about St. Helena. And she didn't think it was because of that no-count hoodoo man.

The sky clouded over, making an already dark night even darker. Sometimes it was like being blind; then Annabelle used Pa's pole out in front of her, and poked it over to the sides, to find or make a path. Cloudy was good for her purposes, not good as dark of the moon but almost. She had no complaint, none at all; it was like the darker gods was helping her this night.

She stopped trying to see her way through the deep woods and turned instead to her inner eye that was guided by the power. Soon she could see as well as feel it in her mind, a shiny silver line that made a path for her feet until, sometime around the middlenight, Annabelle found the place she was seeking. The right place for George's wukkum.

She knelt down and opened up the juju cloth, felt around till she'd found a big fat tallow candle and a lucifer, whose sulfur head she struck to a flame, then put the flame to the wick. After that she took everything else out of the cloth and put it all over to one side; shook out the cloth good; arranged it and smoothed it over a level place on the ground . . . and then she sat down cross-legged right in the middle of the purple juju cloth.

In Annabelle's mind now everything she did became very precise, a part of a ritual handed down to her through a long, long line of Africans, of whom the last had been her pa. With each motion her breath deepened and grew more regular.

She took a bundle of little switches tied up to mekum wisky-broom, and cleaned the ground in a half circle all around where she sat. Then she placed the candle slap-dab in front of her, said a few words, moved it over to the right. The black feather she put at the base of the candle. The seven stones went over to her left, running up in a diagonal line. Directly in front of her she put two small glass bottles, both with tight stoppers in their necks. One held clear, pure water. The other, an inky, black liquid. Last, in front of the bottles she placed a shallow scoop of white bone. The old wooden bowl in which these things had nestled she left off to one side.

The black liquid was poisonous. Annabelle had cooked it herself over days, distilling the poison from the black gills on the undersides of a thousand deadly mushrooms, mixing it with the darkest blue dye of indigo, stirring and cooking until it all turned black. The bone was human, from a woman's pelvis—that's where its curved shape came from—and where the bone itself came from, Annabelle hadn't asked when Pa handed it down to her.

She took the bone in her hand, turned her profile to the candlelight and raised her head. Her eyes grew wide as her trance deepened, and with the bone she began to dig in the soft earth at the edge of her cleared semicircle. As she dug, she slowly rocked back and forth. She hummed.

Wukkum called the spirits of the dead to come back, to walk the earth for a certain while, to do for a living person something that person could not do. Different words, different objects, a different focus in the mind called up a different spirit; Annabelle recognized them, and knew each spirit's nature by how it felt to her when it came. Some were male and some female; some good and some bad; some seemed as large as a mountain, and some as small as a frog. Sometimes the large ones were as harmless as a big bag of wind, while the little ones were as deadly as scorpions.

For George, Annabelle would call the most powerful spirit she knew. This one was powerful with the wound-up tightness that comes from being very small, and with the strength that comes of being pure, as only the very young are pure. This one was dangerous too, because it had died before ever learning right from wrong, before being able to discriminate as to who or what was good, and who or what was not. Most of all this one was deadly destructive because this spirit knew only one thing: Its death had been unfair, and so the spirit was angry and vengeful. Once joined to the task of a wukkum, it swept away everything between it and its goal. And because it was so pure, its anger so righteous, no other spirit would respond to a call to help contain it.

Annabelle worked and worked at the earth until she had dug a fair mound with her human bone. Constantly humming, she piled the dirt into the old wooden bowl she'd set aside. Then she patiently filled in the hole left in the ground with the leaves and pine needles she'd swept up, until the hole was invisible.

She was too deep in trance to notice, but the woods around her had gone silent. The animals and insects that make noises in the night had fled from the thin black woman in her circle of candlelight—fled not so much from the light as from an invisible wall around her that bristled with the strength of her purpose. The air was thick, heavy and still.

Sitting on the purple cloth with her legs crossed, she took the bowl of earth into her lap and bent over it, humming, warming the bowl and its contents with the warmth of her own body. Finally she felt ready and murmured words in a language that was lost, even to her, except for the sounds and how to make them with her tongue. She knew only what the words would do, that they would do it soon, and that once this wukkum came to pass it could not be stopped.

She reached for the bottle of black liquid, removed the stopper and poured the liquid into the earth that rested in the bowl on her lap. Together with the poison, for enhancing destructive power, she also poured all the love and longing that had gone into the making of her son. Hate and love, love and hate, all bound up together.

She mixed with both hands and sifted through her thin fingers, working and working the earth, until the black poison had made the earth all black and sticky. She rolled it into a ball. Rolled and shaped and molded: arms, legs, trunk, head emerged; tiny nose and mouth, curves of ears, two holes for the eyes.

Annabelle's wukkum: the Wicketty Chile.

She set down the bowl with the earth-mud figure still inside, bent forward and picked up the seven stones, which she made into a circle on the ground directly in front of where she sat. At one side of the circle she left a wider space between two of the stones—a gap, like a door.

Very carefully, with both hands Annabelle lifted the earth-mud figure and set it down in the exact middle of the circle. She worked it a little more to be sure it would stand and not break apart before its job was done.

When she was satisfied she picked up the raven feather, closed her eyes and breathed in the deep, deep breaths that would take her far away inside herself, so far that she turned herself inside out and got lost in a place not-here; a place she knew, she'd been there before, but she had no name for it.

Then she chanted, mumbling, words Pa had taught her. She opened her eyes and stroked the earth-mud figure with the raven feather all over. She trembled, she shook, and finally she said aloud in a deep, resonant voice: "Come yuh, Wicketty Chile!"

ST. HELENA ISLAND

Today was the most successful and exhilarating experience I've had in a long time. What a pity it couldn't have ended better, but that was not my fault. It was Jackson's. If he were not behaving badly, I could have had the perfect ending I'd more than earned to top off my perfect day.

Jackson has been giving me sidelong looks, calculating glances. Furtive, you might say. I think he's plotting something, which means I can't trust him out of my sight anymore. Pity.

I need my man Jack, and I thought he understood how he needs me, that we were in a way a team. But then last week he had to go whispering behind my back with his ladyfriend, saying that word "monster." Of course I had to kill her after that, but I spared *him*. What better truth could there be of my essential fairness? I swear it is the most vexing thing in the world to be so misunderstood.

At any rate, I couldn't very well leave him loose with our boat in Hilton Head Harbor all day long while I was busy with other things. I expect even Jackson has heard of Robert Smalls, a slave who last year up in Charleston piloted himself and his massa's riverboat right out of the Confederacy, on over to the Union side. One presumes his massa wasn't watching. Overnight Smalls got his freedom and a certain amount of fame. A thing like that can give ideas to a smart black man like Jackson.

So I locked him in when I left early this morning.

Jackson being my one and only way to travel the damned creeks without getting lost, leaving him behind meant I had a long horseback ride over to the other side of St. Helena, followed by the iffy business of hiring a boat on the spot to take me down Port Royal Sound to Hilton Head, and the same in reverse for my return trip. Land travel is not the efficient way to go from one sea island to another—it always takes at least twice as long.

Nevertheless I did it, and it was most gratifying to find,

upon my arrival among all the military at Hilton Head, how quickly I was able to blend in just by wearing my old uniform and a few well-chosen professional accessories. Nobody questioned my presence. I actually enjoyed myself! And in a few hours, I was able to accomplish everything I'd set out to do.

Well, *almost* everything. Without Jackson to assist me I have no way of transporting whole specimens. But plenty will be transferred to the convalescent hospitals in Beaufort, so I'll have another chance. Jackson too will have his last chance to help me, under my watchful eye. The man needs a good talking-to; perhaps that will straighten him up.

Oh yes: the letter. I did deliver it. My heart pounded in my chest in a very exciting way when I slipped it under Miss Clara Barton's door with my own hand.

I didn't stay after that. I would have liked to linger, watching, until Clara came into her room; I'd have liked to peek through her window and see the expression on her face as she read it (I was sure she *would* read it, because letters are so important to her life); in short it would have been an interesting diversion to spend a few more hours as a Peeping Tom.

But only if I could have had a guarantee I'd not be caught. As there was no such guarantee, I decided to be satisfied with all the many good things I had already accomplished, and to head on home.

Everything had worked out splendidly, until I was about three-quarters of the way across St. Helena on my way back home to the Coffin Place. But then the twilight sky started to cloud over. I should have had at least another half hour of early evening light, but the clouds came and brought full dark too soon.

I broke out one of the lanterns from my saddlebags and slowed the horse to a walk so that I could hold up the light to see landmarks, where the sidepaths branched and so on. But walking the horse was much too slow, it would take all night at this pace, I thought . . . and I had no intention of trudging across St. Helena island all night long.

Not to mention that as soon as it got full dark the whole woodland contingent of frogs started singing their nerve-rending songs. I can't abide the ugly, slimy creatures. Not to mention that at any pace slower than a trot, the ever-annoying bugs will light on every single inch of one's exposed skin. And they bite.

Nor had I fully realized, until the darkness forced us to slow down, how very tired I was.

That was when it occurred to me (city fellow that I am by experience, but I'm a fast learner) that if I gave the horse his head, he might very likely know his own way home. This horse was a Coffin animal, one of several that Mr. Coffin, apparently a very wealthy man, had left behind.

A brilliant inspiration on my part, if I do say so myself. The horse did indeed know his way home, and once I'd released my tight hold on the reins and thus the pressure on the bit in his mouth, the beast got right to proving it. Trust a dumb animal to do anything in a hurry if there's food in the offing at the other end.

Quite often this applies to the human animal as well, as any scientist will tell you. (Though no human is dumb enough to take a bit in the mouth; I know because I've tried it on a few.)

However fleet of foot—or hoof—the horse might have been, the sky above had turned black as pitch when we entered the long, straight alley—or as the French say, *allée*—that leads from the road up to my place named Coffin. Now alongside that alley someone, an early Coffin, I presume, had planted rows of those live oaks that grow so monstrously twisted. In the light of my swinging lantern as we galloped by, they looked as if they really *were* alive. As if they were moving not as trees move, but as people do, with purpose.

I couldn't help but think about Jackson and his superstitions, how he doesn't like to go outside the house after dark, and won't go into the woods after sundown unless he's forced to it. I wondered about the horse too, if he was galloping out of terror, or if he was just very hungry after having been tied to a hitching post opposite Cat Island Landing all day long.

"Nonsense," I muttered to myself. The horse's ears flicked back, so I kept quiet and merely thought the rest of what I'd been about to say: *No wonder the Gullahs are so superstitious. Anybody consigned to live their whole lives in surroundings as strange as these sea islands is bound to go strange after a while.*

Still it was the most peculiar thing: Just as we were literally almost out of the woods that grow right up to the live oaks on either side of the long alley, something made me turn my head. I got a chill, what the French call a *frisson,* and without meaning to or consciously thinking about it, I was lifting the lantern high with one hand and pulling back on the reins with the other hand to slow the horse.

I quit that very quickly, I can tell you, but we'd already lost a bit of speed. Enough for me to swear that something *did* move out there past the twisted oaks. The strange thing was, I didn't see it so much as I felt it. How can you see a moving patch of darkness? How do you know if it's really following you, or if it's only in your mind?

HILTON HEAD ISLAND

"Who *is* he?" Clara asked John Elwell, when she could not stay away from the topic any longer no matter how she tried.

"Ah, my dear," John confessed, now stroking that hair he'd so often wanted to touch, "I don't think I can tell you that. What was the man's name again?"

"Dr. Fontaine, Claude Fontaine."

John chuckled.

"He said he's a colonel."

She sat on a footstool next to his couch. For the brief time Clara had allowed herself to stay in his arms, she'd really felt as if she had found a home.

But only a temporary home: she had to force her usual caution.

"I thought there was something wrong with his uniform," she added.

"In what way?" John made himself leave her unexpectedly long, luxuriant hair alone for a while. He pushed back against his pillows and folded his hands, determined to pay better attention.

"I'm not exactly sure. It seemed old, out of date, not quite right."

"But he's Union Army?"

"I suppose so, he wore Union blue. As for service stripes, marks of rank and all that—well, I confess I had other things on my mind. I'm sure if he said he's a colonel then he really is. It was just a vague impression I had, that there was something wrong with his uniform. As if it might have belonged to someone else in his family and he'd pressed it into service. Of course," she turned more toward John, propped her elbow on the edge of the couch and her chin in her hand, "what I really want to know is if we can't find some reason or excuse to toss Dr. Fontaine right out of here!"

Her dark eyes glittered mischievously.

John laughed again, but with restraint; he did not want anyone to hear him beyond these four walls, did not want any of those feet that constantly tramped to and fro on the porch outside to stop in front of his room, or any soldier's calloused hand to come knocking on his door. He wanted this time to be his with Clara alone, wanted as much of her as possible, for as long as possible.

"Don't worry," he said, "the *Comstock* will be off again as soon as all the wounded have been unloaded, and I expect the doctor will go with the ship."

"Unload the wounded? But where will we put them?" Clara looked alarmed, and suddenly extremely alert, as if she had to run right out and find beds for three hundred or more soldiers.

She was probably capable of doing it, if she really had to, John thought.

He reached out and touched her hair again, tenderly. "Don't worry, Bird, we don't have to take care of them here on Hilton Head. This headquarters is a supply station and a clearinghouse for troops on their way somewhere else in the Department of the South. Sick or well, we check them in and send them on their way. The men you were tending to-day will go on up to Beaufort. There are three convalescent hospitals there. I expect there will be room enough to take care of them."

"Oh, I didn't know."

"Of course you didn't. I forget how little time you've been here," John murmured. "It seems . . ."

He stopped himself, because what he'd been about to say was *It seems my life began all over again the day you walked into this room, and nothing from before then is important anymore.*

But he couldn't say that. It was too much, too soon; in some ways Clara really was like a little bird—he was afraid if he moved too suddenly or too fast, she would fly away. So he held the thought in his mind, and hoped she might read it in his eyes.

But she did something else entirely. She picked up on his words and gave them a whole new twist: *"It seems* they have sent me to the wrong place."

John felt as if she'd stabbed him in the heart. It was a hurt worse than the leg now so rapidly mending.

"I belong at the front," she explained, reaching for his hand. "That's what my pass says, and you have no idea how hard that was to get. The whole point of what I'm doing in this war, John, is to provide the things the government hasn't provided, one way or another, to those who've just been in battle."

"I know. I've seen your pass, and all your papers, including that remarkable letter written on your behalf by the Sanitary Commission. It says that within six weeks of your first visit to their headquarters outside of Washington, you had raised two warehouses full of various supplies. Two whole warehouses! Is that really true, Clara?"

He was trying to understand her. He'd thought they might be moving toward tenderness, but suddenly she seemed distant. Not physically; physically she sat as she had before—she even held his hand—and yet in her mind she'd gone someplace he couldn't fathom.

"Yes, it's true," she said. "I'm glad you never had to see the condition they were in when I was there. To think those people were responsible for all the medical needs of our good soldiers!"

She looked directly at him once again, the expression in her eyes no longer playful but somber. "It was after Miss Dix rejected me for a nurse that I paid them my visit—in spite of her I was determined to find a way to serve, you see. They call themselves 'sanitary,' but they didn't even have the most basic things for our boys in blue! No toothbrushes, for heaven's sake! Not even a bar of soap. Not even—so many other things I can't begin to name them off. In the hospitals men were sleeping two to a bed, *not* because they didn't have enough cots, but because the Sanitary Commission hadn't procured them enough *blankets*. It was disgraceful!"

"So you went out and got blankets. Two warehouses full of them."

"I know a lot of people," Clara said simply, "and they all wanted to help. They've been helping ever since. Someone tells someone else, it spreads, it grows. Helping this way is something almost anyone can do."

"But not almost anyone could organize it."

Clara either didn't hear him, or considered her own role unimportant, because she continued: "You may see only one short, unremarkable, tolerably educated spinster here, but I represent the efforts of hundreds back in the Northeast. And if I can't get to the front where my donated goods and I belong, then I'm not helping much, am I?"

"Spinster? *Spinster?*" John couldn't help himself—good-humored laughter welled up from deep in his chest.

Clara dropped his hand, and balled her own into two little fists she planted on her hips. She tossed her head to remove an errant strand of hair from her eyes, and two spots of pink bloomed right along her high cheekbones, a rarity he'd never seen before.

"For pity's sake, Colonel, why pick on *that*? I don't see what's so funny about an unmarried woman past forty years of age. What else should I call myself? At least 'spinster' is less offensive than 'old maid.' "

"We are almost of an age, you and I. Did you know that, Bird?"

"That's beside the point," she said. She seemed confused again, a little flustered. The pink remained.

He said: "Not that you don't look at least ten years younger—and right at this moment, you seem younger still. You amaze me, Clara."

She did look, at least for the moment, almost like a schoolgirl; apparently in her display of emotion she'd embarrassed herself, and the effect was far more charming than anything she could ever have calculated.

"John, I think you are trying to change the subject."

He grasped her right hand and, tugging her toward him, held her fingers tightly curled within his own. This time he didn't intend to let go.

John Elwell was about to commit a monstrous breach of etiquette—but he could forgive himself and, he hoped, so could she. The war changed everything. It taught you new life lessons fast and it taught you hard: The present moment is all you have, with perhaps a whisper of hope for tomorrow. Not one of them could look farther into the future than that.

"Yes," he confirmed, relishing the way her curled fingers trembled and grew hot beneath his own, "I am changing the subject. I want to talk about us. I want to know why you have never married. That is a mystery unfathomable to me."

Clara knew how she should respond, the answer even she herself expected she should give. But she gazed at that gentle face, which was beginning to fill out and to lose its gauntness, and for the first time in her life she thought: *Why did this have to happen now, when we are both too old for it? Why couldn't I have met this man when we were young, and before he was married to someone else?*

So she said, suddenly coquettish: "I'll make a bargain

with you, Colonel Elwell. You tell me what is really going on in the Department of the South, where the nearest front lines are and how I may get there; then in return I will tell you why I've never married."

"All right," John agreed, mightily amused by this odd bargain, and relieved she hadn't taken offense, "but you must go first."

"I don't see why! Especially when there's one hospital ship already in the harbor, and another was anchored out beyond the breakwater the last I saw, and surely there will be more coming tomorrow. There is some urgency to that, surely, sir. Whereas the state of my spinsterhood is quite stable and the reasons for it can be related at any time!"

"You must go first because, to begin with, there will be no more hospital ships tomorrow, or any day soon."

"No?" Clara was shocked. She'd expected a huge battle, many casualties, even though she understood the Union had withdrawn; but granted, she knew nothing whatever about naval matters. All her experience had been on land, with marching and mounted troops.

Then she remembered: "There was a young sailor I cared for on the *Comstock*, a gunner on a monitor. He kept saying, 'We never had a chance.' And from some other things he said, it sounded as if perhaps his ship never even got a shot off. Something about the Rebels' guns having too great a range?"

"That's right. That battle to take Charleston Harbor was declared over almost as soon as it began." John shrugged; he understood the necessity of this war, but its tactics and the endless posing of the top command bored him. "Certainly retreat has its humiliating side, but by breaking off as soon as they understood they couldn't win, a lot of lives were saved. That's why there's only the one hospital ship."

"I see."

"General Hunter, the commandant—"

"I know General Hunter," Clara interrupted eagerly. Here at last was someone who could help her!

"General Hunter is on that other ship out in the breakwater. He lives here in the house up on the rise, the one with the flag. He'll come in tomorrow, and there are other officers onboard that ship with him. I heard Gillmore is arriving from the field also. Tactics will be discussed for days, and I expect at least some of it will go on right here in this room because they'll need me and I'm not able to get around yet—

"And all that, my dear, is why you must go first."

"Oh."

Clara felt her cheeks color again. It was so ridiculous— she'd learned to control blushes years ago, but here it was happening and she couldn't do a thing to stop it.

"I forget," she teased, "what was it you wanted to know?"

He coaxed her, as she wanted, and she told him the truth. All of it, including that awful time twenty years ago when she'd thought her life would never be worth living, and she'd wished herself dead.

It was late when Clara returned to her own room, wrapped in the warmth of John Elwell's warm regard. She turned the wick down low on the lamp and went to the back window, knowing she wouldn't sleep yet, although she was very tired.

She pulled back the curtains and opened the window wide, letting in a delightful, cool burst of air, full of salt, straight off the Atlantic. But there was nothing to see out there, no moon waxing or waning toward its next phase, no stars, no interestingly shaped little clouds moving across a starry field. Nothing whatever. The sky was black as the deepest funeral pall.

How odd, she thought; if the weather-watcher had cried storm warnings, she hadn't heard him.

Clara stood by the window for a few moments anyway, savoring the freshness of the air; but it was a mistake. Somehow the black sky and the open window dissolved away, too soon, the warm glow of the time she'd spent with John.

Precious hours, she thought, closing both the window and the curtains. *Who knows when we may have such precious hours again?*

She sat on the edge of the bed and braided her hair. Thinking how gently he'd stroked it, after remarking on its length—for he'd never seen her hair down before tonight—she smiled.

Then she gazed idly down and her smile disappeared, instantly replaced by an expression of horror: *That letter!*

She'd forgotten it but now there it was, on the floor halfway under her bed, where she'd kicked it.

I just won't read it.

She picked up the elegant, neatly folded paper gingerly, like the distasteful object it was, and put it in the top dresser drawer.

Out of sight, out of mind.

She blew out the lamp, took off her shoes and stockings and skirt in the dark; climbed into bed beneath the covers wearing her blouse, chemise and petticoat.

She tried to sleep, but sleep would not come. She felt creepy all over, as if a malevolent presence were inhabiting the room with her.

How ridiculous! I'm exhausted. I only want to sleep.

She really didn't want to get up again, go to the bother of lighting the lamp, and so on. Most of all, she most definitely did not want to read that letter, not now, not ever, no matter what it said.

But it might be from someone else. Someone who just happens to have similar handwriting, and similar paper.

"That does it," Clara grumbled. She knew the likelihood of such a thing was somewhere around that of having snow in the Sea Islands in August.

Or tomorrow, for that matter, she thought as she sat up and put her feet to the floor. It had grown uncommonly hot and stuffy in her room with the windows all closed. Yet for some reason she very definitely did *not* want to open them.

She felt her way across the floor to the chest of drawers, found the lamp on top and a tin box of matches, removed the glass chimney and lit the wick, replaced the chimney. So tired, she had to be very careful. Opened the drawer, took out the letter and unfolded it. Of course it was from *him.* She'd never really believed it would prove otherwise.

The first line said: *I knew sooner or later we would be together, so imagine my delight when I heard that you'd made it so much easier for me.* Her stomach turned over; she thought she'd be sick.

He was *here? Right here?* How was that possible?

The letter was full of vile suggestions that made her skin crawl. She scanned rapidly, in case it contained any clues to the man's identity, or to where, exactly, *here* might be. But there were none.

The last line said: *I can see you, Clara, any time I want.*

"Oh God!" she cried.

But then Clara surprised herself. Instead of burning the letter as she had the others, or tearing it up into little pieces since she had no fire in her room, she decided that she would keep it. Malevolence and all. Clara Barton was not a superstitious person, and she wasn't going to let anything, no matter how vile, turn her into one.

Pieces of paper can't hurt you, she thought.

But still she put the letter in the back of her Bible; and what was more, she took the time to find a soft old shawl, much worn and dearly loved, in which she wrapped the Bible and its burden before hiding them away in her bottom drawer.

As she climbed into bed once more, this time leaving her lamp turned down low—wasting scarce kerosene for some silly comfort—Clara made herself a promise: *I will find that man. I will expose his vileness to the world, and his own letters will be my witness!*

May-June 1863

Chapter 7

I observed that something was going on here in Beaufort. There were entirely too many people on the streets for an ordinary weekday afternoon.

After almost two whole weeks of bad weather, on this first fair day I'd come up to town to reconnoiter the hospitals for whole-specimen acquisition. I'd taken them only from field hospitals in the past, where conditions are noisy, confusing and disorganized. I'd known, of course, that a convalescing hospital would present an entirely different situation, but what I hadn't expected was crowds in the streets themselves.

Yes, something was definitely going on; I just wished I knew what. I'd spent entirely too much time isolated out at the Coffin Place with nobody for conversation but Jackson—who didn't have much to say to me these days. Or I to him, for that matter. I can't abide sullenness, especially in a subordinate.

As I strolled along Church Street it occurred to me that I might do well to acquire a second residence here in

Beaufort, a modest little house. Especially if there were any remaining as contraband, which meant with occupancy alone one could claim it.

I tucked that idea away for further consideration at a later time. For now I must remain focused on my reconnaissance.

Old Beaufort seemed to have acquired a good number of new people. Why? And why now? Those were the questions.

The newcomers were almost all military in one way or another, and many were women, healthy, pink-cheeked and well fed: officers' wives. When the wives come, you know their husbands expect to be around for a good long while. How worrisome.

I shook my head gloomily at this thought, and walked on another block. The weather was warm and sunny, and the air had that Southern softness that feels sometimes caressing and sometimes cloying, depending upon the interaction of its water content with the ambient temperature. I have heard people—ladies especially—comment upon this quality of Low Country air as if it were somehow romantic, but it is not, it is purely a chemical thing.

I was on my way from the Freemen's Clinic, where I often volunteer my time (it makes a marvelous cover for certain other operations), to the largest of the three hospitals, which is in a mansion on Bay Street formerly owned by another doctor, this one by the name of Jenkins. The Freemen's Clinic, considering the nature of its clientele, is located in the poorer section of town and so I had a walk of several blocks ahead of me.

At John Cross Tavern, when I stopped in before my clinic duty, I heard this influx of people into Beaufort had begun soon after the most recent, perennially abortive attempt by the Union to take Charleston. In other words, when the *Comstock* came into Hilton Head and allowed me to do such an excellent job of restocking my supplies. The gossip had it that there must be some large new military action in the planning stages, for people had continued to come while April turned into May. The town, which had been half deserted ever since the wealthy landowners cleared out in favor of the deeper reaches of the Confederacy, was filling up again—this time, it seemed, entirely with Union Army.

All these new faces made me nervous. Their presence could interfere with my work, particularly if crowded conditions turned out to interfere with my already-delayed acquisition of whole specimens.

It was the weather that had already delayed me: There's been entirely too much rain. I can't be transporting specimens in the rain; they're too fragile, and the whole point of getting new ones is that they should be in the best possible shape and last for a while. As if that weren't enough, it rained so hard and so long that it became a real chore and a bother to take care of the specimens I already have.

When I complained about the weather, and quite justifiably too, Jackson remarked it always rains in April. To which I replied there had been some miscalculation on the part of nature because we hardly need more rain around here, this place being already nine-tenths water. I swear after a while one's very soul gets soggy.

Not that I believe I have a soul, but lately certain . . . events have made me wonder if there may not be something to the supernatural after all.

But I didn't want to think about that.

Jackson would probably say I do have a soul and it is damned. Since I stopped him from calling me a monster,

I've heard him muttering to himself a few times the word "debbil" instead.

Actually, I rather like that. Black men, and other primitive races, have always thought white men were either devils or angels. I know which one I'd rather be.

As if right on cue, I passed the desecrated building Jackson calls the "piskybibble" church. I saw a hog rooting around in the graveyard, which made me smile. The church doors hung open like toothless mouths gaping on shadows, and the windows had all been broken out long before I came here. I heard the Confederates did that themselves, to get at the lead in the stained glass in order to melt it down and make rifle bullets. Last winter some Union soldiers chopped up the pews for firewood. They'd vandalized the graveyard first thing upon seizing the town, of course. Such vandalism would appear to be a right soldiers expect to inflict upon conquered territory since time immemorial.

I winked at a fallen marble angel in the church graveyard as I turned the corner and continued on by.

Enough of musing. I checked my pocket watch: four o'clock in the afternoon, and high time for more reconnoitering.

Already men, most of them in uniform, were hanging out as if they'd reached the end of a workday. They lounged on the long porches of the big houses, leaning with their elbows on the railings, smoking and drinking and making the kind of obnoxious remarks men think it necessary to trade with one another. I've never seen the point in it—the remarks, I mean; smoking and drinking are fine activities in themselves, when one has the time and the money.

Dr. Jenkins, who'd owned the house on the corner of Bay and Charles streets that was my destination, certainly once had both time and money. He must have been quite the man; they say he invested his medical fees in land and slaves—that is supposedly how he became prosperous enough to buy this mansion a couple of years before the war started. Knowing something of medical practice, and how much it does and does not pay, I suspected the good Dr. J. of making his money otherwise.

Idly I wondered if, wherever he might be, he would think it ironically appropriate that the Yankees had turned his house into a convalescing hospital for wounded Union soldiers.

Probably not. But I did.

However, after having passed so many occupied buildings on the way here, I didn't think I was going to be able to get any whole specimens from this largest of Beaufort's three hospitals. There were just too many people around, who would see and might get suspicious.

Oh, but this must have made a grand house, and now it made a grand hospital too. I stood on the corner and looked up, counting windows. An all-too-familiar ambiance emanated from the building, I swear it did; it embraced me and pulled me in.

I found myself climbing the steps to the porch, where bandaged, mutilated men sat in chairs, some with wheels and some without, and dozed in the afternoon sun. There arose from somewhere among them a vague stench of putrefaction, evidence of growing gangrene that would soon require attention—but for the most part the breeze off the river just across Bay Street blew the odor away.

This was a real hospital—not like those butcher shops that pass for hospitals out in the field, where I got in trouble. This may have been only a doctor's residence and party palace until two years ago, but now it was a hospital real enough for me. I could not resist. I went on in. I should not have done it, but I did.

Later, upon leaving that excellent hospital, I abandoned my plans to visit the other two, which are located out on the Point. They're more isolated, more easily accessible by water and might prove a better opportunity for me in spite of their smaller number of patients. But that inspection would have to wait for another day.

I could not trust myself to endure more now. I know my limits.

So instead of proceeding to the Point, I went across the street and sat on a bench facing the river. It was important that I keep very still until the screams stopped inside my head. Oh, I wasn't experiencing echoes of any screams from the hospital, quite the opposite—that place was almost as quiet as a tomb, compared with what happens in the field. No, the screams I heard in my head were entirely within me.

I have learned to scream in silence.

Make no mistake: I am not insane.

Some people *said* I was insane, when they stripped me of my right to practice medicine and ripped the insignia of rank from my uniform coat of blue. Poor, deluded souls, they believed they were being kind, as if a presumption of insanity would somehow absolve me. I do not understand such notions of kindness.

They were idiots. *They* were the ones in need of absolution, not I.

I have a vision, and a mission, and the brilliance to accomplish it, and *I will*—but to *think* how much faster I could move ahead if only I had a free hand to conduct my experiments in that hospital across the street!

Why not? Why shouldn't I? Why can no one understand?

That was how my head howled.

I howled to think of all those potential specimens just going to waste, when most of them would only die anyway. And even if they recovered they would lead the half-lives of half a person, which was about what they had left of their former selves.

I would make them whole again.

Yes, that is my mission and my vision. It can be done, I know it can. It only stands to reason that an arm or leg, hand or foot that is essentially undamaged can be hooked up to a blood supply and made to live and be useful once more.

Not only would I make some people whole again, but others I would not cut up in the first place. Every surgeon I've ever seen in action in this war is nothing but a butcher. Every one, that is, except myself. They see a damaged limb, first thing they do is chop it off. Not I!

I'm certain they're often chopping off arms and legs that could be put back together with some careful stitching and matching up of the broken bits of bone. The problem is, one must be a fast worker in general and a fast stitcher in particular in order to get it all done before the wounded man bleeds to death. Now I ask you, how can any surgeon— even one who is as good with his hands as I am—become fast enough at this exacting work without *practice?*

My fellow physicians would not let me practice. They insisted I must become a mere butcher like them. They all but accused me of being a murderer, just because the men I was practicing my technique upon kept running out of blood before I'd finished.

I turned my head and looked longingly over my shoulder at that mansion/hospital, glowing in the afternoon sun. I thought: *Give me a place like that and some nurses with strong hands and strong stomachs to help me, keep it stocked with supplies and specimens, and in a year or two I'll change the course of medical history.*

It was going to take me so much longer to do it on my own. I sat shaking with anger at the injustice of it all.

Eventually I noticed, about five feet over to my right, a black boy who stood throwing stones into the river to amuse himself. Every now and then a startled fish jumped, and the boy laughed.

I wondered how long he'd been there. I didn't recall seeing him come up, or I would have waved him away. I frowned with further effort to recall, but still I couldn't.

These blank moments happen to me sometimes. I don't know why, but they leave me weak as a kitten for a while after.

I decided it was fortunate the boy was there—Lady Luck taking care of me when I most needed it—and I called out:

"Hey, boy!"

I judged him somewhere around twelve to fourteen—he was rather tall and lanky, skinny like most boys that age. Most interesting was the fact that he was both clean and reasonably neatly dressed.

He was also cautious. He looked at me, his eyeballs bluish-white and round in his black face, but he didn't move other than to stop his hand in midthrow.

"You callin' me, mistuh?" he asked.

"Yes, I am. Want to make some money?"

The word "money" got his attention, as I'd expected. He came a few feet closer to where I still sat, on the bench facing the river. But now I'd twisted around sideways to face him.

"What you wants me to do?" He tipped his head to one side in a curiously charming way.

I thought of taking him . . .

But I was so tired.

I said, "I'll pay you a penny to go up to the ferry landing where I left my horse, untie him and walk him back here to me."

He said somberly, and I thought a trifle regretfully, "Nossuh, cain't do that."

"Two pennies."

He scratched his head, looked over his shoulder at something, I wasn't quite sure what, and then looked down at his feet.

I upped the ante, even though it was outrageous, just to see what he would do: "A five-cent piece."

He looked over his shoulder again. I could see reflected in his body the very moment in which he made up his mind, because his backbone straightened, and his head—which was so beautifully shaped; he would soon grow into a very fine specimen indeed—his head came elegantly up on his neck like a flower on a stalk.

"I already got me a job," he declared, "ebry day. Pay me wages, wunct a week."

Suddenly he grinned, and well he might! A boy as young as that, making regular money. Who knows where the wonders will end.

"Well, good for you," I said, though somewhat sarcastically, because this was all very charming but it was not helping me get my horse. Still it amused me to continue, and I asked his name.

"My whole name *Ee*-rasmus, but I likes to be call Razz," he said.

Imagine: A name of such noble and illustrious lineage as Erasmus, and he prefers something that sounds like the forepart of a berry. But that's boys that age for you. I continued to quiz him.

"And for whom do you work, Razz?"

"I works for Miss Clara Barton. She an' Miz Frances Gage an' Miss Mary Gage be gone in that big house crost the street. I be sposed to watch they buggy till they come back."

Well, well, well. How very interesting.

Yet inopportune—I did not want to face Clara Barton yet. Especially not right now.

"I'm sure you will continue to watch that buggy very nicely, Razz," I said, as I got up from the bench and cast a quick glance across the street, where I saw a horse and buggy that had not been there before. I was relieved, however, to see nothing on the porch but the same hodgepodge of chairs and bandaged men.

I wondered what Clara was doing in the hospital, and how long she'd been in there, and how close we had come to crossing paths. I shuddered to think I might have come upon her unaware and unprepared.

"Miss Clara be visitin' the sick," Erasmus offered.

"Then she's in the right place for it," I said, resisting an urge to pet the curly black fur on his perfectly shaped head. "And now, since you won't do it, I'll be on my way to get my horse."

"Clara, you are too quiet," Frances Gage said.

The four of them, Frances and her daughter Mary, Clara

and Erasmus, had returned the buggy to Mary's friend Major Hamilton Scott at Port Royal, with thanks for his kindness. Now at Port Royal Landing they waited for the tide to turn so that they could return to Parris Island. Erasmus was trying his best to be patient and not succeeding very well, but he above all of them knew they couldn't leave yet, because it was his job to pole and row the boat. At low tide there were too many spots near their destination where even a shallow-draft boat might go aground.

Clara looked up at Frances, who was about ten years older and a head taller than she. Frances was also the first woman in whom Clara had ever, on first meeting, felt a kindred spirit. This was such an unexpected blessing, like a balm to her soul.

"I don't believe you'd like what I'm thinking," Clara confessed, making a wry face, "so I'm keeping it to myself."

Because her own mother had shut her out, Clara hardly knew how to form a close relationship with another woman. But with Frances she wanted it and so she was trying, in what she often felt were the equivalent of tiny baby steps.

"Oh, please don't do that," Mary said.

Just as Frances was ten years older, so Mary was ten years younger than Clara. Mary was as tall as her mother, but there the resemblance ended. Mary tended to an outspoken exuberance, whereas Frances was grave, patient and thoughtful. Mary had a pink-cheeked prettiness, and her light brown hair was so curly that it would not stay flat and straight against her head no matter how hard she bound it. Frances had a kind face, but any pinkness in her cheeks had faded along with the color of her hair; prettiness had gradually given place to strength of character over the years.

"You must give us your opinion, Clara," Mary insisted. "I expect we will more often agree with you than not. And even if we don't, there are few things more satisfying than a lively exchange of ideas!"

Clara was accustomed to Mary's enthusiasm, and for the moment she resisted it.

"There are times when it is better to be quiet," Clara said, gently but definitely, a tone that brooked no argument.

Frances smiled at her impulsive daughter, as she reached out and tucked a wayward, curly strand of hair behind Mary's ear.

"I've been telling her that very thing since she was about three," Frances said.

Frances and Mary had been in the Sea Islands for a little over a year. In anticipation of Emancipation they had left their whole lives behind in Ohio, setting off on their own, private mission of teaching the abandoned slaves to read and write and to do many of the little everyday things that would be required of them by their freedom.

Clara's eyes were opened by the Gages and their work. It was one thing to be an abolitionist in the North, steeped in theory and ethics and high ideas. Quite another to see for yourself the conditions the slaves had been living in for so long, how miraculous it was that they had left any will to survive. It was almost unbelievable how far they had to go, how much to learn.

She'd heard (from the ever-fair-minded Colonel Elwell) there were exceptions, that not all the wealthy plantation owners had mistreated their slaves. But she'd seen no proof yet. The only exception she had personally encountered so far was Erasmus, who was simply exceptional in and of himself.

She watched him wander off, but not far. They couldn't get back to Parris Island without the boy, so she wasn't about to let him out of her sight.

He was scanning the ground, searching for something. Razz had a good eye. In no time at all he bent down, grinning; picked up his prize, held it up for close inspection, rubbed it on his shirt; looked down and made a rueful face at the dirt he'd just smeared on that nice clean cloth.

But then a moment later he'd forgotten and was bending down again.

Clara felt the corners of her mouth twitch. She surmised he was collecting flat, round stones; later he would skip them across the water, a favorite occupation. A way to pass the time.

It seemed to Clara they—herself, Razz, everyone—spent entirely too much time waiting for the tide to turn. And everyone—Razz, Frances, John, Sam Lamb and even her brother David—had explained to her that she'd just have to get used to it, there was no other way here, you came and went with the tides. So she was doing her best to surrender to this slow, nature-driven pace. But for Clara it was hard. She'd let Razz try to teach her how to make the stones skip, but every time she did it they sank straight to the bottom.

She would spend tonight at the Gages' cottage, because they expected it to be full dark by the time they reached Parris Island, and Razz would stay with Annabelle. Privately Clara wasn't so sure of the wisdom of that; she would have thought having a boy in the house would only remind Annabelle all the more of George's absence.

But Annabelle didn't seem to feel that way. She'd crooned and made a fuss over Erasmus from their very first meeting, when Clara had taken him with her to deliver a message from Colonel Elwell. The news that George could not be found—it had not been good news; yet Annabelle had borne up surprisingly well. Perhaps she'd seen Erasmus as some consolation? Clara didn't know, but Annabelle's curiously placid attitude—so at odds with the way the woman had been in the Colonel's quarters that day—disturbed her.

"Tide's turning," Frances quietly remarked. "We can go soon."

Clara nodded.

Mary tapped her foot, like a coquette who for today only has been forced to wear sober clothes. Yet for all her girlish ways, Mary was a scholar and an excellent teacher—it was just that she was of an age where what she wanted most in the world was to marry.

Poor dear, Clara thought, *at past twenty-five it's not likely to happen.*

Clara knew the men who appeared to be attracted to Mary, even the gentlemanly Major Hamilton, would most likely be wanting things other than marriage. Things of which Mary, at least so far, seemed to be blissfully unaware.

Clara thought ruefully: *She cannot stay that way for long.*

Was Major Hamilton married? Clara thought she might make a note to ask someone—even went so far as to reach into her pocket and close her hand upon her notebook. But then she chided herself and let the notebook go. She was becoming worse than her brother!

Mary would have to learn, just as Clara herself had learned.

But Mary was different; Mary *wanted* to get married whereas Clara never had. Mary might get hurt. Almost certainly, she would.

Clara lifted her chin and resolutely didn't listen to a small voice inside that informed her she had been hurt herself; and informed her that moreover *this* time things were different for Clara too.

If only John were not married . . .

She refused to finish the thought.

Erasmus threw the first stone and it skipped gracefully, almost miraculously, so long and straight that Clara nearly lost sight of it before it sank, making a little round vortex in the placid, rising water of Port Royal Sound. The sun, setting behind them, poured out a golden light that made the trees, the marsh grass tall and thin as blades of wheat, the water now flowing swiftly in its channel, look like a scene from a child's illustrated Bible. Clara was filled with nostalgia, tinged by regret for the loss of something—she knew not what. Innocence, she supposed.

She withdrew into herself, wrapped in her own thoughts, and stayed that way through the long trip to the Gages' home.

Chapter 8

Clara had made a cocoon of silence around her mind. To retreat into this self-spun, silken stillness was a kind of protection she had learned to create for herself long ago—how long ago she could not recall, but long before the war—when things became too much for her to bear. As, for the moment, they were. Action she could take; inaction was unbearable to her nature.

Unbearable: the slow, slow pace that was natural to this part of the world, the waiting, waiting, waiting . . .

Waiting for the tides to change.

Waiting for boats to arrive with letters so that she could answer them, only to wait again for another reply. Over and over.

Waiting for news of battles from the other fronts: That was news they seldom got. There were too many Rebel ships, blockade-runners, and far too many Confederate spies. Therefore what news they got could not be trusted—it might have been planted, meant to mislead those Rebels so nearby, crawling through the marshes on islands attached to the mainland south and west of Hilton Head, islands whose very names rang with the sounds of the South: Pinckney, Daufuskie, Tybee. A South Clara hated for its perfidy, for its wealth built on the immorality of keeping slaves. And yet she could not deny the strange beauty of the Low Country. This confused her, and made everything all the more unbearable.

They were all in the boat now, the Gages huddled together in the bow, and Erasmus had the oars out midway. Clara sat alone in the stern with her hand trailing in the water, which felt lukewarm, like a bath, even though true summer had not yet begun. The boat had such a shallow draft that she could feel the water's current beneath her body, a powerful coursing as the strong outgoing tide combined with the young black boy's pull at the oars. Their own motion made a breeze in the still and heavy twilight air, and Clara held her face down and to the side, to catch the coolness of it against her cheeks.

Waiting . . . still waiting . . . waiting for John's leg to heal completely. What would they do then? Would there really be a time of true intimacy for the two of them? Soon he would be able to stand and walk with crutches, then with a brace and a cane. But standing and walking with crutches and braces must be very different from making love . . . at least, the only way Clara knew of making love. She had heard there were other ways, but she had no experience of them. Really very little experience at all. It had never mattered much to her until now, until John. . . .

"I reckon Miss Clara's done gone off in her head somewheres," Erasmus said.

She heard him, but pretended she hadn't.

"She do that sometime," the boy added, "but then she be back just like she never missed a thing."

Mary said quietly, "It's not that important, Mother. Let's just leave her be."

And Clara, with her eyes cast down to the water, felt the coolness of a silvery fish slide against her fingers. She shivered—from the fish, or from her thoughts? She pretended she hadn't heard a word, and silently blessed Erasmus for taking such good care of her.

When Erasmus stood up to pole the boat into the shallow creeks that would lead them through the tall grasses to the dock behind the Gages' little cottage, Clara had to leave her cocoon because it was necessary to trade places with him. For stability with the long pole, he needed to stand in the stern. With her skirts and all, switching places was a tricky maneuver. But they'd done it before and were getting quite good at it. Clara had upset the boat only once, about a week earlier; the experience had been unpleasant enough for her—so many layers of petticoats to dry out—that she was determined not to let it happen again.

"Give a penny," said Mary brightly.

Frances shushed her daughter. "Let our friend have the privacy of her thoughts, miss," she said.

"I confess," Clara said slowly, "that more and more I believe my coming here was a mistake. Weeks have gone by, and I have accomplished nothing."

"You healed the Colonel," Mary pointed out, "and I'd say that's pretty important."

"Even more important," Frances said in a voice so low that it was hard to hear her, "is the hope for a new life that you have given our young friend in the stern. He is extremely bright, you know."

"Yes, I do know. But that kind of thing is more your area of expertise than mine."

"Don't be so hard on yourself, Clara," Frances said. "You have recently recovered from the typhoid, have you not?"

Clara nodded.

"Then perhaps God or his angels," this was Mary's brighter voice and contribution, "thought you needed a rest."

"Perhaps," Clara nodded and then decided to let it be. These two women, good souls that they were, had never been in a battle. They could not imagine how inconsequential everything else in her life had become by comparison. She would not wish such an experience on anyone, yet she'd insisted on having her battlefield pass, she'd been given it, and that gave her a certain sort of job to do. A job she most definitely was not getting done in this wildly beautiful place that teemed with life, not death.

The sun had sunk below the horizon some time ago but an orange glow still lit the sky and turned the water in the creeks to liquid fire. It was a fire made of water that did not burn. Just one more contradiction in a place already full of them.

No, the Gages would never understand, and there was no point in her even trying to tell them.

Without realizing it, Clara had retreated into her cocoon again. In her mind she had gone back months and months, to the days when she had walked along with the Army of the Potomac, sticking with the Massachusetts regiment because she herself was originally from North Oxford, and she knew some of the soldiers. They were less skeptical of her presence than the other regiments—or at least, out of courtesy, they hid it better.

Cornelius Welles, who was chaplain as well as her

assigned companion, walked behind her and sometimes beside her. They had a rickety old wagon filled with whatever Clara had been able to cobble together—she hadn't been very organized in those days, she was just learning her way, where she belonged, what she could and could not do. It was all trial and error. Over and over again she had to show her papers, which naturally she carried in her voluminous pockets. In the evenings, when they stopped for the night, she spent many an hour sewing on buttons for the soldiers by lamplight.

But then had come one night when they didn't stop to rest. Word had passed down the line of the Battle of Bull Run. There was to be a second battle, for which they were all needed, and they must march double time. They marched through the night and into the next day—and then, before Clara knew how it had happened, the noise and stink of war was all around them. The stink came from the thick smoke of gunpowder and cannon fire. It came from human excrement, as bowels of dying men let go. It came from the sharp smell of urine that seemed to be everywhere, as boys became men instantly through necessity and by virtue of their terror wet themselves.

The stink came from blood, and worse than blood, from bloody guts, sometimes still attached, sometimes separated from their former owners. The air became so black and thick with smoke it was impossible to see.

"Back," Cornelius kept yelling into her ear. "Clara, help me get these mules to pull the wagon back or we'll lose our stores!"

It was then that she had grasped for the first time that her place, the place she could do the most good, was not on the battlefield itself but nearby. Out of the line of fire. She'd pulled at the reins of the stubborn mules, who, the more terrified they were, the more they dug in their hoofs and refused to move. Clara screamed and pushed, and dear Corny, usually such a gentleman, had done the same, until finally the mules gave way and the wagon rolled, and they'd found a place among the trees. Out of the way. Halfway, approximately, between the battlefield itself and the farmhouse that had been turned into a field hospital.

Clara had gauze dressings—to those who would live, who had been toppled off stretchers near her feet, she applied them. She had salves, and liniment to clean wounds. She had her calm, steady hands and her clear voice, and her dark eyes full of the compassion that she felt but could not see herself. The soldiers could see it. Cornelius could see it.

He said straight into her ear, because that was the only way anyone could hear: "This is the place where you belong, Clara. With these soldiers who still may live, between the battle itself and the field hospital." Those words had stayed with her; they defined her: *My place is with the wounded soldier, between the battlefield and the hospital.*

When night came, the fighting stopped. For the first time Clara grasped the full meaning of the phrase "the silence was deafening." After all the noise of the guns and cannons and battle cries and crazed, neighing horses, the silence fell on her ears not like a blessing at first, but like an anomaly. An accident. A freak of nature. As if she herself had suddenly gone deaf, and the noise was still there, but she alone could not hear it.

Clara felt disoriented and light-headed. She didn't know what to do, how to continue or where to stop. She had just participated in the Battle of Second Bull Run, where later she learned the entire Army of Virginia had been devastated. Thousands were dead. Thousands more were wounded. Later when the count was taken, it revealed that more than twenty thousand men had fallen on the field that day.

Finally, no more doctors drew her aside and asked her to hold a cloth of chloroform over a soldier's face, or to probe out a bullet with a knife, or to stitch the edges of a wound with black thread, or simply to quiet a hysterical man until he died—which was actually not simple at all until she learned to join in the hysterical man's hallucinations, and to become his mother, his sister, his wife. To answer to their names. To hold his hands or his bloody stumps and kiss his brow and close his eyes with a gentle hand and say, "There, now. Rest."

She had gone then that night, after Second Bull Run, in search of Cornelius because there was something she knew she must do, and by the terms of her battle pass she was not supposed to go on the field alone, without an escort. She had found a heavy kerosene lantern that gave good light from four sides, of the sort that is usually fixed to wagons or carriages at night. She intended to go out on the field and look for the living among the dead.

Cornelius was asleep in a tent, not on a cot but on the bare ground, his collar not even unloosed. It looked as if he had fallen in exhaustion just as he lay, where he lay. But he was not dead; Clara could see the even rise and fall of his narrow chest beneath the brass buttons of his uniform. She left him there, and went on alone.

Clara held the lantern high. She paid no attention to the way her skirts were pulling at her waist because their hems were soaked and heavy with blood, nor to the fact that her shoes squished, not only with water or mud but also with blood. She walked toward the battlefield with her shoulder aching as she held the heavy lantern as high as she could, to cast the greatest pool of light. Her shadow was much bigger than she was herself.

The dead had been piled in rows; not one by one but in heaps. The rows seemed to go on forever. Clara took them one at a time. She listened, grateful for the stillness now, and the quiet. The night was very dark, with clouds obscuring stars and moon. She did not see the figure of a man who hid among the trees at the edge of the field, a man whose help she could most surely have used.

As she walked down each row she listened for the slightest sound: a movement, a gasp, the faintest moan. Using her left hand to bolster her right arm at the elbow, Clara lifted the heavy lantern higher. "If there are any among you still alive," she said, "give me some sign!" Her voice rang through the night air like a bell.

There were responses. How many, she would never remember. She had in her pocket strips of yellow cloth—she had ripped up a tablecloth in that farmhouse that was being used as a hospital. To each man who was still alive, she tied a yellow strip. Every time she did this, she had to put down the lamp. Each time she picked it up again, the lamp seemed heavier.

The figure in the trees watched her, never offered to help, eventually disappeared. She never saw him.

Some men were so near death that she knew there was no point to giving them a yellow strip. Still she stopped for them, put down the lamp and wrote their names in a little notebook she carried in her pocket. That was her first field diary, and the beginning of what she later called her "battle-field scrawl."

Another thing Clara Barton had learned that night after the Battle of Second Bull Run: She could not do all she wanted to do. It simply was not possible. She had limitations on her own strength and she had to accept them. At the point of exhaustion, she held the lantern as high as she could and looked at all the rows of men where she had not yet walked.

Then she had turned away, had gone to her own tent, blown out the lamp, and like Cornelius Welles, she'd slept filthy in her clothes.

The boat bumping the dock felt like a warning that she was about to fall out of her cot, and Clara blinked, and opened her eyes very wide. Her cocoon vanished and with it the memory. Instead of rows of dead soldiers she saw fields of marsh grass, and a navy-blue sky full of stars overhead. Where memory had put a stench in her nostrils, she smelled the salty, fresh scent of the sea coming up to Parris Island through Hilton Head's inlet.

Frances and Mary, mother and daughter, looked at each other and then at Clara with identical questioning expressions on their faces.

"Sorry," Clara said with a smile, "I was only wool-gathering. It's the idleness of these days that makes me like this, I think."

ST. HELENA ISLAND

When I finally reached home after my experience at the convalescing hospital, once again it was after dark.

All the more reason, I thought, to get a small place in town where I can stay overnight. Not being able to trust Jackson on his own for more than an hour or two was taking its toll on my waterborne transportation.

I slammed through the back gate, unlocked the kitchen door and came on into my house.

Let my man Jack stay locked in for a few more hours, let him go without his supper and see how he likes it.

I used to take him with me—or rather, he used to take me in the boat—on clinic days. But I couldn't very well do that anymore now I'd killed his woman so nearby.

Odd they still haven't found her body . . .

I was tired and I wanted to go to bed, but I stumbled back outside, down the path to my laboratory, and made rounds. Like the good doctor I knew myself to be, no matter what *they* had said.

I have a good nose—a good nose is an invaluable aid to a physician and a scientist, as it helps greatly in medical observation.

I paused in unlocking a barred door, reflecting that I should have those words engraved on my tombstone someday: "He was the most excellent observer." I could translate it into Latin—where the "most excellent" would become one of those superlatives that end in *issimus*. Yes, I'd like that.

But back to the observation of the moment: On the other side of that barred door, one of my experiments had taken a turn for the worse. I could tell by the smell of her.

Silently, I went on in.

She was silent too, but not dead yet.

I could hear her breathing: irregular, shallow. Was she unconscious, or asleep? I didn't know. I could have called out, to see if she'd wake, but I didn't. To do so would have been against my own rule.

I don't talk to them, and I don't call an experiment by name.

Laboratory science should be done in an impersonal way. Now if I'd had a whole hospital, with a staff and all . . .

I put my hand to my head, screwed my eyes shut and,

with a supreme effort of will, stopped the screams that had been about to come back.

A moment later I removed my hand, let out a long breath and waited. My head remained clear. Now, where was I?

Oh yes, if I'd had a whole hospital with a staff and free access to as many specimens as I needed for my work, so that I didn't have to do everything down to the last dreary detail myself (except for carrying out slops and burying things; that's what I pay Jackson for), then I might have been able to come into the hospital and do my work. I could go home at the end of the day, go back the next morning and check on my patients by name, as all doctors do.

But the way I was forced to work was entirely different. A man can run a laboratory by himself, but not a whole hospital. So I had my lab and I had my specimens, my experiments, and I kept them all in a row out back of the lab.

I didn't like it, but that was the way it was, and it was easier both for them and for me if I treated my subjects only as specimens for scientific study.

My specimens came in two forms: (a) whole; (b) partial. Whole, meaning they had their heads and all their essential internal organs; partial, meaning a human part in good condition. Such as a hand or a foot, arm or leg. Once I have performed my delicate surgery, two (or more) specimens are united and become an experiment. Someday I expect I'll get to eyes and tongues, maybe fingers and toes, but I haven't gone that far yet.

I hate it when a specimen goes sour on me. This woman smelled very sour indeed. I had to hold my breath against her stench as I checked her over.

I set my lantern up on a high shelf, where it lit most of the chamber, and bent down over a white woman who had pretended to be a man so she could fight as a soldier. But then she got herself shot and her jig was up. She was an embarrassment of course, so they'd put her off by herself to die alone. Like I've said, Lady Luck takes a special care of me—it was easy as pie to carry her off. I doubt anyone has ever missed her.

On this whole specimen I had done my first splice graft. It was very clever, really: I opened a hole of exactly the right size, in exactly the right place, and attached her femoral vein and artery to the vein and artery of an exquisite little foot I took off an abandoned child. The woman was white, the foot was black, but blood is blood. No one will ever convince me otherwise. It's all red for a reason.

"Tsk, tsk," I muttered. That little foot had been doing well, I'd thought. Its color had been good, so I'd thought the graft was taking, whether or not the experiment wanted it there.

But now the little foot appeared dusky and dull in the lamplight. I'd have to wait for morning to be really sure of its condition. The experiment's heart was still pumping, therefore the blood was circulating. That's all the heart is, you know, just a pump.

What could have gone wrong? Perhaps the heart was not pumping regularly, or strongly enough.

I couldn't take the woman's pulse to find out, at least not in the usual way, because the manacles that kept her from clawing at the grafted foot covered her wrists. Nor did I want to touch her neck where the carotid artery ran.

Heat came off her in waves: She had a high fever, one more symptom to add to the stench.

Inside the woman something was dying. Or outside, if it was only the little foot that was dying. I didn't know. I couldn't do a further inspection without daylight. Even then I might not know, which was which, which came first, the chicken or the egg.

Shaking my head, sucking on my cheek, I took the lantern and relocked the door to keep her safe through the rest of the night. Then I finished my rounds uneventfully, the others being much as I'd left them earlier.

Before retiring I closed the windows, as was my habit, to keep out the noxious night air. The night continued to be as warm as the day had been, and after all that rain I was tempted to open the windows again and let the warm air come in. But I didn't; I followed good health practice and kept them closed.

Perhaps due to overstimulation—after all it had been quite a day, especially considering my unanticipated proximity to Miss Clara Barton—I had difficulty falling asleep.

I tossed and turned in my bed. The specimen's foul stench seemed to have settled in my nostrils. I felt as if I were drowning in the smell of death. So I got up and opened the windows. Good health habits be damned, a man has to breathe.

Perhaps everything would have been all right if I had only opened the windows and gone quickly back to bed. If I had only *not* looked outside. But I did.

I shivered. I wished Old Man Coffin, or whoever had built this place, had put up a nice big stout high wall. Preferably of those bricks they make over on Lady's Island. But then I doubted it would have made a difference. Whatever was out there could probably walk through walls, including brick ones.

I was being silly, of course. Challenging myself to see how outlandishly far I could go with this foolishness.

Nevertheless, gooseflesh had risen all along my arms, and every tiny hair upon my body was standing painfully erect. And then the chill came on.

There is no such thing, I told myself firmly, *as a moving cloud of darkness.*

But there was. I had seen it in the woods several times since the first time on the night of that wild ride, when I'd given the horse his head. Whenever I saw it, I had this involuntary physical reaction of the hair standing up all over my body, and the gooseflesh, and the chill. A *physical* reaction.

"It's real," I muttered; "if it causes a physical effect it has to be real."

I didn't want it to be real. Did I?

Dammit, I see it, it's there!

I was caught in a conundrum. I felt that dark thing out there was somehow supernatural in origin. But I do not believe in the supernatural. I most emphatically do not. So if it's supernatural it can't be real. But if it's *real* . . . then *what is it?*

Whatever it was, it had never been this close to the house before and I didn't like it. That was why I wanted a wall, to keep it out. I had thought—or perhaps I'd wished—this thing lived out in the woods. I'd thought it might be the origin of that story the Gullahs use to frighten children, the bugguh-man.

That would make a certain amount of sense, especially considering Jackson's feelings about these woods at night.

Now it is very hard to continue to keep sight of something as elusive as a patch of darkness that moves from place to place of its own accord. It doesn't really have edges, and it's difficult to keep your eye on the most dense part of it, where it might coalesce if it were going to . . . I hated to even think such a thing, but . . . to take on a more definite shape. So when it shifted and moved, at first I thought it had dissolved, just gone away. I know after a while it *does* disappear.

It's just that I don't know where it goes. . . .

Now, I thought, *is a good time to quickly shut the window and close the curtains, and get into bed with the covers over my head. It won't find me that way.* Yes, I know it's childish but that was how I felt.

I looked out the windows again and saw it was still there. It had moved over to a corner of the yard—and in the process it seemed to have grown to about twice the size it had been before.

"This is ridiculous!" I said in my normal tone of voice. "I am imagining this. If I'm imagining it, I can also make it go away."

That was when I noticed how unnaturally silent everything had become.

Night in the Sea Islands is never really silent. Actually I hate the night noises here, especially the insects—they're constantly chirping or squeaking or humming or buzzing, and one cannot entirely get rid of them because they live in the grass and in that layer right beneath the pine needles in the woods. The frogs are worse than the insects. . . .

And yet at this very moment I would have loved to hear a frog.

Just one frog.

The screams started again inside my mind.

Chapter 9

Clara, Mary, Frances and Razz were walking up the long boardwalk from the creekside dock to the Gages' house, which was more of a cottage. Clara wondered who the former owners had been, and how the Gages had come by it, but she didn't like to ask and they had never volunteered the information. The little house was built in the classic four-square style: two rooms on each side, separated by a central hallway. It had one story only, and a small front porch—plus one extra feature that presented some interesting possibilities to Clara's restless mind: a sleeping porch, currently not in use. But with a cot, easy enough for her to acquire, and a few lengths of mosquito netting . . .

Erasmus, walking beside her, interrupted her thoughts. It was such an unusual thing for him to do that Clara stopped in her tracks and had to ask him to repeat his question.

"I said I wants to talk to you, if that's all right. Private-like, before we gets back to Miz Gage's."

"Of course you can." She resumed her steps, more slowly

now. "I think Frances and Mary are far enough ahead of us that they won't hear what we say, if we speak softly. What's on your mind, Razz?"

He pulled at his ear. "Well, I know I gotta stay with Annabelle tonight, an' I really likes Annabelle a lot, so's I don't mind *too* much, but . . ."

"But what? You can tell me anything. I won't repeat it."

"But," he said earnestly, the whites of his eyes shining in the deepening twilight, "there be some mighty strange goings-on there in the nighttimes. Scratches on the roof, an' at the windas. She keep all her windas closed and shuttered *and* she jus' painted 'em blue again, so why she gotta have it so stuffy inside at nights is more'n I can understand. She nail the chimbley top shut, an' paint the whole chimbley blue too!"

"Blue is a nice color," Clara said hesitantly.

Erasmus rolled his so-white eyes. "Blue be the color keeps the sperrits out. At night. Daytimes too, but mostly nights, so's they can't come home to roost."

"Spirits? At Annabelle's?"

"You know her daddy was the Conjuh Man. She be livin' in her daddy house."

"Yes, I know. But Annabelle doesn't conjure, Razz. She just does a little of what us white people would call folk medicine. It's harmless. She's the Praise Leader at her church."

Razz muttered, so that Clara had to bend her head toward his to hear him: "I cain't stay there no more after tonight. I'm scairt, an' that's the truth of it."

After a few moments of astounded silence, during which both their steps slowed almost to a stop, Clara said merely: "I'm glad you told me. I've been wanting to talk to

Annabelle about something anyway, so tonight I'll walk along over there with you. I'd like to see this for myself."

"You won't tell her what I said, please, Miss Clara?"

"Of course not. The most important things for you to remember are: First, I feel honored you told me something I know was hard to tell; and second, that's the mark of trust and a true friendship, which means a lot to me."

"Yes'm," Erasmus said soberly.

"Now we'd best walk a little faster and catch up with the Gages. They'll wonder why we're such slowpokes."

Razz grinned. "Ain't never nuthin' slowpokey about you, Miss Clara. Oney sometimes you has things on you mind, like today."

"Like today, indeed. You're very observant."

He ducked his head, not knowing how to take the compliment.

Clara continued, as they both lengthened their strides, "I know there are many things happening on these islands that I don't understand. And I don't mean just because I don't always understand the language. I mean things like you said, about Annabelle acting strange. Maybe about her son disappearing, though I still think he got on the Underground Railroad and went up north."

Erasmus shook his head. "Not him. She certain."

"Still?" Clara darted the boy a piercing glance.

"Oh yes, Mam, she sure as sure can be."

"And you're sure you'll be all right there just for tonight?"

He nodded. But Clara thought, in spite of the gathering darkness, she could make out a tremble to his chin.

"I'll have a few questions to put to Annabelle on my own, nothing to do with you, you understand. And then I'll explain to her that I need you with me from now on, that tonight will be your last night. Is that satisfactory, Erasmus?"

"Yes'm, Miss Clara."

And now, she thought, *I only have to convince Frances to let me fix up her sleeping porch. I'll have something to seriously occupy my mind during all this infernal waiting.*

Two hours later, Clara felt Frances's mild disapproval as the older woman served her a warmed-over concoction of rice and some spicy things—Clara didn't pay much attention to food, and sometimes it was better anyhow not to know exactly what you were eating. Mary had withdrawn entirely into the bedroom she shared with her mother when Clara visited; Mary was reading, Frances said.

"I am a disappointment to you," Clara began—her preference always being to get a problem right out into the open as soon as possible.

Frances sat down with her at the table, which was not in the kitchen as it would have been in a New England four-room house. Here in the South the point was to get away from the warmth, not near to it, and so the table was in the main room in a corner between two windows. At the moment, one window was closed and the other open only partway, because the night had indeed cooled down considerably.

Clara could not meet Frances's eyes. She wanted more than anything to have the older woman's friendship, but because she'd never had a close woman friend, she didn't know how to go about it. Clara's mother had been no fit role model; and her sister, so much older all the years of her growing up, had been as distant as stars.

Frances sighed. "It's not disappointment, exactly. Though I admit both Mary and I hoped we would have your help with the teaching at least some of the time while you were here. This particular night, however, I'm concerned because you insisted on going to Annabelle's with Erasmus, alone, after dark. That was not a safe thing to do, Clara, now that Parris Island is crawling with all these new recruits who don't have enough to do, and amuse themselves at night by drinking and moving from bonfire to bonfire, destroying the woods."

"I'm not afraid to move alone among soldiers after dark. I do it all the time." The rice concoction was quite good, and Clara was hungry enough that she allowed herself to be distracted by the quality of the older woman's cooking.

Frances sighed again and put her hand to her head, then leaned on her elbow in an attitude of defeated thought.

A few moments later, Clara took several sips of water and said, "Besides, it was necessary for Razz's sake that I talk to Annabelle tonight. It will be his last with her."

"Oh? How do you mean? I thought they were getting along well."

"They are, but I want him with me now, and I have a proposal to put to you. It concerns your sleeping porch, which you've said you do not use."

"We don't. In summertime, when it would be most helpful, the mosquitoes would eat us alive."

Clara ate more rice, then made her proposal. "In return for your letting me and Razz sleep on that porch for a few weeks, I will fix it up for you. I know I can get two cots and enough netting to cover them from the quartermaster's stores. Colonel Elwell will approve it if I ask, and it's for a good cause."

"Oh?"

"To start with, Erasmus says there are strange goings-on at Annabelle's house at night. He's not Gullah, and he's not superstitious, but I must admit that after talking to Annabelle this evening, I myself am rather concerned. For example," Clara leaned forward across the table for emphasis, "tonight I made Annabelle tell me about the other missing children. None of them was as old as George. They were toddlers, mostly. Haven't you heard anything about this, Frances?"

Frances frowned. She said, "Excuse me a moment, Clara," then went into the kitchen and returned with two glasses of lime juice and water, with a little precious sugar added to cut the acid. Then she sat down again, with the frown still upon her brow. She passed one glass over to Clara, then looked her directly in the eyes.

"What I know seems to me a combination of the carelessness that is a by-product of hopelessness, plus a great deal of pure superstition. And what any of it could possibly have to do with you and Erasmus, who are supposed to be concerned with teaching and learning—I thought that was why you had come to us—I cannot imagine."

Clara thought, *This will be difficult for us both, and Frances knows it too; that is why she brought the lime drink.* Nevertheless, she gathered up her sense of purpose and began:

"Bear with me, please, Frances."

Frances nodded.

Clara launched her best effort. "You have heard, I don't doubt, that Colonel Elwell is growing fond of me."

Frances nodded again.

"I am growing more fond of him than I am able to admit, especially to myself. For this reason I need to spend at least half my time away from Headquarters House. I assume you understand this." Clara didn't wait for the nod but it came anyway.

She went on: "Erasmus does need teaching, and you and Mary are the ones to give him that training. I need occupation, but please believe me—I'm not a good teacher. I taught from my fifteenth through my twenty-ninth year, so it isn't as if I haven't tried."

Frances looked troubled, but she only said, "With so many years' experience, you should know. I won't argue with you."

"Thank you. The only thing I've ever really wanted— something I got from my father, I suppose—was to make some sort of a contribution with my life. To leave behind me something of value. This war seems to have given me that opportunity. There is something I'm good at, Frances."

Clara's eyes began to shine.

Frances said, "There are many things you are good at, but you think them of little value unless they are somehow recognized by others."

It was an astute observation, but Clara scarcely heard it.

"I am good at finding what people need, and at providing it for them. I am also good at helping people, who have been separated by this war, to find one another again."

"So all the visiting of the hospitals today—what was that for?"

"It was to confirm what I already suspected: They have enough nurses. They neither need nor want me there. To the nurses I am not a 'real' nurse because I lack Miss Dix's stamp of approval and her training."

"I think you make too much of that, but go on. I can see you have more to say. And so do I, when you've finished."

This time it was Clara who nodded. "I promised again that I would do my best to help find George, and I will . . .

but finally Annabelle told me something that I could grasp. Before now, this has all been some sort of vague, dark ball with no handle by which to take hold. Annabelle said at least a few of those children were last seen at the Freemen's Clinic in Beaufort."

"That's not what I heard at all," Frances protested. "I've heard only good things about that place. I heard—"

Clara interrupted, "You heard only good about the Freemen's Clinic because that's the buckruh version."

Frances persisted, "I heard those children were taken by some monster or devil that lives in the woods on St. Helena. That's what all the Gullahs believe. They don't go out at night anymore. Some of them have taken to tying their children up in their yards on long ropes, like dogs." She muttered, bowing her head, "Better that than losing them, I suppose."

Clara ignored that. "Annabelle told me her people will go to the Freemen's Clinic only when they have no place else to go. More and more they come to her for herbal remedies, when she has none that would be as good as what she calls buckruh medicine. Yet she doesn't like to send them there. When I asked her why, she said she didn't know, it was just a feeling she had."

"Do you trust her feelings?" Frances asked.

Clara squirmed a little. "Well, no, not exactly. Annabelle has become a little strange lately. That's why I want Erasmus to stay with me here from now on, if that is all right with you. I'll see we make enough contribution in return for our keep."

"Of course you may stay here, but—"

"And that is why," Clara went on, coming to a firm conclusion and standing up to emphasize that she was done, "I am going to volunteer at the Freemen's Clinic myself.

There is a great puzzle here, having to do with people—most of them little people, the most precious of all—who are missing. And I intend to solve it."

Clara tossed and turned that night in Mary Gage's comfortable bed. It was unusual for Clara to have a problem falling asleep anywhere, at any time; she could even sleep sitting up, if it was necessary. But she was haunted by things she had not told Frances Gage; haunted by images left in her mind from the visit to Annabelle's cabin; haunted by the striking change in Annabelle herself.

Razz had not exaggerated: He apparently had reason to be scared, if Annabelle's haggard appearance gave any clue to whatever was going on inside that little two-room cabin, or outside it, as Erasmus seemed to think. Upon their arrival, before he'd knocked on the door, he'd held up the lantern to point out all the fresh blue paint around the edges of every door and window, and had whispered: "That be to keep the sperrits on the outside." Then he'd pointed meaningfully toward the roof, to silently remind Clara of what he'd said about the chimney being boarded up and also painted blue.

When she'd knocked and Annabelle opened the door, Clara had tried not to let her shock at the change in the woman show on her own face, but she knew she hadn't succeeded. Always thin, Annabelle was now gaunt; her collarbones protruded so sharply in the round neckline of her dress (also blue) that it was painful to look at her, as if at any moment there might be a sudden flash of white as bone pierced through that thin, aubergine skin.

When she'd accompanied him before, Clara had said good-bye to Erasmus at the cabin door. He had his books with him; her understanding of the time he spent with Annabelle was that they talked some, but mostly he read by lamplight, slept and enjoyed the Gullah style of cooking.

But this time, on impulse and for the boy's sake, Clara had asked if she could come in. Using a tone that scarcely allowed refusal, she'd announced: "I have something of some urgency I want to talk to you about. I prefer to do it inside."

Annabelle, who towered at least a foot taller than Clara, had put one hand to her bony breast in a slightly shocked gesture, and stepped back to allow the smaller woman with the wide skirts to pass—but she'd said nothing. Not "Yes, please come in," not "Welcome to my house." Nothing at all.

Erasmus, looking cautiously from one woman to the next, ducked his head and mumbled, "Evenin', Miss Annabelle," then hurried to the bed that was apparently his, sat right down and turned up the wick on the lamp.

Clara followed him in and noted with a quick glance that, although the cabin had two rooms, there were two single beds, scarcely more than cots, in this front room. The narrow beds were arranged against walls at right angles, and in the corner where they met was a little square table with a lamp on it.

The air was, as Erasmus had said, stuffy although cool, and Clara supposed fresh enough for health, considering there were bound to be cracks in the cheap board-and-batten construction. As her sweeping look around the room continued, she noticed that the door to the second room was not only closed, it was barred with a plank that had to be at least an inch thick; and furthermore it was also locked and chained.

Good manners be damned, Clara thought, and so she

crossed the room to the round table with its two high-backed wood chairs, which looked to be the only place to sit aside from a rocker that faced a fireplace full of dead ashes. Her first words to Annabelle were: "How curious, Annabelle. You have a larger cabin than most people. Two whole rooms. And yet you keep that second room locked and barred off. May I ask why?"

Without invitation Clara sat in a high-backed chair, untied the bonnet she'd worn to keep her ears warm on the cool evening, and put the bonnet on the table. An announcement of her intention to stay a while.

Annabelle took the other chair. She cast a nervous look over her own shoulder in the direction of that locked door, which was not more than three feet from the bed where Erasmus sat and, presumably later at night, slept.

"That room," she said, "binnah my pa's conjuh place. All he stuff still in that place. Mines too. Ebrybody dunna hab eddycashun—I mean, not everybody know the ways to, to—"

Suddenly Annabelle stopped; words apparently had failed her.

Erasmus huddled so closely over the book on his knees that Clara doubted he could possibly be reading it.

She observed, with deliberate calm, "The door looks as if it were barred to keep something *in* that room, as well as locked to keep most people out."

Annabelle covered her face with her hands. Her long, thin fingers shook, and so did her shoulders. Clara felt as if she had done, or said, something very bad to upset the other woman so; but a moment later she also felt as if the temperature inside the cabin had dropped at least ten degrees. Suddenly she knew what Razz meant about "being scairt."

"Annabelle?" Clara asked gently, concerned she had made the woman cry.

But Annabelle had not been crying. Whatever had caused her to quaver and shake, it had not been tears. When she removed her hands from her face and placed them in her lap, the African queen was back—in her posture, in her facial expression and in her voice. Except that she spoke English, not Gullah, and her English was near perfect.

"I did something for my boy, my George. To help find him. I called a powerful spirit, not from here, not from any-place near any of my people, or yours, Miss Clara Barton. The spirits tend to come back to where they first were called, when their job be done. My pa, he wasn't always so careful about sending the spirits back where they came from. Any loose spirits that come around this cabin, they come from Pa's time, not from me. That spirit I called, it's been out there a long time, but I can feel it workin'. I can feel it, because I know I have to control it and call it back when the time is right. But you don't have to worry. No-body have to worry, especially that boy there." She'd glanced then at Erasmus, seated on the bed so near the barred door. "Annabelle will take care of everything."

Clara had gone on then to talk about George, and then had moved from George to the other missing children. She'd probed, almost forcing Annabelle to tell her why the families of the vanished children had given up their efforts to find them. But all the tall woman would say was "Chillun gwine off alluh time. Dey gits drowndid in de crick."

It was fascinating how Annabelle would return to Gul-lah when the subject was one she didn't wish to discuss.

Remembering this now, in Mary's bed, Clara felt again, like an echo, the chill—that strange drop in the tempera-ture of the cabin when Annabelle had hidden her face behind her long fingers. *Why?* Why had it happened then, and only then?

Annabelle would talk about George, but not about the others. Again, why? And most of all, why had she looked so shocked when Clara had announced her own intention to look for both George and the other missing children?

"And one young woman," Clara had added, "I heard has been missing for a few weeks, from Beaufort Town. Do you know anything about her?"

The tall black woman had an answer for that, and she had delivered it standing, as a reminder that her place might be a lowly former slave cabin, but it was Annabelle's home, and it was time for Clara to go.

"Young woman like dat," Annabelle said, "been fair play for buckruh—high buckruh, low buckruh, done mek no nemmind—since Gawd put we on eart. Buckruh 'dultrify mos' everting dey tecch. Now lettum 'lone."

"No," Clara had said clearly, as she stood and tied on her bonnet, "I do not intend to let this alone. I intend to find out what I can. There's something wrong going on here. I can feel it and so can you.

"I have the time to look into it. I have some skill at finding sons, and occasionally even daughters, who are missing from their mothers and their fathers; I have done it with the soldiers in battle, and I don't see why I shouldn't do it here, while I'm waiting for the next battle to start."

With that she had walked over to the door, stared at Razz until he looked up and made eye contact with her, and then Clara had said pointedly to Annabelle, "I appreciate the hospitality you have shown Erasmus, but after tonight I'll want him with me. We'll be fixing a place at the Gages' where the both of us can stay."

Annabelle had protested mightily—that was what had

upset Clara the most. It was, she supposed, the real reason why she couldn't get to sleep. The tall black priestess had poured out Gullah words so rapidly that Clara could not possibly have caught their meaning, only the pleading, supplicatory tone.

Clara had backed out of the door, not understanding, shaking her head. "You do whatever you must do, Annabelle," those had been her parting words, "and I will do the same."

Then Clara had pointed her finger at Erasmus and said: "*You,* I expect to see bright and early, first thing tomorrow morning. There's a lot of work to be done!"

She'd left without waiting for a reply.

Now Clara bunched up the feather pillow to give better support to her neck, lay straight on her back with her hands crossed at her waist like a corpse and willed herself to sleep.

It worked, but all night long she dreamed in Gullah, in mostly incomprehensible words that filled her head with Annabelle's voice and visions of swirling colors, alternating with a darkness so deep and vast it was like nothing Clara had ever seen before.

Upon waking at dawn, she remembered that darkness, and knew there was anger in it. In her dreams, she'd felt it. Huge, frightening, chilling anger. How could that be?

The chill of that anger stayed with Clara all through her ablutions, as she dressed herself for the day. She was up earlier than the others, and so went for a walk to watch the sunrise over the long, dark tongues of marsh grass that seemed to go on infinitely . . . until at last the sun sent forth rays that showed the blue of water, the great Port Royal Sound. Beyond it, Hilton Head with its guardianship of the inlet, and the Atlantic Ocean helped to restore her sense of perspective.

Still Clara couldn't shake the chill, and she began to tick off the possible reasons that such huge anger should have appeared in her dreams. With the greatest reluctance she dragged two words up from the depths where she hid all that bothered her most, and added to them a rare invective. She spoke to herself alone, in the merest whisper: "Those damn letters!"

Yes, the great anger, if it was aimed at her, not only could but almost certainly *must* come from the man who had written her the anonymous letters. Clara had such a huge correspondence. The maintenance of it was her lifeline in more ways than one; she thought of writing letters as an essential part of the job she did for her soldiers, the boys in blue. In all those many, many letters she'd had some experience with people who did not approve of the things she did. But never had any other letters contained the sharp, clever vituperance the anonymous ones exuded—much less their ugly suggestiveness.

Clara glanced back at the Gages' cottage. All around her, everyone and everything lay still. Clara rarely had such moments alone with the freshness of nature, and a new morning to buoy her spirits. But it wasn't working. Her thoughts were preoccupied by an image of the Colonel Dr. Claude Fontaine. By his smile that was more a sneer, which marred his essentially aristocratic features whenever he looked at her. And oh, he did look!

Clara was convinced Claude Fontaine was a Confederate spy. He had all the pseudoaristocratic mannerisms of a certain type of Southerner, the very type whose way of life the Union Army was determined to destroy forever. Yet, she'd heard he had claimed himself a house in Beaufort town like any other Union officer. No one had questioned his right to do so, though the number of decent houses that remained had grown short. From Beaufort, Fontaine was free to come and go as he liked. How easy it would be for a man who knew his way around to slip across the Confederate lines—southward around Savannah, or eastward to Charleston. Still, he had to be available when called upon.

Lately there had been more meetings, all the busyness that suggested plans still unannounced; whenever these meetings occurred, Dr. Fontaine managed to be there.

Was he invited? Was he essential? John Elwell said yes, he was. Dr. Fontaine would be in charge of the medical part of the next phase of operations.

"Whatever that might be," Clara muttered, her head down, watching her step on the rough planks of the boardwalk. She thought, if Fontaine were to have significant responsibilities, someone—John, most likely—should at least get the doctor a decent, unmistakably Union set of blues. Instead Fontaine continued to wear his thrown-together army uniform, the sort often illegitimately assembled by those who had deserted one side for the other.

In this conflict that was so incomprehensible to many people, especially those who lived in the border states, desertions and switching sides were more common than Clara liked to believe. About the war, the patriotic Union cause, all was crystal clear to Clara. She had no doubts. The South could not be allowed to break away. Their leaders' way of life—though almost everyone said General Robert E. Lee was the quintessential gentleman—was an abhorrence. Every last single one of the great Southern fortunes owed more to the work of slaves than to the intelligence of the landowners. Such things were an offense to both God and man. Why couldn't the Rebels see it? How could they cling to something so immoral, so, so . . . outright evil?

Having walked as far as she could go, Clara stood at the edge of the dock with her small fists clinched so tightly, her fingernails pressing half-moons deep into the palms of her hands. Only when she felt the pricks of pain did Clara realize that her own anger had produced rare tears. She shuddered, then wiped her eyes.

The man who had written those letters frightened her. Even though the letters seemed to have stopped coming, she was still afraid. Perhaps all the more so, because the last one had said, *I see you.* . . . The effect of that last letter had been to set up an atmosphere that was like waiting for the other shoe to drop.

Now, whenever she found herself in the same vicinity as Dr. Fontaine, she had to fight down panic. If she was forced to be in the same room with him, it was all she could do not to leave. Yet he had not so much as touched her. He would not speak directly to her unless circumstances forced him to. He usurped her storage space, he wanted her tents, her trucks, her goods . . . and all these things he told John Elwell, vehemently. He did not tell her.

"Oh," she whispered, looking down at the red marks she had made in her own skin, "I pray God he does not want my body, as well."

She turned on her heels quickly, with an audible swish of skirts that summoned a few curious fish to leap at the surface of the shallow water. At another time, the jumping fish would have amused her. Not this morning. This morning, though the sun grew ever brighter and the sky turned an impossibly yearning blue, Clara Barton remembered the threats in the letters. She knew the man who had written them, if he ever took her captive, would toy with her; toying would proceed to torture; torture would end in death. Her death. A bloody death.

So she did not see the beauty of the brightening day. Instead, in the eye of her mind, she saw the cynical, aristocratic sneer that passed for a smile on the narrow face of Dr. Claude Fontaine.

"Nemesis!" she growled, and spat.

Chapter 10

ST. HELENA ISLAND

I have had nights when I was not so sure the sun would ever come up in the morning. And, like most men, I've had nights when the sun came up all too soon. The truly remarkable thing about the sun is that it does always come up. Always.

And takes away the shadows of the night.

By every culture I know, the sun—or shall I say the Sun—is regarded as a masculine deity. The Greeks—or was it the Romans?—had Aurora, of course; I always rather wondered why she was necessary; why should we even need a goddess of the dawn?

But I supposed, on this fine morning when the sun's light came so bright that even filtered as it was through the trees, I could inspect every nook and cranny of my bedroom for the strangely shaped patch of darkness that was no longer there . . . I could be *certain* it was no longer there . . . I supposed Aurora was a kind of handmaiden. Such as Clara Barton might be to me one day.

The morning had a bit of a chill to it, for summer, and I rummaged in a drawer for something to tie around my neck in the manner of a cravat, and as I rummaged, my thoughts were all a splendid, colorful tumble of images. There was me in the role of Apollo, riding in a golden chariot upon a rosy road laid down across the sky by my handmaiden Aurora. . . .

I found a length of navy polka-dotted silk, not too soiled, and began to wind it around my neck without bothering to look in the mirror.

But then who should I encounter in my Apollonian thought mode but Miss Clara Barton, walking along my rosy road through the sky, her wide and always black skirts swinging, as she went along her way in the opposite direction?

"That will never do!" I said aloud. Perhaps a bit too loudly, as I startled some turtledoves foraging outside the window and they took off in a rather distressing flurry of wings. That startled me; my hand jumped; I lost my place at tying the cravat and had to go look in the mirror after all.

My own appearance startled me. Not that I have ever been heavy or even stocky, but I was always firmly fleshed. Until, somehow, this morning. One has become accustomed to the thinness one sees these days everywhere, as hardly anyone has enough food, and only the ladies can hide their shanks under petticoats. We men must make do as best we can, hitching up our britches and tightening our belt buckles. But what I saw in the mirror just now could not be resolved by any hitching or tightening. For a moment I thought I saw a death's head behind the unshaven skin of my own face.

I turned away from the mirror, muttering, "It's a trick of the eye, that's all, a trick of the eye."

And so it was, for when—bravely and resolutely—I turned back to finish the tying of my polka-dotted silk cravat, the foolish image had gone and I was myself again.

On my way to the kitchen, though, I did wish this house had not quite so many corners where shadows might gather, even during the day.

Frances Gage had her doubts about Clara's plan to turn the sleeping porch into a place for herself and Razz to stay three nights a week, but Mary had no such reservations and had soon convinced her mother.

Mary, who was doing most of the teaching of the tall, bright boy, pointed out to her mother that he had already read through most of the schoolbooks they owned. And, knowing her mother's hunger for more books, she suggested, with a sideways look at Clara: "If we have Erasmus here with us instead of at Annabelle's, then perhaps we can persuade him to his own reading. From Miss Penny's library."

"I doubt that," Clara said with one of her small smiles, "for that boy is as honest as the day is long. I believe he would go into the 'big house,' as he calls it, to borrow books, but he would always put them back. I do not think Erasmus will cooperate in your plan to acquire Miss Penny's library for your school. You will have to find some other way."

It was a bright and sunny morning, though having had such bad dreams all night, Clara felt as if she had not slept at all. The three women had just finished breakfast and were tidying up the kitchen when the subject of their conversation arrived at the back door of the cottage, somewhat earlier than usual. His usually happy face was a bit broody.

He knocked and entered in one motion, while glancing back over his shoulder down the long boardwalk. Without preamble he said, "Miss Clara, iffen we be gonna stay here half each week like you said to Annabelle las' night, then you gotta talk to the Colonel about us havin' a boat to our ownselfs. A boat what don't leak."

"I hadn't thought of that," she said, folding the last napkin and placing it on the table—she would have used it again, because the war had made her frugal of everything, including soap and water, but Frances might prefer to wash her napkins after each use.

"Surely Colonel Elwell will have his own boat, and since he has no use for it at present, he may lend it to us. What do you think, Frances?"

"I think," Frances said, in a tone as dry as she was making her hands with a flour-sack dish towel, "the Colonel has never been much interested in the social scene. Even before he fell off his horse—"

"Actually," Clara could not resist making the correction, an important one to her, "it was his horse that tripped and fell on the Colonel. If you will excuse the interruption."

Frances raised her eyebrows, took a handkerchief out of her apron pocket and used it to finish the job the flour-sack towel had been unable to achieve. "Be that as it may, my point is that I have never known the Colonel to leave Hilton Head unless it was to come here, and when he did so it was generally in Captain Lamb's boat. Generally speaking, Colonel Elwell would rather stay in his quarters and read a book than go to a party. I expect he has no use for a boat."

"Whereas Captain Lamb seldom misses a party," Mary contributed.

"I must admit," Clara agreed, "that scenario sounds quite familiar."

Razz, who had been uneasily shifting his weight from foot to foot, now burst out, "Whiles you ladies be talkin' 'bout who goes to parties and who don't, that boat we got down yonder done sprung a leak in the night. Miss Clara, we gots to go now. I means *right* now!"

Clara laughed, and gave Mary and Frances a peck on the cheek each in turn. "You heard him. I'd best obey if I know what's good for me."

"Wait, wait," Frances said, her hands on her hips. "Erasmus, just take our boat and tie the leaking one up behind. We don't need our boat today. We teach here on Parris Island today, St. Helena tomorrow. Yesterday was a holiday for us, don't forget that, miss." She aimed a sharp look at her own daughter, who was in fact staring out the window as if she wished she were getting ready to parade fashionably up and down the streets of Beaufort every single day, like the ever-increasing numbers of officers' wives who seemed to have nothing better to do.

"If you're certain . . ." Clara said.

Frances nodded emphatically.

"Then Razz, you go ahead and tie the boats together. I'll get my bag and be there in just a moment. Wait"—that *word* again!—"have you checked the tide? Isn't it too early?"

"Not if I be careful. An' I do be careful, Miss Clara."

The three women laughed as Razz ran off down the boardwalk, his big feet pounding.

Their pounding set up an echo in Clara's heart as she gathered up the few things she'd brought for the overnight trip and stuffed them into the well-worn needlepoint bag she'd used as a carryall ever since the first time she'd left Washington City for the Civil War and parts unknown.

Along the way back to Hilton Head, with Razz poling as she kneeled in the stern, holding on to keep a steady tension to the rope that pulled the other boat, Clara thought about what she had done, and what she was going to do. Getting a boat for her own use would not be a problem. Captain Lamb was good at things like that.

No, the problem would be with Colonel Elwell. With John. And with herself. John would not want her to go. He wouldn't want her to be away from him three days out of every seven, particularly since he still could not get around and they had an excuse to be together almost constantly.

As for Clara—well, she was like John. Given her choice, she too would have preferred to stay on Hilton Head and read, and let Captain Lamb and Mary Gage, and others like them, go to all the parties.

"Miss Clara, you be all right?" Razz asked without turning around, his eyes watchful and ever checking the depth of his pole.

Her kneeling position was uncomfortable, but she said she was all right . . . because she was far more uncomfortable in her mind, thinking about how she would have to talk to John. What would each of them say about this affection that had grown so strong, yet which they had never openly discussed?

The time is coming, Clara thought, *when John and I will have to speak our minds.*

But a moment later she thought: *Perhaps not. Perhaps, in this land that is ruled by the tides and nature in all her fecundity and ferocity, we should just let ourselves drift, and let whatever happens, happen . . . come what may.*

ST. HELENA ISLAND

I went whistling through the house, ignoring the shadows, working myself up into a gay mood to match the polka dots on my long silk tie. It was necessary to ignore a few cobwebs too. But in spite of my determination to ignore things, I could not help but notice how, in the few occasional patches of sunlight that made it through the windowpanes, dust stood out everywhere, a pervasive soft gray fuzz.

"A woman's hand, that's all I need," I said, "a woman's hand."

Suddenly a perverse image came into my mind, which ordinarily I might have found amusing—but not this time. I saw the severed hands of Jackson's woman, pretty hands I'd had to throw out because the heat and humidity had spoiled the flesh before I could make use of them.

Oh, I'd had plenty of women's hands around this place . . . just not for their usual purposes.

"Hah!" I forced a laugh. It didn't help.

I turned down the hallway toward the back of the house, and turned my mind too, into a better direction.

Clara Barton: She was fastidious, I could tell.

Also, I had heard evidence, even though it was only secondhand: When I'd lurked at edges of conversations in many a battlefield hospital, before I'd found my place here at the Coffin plantation, that was what they always said whenever her name was mentioned: Clara Barton was fastidious.

She was personally neat without being rigid; quite a trick. The lowly soldiers liked her; the doctors did not. The doctors would never have put up with her presence if it hadn't been for that damn congressional battlefield pass, plus the otherwise-unobtainable things she always brought with her—like her oil lamps that night at Antietam.

They'd looked magical all right, that night, like fairy lamps out of some fantastic story. But they had certainly ruined my plans. My supper too, for as I recalled I'd been unable to steal a single thing, not even to eat. I'd gone to bed hungry, and on to the next battle without so much as a snitched packet of gauze. A part of me would always hate her for that.

Not a good thing to think about this morning, no, no.

I ran a finger along the railing of the back stairs, which unlike the back stairs in a Northern house, did not lead down to a basement but merely to the outside.

The railing was dusty of course. Clara wouldn't have permitted that. If she were here, she would dust it. Polish the whole railing. She insisted on keeping things clean, which was what made her a constant irritation to most of the doctors. Doctors did not have time to keep cleaning up.

The point of battlefield medicine was to dig those bullets out and all the surrounding damaged tissue too, get that smashed and mangled limb chopped off, the faster the better, before the infection could set in. There was no time to be mopping up blood—not until the floors got too slick for a doctor to move around the operating slab without his feet slipping.

No time to be washing saws and knives; nobody to do it either, what with all the orderlies running in and out with more bodies on stretchers or else heating the cautery irons. . . .

My thoughts dwindled off to a sudden blank.

Something was wrong. It was too quiet at the back of the house. Also too, too . . . musty and moldy-smelling.

I should be hearing Jackson moving around his domain. I should smell the sausage he liked to cook for breakfast, when we had any, and we did. He knew we did—I'd showed him the links yesterday. Or had it been the day before?

I couldn't remember. How odd!

Well, never mind.

I opened my mouth to call him, but nothing came out. I was struck as dumb now as I had been blank in the head before.

That was when I noticed the padlock was gone from the door.

Impossible! I had the only key. I reached into the pocket of my trousers, and it was there, yes, I had it. Had the *key,* but the whole damn *lock* was gone!

"Impossible!"

This time I said it aloud. I gave the swinging door a vicious kick.

This was the door to the servants' domain, the whole of which I had given over to that ungrateful wretch, Jackson. For a long time I'd trusted him, never thought to lock him in at night until recently.

Devising a lock for this door had not been the easiest thing in the world to do, either. It was a swinging door, of course, because so often in the days when these plantations had been run the right way, servants had had their hands full of things—food, clothes, laundry, brooms, suchlike— when they came and went from the back of the house. So this door had never had an ordinary lock. I'd bought the best old padlock I could find. Of course nobody was making new padlocks during the war—padlocks are made of metal, and all metal these days went into bullets and other forms of ordnance.

It had taken me a long time to find that padlock, and an even longer time to get it put up right. I'm a surgeon, not a locksmith, or a blacksmith. My hands are precise and delicate, but not particularly strong.

Still I had persisted until I'd got it done, and all to keep my man Jack safe. I didn't want him going off and doing something I'd have to punish him for. In my own way, I was fond of him.

Not to mention dependent on him, something said quietly in the back of my mind, something that I did not want to hear.

I stuck out my hand to stop the door from swinging; I'd kicked it so hard it stung my palm with a slap. Then I scrutinized the door carefully. The padlock itself, the chain and the metal plates to which the chain had been attached had been so neatly removed I could not believe my eyes.

I pushed the door all the way open and back, hooked it to the kitchen wall in the open position, so that the sunlight through the windows over the sink illuminated the flat boards of the door, which at one time had been painted a sort of antique green, now much faded. Yes, the tiny holes were there where I'd done my work to place the lock; also there was the faintest impression where the metal plates had been. But that was all.

Jackson was gone. He had gone for good. I knew, without even looking for him.

Somehow I simply could not call out his name. My voice wouldn't come. I wasn't hungry anymore; the thought of breakfast made me feel sick. I wandered from kitchen to butler's pantry to breakfast room to that all-purpose room with long tin-topped tables, where in happier times the women of the house had arranged flowers, and things like that. I felt a pricking in the corners of my eyes.

No Jack.

I went outside, down the trail to my laboratory. I rather expected to see all my glass flasks and phials and test tubes and specimen bottles smashed, perhaps even the stained oak worktables shattered—but they were not. All was unharmed.

I walked down the row of former slave cabins that until lately had housed my specimens, my experiments, every one of which had gone sour and all within the same week.

What week had that been? Last week?

Well, never mind—the point was I needed to replace them. Needed it *badly*. This was my life's work, gone afoul all of a sudden. I'd counted on my man Jack to help me fix it, to straighten everything out.

It was a puzzle, a tremendous puzzle, I must think it through but there seemed to be all this fuzz in my mind, like the dust on the staircase. . . .

I went to Beaufort. I knew that. I'd gone to see where I might safely get more specimens, because so many had died. Those that hadn't were so near death I'd been merciful, and killed them with my own hands. No violence: I only smothered them. Cover the mouth and pinch the nose. When they're too weak to do anything about it anyway there's no muss, no fuss, no bother.

I'd left Jack the task of cleaning out those cabins and burying the dead. It was, after all, his main job.

I looked around. He had done his work well. The cabins were as clean as could be. The graves, wherever he had put them, were not visible from where I stood at the end of the cabin row.

If Jackson were angry with me, why would he do such a perfect job of work?

How could he leave me at night, when he was terrified of the evil spirits that he was convinced inhabited these woods?

Damn it all, how—*how*—when Jackson was confined to the inside, could he have removed that lock on the kitchen door *from the outside*? How could he have done such a perfect job of it, so that only if you looked very, very hard would you know the lock had ever been there at all?

I wondered if I'd walked in my sleep. If I'd done it my-self. It was really the only explanation . . . and yet I had never known myself to sleepwalk. Furthermore, it was im-possible. I would never do such a thing. Why, I'd left myself *alone*. . . .

It was so quiet in these thick woods. The ground beneath my feet was spongy with years upon years of packed dead leaves and whatever else crawled under them. The trees themselves competed with strangling vines and brambles that choked them. The canopy of the tallest live oaks ruled this forest; they were ancient; they were the ones that got to choose what light got in and what stayed out. They were letting precious little light through this morning.

"He'll come back," I said. But I didn't believe it.

Coffin plantation was too big for me to handle alone. I could not even transport specimens and make experiments of them alone. My work *must* continue. There had to be a way.

That was when I remembered George.

Chapter 11

One of the first things I did after laying claim to the Coffin Place for my home and work was to construct a special cage, very large and strong, totally contained within one of the bigger rooms of a house that had plenty of them. The cage was made of iron bars bolted to the floor, and had an octagonal shape—a nice touch, I thought. I was anticipating the day when I would, at last, find a perfect specimen. George turned out to be it. At least, I think his name is George—I try not to call them by name or even to think of them as human, but with this one that is rather difficult.

For one thing, he will not speak at all. It was Jackson who told me the young man's name is George, and that he comes from another island, not St. Helena, which is a very good thing so far as the necessary secrecy is concerned. I would place the boy's age at about eighteen. He is physically perfect in every way—as none of my others have ever been—and that is why George is so important to me. I expect to learn things from him that I have not been able to learn from working with the others.

I had always been forced, of necessity, to take only those who were already sick . . . and it had come to me, as I watched experiment after experiment fail and my subjects die, that my chances of success would surely improve if I could start with someone in the peak of health. That would not have been possible until I found Coffin plantation and was able to take it for my home, and Jackson—Jackson, whom I'd thought was and would continue to be a faithful retainer—with it. My man Jack, strong as an ox, the perfect helper, with no will of his own, so used to obeying the master . . . or so I'd thought. Until this morning.

George, if that was indeed his name, had plenty of space. He was not restricted in any way, except for the bars of his cage. Though he was well over six feet tall, due to the high ceilings of the rooms in the house and the fact that we had made the cage only a few feet short of the walls and ceilings, the young man could stand upright. He was not even chained—although without my man Jack there to help me, I was not sure I could handle George unless he was in chains.

What to do, what to do?

Well, I'd worry about it later. It was always the greatest of pleasures to see George, and I wasn't going to let thoughts of a traitorous Jackson ruin it for me.

I stopped in the kitchen and cooked my perfect specimen's food myself, a mixture of sausage and rice, which was quite good; I had some too, a belated breakfast. I also brought a fresh pitcher of water.

Jackson and I had caught George hunting in our woods one day about a month ago. He was using a homemade spear and a net to stalk a young deer. Doing quite well at it too . . . until he threw the net a bit too far and I stepped out from behind the undergrowth from which I'd been observing him, captured the net and threw it over George instead. With a nod from me, Jackson leapt upon him from behind while I kept him entangled so that he could not draw back his arms enough to throw the spear at me—which he very much wanted to do; I relished the hatred I saw in his eyes.

It was not, you must understand, that I like to be hated. In fact I dislike it intensely, and deeply regret that the important work I must do (for if I do not, who will? Who else has the vision, and the courage?) usually causes my subjects to hate me. No, it was the pure animal strength of the hatred in the young man's eyes that excited me. Here was the strength, the perfect health, that I had been looking for. There was just one problem: I could not break his will.

He wouldn't speak to me, or to Jackson. In fact, he treated my man Jack worse than he did me: He hissed at him, like a snake. The hiss was the only sound he had made thus far. It was eerie, excessively so.

We took away his clothes of course, right away; Jackson had had to knock George—if that was his name—unconscious in order to get him into the cage, and while he was unconscious we took the clothes, which were slightly better than those most Gullahs wore.

The young man was Gullah, there was no doubt about that, from the color of his skin (blacker than night, with a purplish sheen) to the extraordinary length of his digits, both fingers and toes. He had a magnificent body, slender but tall and perfectly formed, with the long, hard muscles of a runner. I gathered he did a lot of running as a hunter. Yet he also had the bunched shoulder muscles of a rower, and so I knew he had a boat somewhere . . . particularly since Jackson had said the young man came from another island. Yet we had never yet found that boat. This continued to worry me. Once again I put it out of my mind.

The room was not locked; there was no need, since the cage was locked in more than one spot, totally secure.

For one slightly insane moment I wondered if the same strangely talented hand that had silently removed the padlock from the kitchen door for Jackson—for I certainly did not think Jackson capable of doing such a job himself—might have been here and removed the cleverly welded joints of the big cage. But not so.

I opened the door with a sigh of relief and smiled, when I saw the young man sitting cross-legged on the floor, right in the middle of the cage, as he so often did. This posture effectively hid his most manly attributes, which were in length as impressive as his digits. George was living truth that the old wives' tales—about the length of a man's digits having a direct relationship to the length of his penis—was true.

I was determined this morning to be my most charming, because I needed badly to secure George's cooperation. If Jackson did not come back, I didn't know what I would do. On the other hand, if Jackson *did* come back, I would never be able to trust him again, and so I should have to kill him, which would be most unpleasant.

I said, "Good morning."

He looked up, but otherwise didn't move an inch. Or even a quarter of an inch. It seemed to me that the hatred in those almost-black eyes burned a little less bright. He ate, though, and that was a good sign; he just wouldn't eat in front of me or Jack. He drank as much water as we gave him. He pissed and shit in a bucket; I examined his output daily and found it normal.

It was true he was getting thinner, but that was not from

lack of nutriment. It was from the loss of muscle tone since he was no longer running and rowing. I wanted that loss of physical strength; I wanted him still healthy, but not able to fight quite so effectively as he had in the beginning.

His hair, though dirty, was a great mass of shining black curls. I knew the shine was from too much oil, that his head would stink and he probably had lice, since he had never been allowed to wash in the time we'd had him. But from a distance those curls were beautiful.

Oh, he would more than do ... once I'd broken that iron will.

I pushed the bowl of rice and sausage, still fragrant, under the bottom of the cage. Then placed the metal pitcher of water outside an opening barely big enough for it to pass through, and I myself stepped back out of the way.

Then I sat down, cross-legged, like him. I had nothing better to do. I would, if necessary, carry on a one-way conversation.

I saw the question in his eyes.

"Oh yes," I said, "I know what you'd like to know. So why don't you ask?"

The great black eyes went opaque.

"Well, for once, since Jackson isn't here—you're wondering where he is, I know, and why your food is late—anyway, since he isn't here, I have no other responsibilities whatsoever at this moment and I can spend all day sitting here talking to you. Or *at* you, if you continue to refuse to talk back.

"Of course, you probably only speak Gullah, but that's all right. I understand most Gullah, even if I can't speak it; and I know perfectly good and well that you Gullahs understand English too, whether you let on or not."

I waited. He still said nothing. But I thought he looked

unusually hungry, probably because his meal was at least two hours late.

"Go on," I said, "eat. What harm can it do to eat while we talk? It's a very civilized thing to do.

"I'm not so sure Jackson will be back," I continued, "so I think you and I should get to be friends. We could help each other. I admit it, I do need help. I am extremely intelligent—what I lack in strength I can make up for in guile. Do you understand guile? It means a particular kind of cleverness: smart, cunning and devious all at the same time. But I am not physically strong, and I have very important work to do that at times requires physical strength."

Still he said nothing, nor had he touched the food, nor opened the little space through the bars that would allow him to bring in his water.

"I have a great deal of money," I lied. Though it was true I had more now than I'd had any time before in my life. "If you will work for me, I'll pay you well. You do understand that you're free now? You're entitled to be paid?"

He nodded! He actually nodded! He had never, ever done anything like that before. But then, in an instant, as if realizing he'd let his guard slip, the opaqueness was back in his eyes.

I decided to get a little tough. Since the beginning, I had always been gentle with him. He was invaluable in being physically perfect—as no others had been—so I had been kind. Anything rough I'd left to Jackson, but now I didn't have Jack anymore.

The voice I had mysteriously acquired in my head reminded me that I had been more than rough with the little ones. They had been useful only for their tiny appendages, best for grafting, and because their small bodies were easily disposed of; it is best to take a graft specimen from a still-living person, and those little ones will squeal. . . .

I shook my head hard, not wanting to think of that, the squealing; it was entirely too much like the screaming I'd had in my mind after visiting the hospital in Beaufort. How long ago had that been? Was it only yesterday? I felt my shoulders begin to shake, and my arms. This would never do.

I stood up, for distraction, and clasped my hands tightly together. Inside his octagonal cage the shining young man remained motionless, not even looking at me now that I'd moved out of his eye range.

I said: "All right. From now on, you work for me. You will be paid, but you have to show me you're worth it. When I think I can trust you, I'll give you your clothes back and you can come out of there. Except, perhaps, at night. There are strange things going on here at night anyway; you're probably better off in there, where at least you are protected."

Having said this, I shuddered again. And he looked up at me. I saw it in his eyes: He knew about the night things.

He knew! I wondered how, and how *much* he knew, and if someday he would tell me. . . .

Without Jackson, time for my future experiments was running short. I had to let this boy know who was boss. Therefore I tried a tougher approach; as I said before, up until now I'd always been gentle with him.

I ordered: "You will tell me your name. NOW!"

He unfolded himself slowly. Standing, he was fully a head taller than I. Suddenly I wished he were sitting down again.

He said, quite clearly, in perfect English, "My name is George."

I was astounded. I had not, really, expected him to comply.

It was the first time I'd heard his voice. A baritone, melodious; though the language was English the curious, dancing cadence of Gullah was still there.

These people seldom had surnames, so I didn't ask.

Instead I said, "Very well. A good beginning. George, do you know who I am?"

"Uh knows," he said, with absolute conviction in his voice.

"What's my name? I want to hear you say it."

"E man whut wuk fuh oonah sez mas' be de debbil."

He meant Jackson, and I was the master, the devil. Interesting.

What interested me so much was not that Jackson had told George I was the devil; I knew Jack had come to believe that, after I'd killed his woman. And of course I'd seen how his fear of me was reinforced by his fear of whatever went on in the woods.

But far more interesting was that George, after the one sentence proclaiming his own name, had gone back to speaking plain Gullah. I thought he did it purposefully, to let me know he was keeping what measure of control he could, when he had precious few choices.

Now George looked me over carefully, up and down, slowly, without insolence or curiosity, just a close inspection. His eyes lingered on my hair.

While he did this, in my turn I wondered what manner of creature I had captured here. Most of the South's former slaves had lost themselves in hopelessness long ago. You could see it in their eyes. The Gullahs of the Sea Islands formed the worst case, being least able to take care of themselves, in the worst health, and so on—which was why so often they'd been left behind.

"To work the fields" was just an excuse. Without an

overseer they couldn't work; they didn't know how. Any ambition to learn had been beaten out of them generations ago. I'd heard it said that the Gullah race, even in their native Africa, were by nature a gentle people—which of course made them perfect targets for predators like the slave-takers. And, I suppose, for me.

Yet here was George, like a perfect throwback to an earlier time, when white men had seen great physical strength in the blacks of Africa, how hard they could work in a climate that was depleting and defeating the South's lily-white landowners. Our forefathers. Hah.

Finally I could stand George's silence no longer.

"So," I challenged, "you've told me what Jackson said. What do *you* say?"

"Uh sez oonuh not *de* debbil. Mebbe oonuh be leetle wicketty debbil lak mos' de high buckruh. *Suh.*"

My blood boiled.

To think I'd been about to give this insolent creature my name! And here I had already offered to pay him money in return for his help in my great work. Little wicked devil, indeed. It had even occurred to me that I might secure his help, as I'd had Jackson's help, which would allow me to spare that perfect body.

But no, he had to go and spoil it all.

That was when I decided to drug George, and to keep him drugged for a long, long time. I would save him for the most dangerous experiment I could think of.

There were plenty of choices along that line; I could take my time.

I said in a voice like ice, "You may call me sir. And as for the rest of it, you will soon find out." Then I turned on my heel and left before my temper could get the better of me.

Chapter 12

HILTON HEAD ISLAND

Clara and John had their first serious quarrel; it had been so unpleasant, so difficult for both of them that she had literally run away into her room, the only place she had any privacy. She had locked the door—something she never, ever did at any camp or field hospital, large or small—and placed the straight chair under the knob for good measure because she was so furious.

Then she'd dragged the rocking chair over by the window, and rocked and rocked and rocked, until at last she had rocked away most of her fury. Yet she'd refused supper when David came knocking, saying through the locked door, chair still under the knob, that she was indisposed.

A few hours later, when John had tapped on their adjoining wall for her to come to him, she had not allowed herself to tap in reply. Not even the three taps that meant a very polite no. She'd sat on her hands like a child to stop herself from doing it, until he did not tap again.

They'd argued because she felt he was treating her like a child, or as so many men treated their mates, like chattel, with no right to a will of her own. As if he could order her personal life as well as he could her life attached to the army.

John had said he did not approve of her plan to spend three days a week working at the Freemen's Clinic in Beaufort, because he had heard the clinic's reputation was fast declining. She had responded that the large houses turned into hospitals had plenty of nurses already, and did not want her there; that nurses in general did not take to Clara Barton because they all knew Dorothea Dix had refused to allow her entry into the Army Nurse Corps.

John had said: "Piffle."

Clara had stamped her foot. Then, recanting, she'd tried to explain how much she needed something more to do than sewing and reading the ladies' magazines well-meaning officers brought her from time to time, from their trips into town. She had no interest whatever in ladies' magazines, and she'd read every book in Headquarters House at least once.

John had refused to even try (at least in Clara's opinion) to understand why waiting for this battle, which they were obviously building up to, was so hard for her. He'd accused her of being a warmonger; well, so, he'd been teasing—yet still the accusation had hurt. From childhood Clara had known all too well that there is always some meanness at the base of teasing, and she hated knowing that her lover had it in him too.

John would not share with her any of the results of the meetings with other officers who now came and went on a daily basis. He would only say, "When it is time, you'll know." He would not respond to her continuing concerns about Dr. Claude Fontaine's not living on the base like everybody else, nor would John take up with Fontaine what

Clara considered the doctor's unreasoning persecution of her. The latest insult from Fontaine had been a letter he'd written over John Elwell's head, requesting Clara's tents—both of them—be assigned to him instead. As yet, apparently, Fontaine had received no reply. John didn't seem to care. All he would say was "Don't worry, Clara. I'll see Fontaine doesn't get your tents; and as for where the man lives, he's an adjunct, not a regular officer, and he may live wherever he chooses."

John had asked, plaintively (though in her reply Clara had flung the word "whining" back at him to get even for his calling her a warmonger), if she could not simply spend the waiting days with him peacefully, reading and talking, and riding out together as soon as he was able, which would not be long now.

Clara had responded: "Idleness is not in my nature." Which was true, but she had sounded even to her own ears like a schoolmarm, or a bluestocking or, what was worse, like her own older sister—at least in the tone of her voice.

Then, thinking to make things better and to gain some ground for understanding, she'd sunk down on the floor by John's daybed and explained that her desire to work at the Free Clinic was only, in a way, a pretext to allow herself some freedom of movement. A way to make the acquaintance of more Gullahs, because she wanted to find out what had happened to the six or so children who had disappeared.

"Annabelle won't cooperate," Clara said to John. "It's not like her. She avoids my questions. She says things like 'Children are always wandering off around here, they fall in the water and drown all the time.' I'm sure that's not true, and anyway, it's not like her to take that attitude."

John frowned, and agreed it did not sound like

Annabelle. But then he said, "Leave the Gullahs be, Clara. I've heard the rumors too, that something strange is going on someplace, one of the islands. Possibly Lady's, maybe St. Helena. They are a superstitious people even in their church, in their kind of Christianity. Annabelle is their leader both in church and out. If Annabelle doesn't want to know what happened to the children, then it's best for you to quell your own curiosity."

Clara jumped up at that, in a swish of skirts, and tapped her foot. "I don't think I can do that, John Elwell. That is not in my nature either. Now, are you going to help me to get a decent boat so that Erasmus and I can safely go back and forth to Parris Island and up into Beaufort town three days a week, or are you not?"

"Not," John said.

And that, apparently, was that. She'd left his room with her chin in the air, the way she raised her head when she quarreled with David.

Clara'd seen, for the first time, John Elwell's iron will. This big man was gentle when he chose to be, but he could be stern.

Well, of course he could be stern, and more: a hard taskmaster if need be, Clara had thought later as she'd rocked and rocked by her window. There is no such thing as a gentle colonel, not even as quartermaster. Perhaps *especially* as quartermaster.

Virtually everyone, military or civilian, tried to steal from the Quartermaster Corps, yet on Hilton Head inventory was seldom lost. John was responsible for that. Even from his sickbed he was in control.

So Clara had to get her boat another way.

At least John hadn't *forbidden* her to leave Hilton Head, and he had the power to do so. She sent Erasmus asking around the base, and then she herself approached Captain Lamb.

Captain Lamb said, "If there were time, the best thing would be to get one of the natives [by this he meant one of the Gullahs or other Negroes on the base—his habit of calling them "natives" irritated her but lately so did most things irritate her] to build you one. We have barely enough here for our own use."

Eventually they'd reached a workable plan: Captain Lamb would order the leaky rowboat repaired that day, and tomorrow Clara and Erasmus could sell it in Beaufort. The captain would give Clara extra money to buy a good boat there, if they could find one.

It was, he said, the best he could do.

BEAUFORT

The tide rose early the next morning, and Clara and Erasmus went with it up Port Royal Sound, and into the Beaufort River.

"I am going to the Freemen's Clinic," she said after they'd docked and tied the boat, "and I want you to do a job for me while I'm working."

The boy's eyes got rounder and rounder as she explained that she was entrusting the job of boat-buying to him, since she herself knew nothing about boats; and she was giving him all this money too.

He was rendered practically speechless by all the responsibility, but he managed to say, "I do the very best job anybody can do, Miss Clara, I promise."

Then Clara walked off in the direction of the poorer part of town, and Erasmus began to patrol the waterfront. He stopped people who looked friendly enough, and asked questions.

He wasn't getting anywhere. Only thing getting anywhere was the sun, which was climbing higher in the sky and getting hotter. Razz figured it must be close to noon.

He climbed up in a big old oak tree, the kind with wide, curving branches that made a good place for a loose-limbed boy to sit hidden in the leafy boughs. The big tree was over to the St. Helena Sound side of Beaufort, way far down by the water, on land that belonged to one of the biggest old houses, which was now a hospital for the Yankees.

As he settled himself, Razz wished Miss Clara would work in *that* hospital—he glanced over his shoulder, where through the leaves he got glimpses of the big pillars and porches, once white but now all weathered to gray—instead of in that Freemen's Clinic. He'd heard bad things about that place. Still, the clinic was free to the black peoples, while the big houses turned into hospitals took only the sodjuhs.

Soldiers, Razz reminded himself. Then he squirmed into position and opened up his gunnysack. He figgered, *figured,* he'd eat the lunch Miss Clara had given him, read one of his books for a while and then go looking for a boat.

Heck, he could even look out for a boat from here, where he sat this very minute. Wasn't totally unheard of for a boat to come washin' up over to St. Helena side with nobody nor nothin' in it. Such a thing as smugglin' was known to go on, and sometimes a body would let their boat go, take a swim for it to hide in the deep woods. Razz could get lucky, find them a boat that way.

He unfolded the wrapper of the sandwich, which was a

mushed-up boiled egg on stale cornbread, and wrinkled his nose in disgust. He hated the smell of boiled eggs. But his ma would have said this ole egg sammitch was better than what he usually ate, on account of eggs is good for you. . . . The thought made him sad.

For a while, slowly chewing and looking down at the choppy water below without really seeing it, Erasmus let himself miss his ma. He felt the tears prick in his eyes and he just let them come, let them run all down his cheeks without even trying to wipe them away. When he'd swallowed a big mouthful of stinky ole egg, he did swipe at his face with the back of one hand, the one that wasn't holding the rest of the sandwich. He was sitting on the gunnysack so's he couldn't lose the two books in it. The books were precious, they belonged to Miss Clara. Long as he sat on 'em, could feel they were there, then that was awright.

Razz blinked back some more tears, chewed some more sammitch and thought about what was happening to him. Tried, for the first time, to understand it. Every since his ma'd left with Miss Penny an' all them, he'd just kep on goin' day to day, kep on workin' on account of he saw what happened to the ones that didn't find some kind of work.

He'd been angry at the old ones for not workin' the cotton, till one old man tole him the driver, what some white peoples called the overseer, had run off up north on the Underground Railway. It was the driver, 'long with the massa, knew what to do, how and when to plant, how to make the cotton grow.

Sure, by theyselfs they could grow maybe one crop on they own, the old man had said, and they could pick it and the women could pull out the seeds, but then what? Who gonna take to the market, wherever that was? Who gonna see they got a fair price? Who even knew what a fair price would be anymore?

Them Yankees thought they was high buckruh, they didn't know nothin' 'bout growin' cotton neither. Miss Penny's plantation, being so far out of the way and just about hidden down the south end of Hilton Head Island, nobody had ever even come to look at it, much less lay claim to it.

Since this war done come, whole world turned upside down. That's how it seemed to Razz. He didn't think about it so much when he worked, and he was always hungry, so he worked to get the food to satisfy the hunger. He ran all the long miles up to the army place at Hilton Head, and all the long miles back, every day. Somewheres in the back of his head he knew he ran not only to get the work and the food, but also because all that running took time. Tired him out too, so he'd sleep of the nights. . . .

And if he was lucky he wouldn't dream about his ma or his pa or when he was little and the world had been a place where you knew—all time you knew—what would happen next.

Razz licked bread crumbs from his fingers. He swung one leg and kicked at the tree limb below the one he was sitting on, kicked gently, still just thinking. He s'posed he might never see his ma again. He s'posed he might could find a better life, now he was learning to read and all. 'Course he wouldn't never abandon Miss Clara, but when she was gone maybe he'd leave too. Maybe he'd go far, far up north, keep on goin' till he found a place where nobody was fightin' nobody.

One thing Erasmus knew for certain: He was no fighter. He warn't scared to fight, but it was a waste. All the way 'round, war was wasteful. He hated waste worse'n anything. Even worse'n boiled egg sammitches.

Making a face as the taste of the sandwich came back on him, Erasmus leaned over to one side and slid the gunnysack out from under his behind. Took out the book he liked the most: the one Miss Clara'd got for him with stories, called *Legends of Africa,* in the olden times. It was mostly about Egypt and pyramids and kings that wore snakes on they heads, but it had a map of the whole of Africa. It had pictures of people with skin the same color as his. They were called Ee-thee-O-pee-ans. Erasmus couldn't read but about half the words without a dictionary, which was too heavy to bring in the gunnysack. But still, he was making progress. What words he didn't know, he could usually pick up on their meaning from the way they went with the rest.

He opened the book to where he'd left off, and that was when he realized there was one other thing he knew for certain: Book learnin' was *not* wasteful. Somehow, every single piece of new stuff a body put in his head, it would fit there somewhere, and connect up with something else, and that way it would grow and keep on growing.

"Make something new, where nothing was there before," Erasmus whispered, only to himself. "Even better would be to make a new, beautiful thing, to take the place of something burned, something ugly, something wasted."

"I gone do that someday. Me, Razz," he said aloud. "I gone do that."

Clara Barton couldn't help but notice that her much-mended, everyday black bodice and skirt were beginning to look rusty. Even the new lace collar she'd tatted herself didn't help much. Among the wives out strolling along the curve of Bay Street, in their pastels and holding their parasols, Clara observed that she looked a good deal like a crow.

She turned the corner onto Charles Street, paused a moment to look up at the windows of the big hospital in the house there and frowned as she recalled her argument with John.

Hah—the corners of her mouth turned up a little (she was beginning to forgive him in spite of herself)—there was even a bird's nest in the eaves of this big house. John's pet name for her was "Bird," or "my little bird." She called him "John-Boy" in return, when she was feeling particularly brave or saucy.

Nest or no, she didn't belong at this hospital but at the Freemen's Clinic, where she was bound.

Annabelle and Frances Gage had both told her the freemen and women got the medical treatment they needed at this clinic without charge. If they could bring in an egg or two, or a scrawny chicken in exchange for treatment, then they would. More likely, though, they had nothing to give; and even after all they'd been through, they were both proud and distrustful. So they didn't come for help until, most often, it was too late.

Frances Gage was the one who'd said something that made up Clara's mind in favor of the clinic over the better hospitals. Frances hadn't been talking about medicine, either, but about teaching. She'd said: "What these Gullahs, and the other former slaves, are most starved for is not even food, it's kindness. Plain, simple kindness. Mary and I have found that even if they are suspicious of you at first—and never forget they're suspicious with good reason—if you are consistently kind, they will come, and come again. Eventually they will bring their friends. It is human kindness, Clara, that will win this war. It's not a war for land or goods or money—at least, not for us. It's a war for the decency that is due to every human soul."

Clara had nodded, a lump in her throat, when Frances put into words what Clara herself had known for a long time now.

This fine May morning, with Erasmus off reading and perhaps even remembering to look for a better boat, Clara kept on walking toward the poorer section of Beaufort, and thinking as she walked. Two years ago she'd started out longing passionately to be able to pick up a rifle and fight. If not for her small stature and decidedly feminine shape, she might have tried to pass for a young man and enlist, as many women did, for various reasons. Clara's reason back then would have been the very simplest: She was angry—passionately angry. She was a New England patriot from a long line of patriots, with one brother who lived and ran a mill in the bloody, rotten South (and therefore tried to pretend there wasn't the imminence and then the presence of war), and another brother, David, who was basically a pacifist. David had always hated fighting of any kind. Little as she was, Clara had always been the scrappy one, the angry one, the one who would rather *do* something, *anything,* rather than do nothing.

But in two years she had learned a lot. She had learned that war was about principles, yes; but it was also about people. She was seldom angry anymore; if she felt anger now, it was most often with the top level of officers on her own side, the Union side, who seemed to her to be prolonging a holocaust almost medieval in its scope, like the burning after a plague that consumed everyone and everything in its path.

Her father, the Old Soldier, would have been shocked: People had begun to matter more to Clara than principles; compassion has become more important than justice. Maybe, like the old Greek statue, Justice really was blind. In a war like this one, that meant the good and the bad suffered equally . . . and yet, somehow the rich still would manage to come out on top when it was over.

Clara grimaced. She was passing the ruined Episcopal church, traditional worshipping place of the richer half of society, especially in the South. And the sight of it shamed her, because it had been her own boys in blue who had thrown the altar stone out in the churchyard—or so she'd heard. Before that, the Confederates had stripped the stained-glass windows of this church of their lead, just as they had done of every church in the whole South, to make bullets.

Yes, Justice must be blind.

The sound of women's voices weeping and moaning reached Clara's ears. She picked up her skirts and petticoats as high as she dared and ran toward the voices.

What in the world?

"Let me through, please, I'm a nurse." She was not afraid to claim the title, even if it was not quite true, when needs must be. "Let me by. Perhaps I can help."

Faces turned to her, heads wrapped in faded bandannas, some with the sooty skin of malnutrition past all hope. Clara counted without even realizing that she was doing it, out of habit: six women, one old man, one middle-aged man, one little boy. About four years old, she guessed. The middle-aged man had a weeping stump where his knee should have been. A mighty stench rose up—too much to come from that stump of a leg. Automatically she reached into her pocket for her notebook and began to write.

Chapter 13

One of the women challenged her as she was noting the date and the numbers and the location—except, as Clara glanced about, she wasn't sure of the location.

"Oonuh werry stranguh to we," said the woman in Gullah. Clara translated automatically. She knew almost all the language now and she loved to hear it, though she could not speak it herself.

"I'm not really a stranger," she explained, "my name is Clara Barton. I'm with"—better not to mention the soldiers; she stopped herself just in time—"I'm a friend of the teachers, Mrs. Frances and Miss Mary Gage, who have the school on Parris Island. They told me about the Freemen's Clinic, and I've come to help. It's nearby, isn't it, the clinic?"

The old man, calmest of any, spoke up. He turned his face toward Clara, though he was nearly blind, with the pale gray of a cataract completely covering one eye and inching inexorably across the other. "Back door to the clinic be up yonduh." He motioned with a cane.

Clara saw now that they were all in an alley that ran

behind a row of small, but not tiny, houses. Each house had three steps up to a back door, and, presumably, a crawl space beneath. The houses were shabby but not dirty.

And yet there was that awful smell . . .

The little boy piped up: "De debbil 'e werryself bin yuh."

The women began once more to moan. Clara shoved her notebook back in her pocket. Quickly assessing the situation she offered her hand to the little boy. He took it.

"Show me," she said.

No one objected. The women moved back to make room for Clara's wide skirts, though she held them close as she could with one hand.

"Ugh!" The sound escaped from Clara involuntarily, in spite of the many, seemingly worse things she'd seen in the past two years.

"Debbil wuk," said the little boy, pointing.

"I'm inclined to agree with you," Clara murmured. She placed herself between the boy and the awful sight on the ground, took both his shoulders in her hands and bent down to look him right in the eyes. "My name's Clara. What's yours?"

"Willyum."

"Willyum, I want you to go right back to your mama now, and you tell her I'm a nurse, and I need to speak to the person in charge. Do you understand?"

Willyum shook his head. No, he didn't understand.

Clara tried again. She was taking shallow breaths, but still her gorge was rising. She'd have a hard time of it not to vomit. "All right, just go tell your mama to get the doctor from the clinic."

This time Willyum's head bobbed a yes, and Clara turned back to look at the horror. The Gullahs seemed to be guarding the body from a distance. They were watching

Clara too. She could, after all, dressed all in black like a crow, be the devil's handmaiden.

The body had been wrapped in some kind of cloth, like the oilcloth sailors use to stay dry, and only recently dug up. Very recently. No coffin. That was why the smell was so bad—decay had begun, but was not yet complete, and so there were still patches and shreds of blackish, greenish flesh, and holes crawling with things Clara would rather not examine too closely.

Yet she felt she had to. If she didn't, perhaps no one else would.

The patches of clothing that remained on the body indicated that she was female. There was half the skirt of a blue dress, and a petticoat with some embroidery that by some strange coincidence had remained intact, a little square of blue flowers on white that had once probably been a ruffle.

Clara ran to the other side of the alley, got as far away as she could and vomited until nothing came up but bile. Then she had dry heaves. A sip of water would have helped, but she had none. Behind her the useless weeping and wailing continued. Where the hell was the damn doctor?

Somewhere in her deep pockets she might have a lozenge; it would be old if she still had one, but never mind. Her back still to the small, wailing crew, she rummaged until her hand closed around a wax-paper-wrapped oval, and she thanked God for it. Strong peppermint, it quickly soothed her heaving esophagus.

Clara turned back to the dead woman, who had no esophagus left. Her head was gone. Some animal—surely those scratch marks in the dirt could not be human?—had dug up the body. And had been interrupted, apparently, while attempting to take away the bones.

"Oh my God!" Clara exclaimed.

Her horror forgotten, overcome by a need to understand what had happened here, she went down on her hands and knees next to the body and began to count the bones.

On her own, Clara had studied human anatomy from a book. She knew how many bones there were supposed to be, and their approximate proper appearance and location. "No animal did this," she said aloud.

She had not noticed that the old blind man had come to stand nearby, leaning his shoulder against the back of a building across the alley but carrying the cane, which he used, as before, to point.

"Right," he said, "no animal did that. I can't see well enough to know exactly what's there, but I know evil when I feel it. Tell me what you see, Miss Clara Barton."

"There should be a doctor here, or a policeman," Clara said out of training and habit, "someone in authority."

The old man made a rough sound deep in his throat, probably the closest he could come, or cared to come, to a laugh. "You think they care what happens to us over here? That Dr. Matheson, the one started this clinic, he comes around maybe once a week at the most these days, and when he's here he doesn't do much doctoring, if you ask me. I think something's happened to him. Maybe he died, or went away. Anyhow, he ain't been here at all for the past two, three weeks. All the nurses but one got called up to the big hospitals when all them new patients came on the big ships. You know about that?"

"Yes. I was there." Clara nodded. She thought maybe a Dr. Matheson had been there too; she seemed to remember David mentioning that name. But the memory was dim, and the situation at hand was urgent.

"Now you gonna tell me what you see, or not? I used to

be a teacher. Used to have a mind that worked sometimes. Still does work sometimes, even if I am just about blind. Maybe, you tell me what you see, between the two of us we can decide what's best to do. Whatever it is, it's best done quickly. Don't you think?"

"Yes, I agree," Clara said, grateful for the old man's good sense. She turned off her feelings and went into that part of herself that walked the battlefields looking for the still-living among the dead, the part that mopped up blood as if it were water and sewed skin as if it were curiously spongy canvas.

"I have no way of knowing how long ago this woman died. But I think she was murdered. The bones of the hands and feet are not here."

"Go on." The old man had lit a pipe and was puffing on it. The aromatic tobacco helped Clara, a lot.

"Nor is her head. But I think that just happened, not when she died, but this morning. I think the person who pulled her out from . . . "

Clara stopped, as the obvious truth hit her for the first time. Still kneeling by the body, she turned to the old man. "Someone wrapped this woman's body in oilcloth, a table-cloth, I think, and buried her in a shallow grave in the crawl space, just beyond the steps, under the clinic. That is, if this building is the clinic."

"It is."

"I don't know enough to be able to say how long ago that was. The body is about half decayed, as if the wrapping kept part of it protected, but rats or something got at the rest, and had begun to gnaw away at it. Still, a lot of the flesh is still present, though putrescent. That's why the smell is so awful. A doctor could probably tell us how long she's been under there." Clara did not want to touch the body, to further unwrap it.

"But she was murdered, you say?"

Clara nodded, though she wasn't sure if the old man could see her nod or not.

"How can you be sure her head was taken today, and not when she died?"

"I suppose I can't, not really. Her spine is almost entirely exposed, so I think the head might have lifted right off. The person who took her head must have been interrupted and not able to finish."

"You think he, or she, came to take the body away?" asked the old teacher.

The women had stopped wailing now. One by one, they had formed a quiet semicircle, listening to the discussion. Only the man with the weeping amputation remained seated up the alley where he had been.

Clara noticed them, but only peripherally. She did glance up long enough to be sure the little boy was half hidden behind his mother. No child should have to see something like this too closely or for too long.

"He dug with his hands," Clara said. "You can see the finger marks."

"They mark ob de debbil claws," said one woman, who crossed herself and spat.

"No," Clara insisted. Superstition had its place, sometimes right next to worship, but this was not superstition's place. She suddenly realized that no matter how much she disliked the task, there was something she had to know. But first she had to ask a question, and so she turned to the old man, because he seemed to have the most sense of the bunch.

"Is there some way we can arrange to give what remains

of this woman's body a decent Christian burial, without anyone else knowing besides us? No military police, no doctors, just take her quietly off and bury her?"

"She learns fast, don't she?" the old man said, to nobody in particular.

Clara took that for yes, and despite her reluctance, began the unpleasant task of unwrapping the rest of the body. Once she'd done it, the conclusion was obvious, and she stated it. "I was mistaken. She was stabbed in the chest. The person who did that also cut off her hands and feet. What he did with them I don't know, but they aren't here.

"I'd say the person who took her head this morning would have carried off all the bones if he could have, if he'd had time. As it is, he's taken the skull, an arm bone, a leg bone and some of the vertebrae."

"Whuss a bertebray, Ma?" whispered the little boy.

"Hush, chile," the mother said, but the old man answered.

"It's a part of your backbone, son. Looks round, like a big spool made out of bone, with a hole in it."

"Whuss the hole fer?"

"I don't rightly know," the teacher admitted.

Clara could have told the little boy, told all of them, about the spinal cord and its bundle of nerves, but she didn't. A picture—a series of moving pictures that told a story—came together in her mind. Right or wrong she didn't know. But she thought two men had fought over this woman. Maybe she was a prostitute. If she'd been a white lady, someone would have reported her missing. One of them had killed her rather than let the other have her. Then the other one, the one who really loved her, had come back and given her a hasty burial, intending to do better one day when he had more time and maybe more money to do it right.

But why cut off her hands and feet?

The old man had crossed the alley, leaning heavily on his cane. Now he put a hand gently under Clara's elbow and urged her to stand. He spoke quietly: "Let's us walk around to the front of the clinic and go in the front door, start all over like none of this ever happened. You say you're a nurse?"

"Yes," *unofficially*—the word she always added to herself when pressed into nursing duty.

"Well, it just so happens my friend Joe here needs a nurse real bad. Welcome to what's left of the Freemen's Clinic, Miss Clara Barton."

"Thank you, Mister, uh—"

"Doctor, but the professorial kind, not the medical kind. I got my doctor's degree up north, long time ago. I'm what they used to call a 'free colored man,' and why I came back to this godforsaken land of slavery I wouldn't know, except a certain lady, over on Lady's Isle, she had my fancy. Name's Dr. Bob Thornhill. My Sally, she died just before the war, so you might say I got stuck here at just exactly the wrong time."

They continued on around the corner of the alley, Clara slowly coming out of a kind of daze caused by too much happening too unexpectedly, too fast. Dr. Thornhill paused long enough to give a few directions, and the women scattered, one to bring something for a winding sheet, one to bring a wagon, another who promised a shovel and a rake. Friend Joe, on crutches, came along so slowly that he fell far behind.

Later, the part Clara couldn't get out of her mind—especially because later she wasn't sure she'd heard Dr. Thornhill right—was what he said about the hands and feet being missing from the body.

"We've seen this kind of thing before."

That was what she'd thought he said.

Perhaps it wasn't a *good* start, but it was *a* start, and it was clear they needed her desperately. Along about noon a young doctor from one of the military hospitals showed up—this one was navy, from the hospital in the big house out on the Point by St. Helena Sound—and he said he'd heard Dr. Matheson had been sick for a couple of weeks. He had an afternoon off, so he'd thought he'd volunteer at the clinic.

Clara almost threw her arms around his neck and kissed him.

Later, walking back to Beaufort Landing and hoping to goodness she was in time for the turning of the tide, she realized she couldn't even remember that doctor's name. But it didn't matter, because one thing was firmly settled in her mind: She would be at the Freemen's Clinic every Monday, Wednesday and Friday, rain or shine. Until battlefield duty called her away.

Colonel Elwell wouldn't like it, and she wouldn't really like leaving him either. But he was a married man, and they were becoming much too close.

Most important of all, though Clara felt dirty, smelly and tired, she also felt as if she had spent her day well. She had been useful to people who needed help she had to give. For her, that was a vast improvement over sewing riding habits and accepting bouquets of flowers from Captain Lamb, while trying at the same time to find a graceful way to decline to walk out with him after supper. Poor Captain Lamb was almost as boring as her brother David.

When she reached the landing, she looked around for Erasmus. She didn't have to look very far. He'd been waiting for her, apparently so impatiently he didn't even want to skip stones. He was practically hopping from one foot to the other with excitement.

"Miss Clara, Miss Clara, I done us the greatest deal in the whole world!" he declared.

Uh-oh, Clara thought. But she said "Oh really? Well, suppose you just show me."

"Yes'm, come and see."

Razz beckoned her to the other side of the landing, grinning so broadly that Clara gladly, willingly let go of all the cares of her day and entered into the boy's joyful mood. Seldom had she ever seen anyone so pleased with himself.

"So, where is it?" Clara looked around. She didn't see a likely candidate for their price range. There were sailboats aplenty, this being St. Helena's side of the landing, and generally conceded to belong more to the navy than to the army, who went down Port Royal Sound to Hilton Head or stopped at Parris Island along the way. Why a navy man, who had to spend all his working hours on the water anyway, would make sailboating his hobby for what little free time he had was totally beyond her. But many of them did.

"You sold our boat," Clara guessed. "I hope you got a good price, and have arranged us a way home."

"No, ma'am, didn't sell it. I traded it. For this boat right here."

Erasmus gestured with a flourish at a boat that, at first glance, she had taken to be one of the sailboats, because it was about the length of the rest. But this one had no sails.

It was a perfect Sea Island boat, the very kind Captain Lamb had said he would have had built if there were time.

"Not oney that, but the fella said call it a even trade. So I got all this money left. Hold out you hand, Miss Clara!"

She did it, automatically, and all the coins and folding money she'd given the boy that morning were returned to her.

It had to be either a miracle or a trick.

"Oh my!" Clara said, at a loss. She suddenly wanted to sit down, but there wasn't anywhere to sit except in the boat, and she wasn't quite ready to do that yet, if ever. She was already wondering what they would have to go through to give it back.

"It was a even trade," Erasmus insisted. He was still grinning, very sure of himself.

Clara knew him well enough by now to believe him, or at least to believe he believed it, so she said: "All right, tell me about it."

"Lessen you wants to get stuck on a sandbar somewheres long between Parris Isle and Hilton Head, I better tell you in the boat on the way home."

"Oh, all right. But if somebody comes after us for taking their boat by mistake, or if there's some kind of misunderstanding, particularly if it involves the police or the sheriff or any branch of the army or navy, I'm going to be very grumpy, because I've had a hard day today."

"I wouldn't do that to you, Miss Clara. I be, I *am* your biggest fan." Razz, who got taller every day or so it seemed, stepped first into the boat and then offered his hand to Clara. He had already stored his precious gunnysack of books under the small front seat. "Besides that," he added as he waited for her to settle in the back, "I don't want to lose my job."

That made Clara laugh.

"This be the smoothest ride you ever had since comin' to Beaufort, I promise you. 'Specially when we gets back to the marshes at the other end. This prow gonna cut that marsh grass like butter."

"I can believe that." She began to relax, to take in the sounds of the water lapping against the boat; to feel the late-afternoon mist rising from the water, cool and pleasant; to hear baby spring frogs peeping in the grass, and small insects chirring. The air itself had a special softness that she had never felt anywhere but here, among the Sea Islands.

She was enjoying herself thoroughly, until Razz's story of his trade for this boat turned her veins to ice.

Chapter 14

BETWEEN BEAUFORT AND PARRIS ISLAND

Having negotiated the crosscurrent successfully until he had their new boat into the channel that carried them swiftly, and it seemed almost effortlessly, with the outgoing tide down Port Royal Sound toward the sea, Razz began the story he'd been waiting for this moment to tell.

"Miss Clara, I swear to you ever' word of this be true, 'bout how I traded that old rowboat for this here one. I had to make a kind of funny promise"—he rolled his eyes back at her over his shoulder for a moment, while continuing to feather the oars lightly in the water, just to keep them on course—"but that part comes last. If'n I was to tell it first—"

"*If*, Razz," Clara corrected rather crossly, reacting to what she sensed would be a serious interruption to her tranquillity, "not *if'n*, just *if*."

"Yes'm. If I was to tell it first, it would ruin the rest of the story. All right?" He looked back at her again, wanting her approval. After all, having obtained this fine boat all on his own was no small thing.

"All right," Clara agreed, smiling to make up for her moment of crossness.

"I was sitting up in a tree over toward the St. Helena side of the Sound, reading my books, and every now to then looking around to see if anybody come along look like they might know about where to get a boat. I mean, if nobody'd come along soon, I'd of gone into town and starting asking 'round, but tell the truth, I was hopin' and prayin' too that I wouldn't have to do that. 'Cause I didn't get anywheres just walkin' up and down the docks this morning, and in town the best places to ast, I mean *ask,* they don't zackly want people like me in there. Know what I mean?"

"I know," Clara agreed quietly. "I'm sorry, Erasmus, to have put you in such a position. I hadn't thought of that."

"Well, it worked out fine, didn't it, 'cause after a while comes along this huge black man, biggest Gullah I ever seen. You know how Gullahs is mostly skinny—they may be tall but they mostly skinny peoples even when times be good—leastways the men. But this Gullah, he almos' a giant. Look like the Lord took two of 'em and made 'em into one.

"I was scairt—"

"Scared."

"I was scared of him at first, just on account of he be so big. But then he sat down on the grass alongside the water. He had this bundle in his arms—he cradle that bundle like a baby."

Clara's heart skipped a beat.

"He rock it, an' he talk an' sing to it, till I think maybe it really was a baby, and I think maybe I like to make friends 'cause he look so sad, and if it was a baby I like to see it—I likes babies mighty fine.

"So I climb down outten the tree, with my gunnysack; he

baby bundle he got wrapped all nice in somethin' like one of them fancy tablecloffs I seen in Miss Penny's dinin' room. Or maybe was one of them lace curtains. Anyway, I wants to see the baby an' cheer the man up. Didn't know yet he had a boat or nothing like that."

Erasmus was quiet for a moment, pulled one oar out of the water and scratched at his ear, then put the oar back and went on, lightly rowing as he talked.

"Really, Miss Clara, that big man look like he had the weight of the whole worl' on his giant shoulders, and like he be strong enough to carry it too, except when he be so sad. Like the Gullah say, 'E yeye duh leak.' "

"He was crying?"

"Yes'm. Zackly. Tears big as . . . as pennies runnin' outen his eyes."

"So what did you do, Razz?"

"Didn't do nothin' really, 'ceptin' I went and set by him. You knows how sometimes you an' me, we just set on the steps of an evenin', not talking nor nothin', just set together, an' it's . . . well, it's nice?"

"Yes. It *is* nice, Razz, to just sit together sometimes and not have to talk. Sometimes a person you can be quiet with is the very best sort of person to know."

"So after a while, the big man stop his tears from fallin' an' he says, 'Hey, boy. Why you set chere wib dis ole man?'—you know, like the Gullah say, oney I can't always talk jes lak 'em, I unnerstands, lak we talk haf an' haf. An' I jes, I mean I *just* said I was sorry he so sad, and didn't know how else to let him know it, so I thought I'd set there with him for a spell. I said I hope his baby be better soon."

"His baby," Clara echoed, as a chill tingled all the way down her back.

Erasmus feathered one oar broad side to the current, and brought the other into the boat. They had reached a place in the Sound where islands began to pop up here and there.

Knowing what she knew about what had happened at the Freemen's Clinic that morning, and about the way the sandy, mud bottom shifted around these islands, Clara understood that Razz could keep his attention either on his story, or on his navigation, but not on both. Razz might not know the whole truth—she certainly hoped he didn't—but his instincts must have told him something serious was going on.

He had chosen to pull the boat over into the lee of an island and she was glad. Over the side he dropped an anchor she hadn't even noticed was there. This boat did indeed have everything . . . except a peaceful history.

Razz turned around on the middle seat to face her as he resumed his story:

"By then I knowed, I knew, it weren't no baby in that fancy cloff. Was too lumpy a shape for a baby, for one reason; and for another, it didn't smell like a baby." He paused, considering while he pulled at his ear. "But I could see he *loved* it like a baby, so that was what I said."

Then he did a very adult thing: He leaned toward Clara, with his feet flat on the bottom of the boat and a few feet apart, leaned with his forearms resting on his thighs, as men so often do, hands together with fingers interlaced between his knees. She saw in him then the man he would someday become.

If he lives, she thought, *if we all live . . .*

Razz said, "Real babies don't always smell so good, but they don't smell like *that*. Not like what he had wrapped there so fine, all in lace."

Clara swallowed a large lump in her throat. Erasmus waited for her to say something, but she didn't. She couldn't.

So he went on: "Then the big man pat he bundle and say, 'My baby be much better soon. She be fine, up in heaven with God an' all 'E Angels ob de Light.'

"And I said I be glad of that. Couldn't think what else to say, so I kept on sittin' next to him, 'cause it didn't seem right to go till he did, not with him mournin' so powerful I could feel the sorrow pour outen that man like water.

"Then jus' when I was thinkin' I'd be too late to find us a boat and all, the man, he ast me where I come from an' what was I doin', and I told him I work for Miss Clara Barton, and my job was to find us a better boat on account of our'n was a old leaky boat stuck up with tar. I didn't tell him where we from, Miss Clara. I thought maybe, what with him so out his mind with grief and all, wouldn't be a good idea."

"He was probably perfectly safe, but still that was wise of you, Erasmus. Go on with the story, please."

"Ain't much more to tell. He ast to see our boat, an' I showed him. Then he showed me this un, and I said it was a beauty all right. He rocked his baby some and then he said would I like to trade boats. I said I surely would, who wouldn't, but it wouldn't be a fair trade. He said it was fair enough for him, because he an' his baby didn't have far to go. The tears come down his face again, and he say after he lay his baby to rest on St. Helena Isle, he never go on the water again, so he won't need no fine boat, a leaky boat would do him good enough. Which be true, on account of we was already on the St. Helena Sound side. He didn't have nowhere near as far to go in that leaky boat as we would of, Miss Clara.

"So we shook hands on it, and called it a even trade."

As if his hand had its own memory of that handshake, Erasmus unclasped his fingers and, probably unconsciously, rubbed his hand hard against the cotton of his trousers.

"That was when he said me and my boss lady, meaning you, had to make him a promise and keep it, or the trade would bring us bad luck."

Again, Clara's heart skipped. She asked:

"And the promise . . . ?"

"We gotta paint the boat blue, first thing, soon's we get home. Can't take her out on the water again till she be painted blue, that's what I promised him."

"Blue," Clara murmured. Now the boat was a glossy dark green, almost black. "Where in the world are we going to get blue paint?"

"No problem," Razz grinned, showing all his dazzling white teeth as he stood up and raised anchor, ready to go again now that the amazing tale had been told. "Miss Annabelle, she got lots of blue paint."

Then he turned his back and took up the oars again.

Clara let the knowledge Erasmus had imparted sink in for a long while. There was no reason, really, except the sheerest of coincidences, that she should be thinking the things she was thinking, and that she should be wondering old-fashioned things about reporting to authorities . . . especially since that morning she had agreed with the others that everything was different now with the war, and it was best to let the poor woman—what was left of her—rest in peace. Best to let the Gullah giant find his own peace, if he could, she supposed. Surely, if he was suffering so much grief, he could not have been the murderer. . . .

No. Definitely not.

Clara made a resolution to put it all out of her mind for good now. The incident was over and done with.

She and Erasmus would keep their promise, and that would be that. Resolutely she turned her attention to the water flowing by, watched the bubbles of fish blowing just beneath its shining surface, and the occasional silver flash as one jumped into the air to catch a fly.

Finally, just before they stopped at Parris Island for Razz to run and get blue paint from Annabelle, Clara asked him:

"Erasmus, what did you think was in the man's bundle, that he called his baby?"

"Was he dead dog, o' course. Dog prob'ly all he had left. Poor man."

It was only later, much later after dark, when the boat had been safely stowed until it could be painted, that Clara realized: She had never asked Erasmus if the giant Gullah man had told him his name.

"It doesn't matter," she whispered to herself as she blew out her lamp and climbed into bed. "It's all over now. May she rest in peace. May we all find peace soon. Very soon."

ST. HELENA ISLAND

I like fine whiskey as much as any man; I keep a good supply of it, in fine brown bottles, because a gentleman should have his whiskey, even if he seldom drinks it.

I seldom drink it because I prefer to have my wits about me.

But along about noon, when I thought about how my perfect specimen, George, had insulted me, and how I needed Jackson's help, *needed* it and he knew it, damn his hide, and yet he'd run away . . . well, I decided a shot of whiskey would be a fine idea.

I took the bottle back to my lonely laboratory with me. I had a little job to do. A special potion to mix for George the Perfect. The point being to dull his wits bit by bit, slowly enough that he didn't notice, without sapping too much of his strength. I wanted him obedient, not weak.

Especially because, if Jackson didn't come back, I had to have another helper.

It did occur to me, as I sipped fine whiskey and concocted up a pinch of this and a dab of that—I've always been a dab hand at drug concoctions—Hah! a fine pun that, *a dab hand*—because I studied the herbs with anyone who would teach me, never turned up my nose at a Root Woman.

Then there was the Creole gal who'd moved herself from New Orleans to New York, an octoroon with skin so pale she might as well have been white. . . . I took another sip of whiskey while I tried to remember her name. Not that she'd have been likely to have used her right name any more than "Marie Laveau" had been that woman's true name, though some swore it was.

They were in the same business, my octoroon and Marie Laveau: voodoo.

It came to me: Josephine, that was the octoroon's name. "Same as Napoleon's queen," she used to say. I'd assured her she was my queen—I was very young then and she was a good teacher, of many things. She wouldn't teach me voodoo spells, but she taught me the herbs, the medicines, the powders. I begged her to and she agreed because I was going to be a doctor. I promised I'd marry her once I could get set up in practice, but then along came the war and saved me from that. Not that I'd have kept the promise anyway, having left New York under a bit of duress long ago. . . .

Now wherever I went, if I stayed long enough, I had my own supply growing: the plants that heal, the seeds that kill, the beautiful petals of flowers that break the mind and the will. And some other things I couldn't think of at the moment because I had to keep my mind on this potion I was making.

Being an all-around, respectable doctor, I had some of the plain, old-fashioned medicines too. Patients expected it, even at as poor a place as the clinic. For instance, I had the aforementioned laudanum (which had been helpful with Jackson on more than one occasion), and I had some miraculous new-fashioned medicines as well. Like choloroform. And ether.

Especially ether. God's gift to surgeons. Yet it was hard to regulate the drip of the ether, and to perform delicate surgical operations at the same time. . . .

This made me think of Clara Barton. I hadn't thought about her for days. Well, at least two days, and that, for me, was a long time. I'd been too busy overseeing the disposal of my latest batch of failed experiments. Failure is always so messy and disgusting. Jackson had been a problem over that, didn't like that part of his job, to bury the failures. It always disturbed me when he was a problem. And of course there had been the night terrors . . . but I wouldn't think of that.

I knocked back another shot of whiskey. Shot glasses are small. A man deserves to get a little drunk on his own property once in a while. Especially when he has good reason.

I got my concoction mixed up to what seemed about right, then went outside and tried it on a squirrel. They'll eat anything. Very useful test subjects, squirrels. I put just a drop on a crust of bread left over from some meal I'd had in the laboratory, and I hadn't long to wait before a bushy-tailed little bugger scampered right up, gobbled it down and flopped right over.

Hmm. Perhaps I'd made it too strong?

I waited for a while, then when I felt about ninety percent sure I wouldn't be bitten, I went and checked to see if the squirrel was alive or dead. It was alive, still nice and warm, its tiny little heart ticking faintly but steadily. When I touched its furry chest to check the heartbeat, the creature opened its eyes. Conscious, then, but either unafraid or afraid but unable to do anything about it. Either way, a good sign—especially taking into consideration the difference in weight between George and the squirrel.

I wrung its neck and slung it as far into the woods as I could, so far I couldn't see where it landed. One can never be too careful. Who knows but what these creatures may have a language they speak among themselves, and if they do, what tales they might tell when a person's back is turned?

"Leave no trail," I pronounced, as I went back into the laboratory.

There I decanted my concoction into a dark-tinted bottle, to protect it from any changes that might be brought about by exposure to light—it's interesting, really, how many poisons will go bad on you if you don't keep them in the dark—and I labeled it "PGP" for "Perfect George Potion." I'd kept a few drops in reserve in a small glass dish, and this I carried carefully into the house by the back door, whistling, suddenly feeling absolutely marvelous, with PGP steady in one hand, while swinging the whiskey bottle gaily by its neck from the other.

"Jack!" I called out as I entered the kitchen. "Wait until you see . . ." and then I remembered he was not there.

This did some damage to my mood, but not much. I was too focused on my own fast-growing plans now to let an inconsequential thing like Jackson's temporary absence bother me. I made a large meal of potatoes and this and that all mixed together in a hash—I am not as good a cook when working with inferior foods as Jackson is, but never mind, it would be edible.

I sipped more whiskey, from a glass of a more gentlemanly size than a shot glass, while the hash cooked. I thought about the importance of my plan and wondered how soon I could get Clara Barton here. Wondered, in particular, if she would stay out of her own willingness to help, once she understood the brilliance of my mission? How much suffering could ultimately be alleviated? How necessary was it to sacrifice the few for the sake of the many? And how *now* was the perfect time for the necessary experimentation, since in the war so many were going to die anyway, no matter what one did?

I rather thought she might understand, and stay with me.

That vision of her came back again to haunt me, as it so often did; except that it had not been a vision—at least not of the sort I'd been seeing lately, an hallucination. No, this vision had been real: Clara in the yard of the farmhouse-turned-field hospital, wringing blood from the hems of her skirt and petticoats. Calmly as a common housewife doing the wash. But oh, there was nothing at all common about Clara Barton.

An about-to-burn smell warned me that the hash was done. I divided it into two unequal portions: a plate with my own third, and a much larger bowl with the other two-thirds for George. Into his bowl went the few drops of PGP I'd brought from the laboratory. This meal would have to last him for both lunch and dinner, because I intended to write another anonymous letter to Clara this afternoon, and deliver it to Headquarters House at twilight, when the guard changes and all sorts of people are slipping in and out before they close the gates for the night.

I supposed the whiskey had made me sentimental, because I stopped in Jackson's neat-as-a-pin room along the way and took a shirt and a pair of cotton drawstring trousers for George. I was giving gifts to my prisoner. Such a good master am I!

Even if one of the gifts was a secret, slipped into his food.

"Compliments of my man Jack," I said as I tossed the shirt and trousers through the bars of the cage. Then I shoved the bowl beneath, took out that morning's empty dish and apologized for forgetting the water.

"I'm sure Jackson will be back in the morning. He'll bring you extra to make up for it then."

George was back to glaring and not talking. Never mind: From the corner of my eye I saw him step into the trousers as I closed the door. He'd be docile soon enough.

David, for once in his life, was about to make things easier for Clara. He had no way of knowing how much easier, however, and after she'd heard him out she neither felt obliged nor wanted to tell him.

Her brother had knocked early on her door, while her hair was still down. He brought biscuits and sausage the way she liked them, without any gravy. She let him in, keenly aware that he was the only man she would allow to see her with her hair down except one other, and him only the one time: John.

Only the one time so far, said that annoying little voice in the back of her head.

"The sausage is such a rare treat, I thought I'd grab some for you before the men took it all," David said.

"Thank you."

She closed the door behind him—another privilege reserved for a brother.

"Have you eaten?" she asked.

He nodded.

"Then join me by the window while I do. I've boiled water in the fireplace for tea. Would you like some?"

"Yes," David nodded. "A fire in May? I thought it was a little hot in here. You could go down and eat with the others, you know."

"And you know I prefer to take my time about my morning ablutions. Hot water boiled quickly over bits of kindling in a fireplace, or over a campfire—it's all the same to me as if someone else has boiled it in the kitchen and put it in a special pot to serve it. Besides, it's hotter when I make it myself. By the time the pot gets around to me in the dining room, or the mess tent, it's seldom more than luke-warm."

She made her tea in a small china pot painted on the out-side with tiny yellow roses, which had come with the room. Clara sometimes wondered to whom the little teapot had belonged before, but these days one never asked. One took whatever was there, and was grateful.

David had already pulled up the room's only other chair to the little round table near the back window, where Clara sat so often now, especially at night, that she never moved her own chair from the spot.

"I have news," David said as soon as she had sat down, which so surprised Clara that she nearly fell off the chair. Usually she had to pry everything out of him, an operation which took approximately forever.

"Some I shouldn't tell you, but I will, because I think you should know from me and not from Elwell, who will no doubt tell you whether he should or not; and some I will tell you because I must. I will proceed with the latter first, if you don't mind."

He was nervous, Clara observed; the more nervous David was, the more formal his speech became. Always.

"I hope it isn't too unpleasant, this news you tell me first, only because you must," said Clara in a dry but neutral tone. At least, she hoped it was neutral enough; she and David had been fighting far too often lately, usually over Colonel Elwell; but at times now it seemed they fought over anything and everything.

"I don't like to do this." David stared out the window, not at her, so that she saw his handsome profile with the cleft chin. He had always been, by far, the best-looking person in the family.

"If Father were alive," David said, "he would be furious."

"In that case, this once let us be glad he's not here. I remember our father's fury as well as you do."

"You couldn't," David said bitterly, hanging his head, "it was never directed at you. You were his favorite."

"Sometimes Father got angry with me, David. But don't forget, I had to deal with Mother. Constantly. And she hated me until the day she died. I think that makes us even; and in any event, these reminiscences are doing no good. Just tell me what you have to tell me and let us be done with it."

"You always were the direct one, weren't you, Clara?" Now he looked at her, which for him was progress.

Clara sat with a knot in her stomach and her tea growing cold, while she forced herself not to say: *While you were always so circumspect that everything you've ever said or done has taken too long; therefore, in the end, you failed.*

She only nodded her head in acquiescence, put the teacup and saucer carefully on the table with a hand that did not shake, and then clasped her fingers together in her lap so tightly that her knuckles turned white.

"I have to leave, permanently," David said all in a rush, "I can't stand it here anymore. You have that black boy to help you, so you don't need me anymore, for anything."

The United States Congress would disagree with you, Clara thought, because her battlefield pass required that she have a commissioned officer with her at all times—but she didn't say that, either.

"I can hardly stand it here myself," she said, "which is why I'm so often gone with Erasmus. And why I have been making plans to spend several days a week in Beaufort, working at a clinic. Since the doctors so often insist on using me as a nurse, I should develop my nursing skills somehow, somewhere. So I have decided to take this opportunity. As I would have told you, had you asked."

"I thought you were with those Gage women," David said, an accusing look in his eyes. "Or else, with *him.*"

"No, in spite of your overactive imagination, brother, I have not often been with *him* lately. In fact he is feeling quite neglected, and will no doubt feel even more so when I've told him of my clinic schedule, which I intend to do later this morning.

"As for the Gages, I am very fond of them both, but they are agreed that I make a poor teacher. I haven't the patience for all the repetition that lessons require, nor am I very good with children."

"Why didn't you tell me all this?"

"Because I become irritated when I know you are avoiding me for reasons that exist only in your head. Also, because I only just yesterday got my plans finally in order.

"Nevertheless, as to your plan to leave: Am I missing something? You're a commissioned officer. You can't just leave without orders. Not unless you plan to go over to the other side and run the risk of being shot for a traitor."

Clara's eyes sparkled. She was teasing him now, as she had when she was little and they'd played with tin soldiers on his counterpane. Poor David—he had been sick most of his life. With him she had learned how to nurse; he'd been her first patient. Now he was well, handsome and strong enough though in his fifties, yet had only the horrors of war for a reward. It hardly seemed fair.

"Senator Wilson was here last night, for the one meeting only. He said to give you his regards, that he was sorry to have missed you."

Clara felt a pang—she was sorry to have missed him as well. But the fact that he'd been there and gone so quickly might mean good news, as far as the war effort went. "Please, go on," she said eagerly.

"The senator has word of where in North Carolina our brother Stephen is most likely imprisoned. As we thought, it's now been confirmed that the Confederates have seized his mill at Bartonsville. All its employees are forced now either to bear arms for the South, or to produce war materials in the mill, which is now being misused for that purpose. Stephen's wife and children have disappeared, gone into hiding, or else they may even be dead."

"We knew all this before, David," Clara reminded him.

"When Cousin Leander dashed through here earlier this month, he told us, but Colonel Elwell would not allow us to leave, because of that abortive battle that never really happened. Don't you remember?"

"Of course I do! But you know as well as I do, Leander is not always reliable. And Elwell doesn't want you to leave for his own personal reasons."

"John will soon be able both to walk and to ride unassisted," Clara said, thinking to defend the Colonel. But her efforts backfired.

"Yes. And he will be able to do *other things* more easily too, I have no doubt, for which he will need you even more, and I'll be damned if I'll be here for that!"

"David!" Clara's face turned scarlet, in a flood of anger and embarrassment that began somewhere between her breasts and flooded upward all the way into her hairline. Most blushing she could and did control, but not this.

With a speed that left her dizzy, Clara's anger turned to sadness instead. She said softly, hopelessly—for Clara was truly in love with John Elwell: "If only you knew him, the whole person, as I do. If only you would put aside your prejudices and give me, your sister, the respect I'm due for the life I've led thus far and will in the future—"

He interrupted. "We've been over all this before, as you've said yourself, and never to any avail, because *he is married.* I am not going to change my mind. What you and he are doing—"

"What you *believe* we are doing; there might be a difference, you know!"

"—is wrong." David's voice rode right over hers, paying no attention whatever to her pleading protest. "I've asked to be relieved of the duty of being your battlefield escort, in favor of going to ransom our brother. Senator Wilson has directed General Gage to honor my request. I leave on the steamer *Oriole,* which is due to drop off supplies this morning and then continue immediately up the coast."

"What do you propose to use for ransom?"

"A letter of false information, which I will exchange for Stephen's freedom."

"I see. So now you are a spy. Well, all right. It could work, and I know you're unhappy here. Let's not fight anymore, David. You know I love you."

"And I love you, Tot." David stood stiff, resolute. He did not open his arms to her. The language of his body did not match the words he said.

"You're leaving so soon!"

"Probably before noon, yes. I have already packed."

Clara threw herself against her older brother's unyielding body, her long, abundant dark hair flowing over his chest, his arms. She hugged until, finally, he relented and hugged her back. He kissed the top of her head and stroked back that long hair, her most beautiful feature, which so few people ever saw. Stroked and smoothed until she was calm and her hair, tidy now, framed her delicate face.

"I will never believe you belong in this war," he said softly, his eyes gazing at her so deeply she felt for a moment that he could take her into himself through those orbs and make her disappear forever. So she looked away.

"You belong in some kind man's home, reading books, sitting by the fire, playing with children at your feet."

"But Father said—"

"I know he gave you his blessing, said to go and fight as if you were the man you've always wanted to be. But he was dying, Clara, when he gave you that blessing. You took advantage of a dying man to get your own way. I love you, but I've had enough, and I've seen enough."

Clara was devastated. She dropped her arms, moved away from her brother and said nothing, did nothing to defend herself.

He turned his back on her and started across the room.

Halfway to the door, he turned back, slipped a folded piece of paper—whose color and texture Clara recognized all too well—from the inside flap of his uniform jacket, and tossed it onto her bed, saying: "By the way, I found this underfoot on my way in the door. Obviously it belongs to you. I've read it. I was, after all, assigned to protect you."

Whereas before she had been scarlet, Clara's skin was now white and cold with a pain she knew would never go away, and would never be resolved. But still she said nothing. She would not apologize for her relationship with John Elwell ever, to anyone. Nor would she ever say one single word, make one single gesture, that would let anyone know for certain the nature of that relationship. Her private thoughts were her own, and would remain so.

Yet as David reached her door, she did find her voice. "There was something more, you said when you came in. Something that you should not tell me, but you would anyway. I want to know, please."

David stood with his back to the door, arms hanging at his sides. "Yes. In the, the heat of the moment, I forgot. You know there are elaborate battle plans being laid."

She nodded. Everybody knew, but the details were being kept secret until the last moment. Even John would not tell her, and no one knew when the "last moment" would be. Only that it would be some time away; this was surmised.

David now said: "I tell you this for your own good: The battle is to begin in one of the summer months. Our army are digging entrenchments for the foot soldiers, and emplacements for cannon, all the way up the barrier islands from here to Charleston. From Edisto Island, along the beaches of James, up Folly and all the way to Morris, where Battery Wagner guards the southern entry to Charleston with cannon that have range our guns cannot hope to match. The summers here are terrible, not just with heat but with hordes of stinging insects and disease-bearing miasmas that rise off the marshes."

"It's . . . almost insane," Clara whispered. "The Rebels will have every advantage, including the advantage nature and geography have given them: that they are accustomed to these summers whereas our boys are not."

"Exactly. Nor is our one battlefield girl—I mean you, Clara."

"I'm not a girl." Her chin, not so cleft as his but with a dent like the print of a large thumb, came up as she declared, "I'm a woman, forty-two years old."

"You're a woman who looks, to those men you call 'boys in blue,' to be about their same age, and who at the moment has no more sense than they, if she doesn't get out of here. I'm telling you this now so that you will have time to get away as quietly and as best you can. You're a volunteer, not even paid, not under orders. You can leave at any time."

"But—"

"No!" David stopped her protest. He did not move from the door, but he held up one hand in warning, and his voice went low, intense.

"You have an enemy here, Clara. One of the doctors, the worst kind of an enemy a woman who does what you do could possibly have. He's of high rank, a colonel from one of the border states who only just recently came over to our side. He is prized for being able to move freely back and forth across the borders, and so he is not always here."

"I've met him. When the hospital ship came, packed

with all those badly wounded navy men. He was the one who ordered me to leave."

"His name is Dr. Claude Fontaine, and he hates you with a passion that is abnormal, considering that he does not know you at all. Does he?"

"No. Of course not. I never met him before that day on the hospital ship, and I would be pleased never to have to see him again."

"Well, I'm sorry to have to tell you—and to ask for your pledge that you will never let it be known that I told you—that Dr. Fontaine has petitioned the Quartermaster Corps to have all your stores, and your two tents, and your wagons, assigned to him. Elwell, of course, denied the petition, so Fontaine went over his head, to someone in Washington. At last night's meeting, Senator Wilson told Colonel Dr. Fontaine that you may be assigned to the Quartermaster Corps, but you are officially attached to the Department of Sanitation, and your presence is necessary, especially in time of battle, to raise the morale of the troops.

"Wilson told Fontaine to desist. But Fontaine—who lost his temper badly, by the way; he appeared to have been drinking before he arrived at the meeting—looked me straight in the eye and said as he stalked out the door, 'You can tell your sister she hasn't heard the last of this. Or seen the last of me.' "

"Oh." An insufficient response, certainly, but all Clara could think of to say.

"Don't thank me, just forget it was I who told you. And if you have any sense at all left, sister, get out as soon as you can."

With that, David immediately turned smartly on his heels, a motion of peculiarly military formality, and left.

Clara forgave him for slamming the door. She couldn't

think he'd done it purposely; it was more as if the wind had taken the door from David's hand, as if Nature herself had slammed the door on Clara, just for emphasis.

John's note, written on the square, pale brown paper he favored, and with his brown ink, was short. And it was sweet. The note said:

> *Dearest Sister, My little bird has not visited this lonely nest in quite a while. She is much missed. Can you not come again soon, bringing your downy comfort? Yours, John-Boy.*

Chapter 15

I came to, rather than woke up.

At first there was a darkness all around me; I had to fight my way out of it, as if I had become encased in a great cob-web, endless and unyielding. It bound me like twine but randomly, and painfully—though I thought the pain was in my mind but not my body.

I was terrified.

Yet my brain began to function and I knew that my unaccustomed drunkenness had done this to me. Had weakened the power of my mind to keep that Darkness at bay.

Whatever that Darkness was, I shuddered to think; I did not want to know, but still something in me was at times as attracted as I was repelled by the thing. . . .

"Stop!" I found my voice.

I sounded feeble, and my voice had been coarsened by last night's whiskey. Yet through power of imagination, or in actuality—who could tell in an experience so strange as this?—I felt that black cobweb lose some of its power to bind me.

It is a hard thing, a very hard thing, for a man unaccustomed to the aftereffects of a day and a night of heavy drinking, to summon the willpower he has squandered away. But I did it. Consciously, through the screaming in my mind that wanted to come out of my mouth and overwhelm the words I intended to say, I pulled together all my strength and yelled out, "STOP, AND BE GONE!"

I'd meant to say also "from me," but I hadn't enough wind, or will, to get out the last two words.

Those I'd said must have been enough, because the darkness around me began to pale, and the threadlike bindings became looser, then transparent like gossamer. The Black Thing lifted up from around me and rose into the air, like a dark cloud. I could not believe my eyes. No longer was it merely "darkness" or even "Darkness," but a Thing. A real Thing whose nature I did not understand.

Surely I must be losing my mind, or already have lost it, I thought, and yet the testimony of my eyesight *was* there: This was *not* an hallucination—I *truly did see* this Thing.

The screaming of my brain had stopped as soon as It began to rise in the air, yet still my head pounded with the sickening pain of a drunken hangover. I blinked, and kept my vision focused on that dark cloud, which hung spread in the air perhaps a foot over my head—but it was a good six feet in circumference. Now, I myself am six feet tall, plus an inch and slightly more, and so I shuddered as I thought the size of that cloud could be no mere coincidence.

"Move off! Get away from me!" I barked, as loudly as I could.

I blinked again. Even if the earth had moved under my feet, I swear I would not have taken my eyes from that cloud. And before my very eyes it did move off, not *up,* but *across* the room, toward a far corner. It liked corners. I already knew that.

I relaxed a bit, expecting the dark mass to dissipate from its corner, as it usually did.

Where I sat, or sprawled, in the front room of my laboratory, I now could see that the newly risen sun sent pale rays of yellow light, rays made visible by the filter of tall trees, across my desk. The very desk on which I'd laid my head when I'd passed out. How many hours before, I could not remember. I had no idea.

The very desk upon which also rested an unfinished scrawl of a letter to Miss Clara Barton. And a quill pen with dried-up ink. Black ink. I felt a prickle at the back of my neck and quickly returned my attention to That Corner.

The cloud had begun to condense, to coalesce, and at the same time to fade in color—first to charcoal, and then to an ever-paler gray. As its shade paled I saw inside the cloud a whirling chaos, as if those ties that had bound me did in fact exist, were some kind of supernatural twine that whirled and turned, not concentrically but in a torment of totally uncontrolled disorder.

Chaos, I'd thought at first—chaos is frightening to a scientist, perhaps the most frightening thing of all—but now I felt a malevolent intentionality coming from the Thing, whatever it was.

For a moment I swear I saw, in the middle of all that wild, whirling mass, the figure of a child. Neither black nor white, this child's color changed as did the color of the material that whirled around it. A kind of eternal idea of an angry child, with fists clenched, and hair on end like stiff spikes, unmoving in the chaotic wind, and eyes that burned like black coals in the fire—coals you know will be red as lava from the center of the earth if you were to break them open. All this I saw.

Then it was gone.

That was the way of the Thing—though I had not before seen it so clearly, seldom in the light of day and never with that hellish child in the middle. It faded, always, before one's eyes.

Which was why, by the time my headache had gone away, I'd convinced myself once more that the Black Thing, as I called it, was an hallucination after all, and only when I was in the worst grip of the most insane madness would I ever consider it to be otherwise.

I work too hard sometimes; that is all. I strain myself. I would have to be more careful in future, especially if I was going to change my long-standing habit and take to the occasional drink.

The drinking had helped quite a bit overall; I would admit to myself, if not to anyone else, that I was excessively nervous these days. It was just that I'd let yesterday's consumption get out of hand, and I must not do that again. Correctly kept under control, alcohol could become an acceptable, gentlemanly type of remedy that I could pursue in public. I must keep that in mind.

I located a powder of my own devising that is good for the headache, or almost any ache in any part of the body—too bad the selling of nostrums was not of more interest to me; I could probably have made a fortune that way—mixed it with water and drank it down quickly, for it was bitter.

A hot liquid would make it act more quickly; pity I had no hot water.

From late spring through early fall, I did not keep a fire going in the laboratory—not in this climate, though farther north I would have. So I went out the door, stretched in the fine sunlight of another lovely day in late May . . . and then I sniffed the air. Morning, it was, but no smell of coffee. So . . . Jackson had not returned yet.

But still he might. He had been gone only one full day and part of another, and that . . . that Thing or hallucination or whatever it was had awakened me only just after dawn. It was early yet, too early to draw firm conclusions.

In the exceedingly industrious way one often works after a night—well, to be truthful, an afternoon and a night, both—of alcoholic indulgence, I fired up the iron stove in the kitchen. The ovens too. As I worked, I kept hearing some kind of raucous bird calls from the woods, which were loud and very annoying. I whistled tunes of my own to drown them out.

I inspected the pantries and the root cellar to see what we had in the way of food, primarily for George. Because even if Jackson did come back—as he surely would; why, the man could hardly tie his shoes without me—still George would be on a "special diet" for some time to come. And that special diet could only be prepared by yours truly.

I found the coffee, without chicory, the way I prefer it, and put together a pot of grounds with water. But when I pried up the round metal burner to inspect the level of the fire before putting the coffeepot on, a flame leaped out at me!

"Pesky little devil," I chuckled, "you almost got me."

Well, the fire had not yet died down enough to put the coffee on, or to start the baking for George, and anyway I had to return to my laboratory. I had forgotten to bring in the PGP, my Perfect George Potion.

Once outside again, I could not fail to notice how much louder was the racket from the birds. The woods were filling up with them, big black crows or ravens. I thought I might even have seen a hawk or two. Carrion birds. Meat eaters.

Dead deer, I thought . . . but the farther I walked along the path toward my lab, the less I liked what was happening out there. Unless my eyes deceived me—and I'd already had quite enough of that for one day, thank you—more black birds had gathered this morning than I'd seen in one place before in my whole life. Not even when Jackson and I were burying failed experiments had we attracted this many of the horrid, noisy black creatures.

"Because Jack and I were there, of course, that's why there weren't so many," I said aloud—as much to hear the sound of my own voice as for any other reason.

But still I didn't like it, and I retrieved the PGP as quickly as possible from the shelf where I thought I'd left it, glad I'd made a label to be sure. Scientific training encourages the formation of careful habits, which is a very good thing. I should have to teach that to my grandchildren someday. If I ever had any. Which of course I would: Clara and I would have children, and they would produce the grandchildren; that was the way it always went.

Provided she stayed with me once I had acquired her, and I didn't have to kill her, of course.

On second thought, as I was leaving the laboratory, I tucked the letter I had been writing to her the night before under my arm. Ink and more paper I had in plenty inside the house, to which I returned posthaste. The noise of the black birds was simply ear-splitting!

Having started badly, the day continued on downhill from there. I got the coffee made, which took care of the rest of my headache; silly me, I thought that was a good sign. But it wasn't.

When I took George water and a strip of dry-cured meat, along with a boiled egg (priceless in town, but I have a large number of chickens penned up that Jackson takes care of—they are very stupid birds, do not try to fly away, and lay eggs with great regularity whether they have a rooster or not, which I find for some reason perversely amusing) . . . as I was saying, when I arrived at the room where George was kept and I opened the door, I had quite a shock.

I thought he was dead, for he was laid out on his back, straight as an arrow on his pallet on the floor of his cage, arms down at his sides, feet together, as if an undertaker had arranged him that way.

I must have put too many drops of PGP in yesterday's hash, I thought.

Have I said that I am, at least somewhat, physically *afraid* of the young man named George? He caught me once off guard, when I thought Jackson had hold of him, but Jackson did not. . . . A most unpleasant memory.

I shifted the basket containing the food and water to my other hand and rubbed my neck, where just over the carotid artery I'd had a deep bruise for a very long time. I still wondered how he'd known to do that. So far as I know, no Gullah yet has ever studied anatomy.

All right, I thought crossly, staring at that stiffly straight body, *just go ahead and be dead and see if I care! It will be a lot less work for me in the end anyway. I can always leave and start over someplace else.*

But the thing was, George was the only physically perfect, healthy one I'd ever captured, and been able to keep to work with. He was totally necessary to my plan, and so was Clara Barton, and the Coffin plantation was perfect even

right down to the name of it, and so I didn't *want* to leave
and start over. Not again!

HILTON HEAD ISLAND

John Elwell looked like a different man than he had six
weeks earlier, when Clara'd first arrived. His full beard—
which had been shaved for easier care during his convales-
cence, when it was hard to bathe much less wash one's
hair—had grown back. Clara rather missed his face. She
teased that he had quite lost the pallor of the poet; he was no
longer the man she'd become so taken with.

True, they read less poetry. But they did other things instead; and if she was less taken *with* him, she was now more
taken *by* him.

John's injury had entirely healed now, except for a limp
that would most likely stay with him, although in time he
might not require a cane. He would continue, too, to have
occasional spells of weakness. This, Clara assumed entirely
without scientific proof, was due to the oddness of the diet
they were all forced to eat. They ate whatever the lighters,
the supply boats, brought—which meant that some weeks
they had little more than rice; others, they'd be brimming
over with fruits and vegetables. The winter, which in this
Southern clime had been over long before Clara's arrival,
had depleted their store of dried salted meat. Fresh meat
was hard to get, and Elwell had told her he craved it.

Some people thought all cravings were the work of the
devil and should be denied; but Clara, who ate so little, occasionally had cravings of her own, even though she did not
care for food in general. She believed the cravings meant

her body needed whatever it craved, and would try to provide it.

But she had no way to provide meat in quantity for John. Or did she?

They stood side by side watching the steamer *Oriole* carry David, and many others, out of Hilton Head Harbor. She felt a heavy sadness because she knew she might well never see him again. Though in past years they had often bickered, they seldom truly fought; and in many ways for all her years, she'd been closer to David than to any other man. Including her father, though she had idolized him.

John draped an arm casually across Clara's shoulder. His cane was in his other hand. He leaned down until his beard tickled her ear and said quietly, so that only she could hear, "Now your watchdog is gone, will you ride with me openly?"

Without looking up, her eyes still locked on the departing steamer, which had now negotiated the strait and made the turn to portside, heading northward, Clara said, "You might have chosen a more diplomatic time to ask me."

John removed his arm from her shoulder and used that hand to rub his beard.

"Forgive me, please, if you feel I'm rushing you. I've had no experience of these things."

"Is that so?" Clara asked sharply, now looking up at him.

"It is."

Clara searched John's clear gray eyes, which seemed all the more transparent for their contrast with his hair, which had darkened as it thickened again with the return of his health. These were eyes, she felt, which could hide nothing from her. She wondered, if he were to become a prisoner of war, if John could hide anything from anyone. As a colonel in the Quartermaster Corps, John Elwell knew from the pattern of moving goods much more than most officers knew. Others knew only pieces; he knew, or could put together whether he had been directly told or not, the whole. If he was caught, the Rebels would torture him; he would lie, and they would look in his eyes and know he was lying.

Because Clara had been staring at him for so long without saying a word, John added quietly and solemnly: "I am not a philanderer, not the way your brother thinks."

"So he talked to you? He has done nothing but lecture me for weeks."

"Words were not necessary between myself and David Barton. I knew the meaning of his particular gaze."

The clump of men and a few women, who had gathered to watch the steamer depart, now began to break up and to go their separate ways. Only John and Clara had not moved; they stared at one another, oblivious to the rest around them. But as the rest were equally oblivious to them, no damage had been done.

"Besides," John continued in his low voice, which had the advantage of not carrying unless he wished it to—a quality he had not known he needed to cultivate until he had become a university teacher and found the students could not hear him beyond the first row—"David talked to Sam Lamb, and Sam tells me everything."

"He read your note," Clara said.

"So he knows."

"The meaning was not too difficult to divine."

John chuckled, then sobered. "I didn't want it to be. Still, I am sorry he read such a private thing."

"I must have gone to bed before you came to my door last night, and because David was at my room this morning early, he found the note before I did."

They stood together alone now at the dock. Their

aloneness, against the water's backdrop, made them conspicuous. Clara was instinctively sensitive about such things, and began to walk, leaving John to follow. She went toward Headquarters House, wanting to be alone in the shelter of her room, regardless of the blue sky above and the sun's warmth.

John's longer stride caught him up with her quickly, though he leaned heavily on his cane. Speed at walking did not yet come easily to him.

He asked, "You are angry, why? Because your brother read our private business, or because I wrote of it?"

Clara shook her head. "I'm not angry. I'm sad and unhappy and confused right now. David is my brother, the closest to me in age, and we parted not on the best of terms."

"Because of me."

"No, not because of you, but because of *me,* because of what I have become. David taught me to shoot, did you know that?"

"The need to know such a thing has fortunately never arisen." John rubbed at his beard again. He wondered where this conversation was going, and how he could steer it the right way. Or at least, in the way he wanted it to go.

"Well, now you know. I told you about my mother, how she hated me. How she hadn't wanted any more children and didn't think she could have any more, but then I came along. By the end of her life, I believe she hated us all."

"She may have been unbalanced in her mind," John said.

"She was always consumed with anger, and never missed an opportunity to show it."

John stopped walking just short of the steps that would take them to the first level of porches at Headquarters House. He touched Clara's arm, to halt her too.

"Clara, I'm lost. What are we really talking about?"

She looked into his clear eyes and wanted to cry. "I really don't know. Before he left, David said I had always wanted to be a man, and I myself would have said, until quite recently, that he was right, it was true. I'm a crack shot, with both pistol and rifle. I wouldn't consider riding any way but astride; no more ridiculous contraption has ever been invented than the sidesaddle."

"Unless you consider the chastity belt," John remarked.

"I'm being serious. Don't make light when I'm being serious." Clara glowered—something she did so seldom that John physically backed off a step. But only one step.

"I won't. I promise. But please permit me to say that you would be wasted as a man. You are the most extraordinary woman I have ever known. I don't believe another one like you exists anywhere in the universe. I mean that, truly."

"Oh John!" Clara said, biting her lower lip until it turned white, and then she burst into tears and ran up the stairs. She went into her room, closed the door, and for the second time in all her two years of military service, locked the door behind her.

John Elwell was bewildered.

So was Erasmus when he came later on, toward evening, to tell Clara that their new boat would need two coats of the blue paint, because that dark greeny-black was too hard to cover with only one. He knocked on her door, he called out, he even dared to try the knob. But the door was locked, she didn't answer him, and the boy went away with a troubled heart.

Miss Clara would not lock her door, he knew, unless something was very, very wrong.

Razz had worked hard and he was hungry, so he went in search of Captain Lamb.

"Miss Clara done lock her door," he said, explaining what had happened, what he'd done all day, and that it was time now for him to leave. He followed the captain to the building in back of the mess tent, where the food was cooked.

"She be sick?" He finally asked the question that troubled him the most.

"No, Erasmus," Captain Lamb replied. "I think she is only sad because her brother left today on a dangerous mission. She knows she may never see him again."

"I unnerstan' now," Erasmus said, nodding.

He said no more, but thanked Captain Lamb for whatever food was in the sack he gave him without even looking at it, and started running, more slowly than usual, toward home.

Razz was only fourteen but he did understand why Clara had chosen to be alone and to lock her door; he understood in that deep-down place inside himself, where he hated to go. He figured that was where Miss Clara was now too, in that deep-down place. In that place, when you heard people call your name, you didn't answer; when they came to your door, all you wanted was for them to go away and leave you be.

He ran along the hard-packed sand near the edge of the water, where the running was easier. Sandpipers, picking out the periwinkles, scattered from his path but he was so used to the little birds, he didn't even see them.

Halfway home, Razz heard a rumble of thunder, although the sky was still clear overhead, and he picked up his pace. He was glad he'd hidden their new boat under a tarp, propped up on poles so it wouldn't stick to the paint. And it was under the lean-to next to Miss Clara's storage building. He didn't think the boat would get wet and ruin all his hard work, on account of he'd prepared for rain.

All day long Razz had felt a storm was coming.

ST. HELENA ISLAND

If Jackson didn't come back, then time was running out for me here at the Coffin plantation. I guess I'd known that yesterday, been trying to accept it—that was part, not the whole thing but a part, of why I'd gotten drunk.

I wouldn't find another willing helper, not like he'd been in the beginning. They didn't exist anymore, and it was people like me who were responsible for that.

The slaves hadn't been free long, but they'd been quick to learn that the white men who came down from the North, while they might not be any *better* as people go, were *different*. We weren't as, as—what was the right word?—as *merciless* as their slave masters.

Especially not in a physical way. We weren't quite so likely to shred the skin of a black man's back with a bull-whip until he bled to death, for example. Or to force a woman, who'd tried running away with her baby to join her husband, who'd been sold to another plantation, to stand in a fire with the baby in her arms until they both were scorched. That woman fell in the flames with the baby in her arms, the baby's hair caught fire, and it was all over after that for the baby.

But not for the woman. God knows how she survived the infection that must have followed. I've seen her scars. She weaves hats and baskets out of palmetto leaves now and sells them on Prince Street in Beaufort all year-round. Never speaks, but if you cheat her of as little as a penny, she'll give you an evil eye that'll make that penny come right up out of your pocket and into her hand on its own. I swear. That's the only time she ever looks at another human being, if you try to cheat her. Otherwise she stares off in the distance. Doesn't even watch her own hands as she weaves.

Those bluestocking busybodies like the Gages, mother and daughter, teaching people how to read and write and count money, how to figure out how much they should be paid for this and that, and pay out for other things in turn— they were changing people and things. They felt like they weren't getting anywhere, at parties I'd heard them say so, but it wasn't true. They were getting somewhere . . . it was just that nobody knew how far, how fast.

Then there were smart black people, like that Robert Smalls who'd gone turncoat and escaped with his whole family on his massa's boat, through the Union lines. Now Smalls was a big Union spy and an even bigger local hero. There were probably others too, but that was all I could think of now.

These things were having their effect. It was hard to find anybody now who'd be in awe of me, as Jackson had been in the beginning. Impossible to find someone who would do exactly as he was told. And that was why I had to drug George—if I hadn't made a mistake and killed him already.

That was why I'd have to start spending more time at the Freemen's Clinic. That was why pretty soon there'd be a new round of stories about "Bugguh-Man, 'E tek'um chillun fum St. Helena Isle." I wouldn't "tek'um" from St. Helena again, though. There were too many stories now. I'd have to find another way. But the hospitals were out, no longer possible without Jackson to help me.

All these things had been coming together for me

yesterday, though in a somewhat drunken haze. I saw, if only vaguely, a different way to continue my work. But none of it could happen without George. He was the key to everything.

Everything would be much better too if Jackson would come home. I might have to keep him on a long chain, or locked in the house, but he could still cook and take care of the horse and feed the chickens.

As I thought about my man Jack, I realized I had something in my right eye. It was watering for no reason. I put the basket down to wipe my eye on the tail of my shirt . . . and all of a sudden, straight as a shot, George sat up!

"Water!" was all he said. Croaked it, actually.

But that was enough. I still had my project going; my great mission would not be lost after all.

All the rest of the morning I cooked, scientifically. It was interesting, an intellectual challenge to calculate exactly how much PGP to put into each pan of cornbread, and to number them progressively so they wouldn't get mixed up. A challenge, to soak a dried Virginia ham and do similar calculations; I rather thought I might cook it and serve it in portions over time, injecting the portions with a syringe.

As I dimly recalled my mother once having said something about soaking hams overnight, I decided if we were to have anything worth eating tonight without my going out—and I didn't want to go out quite yet, until I got this matter under control—I should catch and kill and cook a couple of the chickens.

I suppose it was about two in the afternoon when I began to drink a new bottle of whiskey. (I had finished the first one, I am embarrassed to say, the night before.) I had a little whiskey, went out and fed and watered the horse—which was not as easy as I thought it would be. Then I went after the chickens.

The chickens proved to be both easy and boring. I fed them first, killed a couple by twisting their necks; they were easy to catch, while pecking at the feed on the ground. I was tempted to kill a few more, just for the fun of it, but I counted the ones we had left and understood why Jackson had said we needed to get a rooster if we expected to have enough chickens to last out the rest of the year.

Cutting up people is interesting. More than that, it is fascinating. People have so many layers inside, and glistening membranes of different colors, delicate veins and arteries, and if one dissects well enough, nerves running through like the most fragile fan tracery. . . .

Then there are the human organs, so compactly and precisely situated that it must have taken a genius to figure it all out. That story about Baron Frankenstein's monster, you know? Forget it. Once you unpack a human being, you can never get it all back in. Not even I can do it.

Now a chicken, by contrast, is supremely boring. For one thing, chickens, once you have washed the blood away, are almost all the same boring yellowish-pink inside. They must be plucked of all their feathers, which is a nasty task indeed. It might be worth it if, once the feathers were gone, one could open up the chicken and find something truly interesting. But compared with a human being, a chicken is disgustingly primitive. It eats, digests and shits; has the parts necessary for these functions, and that's about it. Only the ovaries, where the eggs form, are slightly interesting. The feet are no good for anything (except in voodoo, I remembered from my days with the octoroon), the head is no good for anything, not having a brain worth eating, and the wings are not much good either as there is almost no meat on them at all.

Still I cut them up as carefully as if I were doing fine surgery, disposed of the mess, including the feathers, and baked one plain for myself and the other injected, according to a table or sort of map that I made up, for George.

I drank a little whiskey while doing this, but not much.

I was pleased to find myself a very neat cook; after washing my hands and removing Jackson's big apron, I did not even have to change my clothes.

The chickens should take about an hour to bake. I intended to use that time to rewrite my previous night's letter to Clara Barton, of which I could not remember one word. I took my whiskey bottle, and a fine, low cut-glass tumbler that I had found on an upper shelf, obviously forgotten by some fleeing Coffin, as it was the type used for company-best, into the library. The library is at the back of the house and so I lit the lamps, although it was not yet four o'clock. The woods cut off the light from that room and make it rather dark, although the walls are half windows, the long kind that go all the way down to the floor.

I found that hard to understand, as all these great windows looked out onto was trees. But I hadn't built the place, and there is no accounting for another's taste.

The room was stuffy. Reluctantly, I opened a window. Immediately my ears were assaulted by the cries of the carrion birds, still occupied, I supposed, by the dead deer. I decided I should have to go out and scare them off.

I am a poor shot, but I felt I needed a weapon to frighten the birds away. So I took my Union Army officer's sword, which I keep handily on the library mantel anyway, and set off to get rid of the damn birds. A large swallow of whiskey for fortification sent me nicely on my way.

Jackson was right about these woods: They were haunted. I felt as if I were being stalked. As if there were many pairs of eyes on me. Yet whenever I whirled quickly to look, there was never anyone there.

I'm good in the woods and I know it. I could never have survived as a smuggler and a scavenger after they pushed me out of my rightful place as a surgeon, if I were not good at being the stalker, as well as at knowing when I am the stalkee.

Yet in my very own woods, I mean in the woods of the Coffin plantation, I could not tell either where I was, or who else was there. I knew only there were other presences in those woods, not just my own. It was not the animals, who became quiet as I moved along equally quietly, with my sword in hand, down by my side where it would not be noticeable, yet ready to strike in a second.

I followed the black birds to find my dead quarry. It was easy, because as I approached they sensed my coming, and rose into the air with their raucous voices and a great flapping of their black wings. I brought up my sword, ready to wave it in a circle overhead in case any of the birds should take into mind to swoop down and attack me—there were so many that, even with the sword, I would have been virtually defenseless—yet fortunately, they did not. Even the biggest ones, which looked like a form of vulture to me, with a wingspan of at least four feet, merely rose into the air and flew away.

Finally I had reached the place where the birds had gathered. Vainly I searched the ground for the dead deer. Or perhaps it was even a bear. There are black bears in these woods, they say, though I have never seen one.

All I found was a crude wooden cross, such as a child might make: two wooden sticks tied together with a strip of blue cloth. I inspected the ground around the cross more closely. I thought it had been recently dug, but deeply, and it was well tamped down. Probably the grave of some child's pet. If it had not been dug up yet, then it was not likely to be. This innocent little grave was not the source of my problem.

Just then something cold and slimy fell down the back of my neck, into the collar of my shirt. I felt it slide down my back, like a slug, and all I could think of was that I had to get it off me! I have a particular fear and dislike of leeches, with good reason: We used to try them on each other in medical school, and I could never stand the things on me. I would run out of the room screaming, unable to take the slimy things attached to me more than a few seconds. This made me the butt of a few jokes, but still that was far preferable to having to endure their presence.

This felt the same, although the thing, whatever it was, had now slid down my back almost as far as my belt. The belt, fortunately, would stop it.

I threw down my sword and tore off my shirt, shook myself all over like a dog, but the thing clung. I had to reach around and tear it off with the fingers of my right hand.

As soon as I touched it, even as my senses recoiled, I knew: This was no slug. It was not animal in origin. This, this—Thing—that I held in my hand had once been a part of a human being.

It was eye jelly, not with the iris, not recognizable to anyone but to someone like me, from deep in the back of the eye socket. Human eye jelly, from deep in the eye, a bit that remained to drip down my shirt when the birds had flown away.

I looked up, and there was Jackson. My man Jack. He had hanged himself by a thick rope, the sort used to tie up boats to the docks. Already the birds had eaten him almost to pieces. Except for the eyes and lips, they'd left his face mostly alone. Instead, the birds had gone for the soft parts, the ones that are easy to tear out. They'd opened him up, belly first, pecking out the entrails until they spilled down almost to his feet, to get at the stomach. Jackson's heart was gone, and his liver pecked half to pieces. Those sharp little beaks had gone between the ribs as if they were nothing, to get at the delicate tissues of the lights, sometimes called the lungs. The engine that, driven by the heart, makes us breathe and gives us life.

There was no point in cutting Jackson down. In another day or two, the birds would have him picked clean down to the bone. It would be safer just to let it happen.

It was getting dark in the woods now, truly dark, and I heard a rumble of thunder. Half blind, maybe even with tears, though I couldn't really tell, I searched through dry leaves and slick pine needles and other things I didn't want to think about, until I found my sword.

Once, and once only, I looked back. I called out, in case he could hear me, wherever his tormented soul might be: "You should have stayed faithful to me, my man Jack!"

After saying that, I felt better.

It wasn't until a long time later that I thought about that little grave beneath where he'd hung himself, the grave with the small cross made out of sticks and tied with a strip of blue cloth. But the blue cloth did stick in my mind, the color of it, just always hanging around there in the background. I knew I'd seen it before. But it took me a long time to remember that exact blue dress, and to whom it had belonged, and what I'd done to her.

Chapter 16

From her window, where she had a view across the narrow north end of the island to the open Atlantic, Clara watched the storm come. It rose up from the southeast, which later she heard was unusual for this time of year.

She did not care to learn the rhythms of nature in this part of the world; once she had gone from here, she would never return again unless she had to, and then certainly not to live. Her short time on Hilton Head had brought her the terrible ups and downs of great happiness, but a happiness impossible to keep; and the very real possibility that she had lost the love and understanding of her brother at the worst of all times, when she might never see him again and be able, somehow, to make it up to him. She would stay until her job was done, until God let her go.

"God's will be done," she murmured by her window.

The dark gray curtains of rain, advancing across the ocean, matched an equal march of dark gray premonitions in her heart, and in her mind as well. She sat by that window with her door locked, never answering a knock or a call, and for the first time since its beginning two years earlier, she questioned the value not only of this war, but of all war.

When great bolts of lightning came streaking through shifting draperies of rain to strike the water far off, Clara wanted to jump up and shout "Yes!"—but she did not know why. She merely continued to watch the storm move closer, until the clouds turned darker and took on sinister shapes; until the lightning forked in every direction and lit the night sky in a most unnatural way.

She heard someone climb to the top of the roof and remove the flagpole; at least, she assumed that was the source of the footsteps she heard over her head. She hoped so. When the lightning came overhead it would be likely to strike the object tallest, highest on the island—and that was the flag that generally flew from the top of Headquarters House, which sat squarely atop the closest thing to a hill this low, Low Country had to offer.

At last when the storm lashed the island with its fury, she became afraid to stay by the window. By the light of a single candle she let down her hair and brushed it, took off her corset but left on her skirt and petticoats, and put on a loose smock meant for day wear. There was always the possibility that they would have to evacuate the house during the night. It wasn't the season for hurricanes—at least, she didn't think it was—yet she had never seen a storm so wild as this one, from so close that she felt she was right in it.

She blew her candle out and got into bed, under a light summer blanket. Though this storm was fierce it brought with it not cold, but a kind of suffocation of the air, as if all were turned to water and she had not the gills to breathe.

• • •

To Clara's own surprise, she fell asleep and slept through the night, through all the lightning and the thunder. Morning did not, however, bring an end to the rain that drummed endlessly on the roof right overhead.

John knocked on the wall, his signal: two short knocks, a pause and then another. If she knocked once, it meant she would come to him or send a note; if she knocked twice, it meant he should come to her.

Clara did not knock at all. She made a small fire in her fireplace and heated water for tea.

When Captain Lamb came to ask if he might bring her breakfast, she went to the door in her smock with her hair hanging down, and opened it a scant two inches. She said she was not well, and planned to spend the day in bed. She had water and tinned biscuits and would require nothing more, thank you.

Clara started to close the door, then hesitated and with her eyes downcast asked if Captain Lamb would kindly give her regards to the Colonel and assure him that she had only a minor illness; she was sure she would be better soon and he was not to be concerned about her.

Gratefully, at last she closed the door and locked it again. She had been so tempted to ask Captain Lamb to come in out of the rain—the poor man had looked like a drenched poodle dog, with his curly blond hair and beard escaping, dripping, from beneath an entirely insufficiently brimmed uniform hat.

What this weather required was nothing less than stout New England fishermen's garb . . . except they would all smother in it. The air still felt too thick to breathe.

• • •

Erasmus believed he was scairt of only one thing in this world: them hags he'd heard from time to time tryin' to come down the chimbley at Miss Annabelle's house, wantin' to git in that other room where she didn't ever let him go see what was in there.

Everybody knew her pa'd been the Conjuh Man, and Annabelle could conjuh some herself whenever she wanted to, so that was enough for Erasmus. He hadn't wanted to see what was in the room after that, and he hadn't wanted to see what was on the roof at nights neither, so he was glad now he got to sleep instead at the Gages' on the same sleeping porch with Miss Clara.

He'd thought, though, that he could face anything else until came this here big storm. He'd reached Miss Penny's gates just about the time of the first lightnin' strike. He didn't even stop to think about going into the kitchen outbuilding, where he usually stayed. He went on in the big house through one of them long windows somebody'd left unlocked, and ran through the dark rooms, around the shrouded furniture they'd left behind that looked a lot like ghosts if you let yourself get to thinking on it much, which he didn't, until he reached the library.

It was hunger for the books, since he'd started learning to read, that had led Erasmus to look for a safe way—not a thievin' type of way—into the house. The unlocked window went from one of the bedrooms out onto the second-story level of the porch, and when he came in the house that way, he always locked it after himself. When he left by that way, he left it unlocked. He never touched anything but the books. Never even sat at the library reading table. He sat on the floor, which was bare because they'd taken the rugs with them when they'd gone.

But they'd left behind big oil lamps with hurricane

shades, and plenty of lamp oil in a storage cabinet right there in the library. No lucifer matches, but Razz could get plenty of them from work at the army base. All the men had them, and would toss him a whole box if he asked for one light.

Erasmus spent most of the stormy night reading a big book by a man named Charles Dickens, about a boy name of Oliver Twist who lived in London, England. This Oliver had such a mess of troubles that soon Erasmus was reading faster and faster, looking up fewer words in the big dictionary, figuring out their meaning from what was going on in the story because he didn't want to take the time to stop. He had to find out what would happen next.

It was the first novel Razz had ever read. He forgot about the storm; he cared more about Oliver than he did about himself, and he read until his eyes were closing and he knew he had to blow out the lamp or else he might knock it over in the night and catch the house on fire. He slept wrapped up in the dusty linen cloth draped over the library sofa. But the sofa itself was dry and clean and soft, and he didn't even have time to wonder would Miss Penny forgive him.

Next morning, through the lace curtains at the library window, Erasmus saw the rain still coming down hard. Much too hard to go to the army base. He knew the beach would be a mess until the storm was over, and for quite a while after that; and the road would be too muddy to run on. Wouldn't nobody be doing no work outside this day nohow.

He went back to reading about Oliver Twist. That became a book, and an experience, he would never forget for all his whole life long: He had learned how reading a book can take you away from anywhere, and make you feel like you're somewhere else, and someone else . . . even if only for a little while.

Late in the afternoon of the storm's second day, when all that was left was mostly drizzle, a folded single sheet of ivory paper was slipped under Clara's door.

The surprising thing about it, she thought when she picked it up, because she happened to have been sewing by the fireplace and had seen the paper slide in, was that it was absolutely dry. She recognized the expensive paper, and the elegant handwriting of her name, and she knew the contents inside the folded paper—if she should open it—would be vile.

So she didn't open it. She didn't care anymore. She immediately put it to the flame of her lamp, holding the folded paper carefully by one corner as, with great satisfaction, she watched it take fire. Clara held on to the letter's corner as long as she could, feeling the heat and mentally sending a wish that its anonymous writer would feel that same heat magnified a thousand times, in the flames of hell.

When forced to let go or be burned herself, Clara pitched the remains into the fireplace and watched the thick, expensive paper blacken and curl back upon itself, holding together still but misshapen, as no doubt was its author's mind.

Finally she took the fireplace poker and broke the burned letter into little black pieces, which soon became ashes mixed in with all the others when she kindled a small fire to boil water for her supper tea.

Of course I'd heard that phrase about "courage in a bottle," referring to strong spirits, such as the fine, mellow-yet-fiery stuff I was drinking now. But I never knew it was literally true. *But it is!*

Yes, yes, I must say I am positively overjoyed (except when I think of Jackson, damn his hide—that man not only hanged himself, he sank my boat; there's not hide nor hair of it . . . well, plank nor paint of it . . . to be found at the landing). Where was I?

Oh yes: I am positively overjoyed to say that far from having a difficult time of it with the Black Thing during that terrible storm, I avoided it entirely.

I simply made up a huge fire in the fireplace of the smaller of the two parlors at my house—a delightful room I have never used much although I can't think why—lit all the lamps and took my whiskey and more of the fine cutglass tumblers that I'd found up on a top shelf in there on an elegant liquor cart that had been left in the main parlor.

I gathered up my best stationery and ink, and quill pens with the fine nibs; a couple of my favorite books, and a crocheted afghan that usually resides uselessly at the bottom of my bed.

For some reason, I don't sleep well in my bedroom lately.

George seemed happy enough when I gave him an extra blanket along with enough food and water to last out any storm. He wasn't going to worry me. *Nothing* would worry me: I had made up my mind.

Having told me his name he still had nothing else to say anyway, so I need not be much concerned about George. Not until we reached the part of his treatment where the hypnotics—or the herbals I was feeding him, took hold. Certainly a doctor of medicine of my stature would not himself become involved in hypnotism or mesmerism. Hypnotism and mesmerism are nothing but hokery-pokery, as any decent doctor knows.

A sound mind in a sound body: *Mens sana in corpore sano,* that's the ticket. Who said that? Sounds Greek but the language is Latin. How confusing.

I rode out the night composing my best-yet letter to Miss Clara Barton. If I do say so myself, it was a veritable master-piece of terror inducement. I intended to drive her from fear of her anonymous lover right into my arms. She would soon see that I could be her cherished protector. I mean, cherisher and protector.

Soon I would meet her socially. That would not be diffi-cult to arrange. Letters of invitation went 'round the grow-ing social circles in Beaufort daily, and I—as now owner of one of the largest plantations in the area—had only to let it be known that I wished to be included. The invita-tions would come my way, I was sure of it. I had cultivated an image as a man of reclusive nature, with the sole excep-tion of my good deeds at the Freemen's Clinic. I had insinu-ated, though never said outright, that I was in mourning.

Well, it was true, I *was* in mourning! We all were in a way, weren't we? But I had more reason than most, having been tossed out of my military service and my profession just as I was beginning to make real progress. Now that was something to *really* mourn about!

I'd brooded over that for a while, pausing in my letter to Clara. I drank more whiskey while I brooded, finding that it aided and enhanced the process considerably. Occasion-ally I glanced into the corners of the room, though this small parlor with its light-colored walls, a white-painted chair rail not much faded, and a white-painted ceiling with some kind of ornamental railery below—what do they call that ornamental marking? Something folksy—forks and spoons? eggs and darts?—anyway the point was, the place was light. No dark corners. The Black Thing simply was not here.

Unless it was hiding out in the hallway. . . .

But I didn't think so. I could feel now when it was present, and I did not feel it in the house. Let the lightning crash! Let the thunder roar! I was safe, and happy and warm.

I finished my letter to Clara Barton, folded it over carefully, wrapped it in some waxed paper for tomorrow's delivery, which I would slip off at the last moment, to keep it dry till then. This letter would not go in an envelope, because by experience I now knew that an envelope would make it too thick to slip under her door. But the one paper folded—that would be a snap. I could whisk it right under as I walked by on my way to pay my respects to the Colonel next door, respects which were long overdue. I anticipated not a problem or a worry in the world.

I drank a little more, feeling quite pleased with myself. Things were moving along so well, what with all the new people in town, that I believed I would not have to go to the expense and the bother of taking a small house in Beaufort after all. As any idiot could see, the Union Army was building up to a battle. In such times people move swiftly because you never know what you'll have afterward, do you? It is the best time to win a woman's heart.

One thing they'd forgotten when they took away my rank and my profession: They could not take the contents of my mind. I have always been very, very intelligent. A genius, you might even say.

You might say that of me, but certainly not of many other people in this world. I wasn't worried about anything anymore, nosiree, not I!

I started a list of things to do and the order in which to do them.

At some point I fell asleep; and even though I could not remember having done it, I had gone to sleep in a civilized manner, on the soft silk cushions of the couch, with the crocheted afghan over me.

When I woke in the morning it was still raining, but that did not particularly concern me. I had only the slightest headache, which was quickly cured by a little hair of the dog that bit me, as the fellows at the tavern say.

In a way Jackson had done me a favor by destroying our, I mean *my,* boat—because he'd removed any necessity for choice of transportation. I never much liked going through the marshes, and could not have done it without him anyway. Of course it took me longer to ride across the island and go by ferry from Port Royal to Hilton Head and back. But what did that matter? I knew exactly what I was doing now, and how it would all go, and I had no need to rush.

The horse resisted going out into the weather, but a crack of the whip soon had the creature in line. As for me, I took along a silver flask of whiskey in my pocket, and scarcely noticed the rain.

Though I arrived at Hilton Head somewhat later than I'd anticipated, due to some problem with the ferry, my folded letter slipped under Clara's door slick as butter. And since it was late, and the ferry was going straight back, I skipped my visit to the Colonel and returned right away.

No one paid me any mind. At Headquarters House, they

were all too concerned with keeping their heads down and, presumably, their powder dry.

In the afternoon before the big storm began, Annabelle gathered together her conjuh bag, wrapped it all in the big bandanna with the good juju on it and set off through the woods. She had to find the place across the water, the same place she'd thought was safe enough for the wukkum when she'd done the summoning of the Wicketty Chile. She walked with a stoop to her back that she hadn't had a month ago, and with her father's tall staff carved with animal figures and magic symbols, the staff he'd said come all the way from Africa—though she'd never believed that part. This day she needed her pa's staff not just to chase away any wild animals or curious boys or bad men, but to lean on.

Annabelle was losing her strength. She didn't know if it was physical, if she was getting sick some way like she'd never been sick before, or if it was her constant effort to control the Wicketty Chile she'd set loose on the world, but one or t'other was draining her.

It would be dark when she reached the right place in the woods—you had to call back a powerful sperrit from the exact spot where you called it forth in the first place, if you wanted to put it back where it come from—but the darkness wouldn't bother her. Not nearly so much as it bothered her that she'd let that Wicketty Chile loose on the world.

She didn't doubt the Wicketty thing was doing what it was 'sposed to, even if she hadn't found her George yet; these things take time, sometimes months, sometimes years, and sometimes all they find is bones. Like that poor gal got murdered in the alley behind the clinic in Beaufort the professor man told her about when she went in town to trade some of her pa's old treasures for food.

That second room in her house was like a bank—Pa'd asked folks to pay more for his conjuhs than Annabelle ever had. Sometimes they paid in money and sometimes in things like gold chains and watches and such. She'd been giving her pa's treasures away, little by little, for a long time. Mostly she gave the money coins to her church. But since the war come on, she used other things to trade for food. George didn't know about it. He didn't know nothin' 'bout his grandpappy's wuks; she'd seen to that. She'd kept George out of that room the same way she'd kept Erasmus out.

Annabelle stopped on the path for a minute when she heard the first thunder. It had come from far off. Down to the eastward. Unnatural, that was, a bad portent. She shook her turbanned head and looked up at the sky. Blue as blue could be, but the birds was on the wing. When birds fly home to roost before time, you know a storm's coming. Even if there be not a cloud overhead, that storm be out there somewhere.

She leaned a little harder on Pa's staff and went on. The deeper into the woods she went, the more she felt the magic take her, and her feet only followed. This would be the last time, but she couldn't think about that right now. For now she had to get that Wicketty Chile back . . . because there was enough wickedness in the world already, and she'd been wrong to add more.

She'd been selfish, even if it was with a mother's-love kind of selfishness. That boy Erasmus, he'd taught her that without ever saying a single word, or knowing that she was learning from him, a child, what the world would be like when this war was over.

Annabelle had brought George up in the old Gullah ways. Razz, as he liked to be called, was bringing himself up in new ways. New ways he was finding for himself without even knowing he was doing it. She'd asked him once: "Boy, how you know you gwine do dat t'ing?" ("Dat t'ing" varied from one time to the next, but it was like his trading for the boat—these things just seemed to happen to Razz.)

And he'd replied, with one of his big shrugs, "I know 'cause it's out there, and somebody gonna do it, so's it might as well be me."

Annabelle couldn't teach George any more than she'd already taught him. When he came home—and he *would* come home; she might be losing her faith in the old religion but that much she did know, her George was not dead— but when he came home he would have to teach himself to live in a new world. Whatever it was like when this war be over, it wouldn't be the same as before, not ever again.

So Annabelle had to get the Wicketty Chile back while her faith was still strong enough, before it was too late.

She crossed the creek from Parris Isle to Port Royal; by then the wind was kicking up the waves. It was getting dark. Her feet found the path and led her to the clearing.

Her mind was gone into that place where her pappy'd taught her to go, the place that was neither here nor there but in between, so she saw everything around her but only dimly like through a screen, and the darker the sky got, the more the shine came out of some things and not out of others. The shine came from her footprints, and lay in a circle where she'd dug the dirt before.

The thunder boomed like cannon, but to Annabelle's ears the thunder was not important, so she scarcely heard it. She laid out her bandanna with the good juju on it and sat in the middle, murmuring the words over and over; she arranged her things by touch: the bowl, the feather, the stones . . . but the candle wouldn't burn in the rain. She opened up the hole from which she'd taken the clay to make the Wicketty Chile come to life. It had filled in some, but not all the way; mostly she'd covered it over with leaves and pebbles, which she raked out, and that was good, because the sperrit chile had to go back through this hole, this very hole, to where it'd come from on the other side.

In the pouring rain, lit from time to time by bluish flashes of lightning, Annabelle began to rock back and forth, back and forth as she chanted, protected by the charms around the edges of the cloth on which she sat.

The Chile came. It was a chile with no sex and no color, not boy or girl, not black or white, but a chile made of all the anger and all the hurt of every powerless baby that ever been done wrong to. This Chile knew no good or bad, it knew only one thing: confusion.

The Chile approached in a whirling cloud, throwing off sparks both red and white, with eyes that burned like black coals edged in red fire. It had fed on something, or some-one's anger and confusion, because the chile was plump and healthy-looking, like babies used to be, like they was in pic-tures of the white mamas in long-ago times holdin' they lap-chillun. But 'e were ugly-face, wif 'e mouf all box-up an' 'e hairs stannin' out off 'e haid lak pokeypines.

Annabelle was living now very close to that same in-between place where the Chile lived, and she felt only its confusion, and the anger that hid a terrible fright. She for-got the words to any spells she'd ever been taught—or maybe she remembered them and said them without knowing—because all her knowing now was focused on that Chile and she understood something no one, not even her pa, had ever taught her: That Wicketty Chile's sperrit was being used by Conjuh folk, and that was wrong.

She opened out her arms to the swirling mass that contained the Chile and cried out, her voice ringing out in time with a lightning flash: "Come Yuh to Me! Come Know a Mama's Love!"

The lightning struck a tree across the clearing; the tree split in half and burned, but fast as it burned the rain put out the fire, so that sparks kept rising and rising like fairy lights into the air.

Finally the leaves at the top of the tree caught fire and they too burned like a sparkling crown. The fire jumped from treetop to treetop, but the rain contained it, so that there was no heat, but only light.

Down below the treetops, Annabelle had her arms locked around a squirming, squalling, pinching, hurting baby—a big baby, about the size of a chile four years old. The cloud that had whirled around the baby now whirled around them both, and all those threads of chaos that bound the Chile bound Annabelle too. It hurt. The Chile hurt. And still she hung on. She would not let go.

She rocked and rocked. Into the sperrit that had been the Wicketty Chile, Annabelle poured all the love she could find in her heart and then in her soul; poured it out and poured it out until love poured from her like rain poured from the sky.

The rain put out the sparks from the burning tops of the trees, and the light faded to darkness. The hole in the ground, from which Annabelle had first made the figure to call the Chile from the other side, became a little pool that overflowed with rain, just as Annabelle had overflowed with love. She had poured it all into that Chile and then she'd said: "You not Wicketty no more. Now you go, be free." And she'd opened her arms up, let the Chile go and herself go too. Everything was black, but soft as velvet, and she was floating. . . .

There was a clockwise swirl in the center of the little pool, a small flash of silver, like a fish jumping down instead of up, but into light. The thunder stopped, and so did the lightning. And the rain came down.

Annabelle woke up curled against the base of a huge live oak tree, the kind of trees that are hundreds of years old, with limbs that lay right down on the ground and then grow up again, making a shape like a giant U, and leaves so thick they form a roof. Her bandanna with the good juju on it covered her like a blanket. It wasn't exactly wet, and it wasn't exactly dry either. Her pa's tall staff lay at her feet, near the edge of a small pond that had formed in the clearing where she'd sat last night.

She didn't know how that had happened. She didn't remember crawling to the tree, nor covering herself with the charmed cloth, nor saving her pappy's staff from floating away on that pond, which was almost as big as a little lake. Water filled the whole space where last night the clearing had been.

This morning it was raining still, but not so hard.

The last thing Annabelle remembered was holding on to that Chile Sperrit so tight, so tight, and knowing that it wasn't Wicketty at all, it only needed love. So she'd loved it. That was all she knew.

Except . . . it was gone.

She'd set it free. Not loosed in the world to do mischief,

but free to move on wherever spirits move on to on the other side.

She didn't know where that was. You couldn't have your head half full of the old religion and half full of the Gospels and know what happened when you died. What did it matter?

Annabelle stood up slowly, stretched her arms and legs, stood up tall and straight as a girl, for the first time in a long while. She took the wet white turban off her head and twisted all the water out, shook it open, then draped it over her head like a veil, hanging down to the sides and in the back. She carried her juju cloth over one arm, and the staff in her other hand. All her other things, the magic bowl and the feather and the stones, all those things she used for mekkum and wukkum, they were all gone beneath the surface of that little lake.

She went off and left them there. Annabelle wouldn't be needing them anymore.

Chapter 17

During the second night after the electrical storm the rain had stopped, and at dawn Clara was up at her window and watching the miracle of sunrise gradually lighten the sky, and then the sun itself spread out across the ocean as a streak of vermilion that gradually resolved itself into a round orb too bright for human eyes.

Only then did she turn away.

She was fully rested. She had been writing letters and making lists—her private plans—for most of the previous day and night.

When she heard stirring from the Colonel's room next door she went to their adjoining wall and knocked. His reply was instant.

So was the disappointment on his face when he, in nightshirt and a robe he was in the process of belting as he quietly opened his door, saw that Clara was fully dressed with her hair bound perhaps even more tightly than usual.

He said formally, with a touching uncertainty, "I'm glad to see you're feeling better. Will you come in?"

"No, thank you," Clara replied, "because I'm sure some of the men are up already and will be out and about directly. I've come to say that I am sorry for my behavior on the day my brother left, and I will be happy to ride out with you today, if you like. I believe we have much to discuss."

Then she smiled, a little mischievously.

The attraction between them was so strong that even though they stood at least two feet apart, Clara could feel him pulling at her like a magnet . . . and oh, how she wanted to go into his arms! She had no doubt he felt the same. Yet they each stood their ground.

Colonel Elwell rubbed at his hair, which stood endearingly on end where his head had, until just moments before, lain upon the pillow. He grinned like a boy—a great, bearded boy—and said, "I need a moment to collect my thoughts."

"We may not have all the time in the world," Clara said practically, "but I believe I can stand here another moment. As long as I am still across the threshold, technically on the porch, and you are still in your doorway. In case anyone walks by."

"Ah, yes." The Colonel now rubbed his beard, and for a moment was silent.

In his silence Clara, who always awoke instantly, and since she'd "gone to war" (as she herself thought of it) often found that she was standing on her feet before her eyes had fully opened, reflected that it was a good thing John Elwell served in the Quartermaster Corps. She would hate to have to be on a battlefield at night with him by her side during a surprise attack by the enemy. But then, she thought further, he would be lovely to wake up with, slowly, with whispers of endearment and the little touches of tenderness he so sweetly, sleepily would give. . . .

"I suppose," the Colonel said gravely, "that an inspection of the island by myself, in light of the recent storm, would not be entirely out of order. I will place Captain Lamb in charge of inspecting the headquarters premises, and the inner fort, for damages. After breakfast I'll have a basket lunch prepared and we'll ride out in the late morning. There is a place I came across on a ride not long ago that I've been wanting to show you...." John looked into Clara's eyes and for a moment his voice failed him. "Ah, anyway. It would be a shame if the storm bashed a tree over into it, or—"

"Or," Clara finished for him, "something. That will be more than satisfactory. The days spent in my room gave me the time I needed for contemplation. Perhaps this storm was a blessing in disguise."

"Oh, I've found in this life there are many blessings in disguise." John smiled. "Falling off horses, for example, can sometimes produce the most surprising results."

Clara approved of the way Razz had protected the boat and had kept it, for the most part, dry. While she was eager to tell him the slight alterations in schedule she'd worked out for them, he kept babbling on about *Oliver Twist*.

Finally, she put her own concerns aside and listened to what he was saying—and was glad that she'd done so. Clara felt as if she had at last found the true key to the boy's mind ... and to Miss Penny's library. Which would endear her to the Gages, to whom she already owed so much.

"You prefer a novel, then, to the more factual things you have read?" she asked. "You like a fictional story best, even though you know it isn't true?"

No great reader of novels herself, she found this an

interesting point of view. She made a distinction between "light reading" and other types of reading, and most often was occupied by the other, which for her was more thought-provoking. She was always in pursuit of intellectual fodder for the speeches she wrote out so eloquently and gave in pursuit of the war effort.

"But Miss Clara, the story *do* be true!"

"Is, Razz, *is* true."

"Yes'm, it *is* true, that's what I'm tryin' to say." All this while, Erasmus was stirring and stirring his bucket of blue paint around with a stick. The smell of it got into Clara's nostrils and in her mind merged forever with a lesson she was learning from a fourteen-year-old boy.

"May be," Erasmus was saying, "no boy name of Oliver Twist ever lived, but there be a London, England. I looked it up on the map."

"You did? I'm proud of you!"

He shook his head in frustration. He hadn't said it right, not what he meant to say, and Miss Clara didn't really understand him yet. So he left off stirring the paint and stood up to try harder.

Razz put his hand to his chest, over his heart. He knew he had his hand in the right place, the place he wanted, because he could feel his heart beating hard beneath his fingers, with the importance of this to him. "That whatchacall *novel* be true in *here*. Inside a person. Don't matter whether was ever this gang of pickpockets—"

A new word for him, Clara noted.

"—or did they really have to give they stuff to the bad man or have to eat somethin' call gruel, whatever that be, prob'ly somethin' taste like mush, only worser."

"Worse." Clara's lips curved in a tender smile, as she was impressed by this passionate explanation.

"*Worse.*" Razz hadn't finished and would not be distracted. "What matters is how you feels when you reads it. In your heart you know it's true, that's how things really be. Only you couldn't find the words yourself, you wouldn't of thought of 'em. That Mr. Charles Dickens, he thought how it really be, an' he found the words an' put 'em down in that book, an' now they be there *forever.* Every single time somebody read that story of Oliver Twist, that person know *in here* the truth of how it feels."

Suddenly Clara remembered reading *Ivanhoe* as a girl, and she caught the passion: "Yes! And not only that, but the whole time you're reading that novel, it's as if you've gone there yourself, you're living there with the horses and the knights in armor—"

"Miss Clara, they was horses but no nights in . . . in— what was that you say?"

She laughed. "Never mind, Razz. I was thinking about another book. One that I read when I was about your age. Perhaps someday you might share your secret with me, if I promise not to tell."

"What secret?" Razz turned his head, so that he regarded her from the corners of his eyes.

"Of how to get into Miss Penny's library. I was thinking I might persuade the Gages to let you and me, together, choose one novel from Miss Penny's collection for your regular reading, along with the kind of schoolbooks we've been giving you."

Razz pulled at his ear. "I dunno. If'n I take one of Miss Penny's books out'n the big house, that be like stealin'. Bad enough I went in when my mama there no more."

From the corner of her own eye, Clara saw Captain Lamb approaching with her favorite little mare, bridled and saddled. She resisted the urge to envelop Erasmus in a huge hug she felt he deserved, and said instead, "I have to go now. But I want you to remind me, sometime soon, to tell you the story of Robin Hood."

"Robbin' hood? Yes'm. Were he a pickpocket too, like Oliver Twist?"

Again Clara laughed, waving good-bye as she walked away. She called over her shoulder, "Just wait. You'll find out."

A few moments later, Clara Barton and Colonel John Elwell rode out through the gates of the fort side by side. Ostensibly, they were going to inspect any damage done to the island by the storm. In reality, John wanted only to show Clara Moss Lane, a single track almost hidden by overgrowth at its entrance; but once inside, the lane became more well defined, bordered by a weathered stake-and-pole fence that supported an ancient, endlessly twining vine of briar roses.

At the end of Moss Lane stood a little cottage, in good condition, tiny glass windowpanes intact.

"This is ours," John said, "if you want. Not to live in together, I know we can't do that. But as a . . . a—"

"A trysting place."

John Elwell's face flushed, but the momentarily high color was largely hidden by his beard. "If you will have it, and me, Clara. For as long as we are here on Hilton Head."

Their horses stamped and softly snorted, wanting either to move on or be rid of their burdens. But Clara and John kept their seats, seriously regarding each other, facing one of the most important decisions of their lives. To stop now, or to go ahead? The one way, their eyes said they both wanted, would bring more joy, but along with the joy, more sorrow for the parting that would surely come.

At last Clara said, "What I'd really like to know, John Elwell, is why we could not have met twenty years ago."

Soon the month of June was upon them, and it passed all too quickly.

John accepted a compromise from Clara: In return for Moss Lane cottage, he suffered her absence two days a week, rather than the three she'd originally planned. Erasmus used their boat, which Clara had assured him would belong to him alone when she was assigned to leave the island, to go by himself on the third day to the Gages to make the three days of schooling they'd agreed upon. He objected to taking the boat alone, but when Clara herself painted in big white letters on the back of the boat, "THE RAZZ," he finally believed her.

After that, he stopped calling it "Miss Clara's boat" and said "our boat," just as she did. Clara told him the story of Robin Hood, along with the correct spelling; but he stubbornly refused to apply the moral of the tale to Miss Penny. He would not bring one of Miss Penny's novels out of the big house for anything, so Frances Gage assigned him novels to read for homework.

A strangely subdued Annabelle, though she had willingly supplied the blue paint for the boat, had nothing whatever to say about its new name.

"She sad 'bout her son," Razz said. "He been gone three months now; they done found Annabelle's boat what he was sailing in, but not George. I think maybe she thinking he runned away up north, gone on foot. That's why she be so sad."

So every Monday and Friday, Clara worked at the Freemen's Clinic, where more and more people began to come once word got around that she would be there regularly. She heard that the clinic's mainstay physician, Dr. Matheson, had recently been ill and was now on the mend; he came in more often now, but so far never on a day when she was there. She still had not met him, and began to think he was a myth.

Other army nurses, hearing of the greater need, came and helped out. The clinic was not exactly flourishing, for there is no cure for malnutrition except food, and that was in short supply. But minor ills were being remedied, and injuries healed, and altogether they did the best they could.

Clara continued to have one problem that she never mentioned to anyone: Those army nurses who had been trained by Miss Dix, and who knew that Clara had been rejected from the nursing corps, did nothing to help Clara improve her nursing skills. They avoided her instead.

And so, once again, Clara Barton had to teach herself by trial, some error and much observation. She was still the outsider, still largely alone.

BEAUFORT

I knew that she would come to me! And she already has, though she doesn't know it yet. I know my Clara is working at the Freemen's Clinic every Monday and Friday. Without her knowledge, I've watched her black boy bring her to and fro in a smartly painted blue boat, the type that is so common around here, sharp-nosed and flat and so on, christened with the odd name *The Razz.* I once tried to make friends with that boy, and would again, but he accompanies her to the clinic and doesn't appear again until it is time to take her home.

Asking around John Cross's Tavern, I found out she stays on Parris Island Monday and Friday nights after work, with those hideous Gage women. So I can't get to her then. A pity. That would have been easiest.

Of course I could still do it, start working at the clinic myself on her days there; I thought about it, but I'd have to get rid of the boy, and that would set her against me. I don't want that. I want her to understand my great work and to join me in it.

Time is growing short. Something must be done soon or it will be too late, because the buildup of military strength in these islands south of Charleston is impressive to behold. The Rebs must be shaking in their boots. (I say this sarcastically, of course. I once saw a Reb shot dead, stand right up and shoot his killer before falling down again and breathing his last.)

No, the danger is not that the Rebels will be fooled into thinking that the Union Army will march overland to take Charleston from behind, so to speak; the danger is that the battle, when it comes, will be another disaster and then Clara Barton will be sent on elsewhere, and I shall have to find her again.

I sat in the small parlor, Coffin plantation's brightest room—why *is* it I have such trouble remembering this is *my* house?—sipping whiskey and ticking off points on the list of plans I'd made that night a few weeks ago. The night of the storm, when I'd found out for certain that the whiskey keeps that Dark Thing away. I'm sure it does, because I haven't seen it since. Of course I also keep to this room now; it has become my favorite, as there is no sense tempting fate when things are going well. And if I spend my days a little tipsy, well, that's a gentleman's privilege, isn't it?

I daresay half the country stays tipsy these days or we should all be stark raving mad.

I needed Clara and I needed her soon, because George was almost ready. By accident I'd added a new ingredient to his concoction—to be truthful, I didn't even know what the new ingredient was, which meant that when the current batch ran out I might have a problem—which had the effect of making him ravenously hungry. Therefore he would eat anything I gave him, in as large quantity as it was given. He drank great amounts of water too. But he no longer had sufficient energy or initiative to react when I went into his cage to do the nasty job of emptying his slop jar. Very soon now I would be able to command him to do it himself, and he would. I did not think I would even need to chain him. If ever there was a prime specimen in most excellent condition to receive transplantation, George was it.

I had taken two children off Lady's Isle, from the school yard of that new school there for the former slaves. Both girls. I kept them sleeping most of the time with powerful drugs that would destroy their minds—drugs distilled from the crushing of plants from my own garden, so no one would ever be the wiser. I didn't need the girls' minds, I needed their body parts.

I decided to give a party. A money-raising event for the Freemen's Clinic! Now there was a good idea. The rumor was that Clara Barton was being squired about by that namby-pamby goody-goody Colonel John Elwell. The world would have been a better place if he had died instead of only breaking his leg. A quartermaster who is too honest is no help to anyone except the government, and John Elwell was nothing but honest.

Yet, a married officer, and still squiring Clara about? Perhaps there were limits to his honesty. Well—I took another sip of whiskey—there was no sense worrying about that. She'd be mine soon enough.

I would hire the ballroom in Beaufort's only remaining hotel and set the date for my party one week hence: June 21. I commenced immediately to print out the invitations myself, in black ink and upright calligraphy. If I wrote in my own customarily elegant hand, Clara would be sure to recognize me as her anonymous letter-writer. That would never do!

Dr. Revel Matheson delivered his party invitations, by hand, to all the workers at his clinic. It happened that the day he made his deliveries, Monday, June 16, Clara Barton was the only nurse on duty; and so, under less than ideal circumstances, she met him for the first time.

He came in through the back door, which immediately set her on edge because only staff were supposed to use that door, and her only helper—a young intern just learning his skills—had been called back to his hospital. The intern must have carelessly left that door unlocked.

"Oh!" she said, having already reached for the rifle they kept to hand. "You startled me! What is your business here, sir? If you require treatment, please go into the front room and take a seat. There are several others ahead of you."

"Good heavens, no! I'm not here as a patient—I own the place! I'm Dr. Revel Matheson, originally a volunteer here at the clinic, now owner. Not that that means anything, since no one has money anymore to pay."

This statement was not quite true. He was not the owner; it was more that the other doctors had just somehow . . .

stopped coming. He didn't know why. Or had he known at one time? He couldn't remember.

"Now let's see," he went on, as he noted she had one hand still on the gun and the other holding a piece of gauze to a bloody gash along a Gullah woman's collarbone, "since this is a Monday, you'd be . . . let me guess . . . Miss Clara Barton?"

Revel smiled his most charming smile; but unfortunately at the very same moment he developed a tic in his right eye.

"Yes, I'm Clara Barton. Pleased to meet you, Dr. Matheson. I heard you'd been ill. I hope you're feeling better now."

She still kept her hand on the rifle; in an instant she could snap it into firing position. She didn't trust this man, though it was true he did not look well. His skin had a sickly pallor, and his face was hollow-cheeked. His eyes were bloodshot, and even from a distance of several feet he smelled faintly of whiskey. The latter point, truth to tell, was not unusual around noon in Beaufort town. Whether Matheson—if this *was* truly Matheson—was self-medicating or had a problem with liquor was impossible to tell.

"I believe you met my brother David when the hospital ship was in harbor a couple of months ago," Clara said, still mistrusting, stalling for time.

David had described Dr. Matheson as thin yet muscular, with dark red hair and beard. This man had not much more than skin over bones. However, his hair was a striking dark red.

"Ah yes," Revel said, a clear picture presenting itself to his sometimes befuddled mind, "David Barton, tall fellow, good-looking, dark hair, somewhat insolent. Resented being asked to get me some supplies, when there I was up to my elbows in surgery!"

Clara relaxed, smiled a little and let the gun rest again in its customary spot against the wall. Though not very flattering, it was a good description of David and matched what he had told her at the time.

Like any well-trained nurse, Clara stepped away from her patient, whose body had stiffened during this exchange. "Would you prefer to take over, Doctor?" Clara asked.

"No, please continue," Revel said. He leaned against the nearest examination table and loosened his silk string tie, and undid the top button of his shirt. "I'll watch your, uh, technique."

Clara felt that he was watching more than her technique as she finished her washing and bandaging of the woman's shoulder, then gave her a small jar of salve. "This will help the healing, if you rub it on once a day, and put on a clean bandage. Any clean piece of cloth will do. I'd give you some gauze, but we are in short supply. I'm sorry. Do you understand?"

"Unnerstan'. Thankee, missus."

"Come back here next week and let me see how your shoulder is healing, all right?"

"Aw ri'. Uh come yuh."

Clara went with the woman to the door, and told the two men and one woman in the outer room that they must wait a little longer, since she had to speak with the doctor for a few moments.

"That be Doc Math'son?" the older of the two men asked. His skin was the color of ash, and his hair was a grizzled white, cut close to his head.

Clara nodded, saying nothing more. She had noted the fear that sprang up in the old man's eyes.

She watched helplessly as first the old man, and then the other, younger man, got up and left without a word. The woman remained where she was, which Clara was relieved to see, because the woman was far into pregnancy and probably had not yet seen a doctor.

Clara placed a reassuring hand on the woman's shoulder. "I'll be with you soon, I promise."

HILTON HEAD ISLAND

"Here is the invitation," Clara said to John the next day. "You will go with me, won't you?"

"Of course I will," John grinned, "especially since I received my own invitation to the same party by a messenger off the ferry this morning." He held up an envelope identical to Clara's. "He's a peculiar fellow, Matheson. I don't know much about him. I'd enjoy an opportunity to get to know him better."

"Hmm," Clara said. She spread her skirts carefully, because she was wearing a hoop that made her waist look tiny—a small vanity she allowed herself, especially as John enjoyed it—and sat in the armless rocker. They were in the Colonel's room at Headquarters House.

"Hmm, what?"

"I'm thinking. I'll come out with it in a minute."

"Well, while you're thinking, I'll tell you what I'm thinking. Shall I? Or will it disturb your thought processes?"

"No, go ahead."

"I'm wondering why Matheson is having his party at the hotel, which is rather shabby even though it's the only one we've got left, when he's taken over one of the largest and formerly grandest plantations on St. Helena Island. He laid claim to the Coffin Place almost a year ago, under that squatters law, and he's had no challengers. Technically, Coffin plantation belongs to him now. I've always wanted to see the place. It's true he has a reputation as something of a recluse—"

Clara interrupted, because John was such a raconteur that sometimes one had to interrupt him in order to get a word in edgewise.

"That's easy enough to answer. He's a bachelor and he doesn't have any help. He had a handyman, the only one who stayed on the plantation after the Coffin family went inland. All the others ran away."

"I didn't know that, about the others running away. That was a solidly run plantation, from all I've heard. They had one of the best drivers in the islands."

"I wouldn't know anything about that. All I know is that only this one man named Jackson stayed to help Revel—"

"Oh my. It's 'Revel' already, is it? Am I about to have a rival?" John teased. If they'd been at Moss Lane Cottage, he would have whisked Clara up in his arms and sat her in his lap. He longed to do that here and now.

"Don't be silly. The man's practically falling apart. This handyman of his, Jackson, died recently, and now Revel's taking care of the whole place by himself. So he has to have the party at the hotel."

"Why doesn't he just hire some help?"

"It seems there's a story about the woods around the Coffin plantation being haunted. It keeps the Gullahs away."

"Somebody see a Plateye in the woods?"

"A *what*?"

"Clara Barton, you mean to tell me that your young friend Erasmus—who seems to be coming along nicely, by the way—hasn't told you about the Plateye?"

"Good heavens, no. It sounds like . . . like an animal

from some exotic place like the Galápagos Islands. Or Australia."

"No, that's a platypus. From Australia. A Plateye is a certain kind of ghost that lives in the woods and has eyes that shine silver in the dark."

"Oh. I'm glad we got that cleared up." Clara rocked and smiled. Never in her life had she known a more lively or entertaining conversational partner than John Elwell. "Shall I continue about Dr. Matheson?"

"Please do."

"One of the reasons Revel is giving the party is to let the folk of Beaufort society know that he, at least, is alive and well. I expect he may find some family or officers who can help him acquire at least a cook and a maid. I hope he does get someone soon, because he obviously needs help. It's no wonder that clinic was on its last legs when I first went to work there."

"Whereas now it's flourishing?"

"Not exactly flourishing. But you know, John, working at the clinic is in a way a selfish move on my part. I need the experience. I'm not really a nurse. When that doctor who has it in for me, what's his name—"

"Fontaine. Don't you worry about him. As long as you have Senator Wilson behind you, he can't do a thing."

"But I *do* worry, because once we're in battle, if Fontaine demands that I assist him and I don't do everything just right, I could be in serious trouble. I keep telling people I'm not a nurse, but it doesn't matter. They need me anyway."

John got up from the straight-backed chair where he'd been seated, went to the screen door that led to the long front porch and looked left and right. He saw the coast was clear, came back and stood behind Clara's chair, tipped her head back and kissed her with their mouths upside down.

His thumb just exactly fit the indentation in her chin, as if it had been made to go there.

Clara shivered. "I love the way you do that," she whispered.

"Yes," John whispered back, "so do I."

Then they heard the sound of steps on the stairs, and with a sigh, John resumed his seat.

After a moment he reminded Clara: "You never did tell me the reason for your 'hmm.'"

"Oh. Well, it was because you said Revel Matheson is peculiar. I think he's more on the pathetic side than peculiar. But something happened after he left that did disturb me.

"I examined a woman I think is probably seven or eight months pregnant. She lives in town, and has no women kin to help her deliver her child, or money or anything to pay the midwife. She asked would I come when she had the baby, and I had to explain to her how far away I live. Then she broke down in tears, and begged me to get one of the other nurses to bring her baby into the world if it started to come on a day I wasn't there. I said I'd try, but that wasn't good enough for her.

"She said such a terrible thing, John. She pleaded with me not to let Dr. Matheson deliver her baby. She called him a monster and said he eats children."

Chapter 18

HILTON HEAD

"Oh, thank heaven! This is wonderful, just simply wonderful!" Clara exclaimed.

Erasmus was less enthusiastic. He was helping Clara move into her storage shed box after box they'd loaded onto her wagon, off one of the two ships that had just arrived from Boston. To him this was pure hard work, and boring. Without knowing it, he'd made a significant transition: Erasmus had become a true student, happiest when he was learning, reading, writing. Things that only a few months ago he never would have thought he'd been doing regularly had now become the most important part of his life.

One of the newly arrived ships held supplies, and many boxes of them were from Clara's friends and the large number of people to whom she unceasingly wrote, asking for the small but important items the government seemed to forget soldiers needed. Soap, for instance. Lamps of any kind, especially glass-enclosed carriage lamps refitted so that they could be carried by hand in bad weather, were highly prized.

The other ship was a troop transport, which to Clara's equal joy brought Massachusetts soldiers, including the all-Negro 54th Regiment, about which they'd all heard so much. The 54th Massachusetts had a reputation for bravery and hard training that many people—including those who claimed no prejudice—had believed persons of African lineage could not possibly achieve. She hoped she'd have time for reunions with old friends among the boys in blue before they were dispatched into the field.

But the source of her current excitement was none of these: It was a box of lightweight, white and pastel-colored cloth that had been sent by her friend Mary Norton.

Razz, who was growing like weed, dropped his present burden into one of the few free spaces left in Clara's storage shed, then came and looked over her shoulder. He remembered his ma and cloth like this, remembered that new-cloth smell, and he swiped at his eyes quickly, before the tears that always pricked when he thought about Ma could fully form.

"You gonna make you some dresses, Miss Clara?"

"Yes," she said, "because of the climate here, I'm forced to give up my uniform."

"But you don't wear no uniform."

"Of a sort, I do. I always wear black, as I expect you've noticed. I do that because I'm in mourning for the loss of our country's unity, and for the loss of so many lives in this war."

Erasmus shrugged, and went out for the last load of boxes from the wagon. Women's clothes—or any clothes for that matter—were not of interest to him. On his way out he remarked, "Much cloth as you got there, you gonna need you some help. You be makin' dresses all summer long."

Clara thought she would have time. Though the arrival of more and more troops made it seem as if battle were imminent, and the islands between Hilton Head and Morris, which was closest to Charleston, were filling up with tents and men, Clara knew that for the most part this troop movement was a ruse.

She no longer sat quietly listening during the incessant meetings that took place in Colonel Elwell's rooms at night, because Dr. Fontaine was often there. Convinced that he was the source of her anonymous letters—a conviction supported by the fact that every time she chanced upon him in passing, he both glared and leered at her without making even the slightest pretense at politeness—she avoided the meetings and anyplace else where he might be present.

Every night now, she could sew, and much of the daytime too. Sewing was the only traditional feminine skill in which Clara truly met her own high expectations. Her excellent eyesight and tiny but efficient and strong fingers were a great help, as she made, and continuously repaired, all her clothing by her own hand. Dressmakers were expensive, a mere memory of the dim past.

"Oh good!" Clara was exclaiming as Razz came in again.

"These here be the last two boxes," he said.

"These are the last two boxes," Clara corrected. She and Erasmus had an agreement about her correcting him. He had told her of his dream of going north once he had some education, and she had said it would be a great help if he learned to speak white people's English "like the high buckruh." The speaking part was coming much harder to him than the reading part.

"Yes'm. These are the last two boxes. Now what you got there? That be—that is a mighty pretty color, Miss Clara."

"Oh, but how could she know I'd need something like

this?" Clara was still so transported with joy that she'd hardly heard Erasmus.

The length of cloth she pulled out of its box and held up against her body was rose-colored sateen—a kind of shiny cotton that would have been looked down upon before the war, but not now. When well sewn, the sateen would make a party dress that would look enough like satin to get by.

"Makes the roses come in you cheeks," said Erasmus. "I mean, *your* cheeks." He grinned and ducked his head, as afraid she might give him a tap on it for being too bold.

But Clara only grinned back. She said, "Thank you, Razz. The Colonel and I have agreed to go to a party on Saturday, and I was wondering what on earth I'd wear. I know that Frances and Mary Gage are making themselves dresses with panels of lace from a tablecloth, but the only thing even close to a party dress I brought with me is heavy black silk, and I would wilt in it."

"Women sure are different," Razz remarked.

Clara laughed. "Just you wait. You're going to be learning more and more about that as the years go by, young man."

The night meetings continued and Clara sewed every minute that she wasn't with John. The two of them, sensing that time was growing shorter than either liked to admit, slipped away to Moss Lane on as many afternoons as they could, and there he told her details of the elaborate plans for taking Charleston.

"While the Rebs are distracted by the troops coming overland from Edisto and James and Wadmalaw islands, we will have men hidden in entrenchments on the beaches," he told her one day.

She asked where they intended to put the tents for the wounded soldiers, since that was where she would need to be, and John confessed they had not yet decided. Troops were still moving, and every night brought some new piece of the plan. General Gillmore had recently been put in charge over all.

"Gillmore is a doer more than a talker," Clara commented. "With him in charge, I expect we'll see action soon."

John reached for her, and did not respond, except to begin removing the pins from her hair.

Though its main ornamentation was confined to a row of smocking around a neckline that dipped daringly low, Clara judged her rose-colored party dress to be a success. She could hardly wait to wear it.

Not even the disturbing rumors she had heard at the clinic, about children disappearing from Lady's Island amid renewed talk about the "Bugguh-Man," could distract her from the rare excitement of a real party, and the real pleasure of going openly with Colonel Elwell as her escort.

She had delivered the Gullah woman's baby herself on Friday afternoon, late, and she and Razz had a time of it getting down to Parris Island without going to ground on a mudflat in the marshes. They returned to Hilton Head on Saturday morning as early as the tide permitted.

Clara was startled when Razz said, as he poled the boat through the shallow waters that threaded the green marsh grass like a tangle of snakes, "Miss Annabelle asked me to invite you to come to the Praise House on Sunday. Miz Frances and Miss Mary'll be there too."

Oh dear, Clara thought, while at the same time she

noticed that the contractions of popular speech came more easily to Erasmus than the more formal grammatical constructions. She made a mental note of that, as she took his education very seriously indeed.

"I don't see how I can do that, Razz. You know there is the party in Beaufort tonight, and the Colonel has arranged for us to stay overnight with a Lieutenant Colonel Connor and his wife, who have a house in town. I don't believe I can possibly make it down to Parris Island by midmorning."

"In summertimes, the meetings at the Praise House be, um, *are* at night. On account of it being cooler then. So's we could do it. The Colonel could come too, if he wanted, but she just asked for you special to come. You could stay the Sunday night with the Gages and we could go on to the clinic in Beaufort next morning, like always."

"I suppose it is important, for her to ask that I come," Clara mumbled, thinking to herself.

Clara had been to the Praise House only once before, and in spite of the fact that the "Shouts" were hardly her kind of worship, she had enjoyed hearing Annabelle lead. Watching was something else; the tiny cabin that was called the Praise "House" had been so crowded that at times she'd thought she might faint for lack of air, and she hadn't been able to see anything of Annabelle except the top of her head—and that only because of Annabelle's height. Back then she hadn't understood Gullah very well; she would understand more now.

Besides, she owed Annabelle a great deal for taking good care of Razz earlier and last, she realized with a pang of guilt that Erasmus had said Annabelle wasn't herself these days. But Clara had become so wrapped up in John that she hadn't even been to see for herself what Erasmus meant.

"I'll be happy to come. I'm sure we can work it out

somehow. I doubt John—I mean Colonel Elwell—will be able to, but I can go with you. How is Annabelle, Erasmus? Is she feeling any better?"

"Yes'm. I think so. She's been cleaning out that other room at her house like nothin' you ever saw. You know, that room with the stuff belonged to her pappy, who were, was, the Conjuh Man."

"What's she doing with the things? I thought . . . I don't know much about it, but don't those things have, well, spells and such on them?"

Razz chuckled. He had a man's chuckle now, deep and rich. "Some of her pappy's things she's been giving away to that no-account fella on Lady's Island who thinks he can conjuh. But he can't, and everybody knows it. I think she only gives him stuff that don't—"

"Doesn't."

"—doesn't matter much. The rest, I don't know."

Their boat was approaching Hilton Head now, and Razz sat down facing Clara, letting them drift on the deeper water because the dock was crowded. He asked, "You know about Root Work, Miss Clara?"

"No, not much. Only that it's a little like voodoo magic, and most Yankees have heard about voodoo."

"Well, this be—is—a little different. Like if a woman finds out her man's been cheatin' on her, she'll go to the Conjuh Man, or the Conjuh Woman, and they call up a hag to ride him till he calm down. Hags needs a place to roost when they not workin', and they likes bedposts and tops of houses. Mostly they comes, I mean they *come* down chimneys to get in the house. And once they, their work is done, the Conjuh Man gotta send the hag back to the Other Side. But there's lots of them don't ever get sent back. They just hangs around causing trouble.

"So folks say Miss Annabelle, she's been working mighty hard to send back every hag her pappy let loose."

"Well, good for her!" Clara exclaimed, not knowing what words, exactly, were called for.

Erasmus unfolded his long legs and took up the pole again, now that there was an open space at the dock. As he stood he said, his back once more toward Clara, "I think tomorrow night at the Praise House, Miss Annabelle gonna make some kind of talk about that, what-all she's been up to lately. Tell you the truth, Miss Clara, I think Miss Annabelle gonna leave us and go looking herself for her boy."

BEAUFORT

My party is a great success. But then of course I knew it would be, since I planned it so carefully myself, down to the very last detail.

I am playing the consummate host; I even went especially to a barber in town and had my hair trimmed and a professional shave. My hands shake lately, and I didn't want to take any chance of little nicks or cuts before the big event.

There is only one problem I will admit to: The officers in their dress uniforms, all decked out in their medals and ribbons of service—they anger me so that I can hardly contain myself. *I* should be able to wear the same uniform! *I should look even more resplendent than they!* The military judges who stripped me of my rank and privileges, may they burn in hell forever. And may they burn on earth first.

Quite likely they will. Quite likely no one will win this bloody war; it will continue until everyone is dead on both sides, and it will serve them right.

These were not good thoughts for me to be thinking on

such a night as this, when I must watch my alcohol consumption. I needed whiskey to calm my anger, and some privacy to pull myself together. I had my silver flask in my pocket so I went outside, where things were almost as gay and as light as inside; but eventually I found a dark corner with a bush which stank of urine where someone had recently relieved himself. I ignored the smell, which at any rate would keep other people away as they would assume I was urinating also, and would grant me some privacy.

See what money hath wrought! I thought, when I was more myself again, and went back into the hotel ballroom. The women, wearing wide hoops beneath their skirts, looked like candy confections, or bell-shaped cakes with frills on top, in colors of pink and sky-blue, pale yellows and greens. Only Frances Gage, like an aging old parrot, wore a hideous dress alternating stripes of lace with some moldy old dark green material.

Her daughter, who has an odious personality but is pretty enough, was dressed daringly, entirely in lace over an underdress such a pale pink that from a distance one might think she wore the garment over her bare skin. The effect was, how shall I say? Tantalizing. Mary Gage has a steady beau, however. He never leaves her side. Pity. Otherwise it might be fun to trifle with her.

The word had gotten 'round, as I'd intended, about my need for domestic help. I kept a piece of paper in my pocket, folded like an accordion, and in a tiny scrawl quite unlike my normally legible writing, I made note of the few names offered me.

All the while I kept an eye on Clara Barton, who tonight was a Rose, the very Platonic essence of that most beautiful of all flowers. She glowed like a roseate beacon—and yet I could not go near her, for she had come accompanied by her own Cerberus—in the form of Colonel John Elwell.

He was famous as a storyteller and could, and did, go on for hours; worst of all, he attracted a crowd. Clara had not left his side all evening, and I could swear they were holding hands under the table. It was more than I could bear to look at her with him. I had to get her away, *had* to . . . and yet, how?

How does the saying go—after the darkness, there is always a dawn? Every head has a cloudy lining? No, a silver lining . . . I get muddled sometimes. Muddled or not, it is true that sometimes when everything seems the most impossible, something will happen to surprise you. Which is why I used to think myself favored by Lady Luck, but I had been much disappointed in my Lady Luck recently, for she had been letting me down badly, yes indeed she had and shame on her. . . .

I was becoming befuddled again. The main thing was I had to pay attention now, pay very, *very* close attention, because there was somebody who had just come into the main door of the ballroom whom I most certainly had not invited. No, *no, NO!*

He could not be here. Not not not.

He knows me. He knew me. He might know me still, in spite of my newly clean-shaven face and the streak of gray that has suddenly appeared from nowhere in my hair. . . . And the fact that I've changed my name several times. I can't even remember what name I was using the last time I saw him, but I do remember that he almost caught me, it was only by the breadth of a hare or a hair, some animal in the woods—he stumbled and fell, gave out a shout but I was too fast for him. . . .

I'm not that fast anymore.

I couldn't chance it. If he recognized me it could all be over in an instant, in a flash, in a puff of smoke. Not here, not now!

I cursed Lady Luck for bringing Dr. Claude Fontaine into the ballroom, into my party, when he had not even been invited.

Horrible, vain, pseudoaristocratic man; why, he didn't even live in town. Or did he? Come to think of it, I didn't know where he lived.

But I did know I could not stay in the same room with him.

I turned my back, put one hand to the back of my head—curse this hair's telltale color—I'll be better off when it's all turned gray, or perhaps I should shave my head entirely, pretend I'm bald. Yes, that's it, but it won't help very much now, will it?

So as I say I turned my back to the room and put one hand to the back of my head as if to smooth down my hair, and then I took the curving staircase at one side of the room up to the second level. There were chairs up there, which should have been gilt-wood ball chairs but these were some inferior hodgepodge occupied by the biddies too old to want to dance . . . and there weren't many of them, I'll tell you that.

If the times had been right, by which I mean if there hadn't been a war going on, there would have been palmettos in pots and giant ferns on stands that one might conceal oneself at least partially behind, but these times weren't right, not by a long shot—hah! in the midst of all a pun: *a long shot*—I do remain so clever even under stress. Ah! And there, just as I'd thought: French doors to a balcony. Closed because of the hospital building right next door, to keep the noise level down, don't you know.

But they were not locked. And as I said, every head has a silver lining because I went out there—and my Lady Luck had not deserted me after all. Ahhh indeed. I was alone. Blessedly, safely alone.

The night air was soft. There were four chairs, arranged two by two at opposite ends of the balcony. I took the farthest away and sank into it gratefully. Reached into my pocket and took out the silver flask; though it was almost empty, there was enough for a nip. And then, oh then, the miracle happened!

The French door opened, tentatively, one side only. I heard a feminine sigh of relief, that I could swear must have been the equal of my own, and then *she* came out onto the balcony. The Rose. The Perfect Rose.

I would like to say that she brought that roseate glow with her, but that would be an exaggeration. In truth it was quite dark, especially by contrast to the light that could be seen through the glass of the French doors, so that the corner spaces seemed all the darker by comparison. For the moment, no doubt, Clara Barton believed herself alone.

I had to make a swift decision: Should I be the gentleman and announce myself? Or should I lurk and hope she decided to sit on the other side and fail to notice me?

Good training, or good luck, won out. I cleared my throat to give a bit of polite warning; her head moved slightly—I saw her face in perfect dark profile, like the silhouettes one can buy cut out by an artist on the street—just enough to let me know she was startled, and I announced myself by immediately standing and saying, "Revel Matheson, your host, at your service. Miss Barton, isn't it? I was taking a bit of a rest and getting some fresh air. Will you join me? Here, have a seat, do!"

That voice inside my head that tells me the right things to do hadn't been working too well lately, but dimly I heard it tell me to slow down, don't overdo, don't overwhelm the woman.

"I should be glad to sit a while," she said after a slight hesitation.

There was a big fuss with the chairs, because they had arms and she had hoops, and the two don't go together at all; she said, "I'll stand, thank you," but then I saw one of the chairs on the *other* side of the balcony was the armless kind, and so I went and got it and substituted it for the one I'd been sitting in before . . . thus placing Clara in the very darkest corner. A nice bit of work, if I do say so myself.

Do you know, she even said, "Thank you!" Amazing. "This is perfect. Really perfect," she reiterated.

Oh yes my luck was back in spades. "I'm glad you approve," I said smoothly.

We exchanged some of the more usual niceties, such as what a lovely party I'd put together and so on. I thought to feign a cough and remark that it had taken quite a bit out of me, having recently been ill and all, and that was why I'd decided to get away for a bit. Then she said I mustn't worry because everyone was having such fun they wouldn't notice—adding, in the *sweetest* way, that that was the mark of a party where the host has done his part perfectly, that he can disappear and his absence not be noticed.

I was charmed.

But I was also a bundle of nerves. Sweat was pouring from my brow, down my neck and into my shirt collar. I was thankful for the darkness, and that I was the one with my back to the light now so that she could see me only in silhouette.

We were silent for a moment; both of us felt uncomfortable; we both started to speak at the exact same moment and then Clara laughed, a charming laugh that was lower and heartier than one might have thought such a tiny woman would have.

"You first," I said gallantly.

"I shouldn't," she said. The light from the doorway lit her eyes, just a golden glint in her eyes, which were dark as the night surrounding us.

"Shouldn't what? Of course you should, whatever it is; you should do whatever you want." It seemed I had not forgotten how to flirt, after all.

Clara lowered her voice and leaned slightly toward me. I couldn't help but notice the neckline of her dress curved low. Delightfully so.

"There is a man in there I simply could not bear to see, that's really why I came out here. But he's probably a friend of yours—he must be, mustn't he, or he wouldn't be here? So I was about to say something very impolite and I apologize."

"There's certainly no need to apologize for something you didn't say." I was dying to know who she meant.

I leaned closer, pitched my voice even lower. A cozy twosome.

"Actually, there's a man here I didn't invite. I suppose he may have—well, really he must have come as someone's guest, because although he's a loathsome bastard (begging your pardon for my language and none too humble opinion), one cannot say the man is ill-bred. He wouldn't have come if someone hadn't led him to believe he would be welcome. He does know his manners, and his place. Which extremely unfortunately is generally at or quite near the top."

"But *you* didn't invite him?"

"No, never."

"I wonder if we're talking about the same person," Clara mused. Then she recovered herself, saying, "Oh dear, I'm not a gossip or a snoop. I'm afraid I've been quite impolite, after all. It's just that, that—"

Was that a tear forming, shining at the corner of her lovely dark eye? I held my breath, shivering in spite of the warm air, wishing with all my heart I could lick it off with my tongue. We had the beginning of something here, I knew it. I could *feel* it!

I whispered, leaning so close I almost could have licked away that tear if I'd wanted to: "I'll tell you if you'll tell me. I came out here to avoid him too."

Clara shook her head. She'd done her hair differently tonight, I noticed for the first time. It was pulled back from her face as severely as ever, but instead of braids tightly wound around her head, she had a topknot of curls, with a few cascading down . . . and these few bounced with the sharp movement of her head.

"I really can't. It would be such bad manners I should never be able to forgive myself. I'm afraid there are times you bring out the worst in me, Dr. Matheson. Such as when I almost shot you, remember?"

"Don't try to change the subject. I like the other one better," I whispered again; unfortunately this time my whisper came out rather like a hiss—but conversely, fortunately, she didn't seem to notice. "It's Claude Fontaine," I said, "Colonel Dr. Claude Fontaine, who thinks he is, or should be, the most powerful being in the universe, next to God!"

Clara put her hand on her bosom, charmingly. "I don't believe it! You're a doctor too, and you don't like him either?"

I leaned back in my chair and crossed both my arms and my ankles. This was an opportunity too good to be missed. If I had plotted, schemed, arranged and contrived, I could not have had it work out better.

"It's *because* he's a doctor that I don't like him. My dear, if you only knew . . ." And then I proceeded to tell her.

Of course, I made up quite a bit of it. But nothing more than he deserved.

Chapter 19

There is a place in the Bible that says, in the language of the time of England's King James, "Thou shalt love the Lord thy God with all thy heart, with all thy soul, with all thy mind, and with all thy strength."

The Gullah language is about as different from that version of the king's English as any two dialects of the supposedly same language can be, but it struck Clara, as she stood at the back of the stifling Praise House and watched and listened and moved to the irresistible rhythm of the Shout, that the Gullahs worshiped in just exactly the way the Bible said to love God.

Because she was so short, she was really lost in this crowd. Annabelle had a platform to stand on, which Clara didn't remember from before, but still she could get only occasional glimpses of the leader's face as the others in front of her shifted and shuffled in a motion that seemed to come not only from their bodies but more so from their souls.

The chanted words were such pure Gullah, first lined out by Annabelle and then repeated by the others, that

Clara gave up listening for their precise meaning, and lost herself instead in an experience so unlike anything she had ever known before that she had nothing with which to compare it. The "music" was embedded in the very sounds of the words. There was a cadence she had never heard any-where else before coming to these islands. And the people poured them out in a kind of innocent passion that was stunning to behold.

Clara's background, her training, the very clothes she wore prevented her from joining with them. Never, ever, could she abandon herself that way. Yet she admired, and she longed, and she understood that the engine driving this great wheel of worship, which turned and turned in place while burning with emotion, was Annabelle, the Shout leader. The occasional glimpses of Annabelle's face showed a woman who had, in the space of a few weeks, grown somehow both gaunt and exalted.

If she had not had the wall at her back, Clara would have fallen for the dizziness that overtook her. The height of the emotions in the small house of worship—it could not have been more than twenty feet square, if that—was more than she could stand. Mary Gage was quietly weeping. Frances alone seemed unaffected by it all, as if in self-protection she had gone off someplace in her mind.

Razz, though he was not Gullah by birth, had no trouble with participation. His skin might be a different tone, but he had the moves and the innocence and the words right along with the rest of them. Shy at first, he had stayed by Clara's side until she saw him make eye contact with Annabelle; then Clara gave him a little push, whispered, "Go on!" and off he went into the shuffle and the shout, the stamp, the whole great movement that in some way made

Clara think of Ezekiel's fiery vision of "a wheel within a wheel."

Annabelle stopped, holding both hands high over her head. This apparently was a sign to the others that the Praise Leader would speak. Like a sermon, Clara supposed.

In such pure Gullah that Clara had to translate most of it in her head, Annabelle said:

"You all know my father" [she used the formal word, but pronounced it 'faddah'] "was the Conjuh Man for our people here on Parris Isle. When he died, he passed on that gift, and that burden of his knowledge, to me.

"You all know too, my son, George, has disappeared. Some people, mostly the white people and the soldiers at the headquarters on Hilton Head, think George has gone to live up north now, where things are supposed to be better than they are here. But I have a tie to my son, a tie in here [she touched her turbanned head] and in here [she put her hand over her heart] that tells me George is still alive, and he is in trouble. He needs help. Wherever he is, he can't get loose. I feel him bound in chains. Maybe these chains are real, maybe not, but that's what I feel.

"Now I have a confession to make to all of you, and when I'm done, not tonight but after a while goes by, you can decide do you still want me to lead the Shout. Do you still want me for your Praise Leader."

The people began to move restlessly and to murmur.

Annabelle held up her hands again. She went on, still in that pure, musical Gullah that was hard for Clara to interpret:

"All these years since Pa died, I been caught with one foot in the old religion and one foot in the new. Since my boy, my George, has been gone it's been harder than before to know what to do.

"I did a big conjuh for George. Biggest I ever done. Maybe even bigger than any Pa ever done. Maybe it worked, maybe it didn't, I don't know. All I know is how I feel—I, me, Annabelle.

"Sometime after that big conjuh, I started to feel that calling the spirits back to make them work for us is wrong. We didn't know any better before, but we do know better now. So I called that big spirit I'd conjuhed up back to me, and I made the peace with that spirit, and sent it on back wherever it belongs. Then I made a peace with God . . . and I've been trying to make peace with myself. But it's hard.

"Gullah peoples, if you want me for your Praise Leader, I be honored to serve. But I already renounced the conjuring. I'm not the Conjuh Woman any more."

Annabelle waited out the shouts, the moans, the questions and protests, all silently. When the people saw she wouldn't answer, all of its own, a striking silence took the room.

Annabelle's hands went up again. When she spoke, her voice held a tone of finality:

"You all invited now to take up a torch outside the door, and light it from mine; then we go" [Annabelle said 'binnah gwine go,' which slowed Clara on her translation] "to the house what was my father's house, and now my house. Too many spirits been called up 'round there. That house must be burned to the ground. I intend to do it myself, but as many of you as wants can come along and help, and watch it burn. If you burn it and if you watch, then you say your silent prayers to send the spirits on up to heaven.

"I got a place to stay. I got my faith in God and the Ma Mary and Jesus, all the way back to when he were a leetle lap-chile like my boy. I'm gwine to find George and bring him home. I don't care what it takes. And those who wants to help with that, you can come along there too."

Clara was one of the first out the door of the Praise House. She took a torch.

Erasmus, for all that he'd slept some nights at Annabelle's house, had heard nothing about any of this from her, and he was deeply offended for some reason Clara didn't understand. He went home with both the Gages, and was already asleep on his pallet on the sleeping porch when Clara got home. The whole house was quiet as she finally crept into bed.

Clara Barton was the only white woman on Parris Island who tossed her torch onto the roof of the Conjuh Man's house, that had also been Annabelle's house, and stayed to watch it burn.

Finally, when it was clear that the burning would take all night, and no trees would catch fire, Clara went to Annabelle and enveloped her in a wordless hug. She was surprised by the strength with which Annabelle clung to her.

"You'll find him," Clara said with conviction, "I know you will."

Annabelle replied, "I'll find him or I'll die trying, because I'm not coming home without him."

HILTON HEAD

Erasmus still wasn't talking the next morning. Every effort Clara made to start a conversation, to get him to tell her what was wrong, produced only a shake of the tall boy's head.

Finally, as they waited their turn to dock and the management of the boat did not require his attention, Razz turned on Clara and said fiercely, "I gots to think on it, all right? It's like last night somethin' died, and weren't nothing borned to take the place of it."

Clara swallowed hard. She was a white woman; she hadn't seen it that way. All she could think to say was "I'm sorry."

"It not be your fault, Miss Clara," Razz said, more quietly now, with his head down. But then he looked directly at her, into her eyes, as he so seldom did, and said: "On the other hand, maybe it do. Like I said, I gots to think on it. I'm goin' back home to Miss Penny's for a whiles."

All his good English had just disappeared, Clara thought sadly. But perhaps, when he felt better, it would come back.

Somewhat grudgingly, as he handed her out of the boat, Erasmus said, "Iffen you needs me, Miss Clara, afore I comes back on my own, you can send for me. You been mighty good to me an' I ain't gonna forget."

No sooner than Clara had arrived in her room and splashed her face and hands with cool water she poured from the pitcher into the bowl at the washstand, Captain Lamb knocked on her door. She recognized the softness of his characteristic tap.

"Come in, Sam," she said immediately, with her face still wet, her hand reaching for a towel cloth.

"Colonel wants you right away in his quarters, before the others come." Captain Lamb, usually the most calm and amiable of them all, was visibly agitated.

"Others?" Clara dried her face and ran her fingers back through her hair at the sides, to be sure all was still fastened securely.

"He'll explain. Just come now, please."

John Elwell, in full uniform, paced the floor of the room he used as an office. Like Sam, John was known for his gentle nature, and so Clara immediately knew something had happened.

He didn't give her time to ask. "General Gillmore is on his way. He will arrive quietly, as a regular passenger on the *Arago*. But behind him, farther out to sea where they cannot be seen except at most as dots on the horizon, there will be other ships. Gunships. Monitors.

"I have been ordered to Edisto to begin the process of supervising supply transport into the field. I'll take my horse; Edisto and James are big islands and I can do much, and faster, on horseback. I'll return to you here as often as I can."

Clara nodded. Now that the moment had arrived, her heart had risen into her throat and made a lump like a rock that prevented speech.

John Elwell went on: "I've ordered you an ambulance. Heavy casualties are expected. I've also posted orders regarding your two trucks, two tents and boxes of stores. You may choose your own men to work with you, as many as you think you'll need. I trust your judgment to make wise choices. But not the boy. Erasmus may not come with you, because he is not an enlisted man . . . and because I think he has a bright future and I don't want to see him hurt or killed."

Again Clara nodded. This time she found her voice. "So," she said, "it has begun."

"Yes, indeed."

Clara stood at the railing of the veranda outside her room some time later, watched John mount his horse and walk the animal slowly toward the fort's inner gates. Others also on horseback, each off for some separate mission she knew nothing about, fell in line behind him.

Clara could feel John's heart pulling at hers, almost a physical thing; fanciful as this seemed, she would have sworn that it was so. She would not have been too surprised, in this strange, fecund, bewildering land of the Sea Islands, to see her breast open bloodlessly, magically, and her beating heart waft out on a web of pink veins spread like wings—*the wings of John's Bird*—to follow after him.

He sat strong in his saddle and taller than the others— this same man who'd been weak and pale as a poet when they'd first met. His back was straight. His abundant beard spilled down over the high collar of his uniform in such quantity that even from behind, she could see the dark hair that looked coarse and yet was soft, hair that had more than once obediently curled around her finger.

Turn around, look at me, look at me! she longed to cry out. She knew she should not even be thinking the words, yet she thought more:

Let me see your dear face one more time. . . .

She knew better, knew John had to keep his focus now on whatever the men had discussed after she'd taken her leave of him, in his office. It seemed now as if that had been eons ago, but it had not. She had lost track of the time. She recalled only how passionately he had kissed her good-bye in spite of the risk that they might be seen, and how she had opened her mouth, her throat, her whole soul to him, to let him go as deep within her body as he might go. Yet still it had not been enough.

Never enough.

Her mind was numb.

Somewhere in its dim recesses, behind a learned

numbness, a picture was cracking—the picture of the only marriage she had ever closely observed: her glowering mother, her silent father.

With John it would not be like that. . . .

John had reached the gates now. The precautions of war had already begun: For the first time since her arrival, the inner gates had been closed and bolted through in clear daylight. It was a sign. The sign she had waited for, for so long.

Clara watched the guards draw back the bolts. The bolts were heavy and slow to move, but silent. They had been oiled.

Anointed for battle, Clara thought.

More guards forced back the huge outer gates. She heard them scrape the ground.

In that very moment, John Elwell braced his legs in the stirrups, raised his upper body so that he could turn halfway 'round, and he raised his eyes to Clara Barton. He pierced her through with that gaze, yet she clung to the pain and the joy of it, that he should turn to her in full view of his company of men.

With the reins in his left hand, he removed the brimmed uniform hat with his right, and held it over his heart. His eyes never left hers as he raised his voice and called out:

"If it were not for you, Miss Clara Barton, I would not be able to sit this horse, my leg would not take the weight pressing my foot to the stirrup and I could not ride out of here today. God be with you, as he is with all angels!"

"And with you, Jo—" she began, her voice high and clear, but she caught herself just in time: "God be with you, Colonel, and with all the men!"

Clara forced a smile. She raised her hand, palm out, not so much a wave as a pledge. To what, she was not sure.

The men waved, and John clamped his hat on his head, gave the horse his heels. This time he did not look back.

Clara still stood with her hand up, turned palm out. Though she was all alone on the veranda with not a soul to hear her, she whispered: "Please, God, keep him, keep *them,* safe."

That night, for the first time since the war had begun, and she had taken up her own cause in it, Clara was unable to harden her heart before battle. She knew how. She knew she must. And yet she could not.

Tears would not stop coming—a physical and emotional thing so unusual that she could not believe how little power she had over it, and how much it had over her.

She kept hearing John's voice in her mind, saying the same thing he'd said their last afternoon together at Moss Lane cottage: "I love you, Clara."

"Shhh—" she'd said, more than once, but he wouldn't shush.

"When this war is over, I want to be with you. I'm a lawyer as well as a doctor, you know that; I can fix it."

"John, shhh—"

"I have money put away. I have land in Maine, beautiful land by the sea, where you and I can go. Tell me you want me, say the words."

Her head lay against his chest, as always after they'd physically loved one another. She felt the rumble in his chest as he spoke, she heard his heart beat, yet she dared not believe.

Silently she recited what she knew to be true: *War changes and heightens everything, every emotion. When the war is over he will not see me the same way, and he will want his wife again. I must not believe him, I must not, I must not. . . .*

"Clara?" John had asked, raising up on one elbow so that she had to raise her chin to look at him. "Did you hear me?"

She'd nodded, unable to speak.

"Say the words you know I want to hear, the words you've never said," he insisted, wrapping her up in his arms, rocking with her, his bearded chin to the top of her head. "I can't bear to lose you."

"Nor I, you," Clara had said at last.

But those were not the words he had wanted to hear, and she knew it.

Now Clara had wet every handkerchief she owned and so she filled her pillow with tears. She rolled her head from side to side, but there was no relief from his voice in her mind: *Say the words!*

"I love you, I want to live with you and be married when we can": Those were the words John Elwell wanted.

Clara had not said them.

In the dead of night exhaustion set in at last and stopped her crying. She slid off the bed, onto her knees, leaning up against the crumpled sheets with her hands folded like a praying child. But she didn't say her prayers, she only held the posture. That was the best she could do. Clara Barton was not sure that she knew how to love one man, intimately, forever.

What she did know was that when the sun came up in the morning, she must be dressed and ready for whatever came, whether that be battle or another day of waiting in the stifling summer heat.

And she was.

July and August

1863

At daylight the guns commenced to fire upon Morris Island, we landed troops, shelled the entrances and charged the entrenchments . . . [the rest of this day's entry, and those of the succeeding eight days, are unfortunately almost entirely illegible.]

—JULY 10, 1863: FIRST DAY OF
THE BATTLE OF BATTERY WAGNER

FROM CLARA BARTON'S UNPUBLISHED DIARY

Chapter 20

General Gillmore was only the first of many commanding and high-ranking officers who arrived to be processed through Hilton Head, as the official entry point to the Department of the South. They had one determined goal this time, and one goal only: to break the Confederacy's hold over its last port, Charleston Harbor.

Blockade-runners, who were locally regarded by the Rebs as heroes for their daring tactics and fast ships, daily broke through the ring of Union Navy that blocked the harbor just outside the range of all the land-based cannon. The runners brought much-needed supplies through Charleston; supplies which then spread out by frustratingly random paths inland through South Carolina, Georgia, north Florida and eastern Alabama.

The inland areas were still controlled by the Rebels, though the Union held the ports: Georgetown; Port Royal and, beyond it, Beaufort; and Savannah. But not Charleston, which rankled all the top officers of the Union military no end.

Blessings bestowed either by a purposeful God, or accidental geography, had made Charleston almost unapproachable. First, there was an island right in the middle of the entrance to the harbor, crowned by Fort Sumter, aging but unbowed. There were forts with gun emplacements on headlands both to the north and south. And the space between those headland forts was narrow, with complex, shifting currents best known to local sailors; best navigated by the swift, sleek boats of native, Southern build. The heavier, more lumbering Union Navy had a hard time in those channels, as they had more than once found out.

The fort at the southern headland of Charleston Harbor that the Union Army and Navy had targeted was called Battery Wagner, and it was located on Morris Island.

The meetings of the top officers gathering on Hilton Head went on incessantly. Through the adjoining wall, Clara heard masculine voices droning on late into every night; often she would hear them as soon as she awoke at dawn, as well, and she'd wonder if they'd talked the night through. She supposed the colonels and the generals and an admiral or two were all running on pure, raw nerves that wouldn't allow sleep. But if they were wise, they would have learned ways to calm themselves to sleep now, because later they would have no opportunity, and the lack of rest would slow them down.

She had argued this often, to no avail, so she simply went about her own business and used her own methods to induce rest. Which, she admitted, was not an easy thing to do these days for anyone, herself included.

The remainder of June passed quickly, as clock and calendar mark the hours and the days. But her subjective sense of time passing was something else: heavy, and oh so slow.

John Elwell's voice was not yet among those that met in his room next door. As head quartermaster, he had sole responsibility for setting up supply lines in virtually full view of the enemy, because the Confederates held all the higher ground around Charleston. Theirs was every side except the water. Supplies and munitions had to be moved at night, in the dark, and silently.

John's first rides to Edisto and James Islands were for reconnaissance only; everyone—said Captain Lamb, who was as usual Clara's main source of information—expected him to return fairly quickly. A few days, at most. In physical distance, it was not that far. Yet days stretched into weeks and still he did not return.

The powerful newcomers, such as General Gillmore, shook their heads with impatience. In their view, a considerable possibility existed that the quartermaster was inept, and he was holding up their progress. But those who knew and loved John Elwell, including Clara and all the men who worked under his command, from Lamb on down, were worried that their colonel had been captured, or he and his horse blown up, or shot down.

When at last John Elwell did return he was filthy with dirt, much thinner, his face drawn in lines of worry. Clara had almost given up hope, yet that afternoon she felt a little lift of her heart that urged her to the top of the stairs, where she had stood many times before, inventing reasons that did not exist for her presence there, and then sent her down at last on pointless errands that left her empty-handed and empty-hearted.

Yet this day was different. She stood at the top of the

stairs for seconds only, before certainty set in and down she ran to intercept him.

"Oh John!" she cried. But the men were coming now, his own men closing in so that she could say no more.

He kissed her cheek swiftly, said audibly, "I stink to high heaven," which was true; then whispered into her ear, "The task they've set is impossible. I am weary to the bones."

Then he was gone up the stairs, into the bath, then into a meeting.

And so it went. Colonel Elwell was almost always gone. Those rare times when he was at Hilton Head, he was surrounded by generals and colonels and admirals and captains, all of whom wanted him to do more and do it faster.

Clara became accustomed to not seeing him. At night she seldom cried. It was better this way: so she told herself, and so she told him, but only from the depths of her eyes, whenever their eyes chanced to meet.

Sometimes, from a distance, Clara watched John Elwell now and wondered if it was really true their bodies had met after all, and with such joy. Perhaps Moss Lane Cottage had been only a dream. Oh, the cottage itself existed—Clara had gone there once for reassurance, and she'd found it real enough. But now it was filled with dust and sand, fluffs of down left on the porch by birds that had shed their baby coats from beneath new-grown wings . . . and mouse droppings everywhere.

Long, long days passed slow as sea snails stuck onshore. The sun rose, the sun set, and Clara stayed by her window, sewing. She looked out across Hilton Head's trees to the distant dunes and the all-but-flat Atlantic. The weather stultified her; it stultified them all. Only the insects loved the heat and humidity, in which they thrived, buzzing and biting by day, and at night the palmetto bugs came out:

Giant cockroaches, the length of her little finger and some twice as big around, scuttled audibly across the floors.

Clara learned to go without petticoats, but wore tall white cotton stockings to protect her legs from the bites of sand flies and mosquitoes. She sewed her "summer uniforms" of dove-gray skirts and blouses. For modesty's sake, because the gray material was thin and in the heat she could not bear more than a simple camisole underneath, she made one dark navy vest, to which she gave a slightly military look with double-breasted frog fastenings—as much because she had been sent the trim, but no buttons, as because she liked the look.

Liking or not liking was not something that would occupy anyone's mind now for a long time to come. Clara would not allow herself to be any different. It was time for her to be a soldier in her own way—a way no one else had ever done before.

One dull evening as she sat writing letters, her stocking feet curled up beneath her to avoid the palmetto bugs, Clara heard a small *pop!* of something thrown against her window. Cocking her head, she thought a nearsighted bird had lost its way home to roost. But there it was again: *pop!* This time a thin, flat stone came sailing sideways, harmlessly, into her room. It skittered to rest on the braided rug, after hopping three times.

Erasmus! she thought immediately, and ran to the window. She had not seen him in weeks, nor had she known how to take his absence. She only knew that the sight of Annabelle burning her own house, and perhaps some of what Annabelle had said to her congregation that night, had had a powerful effect on the boy.

Yes! There he was outside the window, motioning her down. His face and body were dimly backlit against the half-moon's rising, and she would recognize the tilt of that head anywhere.

As for the rest of him, that was harder. He seemed to have grown another two feet in less than two months, and he'd filled out through the shoulders as well. That was no boy down there, but a young man.

Clara waved so that he would know she was coming. She left her room quickly, using a ruse she'd perfected during many fruitless watches for John Elwell: In both hands, very carefully, she carried her chamber pot. No one need ever know it was empty. They would keep their distance and no questions would be asked if she ventured farther afield than usual.

"I see," Erasmus said without preliminary greeting as she neared him and shifted the rather ornate porcelain chamber pot to hold under one arm, while reaching out to embrace him with the other, "that there pot's you excuse to get you down here. Mighty smart, Miss Clara." Then he flashed his priceless smile, his teeth as ever a dazzling beacon to his face.

"I am so glad to see you, Razz," she said, honestly, "but I suggest you keep your mouth shut or you'll give your presence away."

"Now how I'm s'posed to talk to you with my mouth shut?" He mumbled, though, and started off toward an untidy row of palmettos that bordered the darker, taller trees. He jerked his thumb in the dark direction: "I come through there. I'll go back that way too. Found a animal hole under the fence—I just made it bigger. After tonight, them on patrol will prob'ly find it. This fort here is locked up tight as a tick on a hog's ear."

Clara nodded. "You should get away from here. The whole island, I mean. And soon."

"I be all right at Miss Penny's. Nobody bother that place, never. I got me food to eat, place to sleep, a whole library of books to read. I be educatin' myself now, Miss Clara."

"I know, but the Union is going to try to take Charleston again, both by land and by sea together. They're recruiting the Gullahs for soldiers, but haven't enough time to train them very well—or so I've heard. They're taking them to Beaufort town."

"I'm no Gullah"—quick flash of smile—"can't nobody make a fighter outen, I mean *out of* a Gullah."

"I know," Clara said, sadly. "But still, most white men don't distinguish among shades of black, Erasmus. I'm afraid someone will find you, force you to sign up, and you may be killed."

The grin turned to a frown. In the pale moonlight among the shadows of the trees, Clara could barely see the expressions that played across her young friend's face. Which was all to the good.

"I'm not no fighter neither," he said, pulling at his ear in an endearingly familiar way. "But Miss Clara, nobody comes near Miss Penny's. They don't like to go near the south end of the island. You know that. It's too close to where the Rebels come and go through the marshes over to Tybee, and all down thataway."

"Still, you must think about leaving." In her earnestness, Clara put her hand on Razz's arm and felt the muscular strength developing there. He was growing up so fast. She hoped his brain could keep up with his body; she expected that it could.

"Maybe," he said, nodding for the first time, drawing the word out in thought.

"You should go to St. Helena, to the free school. They

have a connection to the Underground Railway, and they will get you out."

Razz nodded again. But then he stayed silent for a longish time.

Finally he said, "Don't nobody want to be on St. Helena after dark. They say there be a monster steals chilluns in the nighttime. They say Miss Annabelle, she still lookin' for her George but now she look for these others too."

Erasmus shrugged. "Her George, he done gone on that railway like you said. Besides, this monster, he ònly takes little chilluns, not big boys like me." He tried a lopsided grin that didn't stay long on his face.

"You're not really a boy anymore, certainly not a child. You're almost a man," Clara said. "You were forced to grow up too soon."

"I know," Erasmus responded, digging at a place in the sandy soil with his big toe. He was barefoot, and his tone of voice was sad. "Comes from havin' no ma to fix you up, things like that. And my pa, he gone into battle for certain. Ain't nobody heard from him for a long time. Nobody's tryin' to get messages outen Drayton, anyways inland, anymore. I gotta forget about all that now."

"In the big cities of the North," Clara said to cheer him, "there are public libraries, and private lending libraries where for only a penny or two, you can take any books you want home with you for as long as two weeks!"

"That right?" Familiar cock to the head, flash of a shine in his eyes.

Clara nodded. "That's right." The chamber pot was getting heavy; she shifted it to her other arm.

Erasmus said, "I hear they got jobs, too. Miss Clara, I be, I mean I *am* teaching myself to write. From Miss Penny's books. Can't do no harm, even if they did used to say us black folks got no use to know how to read nor write. But the books, they just sittin' there gettin' dusty. Might as well be learning something from them. Right?"

"Very right."

Within six feet of them a sentry walked by on patrol. He looked over, Clara held up her chamber pot, which was white with tiny light blue flowers, and highly visible in any light at all.

Quick as that, Razz had disappeared into the shadows.

"Where are you?" Clara whispered. "He's gone now."

"I better go too," Erasmus said, stepping halfway out into the moonlight.

Clara bit her bottom lip in frustration. "I wish I had money to give you, but I don't. However, I might be able to get some. Where do you think you might go, and when?"

"I guess I go wherever them Underground Railroad people be sendin' us whatever week I show up," he replied.

"I have an idea," Clara said swiftly, since the border guard had turned and begun his trek back. Nobody took as long to empty a chamber pot as she had been standing here talking. "Wait several days, then go to the Gages' on Parris Island. I may be able to fix it so that you don't even have to go inside their house. Just look for the boat, our boat. Promise me, Erasmus?"

"I promise."

"And remember this: From now on you're *Erasmus,* you're not Razz anymore. That's a boy's name—"

"A slave name. And the real Erasmus was a great teacher. I know now. But I was a boy back then—"

"Now you're not," Clara interrupted. They were so short on time. Guard or no guard, she couldn't stand it. She put down her fancy decoy, stepped forward with her arms open wide, and after a wary moment, Erasmus fitted himself into them for a long hug.

"Parris Isle. For you, Miss Clara. You be careful too," he said. He stepped back, ending the hug without a hint of embarrassment.

Then he was gone.

So Clara had no helper now, but she was not about to call this fact to anyone's attention. It made her life doubly hard. She had to be ever on the ready, not knowing when the orders would come. If John Elwell had clues as to the immediate future, or even the snide Dr. Fontaine, who seemed to be always around lately, and who delighted in tormenting Clara with threats that sometimes contained hints of what was to come, at this time neither one was saying a single useful thing.

The few bits and pieces of information she did have— most of it useless gossip—came from sweet Sam Lamb, whose unceasingly good nature received a severe challenge from the various colonels and generals. High enough in rank himself at captain, he didn't take well to having become their chosen errand boy. But his comings and goings from the secret meetings gave Clara an opportunity to snag him occasionally for a cup of tea behind her (improperly, but these days no one cared) closed door. Sam welcomed these respites as much as Clara valued the information he gave her.

On the thirtieth of June, Sam imparted news that she had both awaited and dreaded:

"The entrenchments for the foot soldiers are still being dug," he said, "but we can estimate now, barring anything like an act of God that whips up the seas and destroys all our work by sending tidal waves over the sands—which shouldn't happen this time of year—that the diggers will reach Morris Island within the next ten days to two weeks. Gunships, monitors mostly, will wait just over the horizon until the attack begins. They have already departed from New York and the Chesapeake.

"Oh, and John should be back any day now. Colonel El-well, begging your pardon," Sam said seriously. He didn't playfully tease either John or Clara now, though there had been a time when he'd wanted more than friendship from Clara for himself. Sam knew about Moss Lane cottage, knew that she and John were lovers; occasionally he let a word or two slip that revealed his knowledge. Since Clara hadn't told him, she supposed John had needed a confidant. She didn't mind. At this point, she wouldn't have minded if the whole world knew . . . especially if the whole world could convince her to say those words he wanted, which she could not say.

"Thank you, Sam," Clara said seriously. She had a far-away look in her dark eyes.

"When you look like that, I always wonder if you can see into the future," Sam remarked.

Clara seemed not to hear, but she had heard. She did not really want to know what the future held, not now. To live from hour to hour, day to day, that was enough in this time of war.

Sam drank the final sip of tea from his cup, put the cup and saucer on the small, round table and sighed.

He said, "I suppose I'll have to get back to them now."

"Stay a little longer," Clara suggested with a smile, forcing herself to play the game for Sam's sake, "and I'll tell you what Madame Clarissa sees in her crystal ball. Reads in the tea leaves."

"How can I refuse such an intriguing invitation?"

Clara took Sam's cup, turned it upside down in the saucer, spun it around and tapped it, as she had seen others do. Then she righted the cup and stared into it, turning it this way and that as she uttered a "Hmmmm . . ." that she allowed to dwindle to silence.

Still looking into the cup, she declared: "I am not looking very far ahead at the moment. But by the fact that before he left, Colonel Elwell asked me to bring my two wagons, both tents and all my supplies, I foresee that those troops now inland will be coming overland as reinforcements, once the first rows of troops have fallen." She looked at Sam for agreement, but like a good second in command, he didn't bat an eye.

So Clara went on:

"John, at least, doesn't think the Battery Wagner will be easily taken."

"Don't forget the ambulance," Sam reminded. "Though I doubt that vehicle will ever make it into your control. Fontaine is livid about it. As he continues to be with his usual complaints. It's just as well John hasn't been present at the most recent meetings."

"You mean I am not to have the ambulance? But I've already found two drivers!" Clara protested.

An ambulance was an enclosed wagon in which the most seriously wounded were transported from the battlefield to the field hospital. Such a vehicle was the very embodiment of her chosen place with the soldiers who had fallen—a place to keep them as comfortable as possible, and to give them hope. She had ridden in the ambulances of the much-larger Army of the Potomac hundreds of times.

"I don't think so." Sam, who seldom had a harsh word to say about anyone, let the look on his face speak for him.

"Clara, you *must* know where Fontaine's dislike of you comes from. You must have crossed him somewhere in the past!"

She shook her head, pushing down the thought of letters written anonymously on creamy white paper. She truly could not remember Dr. Claude Fontaine from anywhere she had ever been—and Clara had a good memory for both names and faces.

"Then," said Sam with a helpless shrug, "he's just a totally unreasonable horse's ass—beg pardon—which is odd for someone who is such a good doctor."

Clara bit her lip but could not stop the corners of her mouth from turning up. In her opinion, Sam had just described Fontaine admirably.

Sam sighed. "Well, in addition to the ambulance, it is my unfortunate duty to tell you that he has requested what he calls real army nurses, and they are to arrive soon."

Ah, there was a blow! But Clara denied it, because she'd expected it would come.

"Generally I get along well with all army nurses," Clara said. "It was only Dorothea Dix herself who didn't like me, because her rules are silly and I said so to her face."

Sam grinned.

Clara continued: "I'm glad the nurses are coming, because we'll need them. As for Dr. Fontaine, I wish I could tell you that I recall meeting him before, serving in some hospital with him, but I genuinely cannot."

"I've heard some people say he changed sides," Sam mused. "I wonder if he could have been on the other side when you did one of those things you've done every now and then which have the effect of drawing attention to yourself. Intended or not."

"That could be so. Though any attention drawn to me

has only proved useful in that it helps me raise more materials for the boys in blue."

And gives me even more letters to write, Clara thought, but didn't say. She'd fallen woefully behind lately.

"I think you should watch out for him," Sam warned, still talking about Fontaine. "He's a good doctor, but I don't like him, and if I had any say about it, he wouldn't be on my staff. Certainly not in the inner circle."

"Perhaps he is a spy for the Union now," Clara said, more charitably than she felt. "Perhaps he *appears* in high esteem because he brought valuable information when he switched sides, and contacts that allow him to renew his information from time to time. But Sam"—Clara leaned forward, perched on the edge of her chair, "you know it's only for show. No one respects spies. Not really."

"Where did you hear that?" Sam asked sharply. "I never said that!"

Clara smiled, and lied through her teeth because she did not wish to encourage any more ill will from Fontaine:

"You were probably too busy doing your real work to listen to idle gossip. I honestly no longer remember when or where I heard it, although I have a feeling it was either in Beaufort or on Parris Island," she said. "Which reminds me: I shall have to be gone overnight. I must go to Beaufort and tell the Freemen's Clinic that my days there are at an end. I'll miss the Gullahs, in spite of everything."

Clara kept to herself a deep regret over the fact that not one single person, Gullah or white, at the clinic or anywhere in Beaufort town, had given her a single useful clue as to what had become of those missing children. Even Erasmus, isolated at Miss Penny's, had heard. The Gullahs would talk to one another, but not to her. Her skin was white; they might like her, but still she was not to be trusted.

It was too bad, because more than anything she'd wanted to organize a search party of trained soldiers, men who would not be afraid to beat every single bush on even the darkest night. Because she doubted, in the end, there would be enough Gullahs who could shed their superstitious fears enough to go into those woods after sundown—Annabelle notwithstanding.

"Everything?" Sam inquired.

"Everything what?" Clara asked, explaining, "For a moment I got distracted in my thoughts."

Sam repeated, "You said 'in spite of everything.' In relation to leaving the Freemen's Clinic."

He had been slumped comfortably in his chair with his feet crossed; now he sat up, matching Clara's posture on the edge of the chair. He sensed teatime was at an end.

Clara looked him straight in the eyes and said, "For most of the Gullahs I saw there, the sad truth is that the only improvement they can expect to their health is death. Which will at least bring an end to their suffering."

He winced. Sometimes Clara Barton could be too brutally honest.

"One more thing, Sam," she said. "I no longer have Erasmus to help me. Nor David. And Cousin Leander, who could if he would, comes and goes."

Sam rubbed his chin, thinking. Finally he nodded, as if he'd resolved something within his own mind. He said:

"You don't need a helper, what you need is a guard—someone strong and intimidating. Because of Fontaine. Don't be concerned, Clara. I'll find someone who will be ready to go with you whenever you want."

"Tomorrow morning, then, to Parris Island. We'll take my blue boat. But we'll have to tow a skiff or a small rowboat for the return trip, because I intend to leave the blue boat with the Gages. It had better be a skiff, I suppose, if I'm to do this in one day. Because of the tides."

"Consider it done."

"Thank you, Captain Lamb," said Clara formally, as she opened her door for him to depart. But then she threw formality to the winds and kissed his cheek, whispering, as he passed her in the doorway, "Thank you most of all for being such a good friend to me."

Clara's new helper was one Private Barefoot, who could not have been more than eighteen if he was a day, and looked as if he had just arrived straight off the farm in a border state. She asked. He replied:

"Kentucky, ma'am."

Private Barefoot was also a very large young fellow, with the perpetually red face of a fair-skinned man overexposed to the sun. He looked as if he could break a hoe, or an enemy, in half with his bare hands. He couldn't meet Clara's eyes, because he'd heard of her and was already in awe of her, so she never found out the color of his eyes.

He also just didn't talk much. Any attempt at conversation clearly embarrassed him, so Clara soon limited her words to giving directions.

She found Frances Gage at home, but not her daughter.

"Mary's gone to say good-bye to her beau," Frances said with a tone of sorrowful resignation. She sat rigidly upright by a window, mending more long white cotton stockings. Only her posture betrayed the tense concern she felt for her child.

She'd once said to Clara, about Mary: "When they grow

up we worry just as much, but it's harder, because we can't hold them and tell them it will be all right; they know too much and don't believe us anymore."

Clara had learned so much from Frances—including the thing about the white stockings: It had been Frances Gage who'd told Clara to go without petticoats in summer, but to keep her legs covered no matter how hot the weather, because the bugs would get up under her skirt and eat her alive if she didn't.

"He finally told her he was married," Clara guessed.

Frances nodded, then looked sharply at Clara. "You knew?"

"No, I only surmised. It is so often the case these days."

"There speaks the voice of experience," said the older woman, sharply. She had never approved of Clara's relationship with John.

"I knew it would not last for John and me," Clara said, "so I was prepared. Now it is over, though he may not think so."

She got up from the chair where she'd been sitting and went to the window, where she pulled back the lace curtain and made a show of peering out at Private Barefoot. All this she did only to give herself time from the pain of her own words.

Frances kept on doggedly sewing, without comment.

Finally Clara was able to turn around and face her older friend. "Mary's situation is not the same, Frances. She wants to marry, so next time perhaps you might intervene. I know I'll never marry, which makes it all quite different."

"So you have said." Frances rolled the white stocking up over her arm, inspected it, found another hole and threaded her needle again.

Clara changed the subject. "I came today specifically to talk to you about Erasmus. And to ask about Annabelle."

"Annabelle's gone and I don't know where," Frances said, adding with a hint of bitterness, "people don't confide in me the way they do you." After a moment's silence, she asked, "You don't suppose Erasmus might have gone with her? I thought they were very fond of one another."

Clara shook her head. "No, he hasn't gone with Annabelle. He was still at Miss Penny's quite recently. He intends to read every book in her library, I think."

At that, Frances smiled, and Clara finally began to relax. She smiled too, but only for a moment. Lately there wasn't much to smile about for any longer than a moment, at most. This particular moment would soon prove to be short indeed.

"I told Erasmus," she said, "he should leave Hilton Head. The battles will begin soon, and from all I have heard, casualties will be heavy."

"That's all the black folk are to these generals," Frances muttered, shaking out the stocking and then rolling it up, "cannon fodder."

"Surely you are mistaken," Clara said in her most formal tone of voice. Her deep patriotism would never allow her to admit such a thing. "It is merely a lack of time to train them properly."

"I won't argue with you, Clara. I learned weeks ago that arguing with you is a waste of time, both yours and mine. I came here to teach the former slaves how to live as free people. You came for one purpose only: to await the next battle. It's true I grew fond of you, but ideologically you and I are as different as night from day, and there's no use pretending otherwise."

Clara's cheeks grew hot, but she held her tongue.

"Now: What, specifically, was it you wanted about Erasmus and Annabelle?" Frances pushed her basket of mending aside with one foot and folded her hands in her lap, like a schoolteacher—which she was—in conference with a wayward pupil. Or, perhaps, a wayward parent.

Clara cleared her throat. Tears pricked at the back of her eyes but she blinked hard and made them go away. Frances Gage's warmth would come her way no more, apparently—and all because both Mary and Clara had been "involved" with married men. That business about ideological differences was, in Clara's opinion, nothing more than a smokescreen. But still, it hurt.

"I believe," Clara said carefully, "that you and I are both agreed Erasmus has a fine mind and a good chance for a profitable future once this war is over."

"*If* he stays alive," Frances commented acerbically. Clara had never seen her dear friend in such a dark mood.

"Yes, that's exactly why I'm here. To do all I can to help Erasmus stay alive. Perhaps it's unfair of me to lean on you in this way, but with battle soon to begin, most of what I can do for him depends on you and Mary, to follow through once I'm gone. If you feel you can't, or you won't, then say so now and I will go elsewhere for help." Clara knew she had sounded harsh, but such a tone seemed the only way to penetrate the mood that enveloped Frances.

Frances said nothing. She sat very still with her hands clasped just as they had been for some time now.

As Frances solidified into the teacher, so too Clara moved into that place inside herself she called her "battle mode," in which her thoughts focused sharply and singly, she worked efficiently and saved her feelings for later in the privacy of her own space—be that space room or tent or simply crouched hidden somewhere in the dark. Therefore she was impatient with Frances, who was wasting her time.

"You know," Clara said, "that when battle starts I will be in the field. Colonel Elwell has insisted that I have a new escort—in fact he's waiting outside right now—a young giant from Kentucky named Barefoot. Erasmus is not to be allowed at headquarters anymore, for his own safety.

"To be as direct as possible, Frances: I would take it as a personal favor if you would continue to teach Erasmus, and keep him safe for as long as he will stay. I have no money right now, but when I get some, I will send it to you for his keep. He may have some interest in the Underground Railway. He wants, most of all, to continue his education, but I should like to see him encouraged to go north."

Frances moved at last: She turned her head to stare out the window. "I wonder," she mused, "what it was Annabelle said to make Erasmus react so violently that night they burned the conjure house."

Clara replied: "He told me, 'It's like something died then, and nothing was born to take its place.' Erasmus is unusually sensitive, for a person of any age. He's probably at least as intelligent as you or I, maybe more than either of us. Only he knows, really, what he meant by his remark. I can only pray that he's still safe at Miss Penny's. That he hasn't done something stupid, like go off looking for his mother or father."

"I agree with you there," Frances said; and Clara thought, *At last!*

Clara went on: "I expect Erasmus senses things, changes for himself and his people and his future, that he has no words for. But he knows they're coming, and he knows how enormous they can be. He wants that future, Frances, he wants to survive! That's why I'm also asking to leave here the blue boat here for him. If he won't or can't take the Railway, perhaps he can use the boat. He can read maps, find the rivers. . . ."

"All right. I'll do it."

Frances rose and so did Clara. They stood a foot apart as if waiting for some signal—but neither knew what it was.

It was Clara, uncharacteristically, who broke first. She reached out for Frances and almost fell into the older woman's arms. "Oh Frances," she sobbed, tears so long held back now flowing freely, "I do love you, and I shall miss you, but we're at *war!*"

Frances let Clara cry, produced a clean handkerchief at the crucial moment, and then said, "Come, now show me where you've put the blue boat."

Sniffling, embarrassed, Clara allowed Frances to take her hand and to guide her out the back door and onto the boardwalk that led to the dock. Soon Private Barefoot was padding softly behind them. He took his bodyguarding seriously, even if the other one was just an old woman.

Frances angled her head toward Clara, until the taller woman's chin touched Clara's temple. Frances said softly, "We each fight our own battles in our own ways. It would be well to remember that."

Stubbornly, but glad to feel close to her friend again, Clara said, "Sometimes there is only *one* right way. *Only one.*"

Frances smiled—not because she believed that, but because it was so like Clara to never give up.

They stopped by the blue boat, which Private Barefoot had tied in the proper place. The skiff they'd towed behind was tied just beyond.

"Yet you don't want Razz—"

"Erasmus," Clara corrected, still sniffling, "he wants to be called by his proper name now."

"—Erasmus, to die fighting for his country. For his freedom."

"That blue boat," said Clara, watching it bob and drift in the water, "may be his freedom. I have taped a letter to him under the seat in the stern. It's wrapped in oilcloth. He'll find it. If he comes."

"He will come," Frances said, "just as surely as you will go into war like a man."

Clara shook her head, a grim expression on her face. "If only they would let me go like a man," she said. "I do what they allow me to do, and that is all."

Having already caught on that spoken communication was not Private Barefoot's favored form, Clara nodded her head in the direction of the skiff. He immediately moved to untie and position the floating platform.

"Good-bye, Frances," Clara said. "I do not know when I shall see you again." She lifted her chin and stepped onto the skiff, which wobbled dangerously for a moment. Frances marveled that it would hold the weight of that young giant; he was almost twice Clara's height. But the skiff held, the giant wielded his pole and Clara kept her head high, never looking back.

Frances Gage would long remember that tilt to her chin as she stepped off the dock, the same woman who not ten minutes earlier had trembled in her arms and shed such copious tears that Frances's cotton blouse was still wet, cool where the faint breeze touched her shoulder.

She's difficult, Frances thought.

She began to walk back toward her cottage. Mary, her daughter, flitted into her mind and out again. Frances was still preoccupied with something about Clara Barton. Something she couldn't quite put her finger on.

"I think the word may be greatness," Frances murmured, looking back down the dock toward the blue boat, and remembering the lift of that small chin.

She turned back toward the cottage, shaking her head, remembering the history she'd learned, and taught when she could. Again her daughter Mary returned to mind, and Frances searched the sky for the angle of the sun; she checked the height of the water against the pilings of the boardwalk for the turning of the tide. Mary would be gone a while longer, but she would come back—Frances had no doubt of that. And someday, Mary would be happy again, as she had been before the cad had admitted he was married.

But the truly great, Frances thought, returning to the lessons of history, *are seldom allowed happiness.*

"I wonder why?" Frances Gage asked, but there was no one to reply, not even the wind.

Chapter 21

She came to the clinic today to say good-bye—not particularly to me, but to those poor souls who show up mainly, I gather, because simply talking to her makes them feel better. She sends them off with a bandage or some virtually useless nostrum, and it is better than nothing in their hopeless lives.

That intern was there too; he's a poor substitute for Clara in most ways, but he does know medicine, I'll give him that. I suppose he will have to learn the hard way that he's trying to save lives that can't be saved. You can't get blood out of a stone, and you can't get nutrition out of what most of these poor Gullahs have available to eat.

God knows I understand about doctors learning things the hard way. I've had more than my turn at that!

But back to a more pleasant subject, Clara Barton: I had a feeling that she would come today, because it is her regular day, so I made sure to be there. I wanted her to say good-bye to me too, with all that dark-eyed earnestness of hers. It was so deliciously ironic to participate in the good-bye ritual, all the while knowing that for the two of us it would not be good-bye at all. It was, instead, merely the ending of one stage of working together and a progression to another, both new and more exciting.

She does not yet know it, of course.

And how extremely delicious it is to think that I have been able to herd her my way with the unwitting cooperation of my old enemy, Colonel Dr. Claude Fontaine. I have more planned there too. With George all nicely subdued, newly docile (I've convinced him we're making ready magnificent new quarters for his mother, about whom he has begun to babble incessantly; in this way he will work unsupervised for short stretches of time, interspersed with spontaneous periods of sleep from which he awakes, apparently, without knowing that he has slept at all), I have been able to lock the house door and the outer gates to the Coffin place, and leave him there alone. The length of time it takes to travel on horseback as opposed to over water is of no trouble to me now, but rather a relief, as going through the marshes always made me nervous, especially all the damn singing, stinging bugs, which are bad enough on land but on the water, unbelievable!

Now, where was I? Oh yes:

Thus in my gentleman's guise I go in and out of the tavern in Beaufort and hear the latest news, and I patrol the hospitals and my clinic as any efficient doctor should. And today not only did I say my false good-bye to Clara—a happy day indeed!—I was able to arrange a new shipment of good Kentucky bourbon whiskey to be delivered at Coffin Landing. Highly illegal of course. But I did it through the fellow at the hotel, who made a nice bundle off running my party. The Marine Officers' Club will never miss a few cartons of whiskey, he tells me, and I am sure he's right.

Besides, I need it now. Whiskey is the ambrosia of the gods to me. No, more than that, it is a cure both Apollonian and Dionysian (Apollo being the one who had the staff with the serpent entwined, which became a symbol for physicians in the Renaissance . . . or was that the Middle Ages? . . . it is sometimes hard for me to remember things these days). No matter. The important thing is that whiskey calms me, it helps me to sleep, it helps me to wake up and get moving in the morning, and if sometimes my hands shake or my mind wanders, why, that is a small price to pay.

Since I began drinking whiskey I have not seen the Black Thing, nor even inexplicable shadows in the woods. Not once. Now I ask you, is that not well worth almost any price? I think so.

HILTON HEAD

John returned around the first of July. By then Clara had gone into full battle-preparation mode, at least mentally. She alternated daylight hours between making sure that her stores of contributed goods, both medical (bandages and the like) and the extras that some thought of as niceties but she thought of as necessities (towels, extra blankets, tooth powder and brushes, etc.), were safe and in readiness, and another activity that she enjoyed more: talking with the soldiers who by now had arrived in droves. Many of those who would be in the front lines, making their way by night and in the twilight and predawn hours, when it was hard to see or be seen, by crawling up the miles of entrenchments on knees and elbows, were now camped on Hilton Head. The main fort had seemed the safest place to put them.

Clara was both overjoyed and sorry to find that her

secret favorite of all the regiments, the 54th Massachusetts, now on Hilton Head, was scheduled to be among the first to leave. The 54th Massachusetts was comprised entirely of free black men from Clara's own home state. Anyone who said men with black skin were less able to drill and fire and fight than whites had never seen this crack regiment in action. They were proud, hardened, tireless and fearless patriots. Clara had many friends among them. And it was the 54th Massachusetts that gave her the certainty that Frances Gage had been wrong when she'd made that unkind remark about "cannon fodder." Clara had seen with her own eyes what time, training and practice could do for a regiment. The color of the men's skin, or whatever they had done before becoming soldiers, had not a thing in the world to do with it!

Out of Clara's pocket came the little notebook in which she always recorded the names of the sick, the dying and the dead, along with their last requests: "Find my brother, my father, my mother, my sisters. . . ." She began to make the rounds, asking her questions, comforting with her hand on a shoulder, adding to and subtracting from her list, which on the whole was sadly growing with names of those missing and presumed dead.

Twice she asked Private Barefoot, who still had not a word to say, but seemed content enough to be her protector, to take her over to Parris Island and once to Edisto—a longer trip. There she repeated her walks and talks through the regiments of soldiers, continuing to make notes. As fewer pages remained in her notebook, she made her writing smaller and smaller.

At night in her room by candlelight, now saving precious kerosene and paraffin for the harder times soon to come, she wrote to the relatives of the soldiers whose fates she had discovered.

One evening on her return from Parris Island, she noticed that the blue boat, on which she'd painted its name, *The Razz,* was not tied in its usual place at the Gages' dock, though the Gages' own boat was there. With all her heart Clara hoped this meant that Erasmus himself had taken it.

"Oh!" she cried out involuntarily.

Private Barefoot glanced quickly at her over his shoulder as he poled along. "Something wrong, ma'am?" he asked, in an excess of volubility.

Clara had stayed late talking to the soldiers and they were dangerously close to getting grounded by the low tide. She hoped the Kentucky boy didn't know that. So she said:

"No, not at all. I was just startled by a thought I had. It was nothing really important, and I'm sorry if I startled you too."

Yet all the way home, in the dwindling light, she kept her keen eyes searching the marshes for a flat blue boat with a sharp prow, a boat that would lie low in the water.

He should paint it again, she thought, *or smear the paint with mud to blend with the surroundings. He will know to do that, and besides, he won't want a boat named* Razz *now.*

She wished Erasmus well, and had confidence that he would be, though she already missed him.

That night Clara heard no voices from Colonel Elwell's quarters. The generals had apparently dispersed, each on his separate way.

Tentatively she knocked on the wall, almost certain that John too would be gone. But he knocked back, using the sign that meant he would come to her, rather than she to him.

Clara had thought only to tell John about Erasmus, how she'd seen the blue boat gone from its slip at their dock. He listened, but not very well, for he was too busy undoing little buttons with his big fingers, swearing every now and then because these were the kind with loops instead of buttonholes. He hated the kind with loops.

He gave up for a moment, and kissed her.

"You were never very good at that," Clara said, mischievously.

John drew back, as if she'd struck him. "I beg your pardon? Perhaps it's only that I've been away too often and am out of practice." He reached for her, determinedly, and clamped his mouth over hers.

When she could breathe again, Clara said, "No, I didn't mean you weren't good at kissing. Heaven knows, you're . . ."

"I'm *what*?" John stared at her with an intensity that seared her. He was John, and yet not John, all the gentleness gone out of him, transmuted into an urgency hot as fire.

"I don't know," she said, lost, "I've never seen you like this before."

He attacked her buttons again, rubbing his head against her breasts, which were free beneath the thin summer fabric of the frock she'd worn for dinner. Only a simple camisole intervened.

"Heaven help me," Clara murmured, burying her hands in his thick hair. She felt his heat, a heat that came up from inside and not from the room around them, and knew he was not in the mood to play, to tease or be teased.

"John, darling . . ." She'd never called him "darling" before, and it got his attention. He raised his head, seemed to see her more clearly than before, and she said in a reasonable tone, "I think it would be best if you lock the door, and I will undo the buttons."

"Damnation!"

It wasn't like him to swear either.

Whatever had changed her John-Boy into this . . . this satyr, it made him cross her room in a movement that seemed no more than a single step, and when he came back he'd shed his uniform trousers precisely in the middle of her rug.

Clara had a way of sealing off her feelings. She'd worked to learn this method over the years, and had perfected it, of necessity, sometime after First Antietam. She pictured her soul, which she thought of as the seat of all emotions and of her real self, as a corridor of such depth that even she did not know where it led—perhaps to God, or perhaps to some inner universe of stars and another kind of life, which could be heaven. But wherever it led, there were emotions along the way . . . and emotions were always dangerous. Each had its opposite. To know real pleasure, you must also have felt pain; to feel joy, you must know sorrow; and so on and on. Too early and too often in her life, Clara had had too much of the wrong side of these emotions.

So she had learned, through concentrating with her eyes closed, to see the long corridor that was her soul. She filled that corridor with a series of doors, each one stronger than the one behind it. The first, deepest inside, wasn't even a proper door: It was only a curtain, sheer as gossamer, made of memory—behind that curtain, a baby gurgled with happiness sometimes but more often cried, and no one came. She had sewn the opening in that gossamer curtain together long ago.

The next one, a real door, was of white paper. . . .

"John . . ." she said. They had undone all their buttons. He was opening all her doors.

What was the opposite of passion, she wondered, as she gave his heat that name, and saw the truth of it in his blood-suffused skin. They were naked and entangled. He'd taken down her hair and undone every braid, yet not allowed her time to brush it; it was all rippled like dark cascades of water; or else it was wild, like Medusa snakes. John's face above his beard was red, either from exertion or from holding back, for he was doing both. Her own skin glowed pink. Or was that only the light from the fire in the fireplace? But there was no fireplace, it was summer. . . .

He picked her up completely in his arms, as if she weighed nothing, as if she were made of something warm and soft and malleable—she thought, *I am pink candle wax*—except that candle wax had no nerve endings and she was all one singing, glorious pleasure nerve. It seemed he could bend her into any position, keep her there as long as he wanted, and no matter what he did she only wanted more; his tongue roamed every inch of her, places no one but she had ever touched, and at first it was frightening and then it was wonderful.

Through all this John said not a word, not a single word; he was all concentration, serious heat; he was a purple arrow aimed at her heart, on a path that went straight through her body. He found a place inside her that turned her mindless and made her gush into his hand. She said, "I think I've lost myself in you," and he said, "Good" . . . and after that she remembered very little except that now she knew passion led to ecstasy.

And what was the opposite of ecstasy?

The opposite of passion is emptiness.
The opposite of ecstasy is despair.

When he was buttoning up the fly of his trousers, Clara reached for the rumpled sheet to cover herself.

John said, "No, I want to remember you just exactly like that. Naked as the day you were born and blushing all over."

She was mute. His wild sex had left her exhausted, bewildered and something else, something more, for which she had no name. Not mere satiation, but . . . happiness? Was *this* happiness?

Her mind began to work again when he was doing up the buttons of his shirt. That was how the wildness had all started, with buttons. Clara giggled.

For the first time that night, John—whose intimacies before had always been so smiling, so gentle—smiled at her giggles.

"All right," he relented, and he sat on the edge of the bed, for in truth he was as limp all over as she, "what's so funny?"

"I was just thinking that all this—whatever it was we did tonight—it all began with *buttons*." Then she let out a peal of laughter like a bell, until she remembered someone might hear and clapped a hand over her mouth. When she had stopped laughing she said, mock-seriously, "Life begins with buttons, you know. Belly buttons."

He grinned, leaned over and kissed her navel.

"I know you liked it," John said, "so don't pretend you didn't."

"But you were so different."

"I know."

"Do you often . . . get like that?"

John just looked at her, sadness slowly filling his eyes.

"I mean, if we were, were . . ."

"Married?" he asked. Not giving her time to answer, he

went on. "I tried more than once in our trysts at Moss Lane to get you to say you loved me, that you would live with me when this insane war is over; perhaps we'd go away together, leave right away and go someplace where nobody is killing anybody, and we wouldn't care whether we were married or not, because you don't care much for convention anyway. Do you, Clara?"

She shook her head, and brought her right hand up unconsciously to cover one breast, and her heart. Behind that gossamer curtain in her soul, that deepest barrier—he'd broken through it tonight but his words just now had brought it back—a baby was crying.

John said, "I could settle money and property on my wife and she'd be content. Divorces can be arranged, you and I could be married. But you'd never say you wanted that. You never did, Clara."

"I'll never marry," she whispered. Whispering the words took all the strength she had.

John had buttoned his last button. He had even put on his shoes. He stood up and turned to face her. His eyes, now fierce again, swept her from head to foot, lingering on the hand that covered her breast and her heart.

He said, "You asked if I often get that way. The answer is no, I don't. I have to be properly inspired. I have two sides to my nature: the gentle one, and the one you saw tonight— a man who needs a woman completely, inside and out. We could get lost in each other, you and I, the way we were for . . . does either of us know how many hours? I never looked at a clock or a watch the whole time, did you?"

Clara shook her head, slowly, silently . . . but inside her soul the white paper door had already closed, so that she couldn't hear the baby cry, and that was a good thing. The next door was made of pierced tin, like the door to a pie safe. . . .

John went on, "We could make the world go away; we could be a new world for each other. You inspire me, and I've been waiting for you to—shall we say—'catch up' for a long time."

"I—"

He held up his hand, a sign for silence. "Tonight I just swept you up and took you with me, but I'll never do it again. Not unless you want the passionate side of my nature that I have seldom shown to anyone, and you let me know that, and you will come with me, and stay with me, all the way."

Clara went mute again. The doors inside her continued to close, all by themselves, one by one. Slowly her chin rose; she felt her skin begin to cool, and she reached for the sheet though he had asked her not to.

His eyes had filled completely with sadness now. They were like great pools of sorrow in a face grown gaunt again, the lines of strain returned. He said, "That's what I thought. Your silence speaks for itself."

John turned away, but with a great effort Clara called out, "Wait, please! I must tell you something. Please, turn around and look at me, John."

He did.

"It's not that I don't want you, it's that I can't have you. I can't have marriage. I don't know why. I only know I cannot do it. There's something missing in me. I can't make myself a wife, anyone's wife. Whether words are said over us or not."

John Elwell came all the way back to the bed, got down on one knee, his good knee, so that his face was level with hers.

"Tell me just one thing, then, Clara Barton."

She nodded.

"Do you love me?"

"Yes, John Elwell, I love you."

He heaved a great sigh, his chest rising, then falling as he exhaled through his nose. But he no longer could look at her. He looked at the floor as he got to his feet and said, "I leave for the battlefront tomorrow. I don't know when I will return, or if I will return, because this Battery Wagner is the most ill-conceived battle I've ever encountered in all my years. It will be worse than my worst nightmares. I don't want to say good-bye, but I know I may never see you again. Even should I live, I'm not sure I could bear it."

The last door in Clara's soul, the one that had taken her the longest to make, that was the heaviest and slowest to both open and shut, was made of steel. She heard her steel door clang shut as John unlocked the door of her room, walked out and pulled it shut behind him.

He was right about Battery Wagner.

And she never saw him again.

Clara was dressed and ready for whatever might occur, but John had left long before dawn. So she had to find Captain Lamb to get her orders, and to learn whatever he could tell her of the battle plan.

He said the 54th Massachusetts would constitute the first wave of men to storm Battery Wagner. They would be covered by cannon fire from Union ships offshore. The 54th had already begun the long crawl north through the entrenchments, followed by more and more men. Photographers and newspaper reporters had been informed, for the great symbolism of having a free black regiment from the

North storm one of the South's most stubbornly resistant targets would be a powerful sign and morale booster to the Union cause.

Unless they are slaughtered, Clara thought, but she did not say. She wanted to ask about the newly recruited local black men, but she did not do that either. Frances and John, separately yet together, had hit their marks.

The field hospital, Sam said, would be set up on Folly Island. They would throw up the tents during the late-night and early-morning hours of the day the first attack was scheduled, which was—God willing—Friday, July 10, 1863.

"Today is Tuesday," Clara said. "Where on Folly Island, to the north or south?"

"Dr. Fontaine will decide. You and Barefoot will go together Thursday late in the evening, taking the ambulance and all your equipment, by barge."

"Horses too?"

"Horses too."

"It must be a very large barge."

"Apparently the Southerners of the previous century used such barges to move their entire households from the inland plantations along the rivers to the sand islands every summertime. The bargemen will be Gullah who have done this before and know the currents. You'll be perfectly safe."

"Perfectly safe," Clara echoed.

But she remembered John Elwell's parting words, and she did not feel perfectly safe.

Chapter 22

It was just after dawn on Friday, July 10. Clara stood on top of the dunes, well back but with binoculars to her eyes. She looked north across Lighthouse Inlet, and waited for the dust and smoke to clear, even as rifle fire began to ring out. She could scarcely hear the latter, as the boom of the cannons still deafened her.

The high magnification of the glasses that Captain Lamb had given her confirmed her worst fear: The 54th Massachusetts had all been killed, to a man. Close on the 54th's heels, the new recruits of freemen, mostly Gullahs, had been sent running in to draw fire, and to meet the same fate. If any one of them still lived, he was being trampled by the third wave of soldiers who now stormed onward, continuously firing their rifles as they clambered up the entrenchments of the silicon-based brick fort known as Battery Wagner.

She had been banished to this place on the dunes by Dr. Claude Fontaine, who had taken one of her tents for his field hospital, which in spite of previously agreed-upon plans, he had placed not on Folly, but on Morris Island. Very close to the scene of the slaughter.

Her one remaining tent and supplies she had pitched at Folly as ordered by Colonel Elwell through his second, Captain Lamb. Elwell was technically her commanding officer, even though she was a civilian. Clara had obeyed orders, whereas Fontaine had made his own, putting himself right at the front.

And Dr. Fontaine had already told her in no uncertain terms that she was to "stay far away from my areas of operation, or you will be forcibly removed." He had brought in army nurses, who were already down at the field hospital. He had also commandeered her ambulance. Without Colonel Elwell present to protest the ambulance taking, Clara was thinking seriously of packing up her wagons before Fontaine could take them too, and removing herself to headquarters at Hilton Head. There was nothing she could do here. Fontaine had said he'd cut her out of this war, and he'd done it without ever telling her or anyone else why, what her offense against him had been.

Clara had never felt more like an outsider—which was saying a great deal, because in truth her whole life long she had felt like an outsider to one extent or another.

The attack on Battery Wagner was clearly not proceeding as planned. Or was it? Had it been some horrible, inhuman part of the plan that the all-black regiment, the 54th Massachusetts, and the new recruits as well, would lay down their lives for the next wave of soldiers to get closer to the fort by using their dead bodies as a bridge, while inside the fort the Rebs reloaded their longer-range cannon?

Surely the high-ranking Union officers, those generals and other men who had met into the late hours next door to her room, must have known that the Confederate cannons had a reach far greater than their own gunships? That the gunships could not, in fact, do what had been promised: provide cover of cannon fire for the 54th?

"Oh God!" Clara cried aloud—to no one, because she had climbed the dunes alone, and stood apart from the few other gawkers. All battles, everywhere, attracted gawkers. Clara personally thought they must all be ghouls, having nothing better to do than watch, as if for entertainment, people kill other people.

"I don't know if that was a prayer or a curse," said a smooth, familiar voice behind her, "but under the circumstances, either one would be appropriate."

"I don't know either," Clara confessed. She brought down the binoculars and spoke to the man who now stood beside her.

"Hello, Revel," she said.

He smiled, but only slightly; this was not much of a morning for smiling. "Do you know, Miss Clara Barton, that is the first time you've ever called me by my given name?"

She put the binoculars to her eyes again, saying, "Perhaps that's because I remember all the things you told me that night we sat on the porch at your party. How you disagreed with the commanding officers, spoke up, and were stripped of your rank and your post simply for disagreeing. How you had felt like an outsider and so had vowed to do your best to serve the survivors of this war off the battlefield."

"Quite true." Revel nodded, as for the moment he had convinced himself that every word he'd told her was indeed the truth. "I am an outsider; but then, so are you. And so was Jesus Christ, and probably the Buddha, though I don't know much about him."

"Neither you nor I belong in such august company," Clara said disgustedly.

She had observed the Union Army withdraw, the men crawling back into the sand trenches, where they were no longer such easy targets. Soon medical corpsmen would begin to clear the bodies of the wounded and the dead, taking them to the field hospital.

She bit her bottom lip hard, to contain her anger, for that was where she belonged! But Fontaine had cut her out. At least the Colonel Dr. Fontaine had located the hospital tents, one of them hers, well. He'd pitched them at an angle that the cannon from the fort could not be trained upon. She wondered if he'd known so precisely where to put the hospital tents because he already had inside knowledge of Battery Wagner.

Clara sighed. She wouldn't be petty. If the doctor was a turncoat, but more soldiers lived because of him, then she must make herself support him wholeheartedly. *After* he returned her tent. And the ambulance.

"I think perhaps you do," Revel said sincerely.

"I'm sorry?" She half turned toward him, realizing that she'd been so engrossed in her own thoughts that she had not paid Dr. Matheson much mind.

He'd noticed her lack of attention, and was just ever the slightest bit annoyed with her for that. After all, he'd gone to a lot of trouble: had dressed himself carefully, had drunk enough whiskey so that his hands did not shake and had done a good job of shaving his once handsome face clean and smooth. Lady Luck was with him this day, he knew it.

He had, while shaving and being forced to look at his gaunt cheeks and haunted eyes, also had moments of wondering if the strain of recent years had been all too much; if he might not have contracted some kind of war-connected disease of the mind. In other words, if he might be going insane. He had these moments of clarity every now and then, but made sure they didn't last long.

He'd drunk his portion of whiskey and felt immediately better. The whole war was insane. Brothers fighting against brothers and for what? To end slavery? He didn't think the slavery matter was quite *it* somehow, not quite the whole reason for the war. No matter that that was now what those in power all said.

But he had no need to be bothered about such things. Ever since they'd kicked him out, the war part was Revel Matheson's problem no longer. He was a doctor, not a politician or an abolitionist, and right now he needed a nurse. He had to keep his focus. His focus was on Clara Barton.

She was saying, "I didn't quite get your reference."

For a moment he didn't understand what she meant, but then he did.

"I think," he said, "perhaps you are entitled to be mentioned in the same sentence with Jesus and Buddha, because you are called the Angel of the Battlefield. Isn't that so?"

"Not today, I'm not," said Clara, perfectly straight-faced. She lifted the hem of her skirt for more sure-footedness and began to descend the dune, on the side away from the water. "Colonel Fontaine has banned me from the field and I lack the stamina to fight him today. There's no point anyway."

"What do you mean?" Revel asked, feigning ignorance.

"Did you see how our gunships are turning, as if to fire upon Fort Sumter? Their range is too short for Battery Wagner. They can offer no support at all; those ships are here only for show.

"Now they turn on Sumter, which is the purest insanity. Sumter's cannon have the same long range as Wagner's. It is impossible to take Charleston by the water, no matter whether it's across the beach or from the sea! When will the men in charge ever learn? How long, in their vanity, will they insist on having control over every single port along the shore when they could just as well—no, strike that— when they could *far better* choke off the supply lines inland?"

She stalked downhill, the little heels of her neat black shoes sliding only slightly, with a small squeak, against the loose sand. She was quick and light on her feet, Miss Clara Barton.

"I'm going home to Hilton Head," she said.

Revel was also quick, and good with his hands. From half a step behind her he said, "I have a better idea," and before she could so much as turn her head to ask what he had in mind, he had pulled a strip of gauze saturated with chloroform from a waxed packet in his pocket and clamped it over her nose and mouth.

ST. HELENA ISLAND, MANY DAYS LATER

"So you see," Revel said earnestly, his eyes burning with passionate belief in his own goals, "it *could* work. It *should* work. And the only reason I can think of why it hasn't so far, why they've all died, is that I've been forced to work with damaged goods."

"Damaged goods?" Clara asked, to keep him talking, though she understood all too well what he meant. She had heard it many times before, even at her own urging.

They sat at an immaculate, long table in a large outbuilding that Revel called his laboratory. She pretended to take a sip of whiskey. She was letting perhaps one drop touch her tongue for every swallow that made its way down his throat. He no longer noticed, though not long ago he'd been encouraging her to "drink up."

"You know how it was," Revel said morosely, having reached that stage of his drunkenness. "I had to take the ones that had been injured and left to die. You know how they used to stack them up against the walls. I saw you go down row after row, finding the ones who were still alive. They spent their last energy talking to you, answering your questions, as if your silly scribbles could make any difference."

My silly scribbles will make a great deal of difference someday, Clara silently vowed, *because I'll find the loved ones of those who died. I swear I'll do it, or die myself!*

"You made it very hard for me more than once, young woman!" Revel insisted. He even shook his finger in her face.

For a moment he looked quite angry. Almost fearsome.

Clara, judging the degree of Revel's drunkenness, along with her knowledge of how much he believed he needed her—she'd lost track of how many days she'd been here, but it no longer mattered—decided it was safe now to ask her most burning question.

She'd waited a long time for this moment. She presented her crucial question in the form of a statement, because she'd learned she could get more accurate information from him that way.

She said: "It was really you who wrote me those anonymous letters. Not Claude Fontaine, as I believed, and as you rather heavily hinted one night."

"Yes, yes!!! I did, I did it all! I was so very clever . . . and I wrote such a fine hand then. . . ." He held out his right hand now, and it was steady, because he'd had a lot to drink.

But he knew if he picked up a pen, or a scalpel, his hand would begin to shake.

Her guess had pleased him, as she'd thought it might. Revel was a volatile drunk. Up one moment and down the next . . . but only when he was in the last, final stage before passing out. Prior to that, he could be dangerous, sustaining and feeding the anger inside him for a long time.

When he was in the angry stage, he would leave the house after locking her into her room. He'd be gone for hours; and on one such occasion, Clara had found an extra set of keys hidden in a corner of her closet, on a ring marked with a small square of blue cloth, with the letter *J* carefully written in black ink. She'd been planning ever since for the right day or night to use those keys—but before her plans had gone very far, Revel got himself lost in the woods on one of his rages. He'd left in such a huff that he'd forgotten his flask, had been without his whiskey for too long and had let himself into her room already begging for help through the door as he'd fumbled with its lock.

Early stages of delirium tremens, Clara'd thought, but Revel was pitiful in his terror . . . and so she'd helped him. She'd put him to bed, tucked the covers tightly over his body to make him feel secure and fed him little sips of whiskey until at last his symptoms had subsided. Yet with every sip she fed him, she'd known she would have left Revel Matheson alone that very night if only George had been fit to travel. George wasn't fit then; but *now* he was— and now George would come with her. Back then it had been too soon.

Unfortunately the downside of that episode, which had left Revel so grateful to Clara that she at least no longer feared for her life, was that the angry, raging stage of his drunkenness seldom took him out of the house anymore.

Some place in his deranged brain remembered the fearful night in the woods, and so now when he raged, he raged at home.

Slowly, patiently, Clara had been learning to manage and to judge the stages of Revel Matheson's drunkenness.

It was too bad, Clara reflected, that the man could not have been thoroughly, completely sane. His great project, or whatever he called it, had merit. He believed that he should be able to take undamaged limbs from one person and attach them to another. A "transplant," he called it.

The first time he'd explained his grand plan, she had protested that people were not vegetables, and immediately regretted her words—because he'd staggered out the door and had come back some moments later with a sprouting potato, shaped distressingly like a human heart. Then he'd delivered a lengthy and only slightly incoherent lecture about how, if the potato could put out new tubers, which act like veins and nerves, into different soil and take root and grow, then human organs should be able to do the same. And Clara had to admit, it made a degree of sense.

Another day, he'd drawn pictures for her with a shaky hand; becoming frustrated with his own performance, he'd left her and gone to get pictures he had done years earlier, detailed anatomical drawings complete with watercolors.

That was the day Clara discovered how much Revel had deteriorated. She didn't know if it was the war that had brought him down, as he claimed, or if the drink had gotten him first. All she knew was that basically his idea was sound and made sense, that he was intelligent beneath his dependence on hard liquor, and that his long-fingered hands had once been capable of considerable skill. The part Revel did not seem to understand was, you couldn't treat human beings the way he had been willing to treat them in order to prove his theories. That kind of misuse of people for medical experimentation had gone out with the Middle Ages.

The other thing she'd understood so clearly upon seeing Revel's earlier drawings was how far the demon alcohol had brought him down. Really, it was shameful and ironic that a man of no conscience whatever should have possessed such superior intellect and surgical skills.

Simple medical skills he had too, drunk as well as almost sober. It took skill to be able to keep a person in the kind of lightly drugged state in which he'd maintained her for days after that first chloroform haze had begun to wear off. And what he'd done to poor George—well, she could only say that, from a pharmacological point of view, George's state had been as brilliantly achieved as it was horrible to observe.

As for herself in the early days of her capture, once she had convinced him that she believed his stories and would be his willing helper, he'd stopped drugging her. And as soon as her mind was clear, she'd set about to learn, and to manage insofar as possible, the stages of his inebriation. Soon she knew with a certainty that once Dr. Revel Matheson passed out, he would remain out for at least three hours; next she'd learned that if she managed to be with him when he came around after that first three hours, convinced him it had been only three minutes, and pressed more drink upon him, that three hours would become four or five. Those were the hours when Clara Barton went to work.

First she had found George—though she hadn't known for certain it was he then; she'd only guessed—heavily sedated. She'd spent a day baking bread, plain bread that she served to him with clear, clean water to begin to wash the drugs out of his system. Next she'd started preparing all water pitchers in advance so that Revel "could be spared that petty chore." Suggesting that she was willing to do anything he might consider beneath him always worked.

Worst had been the day she'd asked to see the other "experimental subjects," the three little girls he kept asleep in the former slave cabins. She had found at least three of St. Helena's missing children—but little good it did either them or her at that moment.

The poor little girls had dwindled to skin and bones—all except one, who'd either been taken later or had had more meat on her bones to begin with. The girls were all alive still, and all in one piece, which was a great blessing. Clara had volunteered to take over what Revel called their "feeding and watering and cleaning the cages, as it were." He seemed to have forgotten why he had originally captured them; he talked often of his experiments, without precisely defining what the experiments were, or would be—which was another blessing.

Later Clara would learn that the Battle of Battery Wagner had been fought and had reached a stalemate during those days when she'd begun to learn the ways of her captor. The Union forces had drawn back into their entrenchments, determined that if they could not break the fort by direct attack, they would put its occupants under siege, which they did do, with eventual success. But it took months, and thousands died. Battery Wagner had turned out to be every bit the nightmare John Elwell had predicted. The Colonel had petitioned for, and had been granted, a transfer—where to, Clara did not later ask, when she'd been told the other news.

So while Clara Barton was fighting out her own quiet battle with the mad Dr. Revel Matheson, the Union Army was starving their enemy to death. But of course she had not known that at the time, and might never have known it if she had not been both patient and clever.

Patiently, slowly she built up the strongest little girl's body to a reliable degree of stamina. She stopped drugging her but continued to let the others sleep, because their condition was so poor. Clara thought the other two little girls were better off not understanding their fate, until rescue came.

Rescue would come; Clara had not the slightest doubt of that in her mind. She spoke to the strongest child in Gullah, and gained her confidence. Her name was Sary—she had probably been christened Sarah, but it was pronounced "Say-ree"—and she lived on St. Helena Island not far from Coffin plantation. When Sary could think and speak again, she told Clara the story of her capture.

The Bugguh-Man, as Sary called him, had already had the other two when she came. Bugguh-Man had caught her one night when she'd stayed out too late and was just walking home alone on a road she'd walked a thousand times. He'd come along on his horse and swept her up, put his hand over her mouth, and she'd been stuck in this place ever since. It was her punishment, Sary had said, for disobeying her mother and staying out after dark.

"Where was I?" Revel suddenly asked, glassy-eyed.

Clara was glad she hadn't left his side yet; she thought he was not quite "out," and she'd been right.

"You were telling me that it was you who wrote me all those letters, not Fontaine," Clara said. Swallowing all her pride and disgust, she leaned closer to him and made her voice husky, seductive.

"Shall I tell you a secret?"

"Please do." He leaned toward her too, his body wavering unsteadily without any awareness of it on his part.

"Sometimes I liked the things you said in your letters. They made me feel . . . excited. A little wicked."

"Ah-hah! I knew you had a little bit of that in you. A high-spirited woman like yourself, afraid of nothing . . ."

Clara suggested, "Let's drink to that!" She poured him a generous measure of good, strong bourbon and topped off her own glass, which she then raised in a toast.

Revel drank deep, talked earnestly for a few moments about George's perfection as a specimen and how he planned to take advantage of that soon, very soon; and then he slid forward onto the table like a boneless baby.

Now he was really gone, and would be for several hours.

After a moment, Clara turned Revel's head to one side, in part to make sure no discomfort would awaken him, and in part to judge for herself how deeply he was unconscious. Then she warmed his glass of whiskey over the candle flame until it reached body temperature, and carefully poured it over him. He didn't stir. She emptied the rest of the whiskey bottle down the length of the long table.

Clara had been planning for this particular night a long, long time. Learning for certain that Revel had written the letters, not Fontaine, only further hardened her heart. She had promised herself she wouldn't leave until she'd learned the truth of that. If Revel had denied writing the letters—though she'd long since found samples of that creamy stationery in both his bedroom and a drawer in his laboratory—when she got out of Coffin plantation, Clara would have gone after Fontaine. Now she didn't have to do that. She was only half glad.

The little girl she'd sent off home yesterday, Sary, had

not returned with help. That was a disappointment; she'd hoped they would be here by now.

The laboratory clock showed midnight. Clara was willing to wait no longer for rescue to come from the outside. She and George had a shaky alliance. He had remembered that he was Annabelle's son, and Clara had convinced him that she was Annabelle's friend. But Revel's drugs had clouded George's mind; some days he remembered everything, and other days he forgot . . . all except for Annabelle. Once his ma's name had come back to him, he'd clung to it. *Annabelle, Ma,*—she'd keep him alive and safe. He said so over and over.

Yet if he was having a bad night, he might not come with her, Annabelle or no Annabelle. Clara hoped George would come but if he did not, then she would escape alone. Even, God help her, if that meant leaving the two, barely alive little girls behind. She needed George to carry them.

Clara was outside the laboratory now, on the dark walkway that led to the main house as she mused over George's state of mind and body. She had no idea what was in the "Perfect George Potion"; Revel wouldn't tell, and after watching him mix it, Clara had to wonder if he had forgotten himself.

There was almost no end to the man's cleverness, which made his insanity all the more a pity. Revel had a little garden, a living, growing pharmacopia of poisonous plants. Obviously he had once known how to use them; knowledge that had been stored in his head and not in any book. Clara wondered how he'd learned, what his sources had been, if he'd had one specific teacher.

In the house now, finding her way by the light of one candle down a long corridor with one hand trailing against the wall to count the doors as she passed, Clara's thoughts went specifically to George. It was possible he might have suffered permanent brain damage. She sincerely hoped not, for tonight—very shortly in fact—George would have his one and only opportunity to confront his jailer, the man who might possibly have robbed Annabelle's son of his mind.

Physically, George was in good enough health, though he had been, at first, seriously overweight. It was ironic that in his always drunken dementia, Dr. Matheson continued to speak of George as if he were the perfect specimen. In a way, George's former physical perfection might be what had saved him for so long—because although Revel Matheson's mind was twisted, he did appreciate the beauty of the human body. It was sickness and deformity beyond redemption that repelled Revel, and made him want to act. Even though his choice of action was wrong.

Because George had a right to confront the man who had harmed him, Clara had come to fetch him. As she touched his doorknob, she admitted that her palms were itching with a desire to forget this step, put her plan into action and run.

George was asleep in the bedroom assigned to him. Whatever drug he'd been fed for so long had made him highly suggestible, and Revel had only to say that this room was where George "belonged" in order to get him to return to it when he had finished the "chores" Dr. Matheson assigned on any given day.

Clara raised her voice: "George, it's Clara. Your mama Annabelle's friend. Annabelle wants you to wake up now."

In George's slowly recovering mind, Annabelle's wishes now exceeded Dr. Matheson's in importance. This had not been so upon Clara's arrival, and she considered it progress.

George claimed his ma came to see him in dreams, and

that it was Annabelle who had saved his life and made "Doc Matheson" crazy for whiskey, by putting a conjure on him.

Clara repeated, "Annabelle wants you to get up now. In a little while, we're going to go on a long walk to find Annabelle, George."

Slowly George turned over onto his side and raised his head. He had Annabelle's skin and eyes, and masses of curling black hair that had not been cut or washed for months, until Clara had arrived to do it for him. She cut George's hair to shoulder length, which made him look a bit like Samson, or as if he deserved a lion skin over one shoulder like that fellow of Greek myth—Hercules. The look slightly intimidated Revel, which was all to the good.

"Find Ma? Oonah gwine tekkum we outen this yere place?" George sat up and rubbed at his eyes with his fists, like a baby. Sleep always seemed to make him regress. It was a curious phenomenon that Clara would someday like to decipher, but not now.

"Yes," she said, "exactly, and we have to be fast about it. Put your clothes on, George."

Revel told Clara he'd kept George nude, chained in a cage like an animal, for a very long time before she'd arrived. Unfortunately, during that time, George had begun to prefer going without his clothes. He still slept nude, but he remembered to dress in pants and shirt most days.

The clothes he had did not really fit him. George said they'd belonged to someone named Jack who'd disappeared a long time ago. Jack had been good to George, but couldn't disobey Doc Matheson, because Jack believed Doc Matheson was "de debbil he ownsef." But George had never believed that. Nothing would convince him that Doc Matheson was anything but an ordinary man, made peculiar by "alkyhol."

George had dressed himself—in a green plaid shirt that didn't button over his broad chest, and thick denim pants that stopped above his ankles but did fasten at the waist. He'd used his chamber pot, unembarrassed, without asking Clara to leave the room.

"Whuh he at?" George asked now.

Clara felt encouraged by the improvement the question showed in George's short-term memory. She had been prepared to remind the young man, to tell him more than once each thing they had to do.

"Doc Matheson is in his laboratory. Take my hand. I'll show you the way." This was the one area in which George showed greatest deficiency. He could not find his way around the house and grounds alone. His sense of direction had been so utterly destroyed that sometimes "up" and "down" baffled him.

Along the way, Clara explained the steps they would take to get out of Coffin plantation and find Annabelle. She was careful to focus on the fact that he had to leave first on his own, and that she would take care of the laboratory and Doc Matheson while George was to carry the two "chillun whut sleep all'ee time."

They reached the laboratory, where Revel was still sprawled out exactly as she'd left him. The man lay seemingly in relative comfort, with his head still turned to one side.

"Go on, George. He's asleep, but he'll hear you. We do hear things in our sleep, and we put them into our dreams, often."

The big young man nodded, as if this were a frequent occurrence and he understood it well. Yet he didn't speak.

Clara pushed: "This is your chance to tell this man

whatever you want to about how he captured you and kept you a prisoner, like an animal in a cage."

George was six feet five inches tall, with broad shoulders, a little too much belly still, and black hair that curled like a bramble bush down to his shoulders. Clara was just under five feet herself, and Revel lay sprawled at waist height on the laboratory table. So George towered over everyone and everything in the room, except some of the more exotic laboratory equipment, such as an enormous flask in a corner that could have held a small human. Clara, for instance. Fortunately, it was empty.

" 'E drunk," George observed, sniffing the air.

"That's true, but it doesn't change anything I've said."

George stared at Revel, who shifted position slightly, moving only his arms. This seemed to satisfy something in George.

He sat down in the chair where Clara had sat not long before, and thus began one of the strangest monologues she'd ever heard. Possibly the strangest ever. Sometimes in the Gullah he vaguely remembered, but more often in the same English with which Matheson had spoken to him, George had his say:

"Doc Matheson, oonuh binnah bad man. Jack told me how you kill ee woman, then mekkum Jack tek ee own woman hands and feet onna boat. You a murderer, you know that? That be a bad thing. Worse thing a man can do, be a murderer."

George leaned closer, wrinkled his nose at the smell, then pulled back. "I 'member me how you not give me nothing to eat for a long time, real long time, 'cause I not talk to you. Not tell oonuh my name.

"Then Annabelle, my ma, she the Conjuh Woman, she come to me in the nighttimes in a dream, an' she say, Eat.

Get strong. She do big wukkum for get George free. So I eats, an' you know what? Annabelle, she better even than my granpappy. She conjuh this big black thing outen nowhere, outen the 'eart, mebbe. I seed it too, wif my own eyen, but I not be scairt like you, 'cause Annabelle, my ma, she tell me in a dream she do dis ting."

George paused, looked at Clara, looked back at Revel, then scratched his head, and for a long moment—so long Clara began to worry about the time—he waited. But then he said: "Now my ma's conjuh done wukked on you, you ain't fitten to talk to no more. You jus' a ole drunk man with lotsa big words, and now my ma's frien', she gone get rid of you. Ain't that right, Miss Clara?"

He looked at Clara, and she beamed. It was the first time George had remembered her name.

"Yes, George," she said, "that's right."

He stood up, decisively. "Then I ain't wastin' no more time on Doc Matheson. He done become a sad specimen he-ownsef."

Clara nodded her understanding.

"You want I should go get them girls what sleep all'ee time, now? Where you want I should tekkum?"

"To the front gate," Clara said. "Do you need help or can you find it? I have keys, we can get out."

"Yes'm, I can do that. I feel good now. I 'member where them little girls be at, an' the path what go fum there to the gate."

He went off, and Clara heaved a great sigh of relief.

Then she got down to the real work.

On her explorations of the laboratory and the house when Revel was asleep, Clara had discovered bottle upon bottle of ether. Revel Matheson was the type of man for whom one of something is never enough; the type who feels most secure about himself and his world when he has a number of matching objects lined up in a row, neatly, in a closet or on a shelf. He had been obsessive in this way, until the alcohol had become more important to him than anything else.

Another thing she had found: She suspected he would have kept such a list because of his obsessiveness, and he had, of the names of the "specimens" he had taken from the various field hospitals where they had been left for dead.

Now she rushed to the drawer in the lab where that leather-bound book was kept—gruesome as its contents were, it was, fortunately, as small as her own diary—and quickly she slipped it into one of her pockets.

The next step was going to be difficult, for she herself could go up in flames.

Clara climbed the lab's small ladder and, one by one, although she begrudged every minute it took to be so careful, she removed a dozen glass bottles of ether. Starting at the back of the laboratory, she removed their glass stoppers, poured out a little of the colorless liquid and quickly backed away, holding her breath the entire time. She worked fast.

Even so, by the time she reached the front room where Revel lay sprawled at the table, she was getting dizzy and had to settle for just leaving the tops off the last three bottles. She took an unlit candle and a sulfur match from her pocket, and last of all removed the glass hurricane shield from the candle that burned on the long table near Revel's head.

Clara ran out of the main laboratory door and quickly took two deep breaths of fresh air. Then she lit her candle with the match, which she struck on the heel of her shoe, and rolled it in through the open door while praying the flame would not go out, then closed the laboratory door behind her.

She ran for the main house as hard as she could.

What Clara Barton did not know was that Sary had done her job. Her ma and pa had sent for Annabelle, and Annabelle had chosen midnight as the time to arrive at the Coffin plantation.

There were ten Gullahs in the rescue party, six men and four women. Annabelle, in a tall turban of brilliant blue that shone by the light of the torch she held aloft—the same kind of torch she'd used to set fire to her house—with her black-purple skin, looked like an avenging goddess of night. The Gullahs walked in long strides, Sary's father carried her.

George, true to his word, waited by the gate with the two sleeping little girls in his arms. Clara was running as fast as her feet would carry her. Even so, she had not run fast enough. She had the keys out, in her hand, when the laboratory exploded. The ground shook like an earthquake, and Clara fell. But George stood firm, legs braced apart as strong as any two trees.

The roar was tremendous, and so was the wind generated by the concussion of the explosion. The sky turned orange, and the tops of trees took fire like lucifers.

Clara scrambled to her feet with keys in hand and, panting, she said, "We've got to get out of here, *now*!"

George smiled. He thought Annabelle had done it. "My ma a great Conjuh Woman," he said proudly. "She be waitin' for us on th' other side. You'll see."

She didn't take time to argue with him; Clara just unlocked the gate and pushed George through ahead of her.

"Run," she commanded, "go fast!"

The walls were brick but the gate was wood, it would burn, that was all she could think. The gate did burn. It burst into flames when they'd gone only about ten feet down the drive.

Halfway up the mile-long tree-lined drive called Coffin Avenue, the party of ten, led by Annabelle, began to run too. They ran toward the house, toward the fire and the light in the sky.

At some point, Clara would never know exactly where, because the explosion had temporarily deafened her and her head felt as if it wanted to leave her neck at any moment, the two groups met. Arms reached out for her, supported her and finally carried her.

Sary wanted to see the other little girls, and George tenderly laid them down in the grass. His eyes lit up, his face cleared and he smiled with a radiance greater than that of the fire in the night sky as he caught sight of his mother. Annabelle had already handed off her torch to another person in the party. She opened her arms and raised her face to the stars as she shouted: "Thanks be to Gawd, and the Ma Mary, I done found my son!"

George and his mother, of equal height, taking into account the turban on her head, wrapped their arms around each other for a long time. Clara watched and felt tears come to her eyes, both from relief and because she shared their joy. Her ears popped, and suddenly she could hear again. To Annabelle's paean of thanks, Clara added a quiet but audible "Amen."

To the big man who carried her in his arms, she said, "Thank you. You can put me down now."

George, with one arm still around his mother's shoulders, said, "My ma saved me with the bigges' conjuh in the whole world!"

Considering the size of the blaze, which had already reached the main house and was quickly turning it into a skeleton of brick window frames and doorways, no one was likely to argue with that.

But Sary, having assured herself that the other little girls were not dead, walked over and stood next to Clara Barton.

"Axshully," Sary said, taking hold of Clara's hand, "weren't Gawd nor the Ma Mary nor a conjuh. Was Miss Clara Barton who done it all."

Epilogue

MISS CLARA BARTON RAISES FLAG
OVER
ANDERSONVILLE CEMETERY

—EXCLUSIVE TO THE *CINCINNATI RECORDER,*
BY ERASMUS TRUE, AUGUST 18, 1865

Today Miss Clara Barton raised the American flag of Stars and Stripes over the cemetery at Andersonville, site of the former prison. Now more than 13,000 soldiers who fought for the Union cause are buried there. As the band played "The Star-Spangled Banner," Miss Barton bowed her head, covered her face with her hands and wept.

Listing of Major Characters

THE HISTORICAL CHARACTERS:

Clara (Clarissa Harlowe) Barton
John Elwell
David Barton
Samuel Lamb
Frances Gage
Mary Gage
General Hunter
General Gillmore

THE FICTIONAL CHARACTERS:

Annabelle
George
Erasmus
Colonel Dr. Claude Fontaine
Dr. Revel Matheson
Jackson
Dr. Bob Thornhill
Major Hamilton Scott

ACKNOWLEDGMENTS

First and deepest thanks must go to my agent, Peter Lampack, without whose support and insights I could never have written this book.

Second I must thank my research assistant, Polly Archer, who is by profession a reference librarian but who tirelessly worked full time for an important period to find and provide for me the original documents, aka primary sources, never before published, which I used heavily for this book. In turn I also thank the unknown librarians at the Library of Congress, the Southern History Collection at the University of North Carolina Library, and at the Smith College Library; these librarians provided me with invaluable photocopies of, in order: Clara Barton's original field notes and diaries for this particular period of 1863; letters to and from Clara from personal friends, especially Mary Norton; John Elwell's own diary, written in his own hand, which contained his private notes to Clara and some of hers, to him.

I want to thank also Kate Miciak and Michael Palgon at Bantam and Doubleday respectively, for their ideas and support on this topic; my former editors Judith Kern at Doubleday and Amanda Powers at Bantam; and Deborah Cowell at Doubleday for helping to bring this project to completion.

— AVA DIANNE DAY

References used in the writing of this book, which may also constitute a reading list for those with further interest in the topic:

In a category all its own, because I relied most heavily on the superb historical documentation of this book:

Oates, Stephen: *A Woman of Valor.* Free Press, 1994.

Other resources, in alphabetical order by author's last name:

Clinton, Catherine: *Civil War Stories.* University of Georgia Press, 1998.

Garrison, Webb: *Civil War Curiosities.* Rutledge Hill Press, 1994.

Geraty, Virginia Mixson: *Gullah fuh Oonuh (Gullah for You), a Guide to the Gullah Language.* Sandlapper Publishing Company, 1997.

Goodwine, Marquetta L.: *Gawd Dun Smile Pun We: Beaufort Isles,* Volume 2 in the Gullah/Geechee series: The Survival of Africa's Seed in the Winds of the Diaspora. Kinship Publications, 1997.

Kozak, Ginnie: *Eve of Emancipation: The Union Occupation of Beaufort and the Sea Islands* (2nd edition). Portsmouth House Press, 1995, 1996.

Pinckney, Roger: *The Beaufort Chronicles: Old Houses, Old Stories.* Pluff Mud Publishing, 1996.

Pinckney, Roger: *Blue Roots: African-American Folk Magic of the Gullah People.* Llewellyn Publications, 2000.

Pryor, Elizabeth Brown: *Clara Barton, Professional Angel.* University of Pennsylvania Press, 1987.

Schwartz, Gerald. *A Woman Doctor's Civil War: Esther Hill Hawks' Diary.* University of South Carolina Press, 1986

AVA DIANNE DAY is the author of six Fremont Jones mysteries, including *The Strange Files of Fremont Jones* and *The Bohemian Murders*. She worked as a psychologist and hospital administrator before beginning her career as a successful mystery writer. She has two grown sons and lives on the north coast of California.